07-07
24/4/20

Please return/renew this item by the last date shown on this label, or on your self-service receipt.

To renew this item, visit **www.librarieswest.org.uk** or contact your library.

Your Borrower number and PIN are required.

LibrariesWest

'A fascinating and absorbing narrative drawn on the landscape of a world descending into savagery'

The Australian

Jane Thynne was born in Venezuela and educated in London. She graduated from Oxford University with a degree in English and joined the BBC as a journalist. She has also worked at the *Sunday Times*, the *Daily Telegraph* and the *Independent*, as well as for numerous British magazines. Jane appears as a broadcaster on Radio 4 and Sky News. She has three children and lives in London.

Also by Jane Thynne

Faith and Beauty
A War of Flowers
The Winter Garden
Black Roses
The Weighing of the Heart
The Shell House
Patrimony

SOLITAIRE

JANE THYNNE

SIMON &
SCHUSTER

London · New York · Sydney · Toronto · New Delhi

A CBS COMPANY

First published in Great Britain by Simon & Schuster UK Ltd, 2016
This paperback edition first published in 2017
A CBS COMPANY

1 3 5 7 9 10 8 6 4 2

Simon & Schuster UK Ltd
1st Floor
222 Gray's Inn Road
London WC1X 8HB

Simon & Schuster Australia, Sydney
Simon & Schuster India, New Delhi

www.simonandschuster.co.uk
www.simonandschuster.com.au
www.simonandschuster.co.in

A CIP catalogue record for this book
is available from the British Library

Paperback ISBN: 978-1-4711-5581-9
eBook ISBN: 978-1-4711-5582-6

Typeset in the UK by M Rules
Printed and bound by CPI Group (UK) Ltd, Croydon, CR0 4YY

MIX
Paper from
responsible sources
FSC® C020471

Simon & Schuster UK Ltd are committed to sourcing paper
that is made from wood grown in sustainable forests and support the Forest
Stewardship Council, the leading international forest certification organisation.
Our books displaying the FSC logo are printed on FSC certified paper.

Love consists in this: that two solitudes meet,
protect, and greet each other.

Rainer Maria Rilke, *Letters to a Young Poet*

I consider it right if small children of Polish families
who show especially good racial characteristics
were apprehended and educated by us in special
institutions and children's homes.

Heinrich Himmler

Diamonds are a girl's best friend.

Anita Loos, *Gentlemen Prefer Blondes*

For Rosemary Thynne
1932–2015

Prologue

Lisbon, July 1940

The Lisbon coastline is famous for its waves. The beaches that stretch along the westernmost peninsula of continental Europe face the full force of the Atlantic Ocean. In winter vast swells batter the rocky outcrops that curl like a jagged spine around the coast, lashing the gullies and roaring up the sandy beaches. Even in summer glassy crests crash against the rocks and send spray arcing into the air, refracted by sunlight into a thousand splinters of quartz. But in the summer of 1940 another kind of tide descended on the city.

A flood of human beings.

Refugees were nothing new to Lisbon. Over the centuries, successive waves of Phoenicians, Romans, Visigoths, Moors and Crusaders had arrived at the farthest edge of the known world, establishing vineyards in the fertile landscape and fishing from the natural harbour. According to legend, Odysseus founded the city after he left Troy and later a young Christopher Columbus studied there, developing an interest in ocean exploration. But in the first summer of the war, it seemed that half the refugees of Europe had fetched up in neutral Lisbon, heading for the freedom of Britain, Africa and America. A million people: Jews, kings and princesses, prisoners on the run, black marketeers, bankers, writers and artists, all desperate to escape as German forces advanced across Europe and the Nazi noose tightened. A jangle of clashing languages filled the streets as travellers waited for exit permits and transit visas to make their tortuous way through lengthy bureaucratic channels. The rich stayed in converted palaces, the poor haunted the shabby cafés and those who couldn't afford even a roof over their heads slept rough in the docks and alleys of the ancient city, kept alive by soup kitchens.

And in the midst of this anxious, shifting population were spies of all kinds. Agents from the Gestapo and MI6, double agents and informers, thronging the bars of cheap hotels, supplementing exile with espionage. Alongside the official spies were a legion of unofficial ones – waiters, bartenders, shop-keepers and gardeners – watching, waiting and informing. For everyone in that crowded, turbulent city, Lisbon was the very end of the world.

Just west of Lisbon, at the plush beach resort of Estoril, at a few minutes after midnight, a young woman was also waiting. Estoril was the destination of choice for the wealthier and more aristocratic of the refugees, with its sapphire waters and well-raked beach festooned with bathing cabins and palm umbrellas. At one end, like an abandoned sandcastle, stood the turreted, mock Gothic folly of a tower.

The town was more than just the Portuguese Riviera, it was the Riviera, Biarritz and Monte Carlo rolled into one, a place jokingly known as the 'Royal Morgue of Europe' for the number of crowned heads and titled people who flocked there, and the biggest attraction was the Hotel Palacio, a handsome building in white limestone, set on one side of a square that enclosed a manicured park, studded with fountains and palm trees. Although the hotel's corridors were hung with photographs of royal and celebrity guests, the grand mirrored salons, gold filigree walls and fretted woodwork had very little to do with the hotel's popularity. That was entirely down to the casino, one of the best in Europe, where the tips were lavish and the rich flocked every night of the week, desperate to wile away their time with roulette, backgammon and *chemin de fer*.

The night was rich and dark, dense as a wedding cake, and the sky powdered with stars. The young woman stood to one side of the casino's pillared door, trying to remain inconspicuous as knots of people drifted through the glass doors and across the thick red carpet to the gaming room. Inside, chandeliers hung on gold painted ropes, bored croupiers raked the tables and a layer of cigar smoke was intercut by musky drifts of Chanel, Lanvin and Worth. The atmosphere was the same as in any casino the world over: joyless, thick with alcohol and moneyed voices. Occasionally the woman would venture out of the shadow and peer past the porters and bellboys, trying to catch a glimpse inside, but each time she hesitated and withdrew again, drawing her silk jacket closer around her. A black, strapless evening gown, decorated with silver faux-Chinese motifs, hung on her like a negligee and a single strand of pearls circled her neck. She had a gleaming drape of charcoal-coloured hair, eggshell skin, a soft pillow of lips, and a face that had broken a hundred hearts.

The night air raised goose bumps on her flesh and she braced herself, as though she could shrug off the shadows like a sable stole. On the opposite side of the square the red neon sign of the casino expanded and contracted like an artery and a short way away the shivering glitter of the sea was advancing and receding, tugging the shingle outwards to America and back to Europe again. Raucous laughter and the crash of bottles rattled from a nearby bar. The splayed branches of pine trees fractured the dark sky and as she stood there shivering, a momentary waft of resin transported her hundreds of miles, back to the pine-scented Grunewald of Berlin.

Berlin. Nothing about her life in that city could have predicted her presence here, all alone, in an unfamiliar town on the far westerly edge of Europe. Not the ranks of teachers at school or the marching and massed parades and gymnastics in the Tiergarten. Not the dancing and singing, nor the nightclubs, nor the stint at the Haus Vaterland, draped across a grand piano, trying to be Marlene Dietrich. At the thought of it she instinctively flexed a leg with the toe pointed and circled it slowly, as though she was warming up for a performance.

It was love that had brought her here. Damned, inconvenient love. She had always imagined herself immune, as though she'd had an injection against it, like you had for a disease. She prided herself on her indifference. Her heart was as hard as a Wehrmacht helmet. Melting eyes and tender protestations glanced off her like raindrops from the windshield of a pale blue Mercedes convertible, the kind she had always dreamed of owning. But somehow, love had undermined her defences and left her stranded here, three countries away from home, frozen, uncomfortable and very afraid.

She shivered again, shuffling toes that were growing slowly numb in her high heels, and tried to calculate the time. She was, in fact, perfectly used to high heels and late nights; back in Berlin, midnight was nothing. Usually, two o'clock in the morning was her favourite time, when everything slowed down and the harsh edges of the city relaxed. Often she would still be out at dawn, when the housewives first appeared at their doors, clutching their dressing gowns to their necks, looking for the milk cart. But on this particular night, the waiting was a strain. A numbing exhaustion was seeping through her body, up from her legs, coaxing her into a waking doze, forcing her to shake herself awake. She wished yet again that she could find a cigarette, but smoking might draw unwelcome attention. Coffee would help, and the bar across the square was still open, its light fizzing over a few plastic tables, yet she dared not desert her post. Instead she took out a chunk of chocolate from her jacket pocket and let it dissolve slowly on her tongue, staring restlessly at the casino from her vantage place in the shadows. It helped that her performer's training had instilled a certain vigilance in her, a hypersensitivity to her surroundings, and she told herself that standing here was no different from waiting in the wings, poised to enter the stage for her moment of action.

It was past three in the morning before there was any sign that her long vigil might not be in vain. A group of men in dinner jackets and patent leather shoes, ladies in gowns and jewels emerged from the casino and stood chatting. She stiffened to attention. They were like a flock of exotic nocturnal creatures, the trill of female voices and the gruff bark of the men rising and falling as cigars were lit up and the women drew furs around their shoulders. Floral perfume carried faintly on the night air. She studied them intently for a while, checking their faces against the image she carried in her head, running through the options, until they broke apart and began to amble across the close-cropped lawn. Now was her moment. She slipped from the shadow and started to move towards them, but even as she did, at the far edge of her peripheral vision she registered a flicker that resolved itself into the shape of two men approaching in her direction. The sight stopped her dead. There was no question who they must be. She knew at once, from the sleek cut of their plainclothes suits, so different from the shapeless grey-green uniform the ordinary Portuguese policemen wore, that they were secret police. The only issue was whether they been watching her and, if so, for how long?

She hesitated for a second, then spurred by panic quickened her pace towards the group in evening wear, down the steps of the casino to the carefully tended lawn, her heels sinking into the grass. Her movement prompted the men in suits to break into a faster walk. They were coming diagonally towards her, seemingly aiming to intercept her long before she managed to meet the people she had come to see.

Rattled, she turned and darted back into the shadow, but the men were only twenty yards away now, jogging in her direction with obvious intent. Where to go? To one side of the casino an alley of stained concrete led down into deeper darkness and on the spur of the moment she gambled and headed in, praying for an escape at the end. But several yards down she found a twelve-foot chain-wire fence that would be impossible to scale. A bad call.

Heart racing, mind flooding with possibilities, she made a swift reverse out of the alley. The two men were nearer now and one of them was walking with his right arm held close to his chest, as though holding something. It was a technique she had heard of. It was helpful in concealing a gun.

She ran blindly, as well as she could in heels, feeling the circle on her back where the bullet would penetrate. In her mind's eye she could see the flash of the gun's muzzle before she heard it because she knew that light travels faster than sound. She could sense her life exploding, far from home, far away from everything she held dear.

She ran into the square, hoping to camouflage herself in the dense shrubbery to one side of the park, but it was too late. Her foot slipped on the grass, still damp from its nightly watering, and she fell awkwardly, hitting the back of her head on an ornamental rock. The men were upon her.

Light spasmed into her eyes, and she raised a hand to cover them. She dabbed a wet streak on the back of her head and tasted the sharp, metallic tang of blood. Pain was beating a tattoo across her temples. She felt the life force leaking from her like champagne from a broken bottle.

Struggling to her feet she stood transfixed, wondering if the palpitations of her heart were visible beneath her silk jacket, and found herself looking into a vulpine face with pockmarked skin and sunken eyes.

'And there was I thinking you were pleased to see us.'

The policeman rocked backwards on his heels. He was smoking a cigarette and stank of cheap tobacco. He spoke bad German. She wondered how he knew.

'I'm in a hurry. I need to get home.'

The second policeman was fat with blackened teeth, pebbledash complexion and a low brow. His face was glossy with the sweat of pursuit and the whites of his eyes were threaded with a red filigree of veins. The pair had the air of a variety act. Fat and thin. Playful and intensely pleased with themselves.

'No time for conversation?'

'Not at this time of night.'

The first man spat out his cigarette stub sideways.

'But *you're* out at night. What kind of lady is out alone so late?'

'The kind who's been working late.'

'Papers.'

'I don't have them on me.'

'That's a crime, you know. What are you doing here?'

'Just waiting for someone.'

'Who?'

'My boyfriend.'

'What's his name?'

'Why do you need to know?'

'Normally, lady, it's us who ask the questions.'

The double act continued. The fat policeman was dull, meat-faced, relishing the repartee.

'So we have a girl with no name and a boyfriend who doesn't have one either. What *do* you have then?'

'I have this.'

She fumbled in her pocket and pressed something into his palm.

'Take this. It's better than any papers.'

The policeman stared for a moment at the object in his hand.

'What the hell is it?'

'Show it to your superior. He'll understand.'

The man laughed and handed it to his colleague. From the casino door, a ribbon of music unravelled in the night air.

'That's if it's yours to begin with. If you're up to what we think, lady, it'll take more than that.'

With a force out of all proportion to the young woman's size, the fat man seized the tender flesh of her upper arm in one meaty fist and wrestled her past the incurious casino guests to a waiting car across the square.

Chapter One

Berlin, June 1940

Berlin was in darkness. Darker than it had any business to be at ten o'clock on a summer night. Darkness that was more than just the absence of light, but was dense and sooty, composed of folded layers of shadow that collected at the base of buildings and shrouded the narrow alleyways and courtyards. Darkness that blackened the granite icebergs of the government ministries in Mitte, with their tunnels and their bunkers and torture cellars that penetrated deep beneath the street. Darkness that had shuttered the shop fronts along the Kurfürstendamm, doused the jittery fluorescence of the theatre district, and extinguished the beacon on the Funkturm, Berlin's famous radio tower. Darkness so thick it felt heavy to breathe. It obliterated the tenements in the outer suburbs and closed every window in the city like the eyes of a corpse. It rolled like smoke across the canal and over the railway tracks that led westwards to Potsdam, eastwards to Lichtenberg and further to the most distant outposts of the Reich.

Berlin in the first summer of the war was drowned in a darkness that penetrated the eyes and tunnelled right to the very recesses of the soul.

Clara Vine came out of the station at Potsdamer Platz and made her way confidently through the gloom. Until recently Potsdamer Platz had been the busiest intersection in Europe, a five-way maelstrom of honking buses and screeching trams, blazing with multicoloured neon, but since last autumn when war broke out, it had been a very different square. Quieter, because the petrol ration had driven almost all private vehicles from the streets, yet much more perilous at night. Soft curses could be heard as people stumbled on cobbles trying to navigate their way by the phosphorescent paint on the kerbstones, or bumped into lamp posts and fire hydrants set in the centre of the pavement. Buses lurched past like ships, their windows painted blue in the funereal murk, their headlights veiled to show the merest crack of light. The only illumination came from the sporadic violet sparks off tram rails and the dancing circles of torchlight that preceded people along the pavement.

Most pedestrians had a pocket torch, its light obediently muffled with turquoise filter paper. You were only supposed to use it intermittently to check the path, and if you left your torch on for too long you would be shouted at for violating the rules of the blackout. But Clara didn't bother with a torch because the route was as familiar to her as her own face. *First left from the station, across the canal, past Lützowstrasse and right at Bülowstrasse towards the arched dome of Nollendorfplatz U-Bahn, then right towards a street that ends in a tree-fringed square, where a red-brick church tower stands like a ship's mast.* She knew every turn and paving, and exactly how many paces it was from the end of her street to the door of her block. She had followed this route for seven years, yet still it felt strange walking through these silent streets. This neighbourhood in the Nollendorfplatz area – known to everyone as Nolli – was once famous for its risqué nightclubs and cabarets, and even after the Nazis arrived it was crammed with restaurants, bars and cafés whose customers spilled out onto the pavement in summer, beneath the rattle of the elevated S-Bahn, chatting until the early hours.

Yet now the only nightly music to be heard was the air-raid siren. For months everyone in Berlin had assumed that enemy planes would confine themselves to military targets, and could never, even if they tried, penetrate the city's formidable battery of anti-aircraft guns. Yet the first raid had come that month, provoking flak like terrible fireworks and searchlights dancing frantically across the sky. Since then, Clara had spent several evenings huddled in her block's damp, odorous shelter, a deep concrete space lined with wooden benches and sandbags. There was a desultory attempt at furniture, a few tables for card games, coarse, itchy blankets that smelled of mould and space for Jews in the hall outside. A couple of times a local stray cat had crept in and found Clara's lap, a skinny black and white creature quite threadbare compared to the plump, assured beasts that had stalked her childhood home – yet the feel of his fur between her fingers was intensely comforting and she unconsciously looked round for him every time the siren sounded.

The only other diversion was her neighbour Franz Engel, a doctor from the Charité hospital, who would entertain her with stories of his patients. Clara would reciprocate with gossip from the Babelsberg film studios where she was under contract as an actress. Never politics – no one speculated about that, and besides, what was there to speculate about? With all foreign news stations and newspapers banned, everyone was of the same opinion. Germany, protected by its alliance with Russia to the east and to the west a neutral America, had marched across Europe at lightning speed. Belgium and Holland had dropped into the Nazis' laps like ripe plums. France had fallen in six short weeks. Now the *Luftschlacht um England,* the air invasion of England, was only weeks away. Hermann Goering, it was said, had the plans for the attack all mapped out. Virulent anti-British propaganda was everywhere. A tide of feverish hatred rose in the city. The British were *Krämervolk* – a nation of shopkeepers – and when troops marched down Unter den Linden they sang the most popular song of the day, *Wir fahren gegen Engeland.* We march against England.

To Clara, Anglo-German by birth and English by upbringing, the idea of her native land under Nazi occupation was a special horror. She had arrived in Berlin at the age of twenty-six after a less than glorious stage career in London, hoping that at Babelsberg she might make a fresh start in films. Yet the past seven years had taught her far more than the talents required for motion pictures. Whereas in England a girl of her background might have learned to type and address letters, to set a table, arrange the silver and make correct conversation

with vicars, in Germany she had acquired far more special-
ized skills. How to pass as a guileless actress amid the highest
echelons of the Third Reich. To listen to the complaints and
confidences of the wives of the senior men, observe their feuds
and mine their every move for evidence of Hitler's intentions.
And to relay every piece of useful information back to her
contacts in the British secret service.

She had learned how to spy.

Yet since war had been declared, her position was more
dangerous than it had ever been. For years her British
heritage had marked her out, but now it was a terrifying vulnerability, a dreadful weakness, and although her Englishness
had been formally renounced and eradicated by a sheaf of
official documentation, the stain of it lingered. And as if that
were not enough, beneath the perilous mark of her ancestry
another, far more damning vulnerability remained. When
she first arrived in Germany, in 1933, she had discovered that
her grandmother, Hannah Neumann, was a Jew. Therefore,
Clara, through her maternal line, was Jewish too. It was a fact
she kept deeply hidden, a secret that would not only end her
career but could threaten her life itself.

Last summer, the family she had not seen for so long, her
father, sister and brother, had all written separately, urging
her to return to England. Her father sent two lines of spiky
script like a military command, Kenneth's letter was full of
brusque, brotherly concern and her elder sister Angela had
filled pages in her elegant, flowery hand, offering a schedule
of tennis parties, bridge evenings, dances and dinners, and all
the chintz-covered safety of the Home Counties.

Yet still Clara hesitated, reluctant to abandon Erich. It was seven years now since his mother, a fellow actress at Babelsberg, died in a suspicious fall and Clara had vowed to care for the orphaned ten-year-old. Since then the relationship between them had grown close, and nothing pleased her more than his company on their weekend outings, watching him develop into a teenager of quick intelligence, debating, relaxing, laughing with him. Then in September the borders of the Reich clanged shut and she lost her chance to leave. She was left with only Erich and a document declaring her a citizen of the German Reich. One she loved dearly, the other she hated more with each passing day.

A chill breeze sliced the night air and she tried to walk faster. Clara always travelled by train now; the little red Opel she had once driven was locked up in a garage in Neukölln and she had been required to surrender its battery. Even if she'd kept it, petrol was impossible to come by. However, the twenty-minute S-Bahn ride from Babelsberg station to the centre of Berlin suited her. It was impossible to read on the train because the windows were fitted with thick blinds fastened to the panes and alternate light bulbs had been removed, leaving only small pools of light above the seating in a zigzag pattern, so Clara had put the leather bag containing the script for a new film to one side as the train swayed on its tracks through the shadowy suburbs. She relished these small moments of solitude where she could exist, unobserved. Everyone did. You saw people on the trams and the trains and the buses, building invisible barriers so they could sink into their thoughts. Nobody looked at each other

if they could help it. Everything was rationed nowadays –
even smiles.

That evening she had been especially late leaving
the studios and the carriage was entirely empty until
Mexikoplatz, when the train braked with a hydraulic sigh,
the doors slid open and a figure walked in through the
gloom. Despite having an entire carriage to choose from
he had approached and settled himself on the wooden seat
directly facing Clara. A brief glance upwards told her that
he was youngish – thirty perhaps. Average build, regular
features, anonymous-looking. *Unassuming.* That was how
she would have described it had she been paying enough
mental attention even to put it in words. He wore a greasy
beige fedora, shabby suit and a white shirt that gleamed
in the blue light. Dark hair, with a widow's peak. Politely
she looked away, but when she glanced back, the man's
eyes remained unflinchingly on her face. Almost certainly
he recognized her – that happened increasingly often –
and was trying to work out exactly why. Most probably
he was ransacking his memory, seeking to place her,
running through a mental list of his acquaintances until
it dawned that she was neither one of his neighbours, nor
a girl in his office, nor the woman who served him in his
local bakery but an actress he had seen on the big screen.
Clara Vine, that was the one, who had starred in *Black
Roses* and *The Pilot's Wife* and *The Stars Shine.* When that
happened, the realization would be generally accompanied
by an embarrassed smile or a sheepish shake of the head.
Sometimes even an autograph request. And yet ... this

man's stare suggested no such mental confusion. His gaze was intent, the mouth steady, the eyes pools of inscrutable shadow. Clara felt a prickle of unease. It was as if he *did* know who she was.

Yet she most certainly did not know him.

Moments passed and the thud of doors echoed down the platform. The man was still staring at her, directly, and then, as the guard's whistle sounded, he moved fractionally forward as though he was about to address her. At that moment a heavily panting woman in a stout tweed suit and woollen stockings slammed open the dividing doors at the end of the carriage and settled herself in the seat next to Clara, giving off a mingled odour of cooking and cheap perfume. The train jerked forward with a pneumatic hiss and began to move.

The woman got out her bag and despite the poor light, which rendered the needles almost invisible, began knitting. Everywhere you went women were knitting now. On every street and in every magazine the jaunty governmental slogan could be seen. *The German Woman Is Knitting Again!* At home and in public places women knitted and knitted as though needles themselves were weapons of war and the nets of wool they created could somehow reach out and wrap themselves round their distant sons and hold them safe.

The man leaned back slightly, placed one leather-gloved hand on each splayed knee, and relocated his stare to a spot just beyond her left shoulder. Clara did the same, focusing on a poster opposite reading *I am a member of the NSV – are you?* while she allowed her mind to drift.

The eye adjusts to darkness, and just as Clara's eye had adjusted over seven years to the placards condemning the Jews, the arrests and disappearances, the police informers in every shop and office, so she had grown accustomed to the darkness that had fallen on her life. The ashy deadness of Berlin suited her, because it matched the leaden monochrome of her existence.

Berlin was a city of absent men, but the man missing from Clara's life would never return. The previous year her lover, Leo Quinn, was reported killed in a shoot-out at the German border, along with Conrad Adler, the German officer who was helping him escape. Leo, the person who first encouraged Clara as a nervous young actress to relay the gossip she encountered in the company of senior Nazis back to British intelligence. Leo, who schooled her in espionage and, in the process, had fallen in love with her.

It had been Mary Harker, an American journalist and Clara's closest friend, who picked up the news of the incident from the press club that evening a year ago and passed it on. Two unnamed enemies of the state, challenged at a border checkpoint, had attempted to escape and been cut down in a hail of fire. Mary had known barely anything of their love affair because Clara and Leo had kept their secret from everyone, so their story had slipped into the past unseen, engulfed by events like a raindrop sliding into a lake.

Perhaps for that reason, or because she had not witnessed his death, Clara found it hard to accept the finality of the event. She had no photograph of Leo. She would never know his last words. When they parted they imagined they would meet up again within days, or at the very least weeks, but instead Leo had disappeared as entirely as his car's red tail lights had vanished that evening from view.

She remembered people telling her about shell shock during the last war. How it would come in waves, and there would be intervals of feeling almost entirely normal, and now she knew that was true, because it was exactly how she felt. At times her whole body ached, as though heartbreak was a physical condition, yet the rest of the time she functioned the same as ever. She had a horror of staying still and did everything she could to keep busy. During the day, acting, getting into costume, in make-up, in the canteen or talking to friends, she was able to shut the thought of Leo away entirely, but at night her sleep was torn with dreams and memories. Frequently she was jolted into wakefulness by a sense that he had returned – even that he was sleeping right next to her – only to fall back into a fitful doze. Or she would lie awake with the same scenes playing over and over in her mind, as if she was caught in some remorseless searchlight she couldn't escape. Insomnia slowed time to a leaden pace. She craved sleep like an addict. Yet every morning she welcomed the moment when she woke up and the world surged in; even if it was a world filled with war, it was still a place where people baked bread, played games and made films – more so now than ever.

Babelsberg, the Hollywood of Europe, was busy. Two thousand people worked on its eight sound stages, turning out the *mélange* of escapist musicals and stalwart military films that was their contribution to the war effort. Clara was relieved to be occupied, even if the work presented its own problems. The bag beside her contained the script of a new film called *Jud Süss* for which she had been asked to audition. Its director, Veit Harlan, was one of Babelsberg's stars and no one turned him down him with impunity, yet a brief glance at the script caused Clara's heart to sink. Although it was set in the eighteenth century, its theme of a ruthless conniving Jew destroying the city of Württemberg could not echo more clearly the sentiments of its originator, Joseph Goebbels.

What the five foot six Goebbels lacked in stature he made up for with the longest title in the Reich – Minister for Propaganda and Public Enlightenment and Head of the Reich Chamber of Culture. For years he had mistrusted Clara. He had had her tailed and investigated. Once he had her arrested and imprisoned. Despite her acquaintance with his wife, Magda, Clara knew Goebbels could never quite shake the conviction that this London-born actress was memorizing the gossip and information she encountered in the circle of the Nazi elite, and relaying it to British intelligence. As ever with Goebbels, his instinct was stronger than his evidence. All the same, she was increasingly careful to avoid him.

Clara carried on through the unlit streets. The walls had a different texture in the darkness, as if they were made of something more solid than mere brick. Anti-Jewish graffiti appeared sporadically like prickly stigmata. She crossed the canal, and turned the corner into Potsdamer Strasse. With dismay she noted that the flags were out again. Each residential block was decked in swastika banners to mark the recent victory in France. Since May, there were more posters and banners than ever. Flags were hung out as regularly as washing on the stucco façades and if any window failed to display one when the order had gone out, a zealous blockwarden would complain. Either a pennant must appear within two hours, or the authorities would. Rudi, the old man who supervised Clara's own block in Winterfeldtstrasse more fiercely than Cerberus guarded the gates of hell, was no exception.

'I'm sorry, Fräulein Vine,' he explained, with not a trace of apology, the last time Clara had neglected to unearth her musty scarlet pennant from its place at the bottom of a drawer. 'You actresses are busy. We all know that. But there's only one Führer and the law's the law.' He tapped his watch. 'As soon as you can, please.'

In the distance she saw a speck of light that formed into a disembodied luminous swastika wavering towards her. It might have seemed something from a horror movie, had Clara not known it was a phosphorescent lapel badge, one of the newly fashionable kind that allowed their wearer to express Party allegiance even in the darkest hours.

The swastika came closer, its wearer a shapeless shadow. She felt a leap of disquiet and picked up her pace. With so many men away from Berlin, those that remained had become emboldened and were given to approaches they would never previously have dared to make. She told herself that there were plenty of people who worked late hours. This man was probably just as eager to get home to his bed as she was.

He was only a few feet from her when a torch beam sliced through the thick darkness. She startled as he obstructed her path and flipped his torch upwards, dazzling her as she raised her hand to shield her eyes. His body blocked the background light. Squinting, she saw it was the man she had noticed before, the one on the train. Dark hair with a widow's peak. Expressionless. Beige fedora. The light of the torch from below made the lines and angles of his face stand out chalky against the blackness.

'Excuse me.'

She sidestepped him and made to walk on but the man sprang to stop her.

'Please get out of my way.'

He moved towards her so that she was forced to edge up closer against the wall and his hand went to his pocket. Panic overwhelmed her and in a reflex she brought the heavy manuscript bag swinging upwards, clashing against his solar plexus, winding him. The man reeled back in surprise, but only for a moment, before stepping forward again, his face looming towards hers.

What did he see when he looked there? A slender woman in a pale blue skirt and a blouse buttoned to the neck beneath a jacket that was a couple of seasons old. A solemn face, thinner than it had been, the girlish roundness gone, but still heart-shaped and framed by wavy chestnut hair that was cut short and fastened with a clip to one side. A straight nose, generous lips outlined with just a trace of blush pink, and brows tweezered into high arches to emphasize eyes of deep blue. If he had looked deeper in those eyes he would have seen a steel harder than any blade, tempered by loss and untarnished by fear, the steel of someone who had already come so close to death that it no longer had the power to frighten her.

A sudden burst of male laughter sounded to their right and both looked round to see twin red glows bobbing towards them. Two cigarettes were approaching, accompanied by their smokers. Their large forms were indistinct, but a glimmer on the pavement showed where the men had applied luminescent paint to the toe of their shoes.

The man in the fedora stiffened, sensing discovery, and stepped back. Clara took the opportunity to break away, running swiftly the few yards round the corner of her own street. She guessed he would not pursue her with other people so close by and she was right. Yet her heart was still hammering as she reached the ochre block at 35, Winterfeldtstrasse and pushed the heavy wooden door.

The dim entrance hall was empty, the tiled floor pitted and rank with bleach. Buckets of sand stood in case of fire and on the notice board Rudi had pinned directions to the air-raid shelter – as if they were needed – alongside a variety of yellowing notices, warnings and threats. A memo from the Propaganda Ministry about an upcoming parade. Fresh protocols from the Reichsluftschutzbund, the air-raid body. Collections for the Winterhilfswerk. Slipping in, Clara decided against taking the elevator, in case the clanking iron cage woke the other residents, and instead trudged up the stone stairway to the fifth floor.

Removing the tiny pebble from the door handle – her precaution against unsolicited guests – she locked it behind her and kicked off her shoes. She adored this apartment. It was perfectly situated and in a lively area. Its single corridor had a bathroom, bedroom and kitchen leading off it and at the end, its glory, a high-ceilinged, book-lined sitting room with a window that looked out over the crooked grey rooftops of Nollendorfplatz, although that window was now patterned with criss-crossed strips of tape to prevent bomb damage. It also contained a desk with a wobbly leg and her old, red velvet armchair, next to a towering pile of books waiting to be read.

She drew the heavy black curtain, switched on the lamp and gazed around her at her beloved possessions and the photographs of her mother and Erich on the mantelpiece, as if drawing comfort from their familiar presence. Sometimes these walls seemed to squeeze her so it was hard to breathe, at other times their embrace enclosed and comforted her. Now was one of these times.

She went into the kitchen, put some water on to boil and moved restlessly about, her pulse still racing, clasping and unclasping her arms around her chest. She wasn't cold, even though coal had run out in May, meaning the apartment was chilly and she couldn't heat the stove. Nor was she hungry, which was lucky because she had not had the chance to shop that day. Rationing had been in force since war broke out, but the complexity of the system, coupled with the scarcity of groceries on offer, meant there were always long queues. Had Clara's Jewish identity been known, her cards would have been printed with a J and her much reduced rations would only be available at the end of the day when most of the food had gone. But then if her Jewish identity was known she would not be in the Reich Chamber of Culture, or in this apartment, or in Berlin for that matter.

She ran her fingers down her throat. There was a rushing sound in her ears. Abstractedly she twirled a lock of hair that fell down into her eyes – a habit she had when thinking – as the implications of her encounter dawned. In recent weeks a spate of attacks had taken place on or near the tracks of Berlin's S-Bahn. A man dubbed the S-Bahn attacker was being held responsible for several assaults that had left women fighting for their lives. The attacks had transfixed the citizens of Berlin and details of each one were relayed with breathless urgency in the local papers. Everything about that evening suggested that Clara had met the same man. The moment on the train when he leaned forward and seemed about to accost her until the Hausfrau with her knitting settled in the seat alongside. The fact that he followed her from the station to her home, only to be interrupted by a pair of pedestrians. Even as she digested the shock she knew it would no doubt reverberate as she reflected on her lucky escape over the next few hours.

She was far too alert to go to bed. She thought of switching on the radio and trying for the BBC. Like everyone else she had a Volksempfänger VE301 on her mantelpiece, a mottled brown mass-produced Bakelite object with an eagle and a swastika on its case and a dial that offered only German frequencies, yet beneath a floorboard in her kitchen she had a hidden shortwave set. The sentence for listening to foreign radio stations had been upgraded to concentration camp or death, but that did not deter her. It helped that she had total trust in her neighbour, Doktor Franz Engel. Often, when they were both in, the confident blast of Beethoven's Sixth Symphony would vibrate through the wall – a private, neighbourly signal to Clara, as clear as any Morse code, that her transgression would be drowned out.

Only last week she had crouched down to hear the slurring bass of Winston Churchill, the new British Prime Minister, addressing the House of Commons, his distant voice crackling from the set like the echo soundings of a submarine.

'*The whole fury and might of the enemy must very soon be turned on us. Upon this battle depends the survival of Christian civilization. Upon it depends our own British life and the long continuity of our institutions and our Empire . . .*'

Yet now she had no appetite for news. Instead she perched on the edge of the velvet armchair, clasping her knees, and tried to make sense of the curious sensation racing through her. It wasn't trauma – it was more like – *excitement*. The inertia she had felt for so long had turned into a thrumming impatience. Something about her encounter in the street – the rush of adrenalin she had felt – had taught her something. She need not go on any longer like this, drifting and dreaming, imprisoned by her loss. The thing she most feared had happened, and if her own life was to have any meaning, the least she could do was to fight back, seize every opportunity to assuage her sorrow and make something worthwhile from the loss of Leo. To collect up all her grief and resentment and with it light a fire to revenge him. In the past months her life had dwindled to such a point that acting was her only occupation. She had promised Leo that she would stay away from the work that he himself had introduced into her life and since last summer she had kept her pledge. She had avoided any contact with the British intelligence services, nor had they contacted her. She remained on the guest list for many a Nazi reception, which meant she still saw the wives of the Nazi elite – Emmy Goering, Magda Goebbels, Annelies von Ribbentrop – and still overheard their gossip about the progress of the war and their husbands' feuds. Yet she had not attempted to relay this information elsewhere. She had abandoned all contact with the British secret services. She had lost all inclination for espionage.

But now she felt a new resolution surge within her.

She realized, although her heart was broken, it was still beating.

Chapter Two

'War's changed a lot of things,' said Mary Harker, as she and Clara stood at the back door of sound stage three in the Babelsberg studios, where a line-up of chorus dancers were practising a basic high-kick number, 'but you'd never have thought it could change basic human anatomy.'

Clara saw her point. Assembled on the sound stage in front of them the chorus line rehearsing the latest musical, *Die grosse Liebe*, seemed so much less elegant than usual. The film was a typical Babelsberg extravaganza, with no expense spared to create an uplifting visual spectacle that would simultaneously remind Germans of the sacrifices of war and invite them to dream of the future. The troupe were dressed as angels, in billowing white chiffon with gauzy wings, yet they possessed all the ethereal elegance of a village football team. Their movements were pantomimed and their routine woodenly regimented, with none of the suggestive sexual undercurrent that chorus girls usually imparted. The blusher on their cheeks was far too exaggerated and their wigs had the comical cast of a bad cartoon. It was all the more extraordinary, given that they were performing alongside the nation's favourite film star, Zarah Leander.

Like everything in the Third Reich, the studio star system was rigorously controlled and that included telling the nation which actress they loved the most. Once it had been decided that Zarah Leander, a statuesque redhead of Swedish origin, should be the Diva of the Third Reich, nothing was left to chance. The studio had issued her with a rigid set of rules dictating her wardrobe, her social life and her press interviews, and no expense was spared on her productions, including this one. She wasn't the first Swede to make her way to Babelsberg; Ingrid Bergman and Greta Garbo had gone before her, but Zarah was the first to stay and make the most of it. She possessed a deep, smoky contralto that got under the skin, an exotic air and an image of unapproachable grandeur. She was also the highest paid artist in the Reich. Which made it all the stranger that the hatchet-faced angelic host surrounding her should be so unappealing. From where Mary and Clara stood, a hundred yards from the dazzle of the arc lights, this chorus line seemed more muscular than usual. Heavier, too. In fact, they seemed almost . . . *male.*

'You know what it is, don't you?'

Another actress, Claudine Hoss, had come up behind them. She pursed her mouth and raised eyebrows that had been darkened in the new method with burnt matchsticks.

'Take a good look.'

As Clara focused more closely on the dancers – the bulky thighs, the rough hands, the shadow of stubble on their faces – reason slowly dawned.

'They're *men*, aren't they?'

'Not just men. They're from the Führer's bodyguard. The cream of the SS.'

'But why?'

'It's Zarah. She's too tall. They need to match her height or she's going to stick out from the chorus line like a bratwurst from a bun.'

For the first time in a year Clara burst out laughing.

'Please God tell me they're not going to sing.'

'They probably only know the Horst Wessel Song,' said Claudine, 'and songs about knives spurting Jewish blood don't sound so good coming from angels, even if they are SS ones.'

'I thought Goebbels had banned drag acts,' gasped Mary, choking down laughter. 'I remember him saying it offended National Socialist sensibilities.'

'I expect they volunteered on account of the stockings,' said Claudine. 'Perhaps they think they can keep them to bribe girls with.'

'They might be right. There's a lot I would do for a pair. These are hopeless.'

They all cast a glance at Mary's legs, which on close inspection had been painted a streaky brown. Liquid stockings came in a jar, but they were pricey.

'At least you're not using gravy powder,' shrugged Claudine, in reference to the cut-price alternative. 'It looks good but you find dogs following you up the street.'

Mary grinned happily. 'Just wait till I write up this story. The SS must be the only people left in Berlin who still get to dress up.'

It was true. Dressing up, since the beginning of the war, had become the stuff of dreams. Once, Germany's glossy magazines had carried patterns for every type of occasion – town clothes and country gear, afternoon dresses and evening gowns, for lunch in town and evenings at the opera. Now there were only articles on make do and mend, tips for making knickers out of old sheets and excitable pieces about second-hand fabrics. Even when one found a pattern, the styles were confined to a miserable, drab selection, with strict stipulations over the amount of cloth allowed and a single shade of the season, which according to the latest edition of *Vogue* was 'storm-coloured'. That made sense.

As if that wasn't bad enough, the newspaper fashion pages were cluttered with government regulations on what a woman's 'normal' wardrobe should resemble. Ladies should own just one dress and petticoat, a single pair of knickers, a lone bra, one pair of stockings and three handkerchiefs. No one need possess more than two pairs of shoes, and if they wanted another pair they needed to provide evidence that the old ones were thoroughly worn out before they could get permission. Clara's wardrobe far exceeded this paltry provision, even if her favourite pink silk dress by Hilda Romatzki was wearing thin, and the others were feeling a little shabby. Yet if her surplus clothing was going to be discovered it would have happened already. If past experience was anything to go by, the Gestapo probably knew the contents of her drawers better than she did.

Claudine pursed her lips. 'What is it they say? In wartime

everything must be put to a different use. I suppose that applies to SS men too.'

The women lingered a while longer, enjoying the comedy of the spectacle, before Clara and Mary wandered out into the sunshine. The grassy lawn at the centre of the Babelsberg studios was a favourite place for actresses to spend their lunchtimes or the break between scenes. It was fringed with willow trees, and that day it was crammed with actors and production staff stretching out in the sun. Yet it was a spot Clara tended to avoid, given that it was overlooked by office windows, and one office in particular: that belonging to Joseph Goebbels. The minister frequently stood at his window feasting his eyes on the suntanned flesh outside, and the idea of his gaze falling on her turned Clara's blood to ice.

'Mind if we keep walking? That's Goebbels' office over there.'

'So you're avoiding him?'

'I've been offered a new film. *Jud Süss*. It's a dreadful script but if I turn it down I'm looking for trouble. I could be arrested. It takes almost nothing these days.'

From her earliest days in Babelsberg, Clara had recognized that acting was a dangerous business. In her second week at the film studio the actor Hans Otto, a Communist, had been arrested in a café by Brown Shirts and beaten to death in Gestapo headquarters when he refused to name his associates. Helga Schmidt, her first friend in the city and Erich's mother, had been thrown from a window for daring to make jokes about Hitler. To turn down a role in one of Goebbels' prestige projects would take either crazy courage or an especially convincing excuse. As yet, Clara had not managed to summon either.

'Or is it you don't want to be seen with a known trouble-maker like me?'

'Don't joke, Mary. It's Goebbels I don't want to see. You, on the other hand . . .'

Clara left her sentence hanging. Mary had, as usual, per-ceived the truth. Even though she was American, and her country uninvolved in Europe's war, she remained a foreign journalist and it was increasingly risky for the pair of them to be seen together. Yet there was practically no one in Berlin whose company Clara preferred. Mary Harker had barely changed in all the time they had known each other, since the days in 1933 when she abandoned her affluent family home in New Jersey and arrived in Germany as a poorly paid stringer for the *New York Evening Post*. She still had the halo of hair springing untidily from her head, ineffectually tamed by a few Kirby grips, in a shade the Germans called *Strassenköterblond*, mongrel blonde, because of the range of colours it contained. American teeth as wide and white as a picket fence. The sun had spattered freckles across her face and her clear hazel eyes were masked by the same heavy spectacles. She still had a habit of speaking her mind, in a drawl that had only deepened over the years from a serious addiction to Marlboro cigarettes, and she retained the burn-ing sense of justice that landed her in frequent conflict with the authorities. And she still, after seven years, was no nearer finding a decent man to share her life.

As far as Clara knew, since Mary's unrequited love for a

British journalist called Rupert Allingham, there had been no one serious. The other foreign correspondents, who, apart from the freelance Stella Fry and the *Chicago Tribune's* Sigrid Schultz, were almost all male, treated her as an equal. She was an experienced, professional, hard-drinking reporter, an acute reader of the power structure in Nazi Germany, and simply one of the guys. That was how they saw her. There had been a few light-hearted affairs – Mary had the ability to make everyone laugh and she was effortlessly relaxed in male company – but no man had yet come between Mary's Remington typewriter and her roving eye for a story.

'You didn't tell me. Why exactly are you here?'

'I wanted to take a look at the camp.'

'A camp? At Babelsberg?'

'Apparently. They've built it round the back of the lots. Deliberately out of the way.'

'What on earth for?'

'To house Polish prisoners.' Mary grimaced. 'Forced labourers.'

Since the invasion of Poland, the country was awash with foreign workers. *Zivilarbeiter.* You distinguished them by the initial P sewn onto their clothes; that was if you hadn't already noticed the starved pallor and fugitive eyes averted whenever a German went by. Public transport, churches and restaurants were out of bounds to them and, most of all, German women. Just in case the women forgot, every library, station and government building was littered with pamphlets warning of the risks of disease and the penalties for any form of fraternization.

35

'Why house prisoners at a film studio?'

'Useful labour. In fact, I'm surprised they needed to call in the SS for Zarah Leander because the word is labourers are going to be used as extras, now that so many actors have been conscripted.'

'Where did you hear that?'

'Straight from the mouth of Joey Goebbels himself. Doesn't mean it's true of course, in fact it usually means the opposite. But seeing as he announced it in the morning press conference at the Ministry of Truth I thought I'd come out here and take a look on the off-chance that for one moment he wasn't lying. It's so rare he lets out anything interesting; I tell you, the nightly blackout has nothing on the information blackout from the Propaganda Ministry. We journalists are starved of news. But you know what?' Mary pointed. 'He was right. There they are.'

On the far wooded edge of the studio grounds a number of workers wearing cast-offs from the prison system were initiating the construction of a series of low, brick-built barracks under the instruction of an SS guard. As Clara and Mary approached they detected, alongside the sound of hacking and sawing, a quite different commotion. At the end of the barracks a makeshift boxing ring had been set up, and two prisoners were being picked to fight. The supervising guard strutted down the lines before pulling out a heavy-set worker with a dense, hairy torso and enormous hands and feet. As the prisoner trudged towards the ring, the guard continued squinting through the throng before selecting a pigeon-chested figure in wire-rimmed glasses.

A jovial throng of Ufa employees had begun to congregate, men with their hands in their pockets, secretaries on their lunch break, and stagehands snatching a moment off work, all relishing an unexpected moment of entertainment. An impromptu boxing match was a welcome interruption to the usual working day.

Once the boxers were in their corners, it was even clearer how mismatched they were. The larger one was jogging, dancing round the ring, making practice feints with his fists as the crowd shouted their appreciation. His opponent sat stripped to his shorts, the towel round his neck barely concealing the ladder of ribs clearly visible beneath his heaving chest. Even before the fight had begun his face was beaded with sweat in anticipation of the pummelling he was about to endure. Sickened, Clara turned away.

'I'm surprised they're not trying to keep this place quiet rather than broadcasting it to the international press.'

'They're proud of it. Goebbels says everything necessary will be done to keep Ufa studios at the peak of its production. Entertainment is more important than ever. Film is the vanguard of the German military. Etcetera, etcetera.'

'I suppose it's better than most of the work they can hope for.'

'Exactly. But while the Poles come here,' Mary's voice dropped, 'the Jews are being sent to replace them.'

'Moved to Poland?'

'Somewhere in the east. For resettlement.'

No one in Berlin could be unaware that the Jews were going somewhere. Those who had not already fled the Reich were now a terrified, hunted people, banned from cafés, restaurants, places of worship, hospitals, cinemas and theatres. Yet not content with removing them from daily life, Hitler had publicly announced his intention to deport them. It was hard to remain ignorant of the trucks making arrests in the Scheunenviertel, the Jewish quarter, or calling at dawn at addresses across the capital.

'What does resettlement mean?'

'I don't know. But I'm determined to find out.'

They sat for a moment, watching the boxing match progress along predictably uneven lines. After the third time the smaller man was knocked down and hoisted to his feet, Clara turned away.

'All I can say is, I pity you having to see Goebbels so often.'

'As it happens, I'm seeing more of him than ever. There's a war going on.'

'I noticed.'

'Not that one.' A small, ironic laugh. 'I mean the war between Goebbels and von Ribbentrop.'

The antagonism between the Propaganda Minister and his opposite number at the Foreign Office was longstanding. Feuds were rife in Nazi circles and anyone hoping to understand the senior men needed to be an archaeologist of arguments, digging deep into the origins of the rivalries that gave the regime its malign energy.

'It's reached absurd levels. First, they established rival foreign press clubs, and now they've taken to scheduling their press conferences at the same time so they clash. Both start at eleven o'clock each morning and we journalists have to choose between them.'

'Some choice,' said Clara, who would always take the option that avoided Goebbels.

'It is. But Joey Goebbels is winning hands down.'

'I can't imagine why.'

'He's hit on a masterstroke. They may starve us of news, but we're not going to starve any other way. He's fixed the ration coupons.'

For some months a complex system of colour-coded cards had been issued by the Reich Rationing Office – blue for meat, yellow for fat and white for sugar. Aryans were allocated more than two thousand calories a day, Poles less than a thousand and Jews around two hundred. Some categories of the population, such as nursing mothers and manual workers, received special concessions.

'There's this system of handing out our ration coupons at the end of every conference – it's a way of making sure the press turns up – and Goebbels has arranged for us to get double rations.'

'Surely double rations are only for coal miners and heavy labourers?'

Mary shrugged nonchalantly.

'Journalism counts as heavy labour, as far as I'm concerned. Sometimes I'm doing a sixteen-hour day. Anyhow, von Ribbentrop can't work out why everyone's opting to attend the Propaganda Ministry briefings instead of his. Say what you like about Mahatma Propagandi, he's clever.'

'There's a lot else I'd say about him first.'

Mary looked at Clara, and her grin faded.

'Are you having a problem with Goebbels? Apart from this film, I mean?'

'Nothing I can't cope with. I'm hoping the war means he's too busy to bother with me any more.'

'And your English heritage?'

'You forget. I'm a citizen of the Reich now, so it needn't be a hindrance.'

Mary knew that Clara had taken German citizenship, and she had a shrewd understanding of why, yet the two of them never spoke of it. It was better that way.

'All the same. Lilian Harvey's gone back to England.'

Like Clara, Lilian Harvey had joint German and English parentage. Although she had been born in Muswell Hill in north London, the actress had been Ufa's favourite blonde bombshell in the last decade until she found the attacks on Jewish colleagues too much to bear and had fled, with plans to quit acting altogether and open a gift shop.

'Something's bothering you.'

'Something's bothering us all.'

'How's the family?'

'They don't write often and I'd need permission to telephone abroad. Besides, I wouldn't risk it.'

'And Erich?'

How swiftly Mary had got to the heart of the matter. She knew intuitively that Erich was the sole reason that Clara had stayed in Berlin, and not only because she paid for the boy's support in his grandmother's apartment.

'Erich is hoping to join the Luftwaffe. Fortunately he

hasn't succeeded yet. I sometimes wonder if I could pull some strings.'

'You mean get him drafted?'

'I mean keep him out.'

'And . . . everything else?'

Clara hesitated. Even now caution prevailed. Even now, when Leo was dead and there was no longer any earthly need to deny what had existed between them. Why was it so hard to allow the truth to bludgeon its way out from the frozen wasteland within? Why could she not even bring herself to say his name?

She gave a light shrug.

'Everything's fine.'

'I still can't believe you're staying.'

Clara frowned. How to explain the new mood of resolution that had woken in her?

'I've managed so far, haven't I?'

Mary took off her spectacles and cleaned them on the edge of her skirt. It was a journalistic trick that generally bought her a little time while she considered how to approach a tricky subject, but Clara was no interviewee, and she knew there was no point probing further. When Clara wanted to keep something private, there was barely any chance of prising it out.

'Well, whatever it is about Goebbels, watch out, won't you?'

'Don't worry. I haven't seen him for months and I'm doing my level best to avoid him.'

They remained a moment in silence, breathing in the

mingled summer scents of cut grass and wood smoke. They had reached that stage of friendship where they knew so much of each other's lives that certain things could stay unsaid, and what remained unknown would never be allowed to come between them. Mary pulled out a packet of Marlboro and flipped the top.

'Have one of these. Bill Shirer brought them back from the States. God, I miss real tobacco. The stuff they sell here makes mud taste good. And you can't scrub the stain off your fingers for weeks.'

They lit up, savouring the toasty flavour, so helpful in deadening hunger pangs.

'In fact, it's not just the cigarettes I miss.'

Mary aimed a sudden, searing glance at her friend.

'The truth is, I'm not sure I can stand it here much longer.'

'*You're* not thinking of leaving?'

Shock made Clara's voice unnaturally loud.

'I don't know how long I can go on dealing with these people. You must hear the stories – one of my German colleagues was arrested last month and taken to Gestapo headquarters. He was beaten to within an inch of his life. His own daughter didn't recognize him when he returned. Another guy, a contact of mine, simply vanished. He never came home and two weeks after he disappeared his wife received his spectacles in the post. Just that. The *Herald Trib* correspondent got thrown out yesterday for suggesting the Germans and the Russians are no longer getting on.'

'But you don't write about the politics.'

Mary Harker's Berlin Life, which ran in the *New York*

Evening Post, was designed to take a sideways look at the city, focusing on everyday 'human interest' stories away from current affairs. Privately Clara had always welcomed this approach, aware that in the realm of political reporting Mary and her visa would be easily parted.

'Everyday life *is* politics now. It's impossible to say where one ends and the other begins.'

Mary didn't need to spell it out. Even among the actors and studio staff Clara knew, people were cracking up. Wondering if they would be denounced or accused, whether the knock would come on their front door and they would join the disappeared, rotting away in prison camps as their relatives mounted ineffectual campaigns for their release. Berlin was a city full of fear, where people watched their backs and hoped the slam of the car door at dawn was for their neighbour, not themselves.

'All of us American correspondents are under intense pressure. It's becoming almost impossible to report objectively. And if the Nazis invade England, the *Post* will want me to embed with the German forces. I don't know if I can bear that. I love your old homeland. I lived there for a while, remember, back in '36? In a pretty cottage in Kent while all that fuss was going on about the King's abdication and the wicked Wallis Simpson.'

She paused and exhaled a luxurious plume of smoke.

'God, that affair was romantic. *It is impossible to discharge the duties of King without the help and support of the woman I love.* And then the Duke went and enraged his nation by coming to Germany on honeymoon.'

Clara smiled wryly.

'I remember.'

She had seen the couple briefly on their Berlin visit, the Duke, tiny and trim, and his new wife Wallis, beady-eyed and swathed in fur like a trapped mink, with a look on her face that said she had never planned ending up on the arm of an ex-King, let alone dragged around Europe, mocked and reviled, far from the fast society she loved. Yet once they were wedded, the couple did everything to keep up appearances. Wallis Simpson was a couturier's dream and the pair were competitive dieters who survived on a regime of olives and cocktail nuts that made their Nazi hosts appear all the more gargantuan.

'I was at a party Goering hosted for them out at his country place, Carinhall. The entire top brass turned out in force. Everyone in England was furious about it. I almost felt sorry for them.'

'Wonder what they'll do now.'

'I'm sure the Duke will be going back to Britain if he hasn't already. He'll want to play his part.'

'Actually . . .' Mary hesitated, relishing the gossip she was about to relay. 'That's not what I heard. Churchill is begging them to come home but word is they're having a very enjoyable time in Europe. The Duchess is digging in her heels. She's refusing to get dragged into the war.'

'Even someone as accustomed to getting her way as Wallis Simpson might find it hard to avoid an international war.'

'I wouldn't bet on it. Wally's American, remember, so she's not involved. And she won't lift a finger to oblige the

British. There's been endless underhand sniping from the Royal Family.'

'Families are good at that kind of thing.'

'Your Royal Family make everyone else look like amateurs.'

'But if the Nazis continue to occupy mainland Europe, they'll have to go. They're English royalty, for heaven's sake. What do they expect will happen?'

'Wallis is a survivor. If she can survive the British Royal Family, she'll certainly manage the Nazis.' Mary stretched out her legs and sighed. 'Anyhow, in the meantime, I'll stay as long as I can. I've been offered a new job.'

'That's fantastic news!'

'It's only a short contract but it's something entirely different. It's radio, Clara, and I think I'm made for it. CBS gave me a test broadcast and I thought I'd freeze to the microphone but as soon as I opened my mouth I got quite carried away and I realized, yes! This is what I'm good at. Talking.'

'You mean no one told you?'

'They've asked me to come up with some short pieces. "Berlin in Wartime". That's why I came to see the camp. Though I think I've seen enough now.'

In the distance a volley of jeers and cheers heralded the end of the boxing match. Two burly prisoners seized the loser by his underarms and were dragging him from the ring, heels scraping on the mud, a line of blood soaking the earth.

Mary ground out the half-smoked Marlboro, placed the stub in her pocket and looked up at the darkening sky.

'I felt a spot of rain, didn't you?'

As they passed the rows of prisoners returning to their work, almost imperceptibly Mary slipped a young man her cigarettes.

'Careful,' said Clara. 'Someone got four months in prison the other day for giving a single cigarette to a Pole, let alone an entire packet.'

Back at the studios they retraced their steps down a corridor and past the sound stage where the Zarah Leander musical was being filmed. As they passed, a hulking six-foot soldier in an angel costume emerged, a cloud of chiffon flapping behind him, head bent awkwardly as he attempted to remove a sparkly earring. His face was coated in Max Factor's Pan-Cake and his lips were a crimson rosebud. He caught the women's eyes on him, coloured, and stalked off with as much dignity as he could muster.

Clara and Mary managed to contain themselves until they were out of earshot, before convulsing with laughter all the way back to the foyer. They were about to pass through the revolving glass door when they were stopped by a bark of command.

'Fräulein Vine! One minute!'

A shrew-featured young man wearing the uniform of an SS-Untersturmführer was marching self-importantly towards them. He clicked heels and pointed an envelope at Clara like a Walther PPK.

'I'm glad to find you. I have an urgent communication for you from Herr Doktor Goebbels.'

He gave her an envelope, which Clara pushed straight into her bag.

'I don't think you understand,' he said officiously. 'You need to read the letter now.'

'And why is that?'

The Untersturmführer made an impatient gesture towards a sleek black Mercedes 320 standing with its engine idling in the studio forecourt.

'The Herr Doktor has sent his car for you. He wants to see you without delay.'

Chapter Three

'Before we leave, girls, *Volksmaske* practice.'

Thirty scrubbed faces, thirty neat heads, thirty pairs of blue eyes so similar they belonged on porcelain dolls, and thirty pairs of hands reached for the canisters at their sides. Katerina Klimpel, jolted from her daydream by a sharp dig in the ribs, did the same. Fräulein Stark, the Mädelführerin, a skeletal figure with anaemic skin stretched like tissue paper across her face, stood with her arm raised and when she dropped it, everyone pulled on their gas masks in the stipulated ten seconds and fastened the loops behind their ears. The masks were bizarre objects, bristling with straps and buckles, and when Katerina peered out through the murky eyepiece she thought Fräulein Stark, with her great circular eyes and long rubber proboscis, resembled some antediluvian reptile from the swamps of Berlin's prehistory, ready to stalk the city streets.

As they took the masks off again and folded them back into their tins, Katerina wondered what the poison gas would look like when it came raining down. Would it resemble a glitter of pollen spiralling in the warm evening air or the smoke that was right now wafting from the bonfire in the park outside? Could it be seen, in the way planes made a scribble of light on a clear blue sky, or would it be sucked invisibly into the ground, swirling up from the earth like marsh gas and causing flowers to wilt? And what about all the animals, the dogs and the cats, would they have *Volksmasken* too?

'And before we leave.'

What followed needed no prompting. The girls sat silently and bent their heads, murmuring the words.

'*Hände falten, Köpfchen senken, immer an Adolf Hitler denken.*' Hands folded, head lowered, thinking always of Adolf Hitler.

It was important to end the weekly session with a Moment of Thought about the Führer, yet whenever they did Katerina could never prevent her mind from wandering. It was always the same. There was something about Hitler she just couldn't focus on. Perhaps it was because she had never seen him – so it was impossible to think of him as a real person. Or that he came in so many different incarnations. She remembered her first induction as a ten-year-old Jungmädel, in a room furnished with a portrait of the Führer on a black stallion, wearing a silver suit of armour. That was her favourite image of him, like something out of a fairy tale, yet most of the time he seemed more of an idea than a human being. An idea that seeped out across the entire Reich, filling up every space, every scene, every mind, like poison gas. No. Not poison! This was exactly why she should never speak her thoughts out loud. She was apt to get things mixed up, or say things that were not what people wanted to hear. Whenever she tried to articulate the images that ran through her mind, they always came out wrong. Perhaps that was because language was designed to express the sentiments that people in authority believed. Like the things Fräulein Stark said. '*The trust of this great nation must be buried deep in your souls.*' Phrases that went right through Katerina's head. Even when Fräulein Stark used ordinary words, like *work* or *freedom*, she managed to make them sound harsh and ugly, as if they were twisted in wrought iron.

That said, Katerina was quite interested in the *Volksgeist*, the spirit that lived inside you and helped you learn your duty to your country, particularly because there was also an evil spirit – a *Geisteskrankheit* – which stopped you from taking pleasure in National Socialism. The good spirit and the bad spirit. That was easy to remember. Yet most of what they learned at the Bund Deutscher Mädel slid through her mind like water through open fingers.

Fortunately, she'd hit on a solution. Whenever she was asked to think of the Führer, she would think of his dog instead. Her friend Heidi's cousin had paid for a hair of Hitler's dog. It came from the vet and it was absolutely authentic. Katerina's own dog was the dearest creature on earth, or she had been before she went. A dog was the first thing Katerina would acquire when she was older, and she liked to amuse herself with endless speculation about breeds and names. So her Moment of Thought was usually a silent prayer that one day she would have another dog, and perhaps a family, and a home of her own.

A general shifting signalled that the Moment of Thought had ended and the BDM girls struck up their leaving song.

We must forge a discipline
Obedience, subordination
Must fill us all because
The nation is within us.

Katerina joined in lustily. She loved this one with its jaunty tune and when she still lived at home she had sung it often, drawing a scornful raised eyebrow from her half-sister Sonja. Originally she had assumed that this was because Sonja was a professional singer. In striking contrast to her personality, Sonja's voice was sweet and gravelly, with a husky, lilting quality that ensured her a loyal following in the city's cabarets and nightclubs. She would perch on a high stool, cigarette in one hand, a feather boa of smoke weaving around her shoulders, and her voice would tie you up in knots and wring you out, even if you had no idea what she was singing about.

Katerina initially assumed Sonja's scorn was directed at her atrocious singing but lately she had realized that it had more to do with the song itself.

It was always hard to tell what Sonja thought, especially about her. It must have been hard seeing her own mother replaced with Katerina's, when Sonja was just twelve years old, and then so shortly afterwards being introduced to a tiny newcomer with a cloudburst of white-blonde hair and shell-pink skin who rapidly became the apple of their father's eye. Perhaps Sonja had felt hostile to Katerina all her life. Or maybe scornful distance was just Sonja's style. It was hard to tell.

She wasn't exactly unfriendly. There were plenty of times when she would entertain her half-sister with songs, or read, or chat to her about actors and actresses, or show her how to apply make-up and quiz her about the girls at school. Sometimes she would arrange for Katerina to watch her perform at the Café Casanova, her lithe body draped over a piano in a dress of golden silk, hair tumbling in glossy waves, singing Noël Coward's *Mad About The Boy* in heavily accented English, with a wistful quality that made you think she was genuinely, hopelessly in love. But there were far more times when Katerina felt like an unwanted encumbrance in her older sister's life. When they were out together, Sonja would stride ahead, her hands clenched into fists in her pockets, while Katerina tagged along behind, her heart freezing over.

She had been born with one leg shorter than the other, its calf muscle puckered as though a giant creature had raked a claw through the flesh, turning the foot slightly inward at the same time. Until recently she had worn an iron caliper until one day Sonja knelt down and removed it.

'If you keep wearing this thing it'll only make your muscles wither.'

'The doctor says I need it!'

'These doctors don't know anything. Start walking without it and you'll be fine. You'll build up the muscle. Like an acrobat, you know? Or a dancer. You want to be a dancer, don't you?'

'But it hurts.'

'Don't be a baby.'

Sonja had disposed of the caliper, without telling Katerina where it was gone, and while she was delighted to abandon the hated thing that rubbed against her leg and made the skin on her calf red and raw, now her entire limb ached more profoundly and her walk was even more hesitant, with the quick dipping gait of a sparrow. Far from becoming a dancer, she couldn't even attempt the sprint in BDM games. But she had not dared ask Sonja to put it back.

Her crippled leg had never mattered to Papi, the man who had raised her single-handedly after her mother died. Herr Otto Klimpel in his immaculate suit with a triangle of white handkerchief peeping over the pocket, a spotted bow tie and a gold watch in his waistcoat. Sometimes Katerina still awoke feeling him swing her up in his strong arms, smelling the pomade on his skin, the musty tobacco from his cigars that was ingrained in the fabric of his suit and the dab of scented wax on his moustache. He had done exactly that the last time she had seen him in December, half an hour before he had arrived at work at the Reichspost building in Leipziger Strasse and fallen to the ground next to his desk, like a great oak crashing to the forest floor.

When Papi died it had been like walking along a sunny pavement and having a trapdoor open up beneath her feet. She was a small moon flung out of the orbit of a parent planet into deep space. The shock was so great that even now Katerina barely comprehended it. What was more, Papi left barely a pfennig.

It was decided, by a distant coterie of aunts and uncles Katerina had rarely met, that she should move out of the house in Wilmersdorf and into a home run by the National Socialist Volkswohlfahrt – the Nazi welfare organization. She could not possibly live with Sonja, who shared a tiny apartment with her friend Bettina, though in truth the shortage of space was the least unsuitable part of Sonja's living arrangements. So Katerina moved instead to an ugly NSV mansion in Lichterfelde where children in need were housed and educated. They weren't all orphans. Some had parents who had been deemed 'unsuitable to care' because they were alcoholics or idiots or incapacitated. Recently there had been others too, who came from far away and had been allocated their own separate quarters and schoolrooms apart from the other children.

The only escape Katerina had was at evenings and weekends when she was allowed to make the twenty-minute train ride across Berlin to attend the social meetings of her BDM group. It was important that you stayed with the same Mädelschaft – the group of girls you had grown up with – because it reinforced sisterhood and loyalty. So twice a week she would sing songs and write letters to the troops or, like tonight, make packages of wool gloves and ear warmers and socks.

The only other escape was visiting Sonja.

The last time she had seen her sister was at the Café Casanova, where Sonja was performing. The communal dressing room, with its pink lights fixed round the mirrors and rubble of rouge and lipstick and Pan-Cake on the dressing table, the smell of perfume and sweat and cigarettes, a tangle of underwear and stockings thrown over the chair, was, to Katerina, the cosiest space on earth. Curled up on the battered armchair in the corner, listening to the chatter of the women, utterly unselfconscious in their hair rollers and underwear, or dressed in feathers and beading and scraps of peach chiffon, was the only place in the world she felt secure and comfortable.

Mostly the women discussed their love affairs, but Katerina noticed that Sonja never joined in. She was funny like that. When Papi died, Katerina had tried to transfer all her affection onto her sister, like an unwanted pet seeking attachment at all costs, but she met only rebuffs.

'Who do you love most in the world, Sonja?'

'None of your business.'

'Well for me, it's you.'

'Let's see how long that lasts.'

'I'll always love you. You're my sister.'

'Up to you.' Sonja shrugged, her lovely, creamy face impassive. They might have been talking about their favourite cake, or whether it was going to rain. Then she sprang up and began applying a layer of lipstick, pursing up her lips in a way that Katerina hoped she too would one day be able to perfect.

'Personally I don't think love exists. It's just a trick to get people to do what you want. Like being hypnotized. Besides, you should never tell anyone what you're thinking, kid. That's a very bad idea.'

Sonja was full of talk like that. Katerina was sure she didn't mean it. And as she never actively tried to dissuade her from visiting, or tried to make her leave, Katerina carried on turning up backstage wherever Sonja was performing, or at the matchbox apartment in Fischerstrasse, basking in the glamour of her big sister's life and absorbing the complex etiquette of womanhood – arranging hair, fixing earrings, tweezing brows. She would drink in snippets of gossip and learn the names of Sonja's friends and associates like one enormous extended family. She knew better than to try to talk about their own, shrunken family, reduced now to the two of them, or to reminisce about their father, and she found if she kept quiet Sonja tolerated her quite well, gave her tea to drink and the odd bread roll and sometimes even asked when she was coming back.

That was until two months ago.

Sonja had gone abroad. Compared to some of her friends who had been drafted into factories or hospitals or department stores, getting a job abroad was paradise. Sonja had explained her trip briefly to Katerina, as if as an afterthought.

'I'll be back in a fortnight. Be good, kid.'

But she wasn't back. Weeks passed without any sign of Sonja, then the other evening, getting off the S-Bahn at Friedrichstrasse on her way to the BDM meeting, Katerina had run into Bettina.

'I'm sorry, Katerina. Has no one told you? Sonja didn't come back. In fact, we don't know where she went. She disappeared.'

Bettina's heart-shaped face creased, partly in sympathy, partly in irritation at being saddled with delivering this awkward message.

'Don't worry, darling, Sonja will be all right. The one thing about your sister is, she knows how to look after herself. Let me know if there's anything you need, hmm?'

The session was winding up. The girls' voices rose in a bright tangle of sound. At the door, handfuls of badges for the Winterhilfswerk were being doled out from a bucket for the girls to distribute during the week and Katerina tried surreptitiously to slip some of hers back. The idea was that they should sell them in a public place, like a railway station, where people would always donate in case they were seen and reported, but even with that stipulation the girls were always given more badges than they could possibly offload. That was intentional because everyone knew their parents would make up the difference rather than expose their offspring to embarrassment. But Katerina had no parents, and the chances of Sonja spending any of her wages on a heap of tin charity badges were next to none.

Especially as she had now vanished without trace.

Chapter Four

The Mercedes passed through the city and headed northeast into a heavily wooded landscape. It was raining in earnest now, drumming on the car roof, dripping down through the dense wall of regimented beech, pine and oak that arched across the narrow road through the forest, blurring the windows and the lowering sky. Very few other cars passed, and the occasional picnic spots with their damp cluster of wooden benches were deserted. A tattered billboard of Hitler, proclaiming *Ein Volk, Ein Führer,* flapped desolately in the breeze, alongside a poster advertising family hikes with the Strength Through Joy foundation. Clara sat in tense silence, trying to make sense of her situation. If Goebbels wanted to see her, surely he could have called her into the Propaganda Ministry in Wilhelmstrasse, or more simply his office at the studios? Yet instead they were heading in precisely the opposite direction, far out of the city.

The expensive Mercedes engine purred deep beneath her, and the aroma of polished leather rose around her, but the chauffeur in front remained impassive. Clara wound down the window and breathed in the air, sharp with pine, heavy with earth and vegetation, trying to gauge where they might be, but the rain had lowered the temperature, making her skin prickle over, so she rolled the window up again, and tried to calm herself.

Then it dawned on her.

When the city of Berlin was informed that it wanted to make a birthday gift to the Propaganda Minister, it came up with a plot of land several miles to the north of the city, close to the small town of Wandlitz. At its centre was the Haus am Bogensee, whose finishing details were designed by Goebbels himself and only completed the previous year. Buried deep in rustic solitude, on the shores of the Bogensee, the house boasted an underground bunker, a cinema and a banqueting hall. But its most important feature was the fact that it was sufficiently far away from Magda and his children that Goebbels could conduct his casting couch meetings in peace.

The roads had been narrowing for some time, tunnelling deeper into the forest, and now the car slowed at the end of a lane, rounded a bend and turned. Two minutes later it was crunching onto the gravel of the house to the energetic barking of dogs.

A guard in a green rain-cape approached, managing to wield an umbrella in one hand and salute with the other.

'*Heil Hitler*!'

He opened the car door, giving Clara her first proper glimpse of the house every actress in the Reich had heard of, even if they had not yet had the misfortune to see it.

*

The Haus am Bogensee had a low-hanging Nordic roof, brown wooden shutters at the windows and whitewashed walls, yet despite its air of rustic simplicity, it was a distinctly ugly edifice. The huge mediaeval gabled entrance, flanked by wrought-iron lanterns and supported by rough stone pillars, was freakishly out of proportion to the low-built, utilitarian style of the building. Floor-to-ceiling French windows led out onto a terrace, speckled with a coating of damp leaves and fringed by thick clusters of silver birch and fir. An ivy-clad stone balustrade surrounded the garden, where a flaking nude of a young woman was posed awkwardly, one hand across her legs, as if longing to cover up. To one side of the entrance the steel doors of a concrete bunker could be seen and in the distance, half hidden by beech, fir and oaks, stretched the grey mass of the Bogensee. Only the soft dripping of the trees and the sharp call of birds pierced the thick silence.

At Clara's approach the heavy wooden front door opened and the smell of wet leaves and overcoats gave way to a mingled aroma of floor polish and cigars. The hall was decorated with a marble bust of the Führer, glowering sightlessly, and a series of heavy-framed photographs of the owner: Goebbels shaking hands with Mussolini at the Olympic Stadium, Goebbels beaming adoringly at Hitler at the Berghof, Goebbels in intimate conversation with the Duke of Windsor, Goebbels with one hand on the arm of Zarah Leander. None, Clara registered, of Goebbels with his wife.

A young man in his thirties, sleek in field grey, with a bundle of manila files under his arm, approached.

'Fräulein Vine. I trust you had a good journey. The Minister asked to see you as soon as you arrived. If you would follow me.'

He led the way along a narrow passage with parquet flooring and modernist brass wall-lamps, and down a gloomy series of steps. Opening the double doors at the bottom, Clara found herself looking into an enormous darkened room with an outsized flickering screen dominated by the giant, maddened figure of Robert Wiene's Expressionist antihero, Dr Caligari. The film of the insane doctor had become famous around the world but had not been shown in Germany since it was banned as a danger to health and safety by the same man who was now viewing it, seated alone in his personal movie theatre.

Joseph Goebbels swivelled round, whipped off his glasses, and raised a hand in half salute. The ghostly Dr Caligari with his wild stare and chalky skin loomed behind him on the screen, casting Goebbels' face in shadow. His position was deliberate, Clara realized; with the light of the screen behind him it was difficult to make out his features.

'So glad you could make it. It's an age since I've seen this film. I find it a little long-winded, but overall a classic, don't you think?'

If this was a test, Clara was taking no chances.

'I'm not sure I ever saw it.'

'Really? You should. Some say it indicates a subconscious need amongst our populace for a leader who will rule with an iron hand. Firm leadership as the only alternative to social chaos. In many ways it was the most important German film of its time, the high point of Expressionism, not to mention a horror masterpiece.'

That much was right, though when Clara had watched the film with apprehension and awe she had reached the opposite conclusion. For her, the shadowy distorted perspective of twisted buildings and spiralling streets was a mirror of the angst-ridden German psyche. The crazed psychiatrist Caligari, transforming into a hypnotist and murderer by night, symbolized an authoritarian state gone mad.

'It's not for everyone of course. Obviously one takes one's responsibility seriously when it comes to protecting the populace – there's a documentary coming out about the Eternal Jew that makes for very alarming viewing, and I've decided that no women will be allowed to watch the closing sequences. But for professionals, it's a different matter. And you are, after all, a professional. I hear Veit Harlan has offered you a role in his new vehicle. *Jud Süss*, isn't it called?'

He knew.

'That's going to be an important movie. Film has a vital place in the vanguard of the German forces. We must fight with words as well as weapons. Have you accepted it?'

'I've only just received the script. I've not had a chance to do much with it yet.'

'Of course. And in normal times, I would urge you to take the role. However . . .'

He rose to his feet. 'These are not normal times and it may be that there are other projects you need to consider.'

'Herr Doktor?'

The familiar dazzling smile stretched over his cadaverous features.

'I'm going to need to explain.'

He led the way out of the cinema, limped swiftly up the steps and into a spacious oak-panelled drawing room laid with Turkish rugs. In one corner a sofa stood, piled with cushions and capacious enough to facilitate any amount of casting. Floor-to-ceiling windows gave a panoramic view of the Bogensee beyond the terrace. Despite it being summer, a fire was burning in the open fireplace and two chairs were pulled up before it. Without turning, Goebbels addressed the aide who had followed silently and slid into the room behind them.

'Leave us alone, Farben. And I mean *alone*.'

The aide clicked heels and melted from sight.

'Sit down, won't you.'

Goebbels settled himself into one of the armchairs with a wince and Clara realized that his right leg was giving him trouble again. A childhood operation had crippled one foot, meaning that Goebbels always walked with a characteristic semi-hobble. The pain it caused him surfaced so reliably with stress that employees at Babelsberg could judge the ferocity of his mood simply by monitoring the extent of his approaching limp.

'Drink?'

A frosted bottle of 1929 Mosel, wrapped in a white napkin, stood on a table at his elbow, two glasses alongside.

'Thank you, yes.'

He poured Clara a glass then leaned back, extending an

arm along the chair and staring into the dancing flames of the log fire. The silence continued so long that eventually she could bear it no longer.

'How is the Frau Doktor?'

The previous year the crisis of Goebbels' affair with a Czech actress had come to a head. Following his wife's demand for a divorce – and Hitler's adamant refusal to countenance such a thing – a pact had been agreed between the couple, witnessed by the Führer himself, pledging that as the First Family of the Reich the couple would endeavour to get along. One result of this, Clara knew from the newspapers, was that Magda was pregnant again. The reconciliation baby would be the sixth in a brood whose neat braids and wholesome, white-smocked innocence were routinely exploited by their father. The Goebbels children were rarely out of the press and their most recent outing on public screens had been in a documentary in which they appeared as a contrast to the misshapen and handicapped children who were such a burden to the Reich.

'My wife is fine. Thank you for asking. If you can call spending all your waking hours playing Solitaire "fine".'

Clara remembered Magda Goebbels' affection for Solitaire, a game she played compulsively, shuffling and sorting the cards, flipping and turning, as if by ordering them she could set her own life to rights again.

'She's a keen bridge player too, isn't she?'

'Yes. There's a whole circle she plays with. They gamble endlessly.'

That Magda should involve herself in gambling was not a

surprise. Bridge, poker, canasta and Skat, games of chance, threat and dare, were now the favourite pastime of high society. Everyone played, from officers in the exclusive Herrenklub to fashionable ladies in the Skagerak Club. When you felt the cards were stacked against you, gambling was a sure way to recapture that fleeting sense of feeling lucky.

'Perhaps you should join them. It would be useful to know what those women spend their time gossiping about, though I suppose I can guess.'

He lit a cigarette and passed it to her, then lit another for himself.

'But I didn't invite you here to discuss trivia, pleasant though it may be. Tell me, do you know who I mean by Walter Schellenberg?'

The name alone was enough to send an ice cube down the spine. Clara did know, but it was probably better if she didn't.

'Could you remind me?'

'Chief of Amt IV of the RSHA.'

Despite the numerical obfuscation beloved of intelligence-speak, Clara knew this meant the Reich Main Security Office, the Nazi intelligence service, of which SS–Sturmbannführer Schellenberg had just been promoted to head the counter-espionage arm. He was the man in charge of rooting out spies in the entire Reich. He was said to be as ambitious as he was good-looking, and he was tackling his new job with formidable zeal.

'I think I might have seen him once. Across a crowded room. But I never had the opportunity to speak to him.'

'Well then. Perhaps your chance has come.'

Goebbels leaned forward, elbows on knees, and lowered his voice.

'I brought you here because this is an extremely confidential matter. It's not the kind of thing I could discuss in my office because it's stuffed with idle secretaries whose ears are flapping and Babelsberg is full of loose-tongued gossips who love nosing in other people's business. And it goes without saying that if a word of this gets out I will hold you personally responsible.'

He paused to examine his nails, buffed regularly by a personal manicurist. Skilled as she was in observing the smallest details, Clara noticed they were bitten to the quick.

'Herr Schellenberg has received intelligence that the Reich Chamber of Culture has a traitor in its ranks.'

'A traitor?' She lowered her glass. 'What kind of traitor?'

'A spy who is liaising with the British. That kind.'

Clara knew her expression was entirely impassive. As an actress she had trained every muscle in her face to register only the emotions she wanted to express, and if her eyes widened at these words, or her cheeks paled, then it was entirely justifiable. Who would not be shocked at such a notion? Yet Goebbels' words terrified her. What was he implying? Was he about to confront her with allegations of her own espionage?

To steady herself, she took a sip and made a show of savouring the crisp white wine, as its undoubtedly hefty price tag deserved.

'Can I ask who this spy might be?'

'One of my favourite artists, I'm afraid.' Goebbels

glowered and twisted his cigarette into a cut-glass ashtray, as if the situation had arisen precisely to vex him.

'Hans Reuber.'

Clara exhaled with relief.

'You know him, of course.'

Everyone knew him. You could hardly escape him. Hans Reuber's face was on ten-foot billboards the length of the Reich. He was a celebrated stage entertainer, and his particular act, a mix of illusions, hypnotism and magic tricks, had become wildly popular in recent years, as the Nazi clampdown on political cabaret and risqué nightclubs made way for more inoffensive entertainment. Posters of Reuber in evening dress, or wearing a turban, or bending suggestively over a prone woman, were everywhere, promising *Screams of laughter every evening!* Despite the comic, ridiculous and downright erotic situations he induced, there was no shortage of willing secretaries and clerks happy to drop into a trance for the amusement of others.

'As Reuber is in the Chamber of Culture he falls under my responsibility, so Schellenberg quite rightly came to me first. He wanted to arrest the fellow straight away, but there's no evidence. If you botch that kind of thing it plays badly with the public. It shakes their faith in the authorities. People like the man. They don't want to hear that he's a traitor. Not without solid evidence and Schellenberg doesn't have that, so I forbade him to act, and he was obliged to listen to me.'

'Of course.'

Clara knew that if Schellenberg had wanted to proceed, he would have done so with or without Goebbels' permission.

The security of the Reich trumped all other concerns, particularly trifling issues of box office popularity. Perhaps the notion of Reuber's treachery was more of a hunch, or a smear. Not a day went by without some public figure being denounced for anti-Nazi tendencies, based on nothing more than malice and professional jealousy.

'However, seeing that Schellenberg had sought my advice, I said I would mull it over, and I had a rather good idea. It involves you.'

Clara felt herself freeze as Goebbels' eyes travelled over her; from the carefully shined shoes that were wearing thin in the sole, over the rose pink summer dress that was several seasons old and patched at the hem, up to the pearl necklace at her throat and the Prussian blue eyes that returned his gaze with perfect equanimity.

'Forgive me if I'm a little puzzled.'

'You're what – thirty-three? And still single.'

Clara's fingers tightened around the stem of her wine glass and she willed herself to remain impassive. Did he know – *could* he know? – about Leo? She felt a fury rise in her gorge – as though Goebbels himself was responsible for Leo's death, even though she knew that was not true, and she forced herself to push it back down.

'I'm not as fortunate as you, Herr Doktor.'

That was careless. Many times over the past seven years the miserable Magda Goebbels had taken Clara into her confidence, with the result that Clara was probably as familiar with Joseph Goebbels' marital shortcomings as he was himself. Her reply grated, even to herself, but he gave a brittle smile.

'No indeed. We can't all be so lucky. Your work, though, must be a consolation.'

Strangely, he was right. After Leo's death, it seemed obvious to Clara that there could never be another man in her life, so shrugging on the shallow, glossy existences of the characters she played was a fantasy, like donning a flimsy piece of lacy couture. Their lives were an escape from the void of her own.

'It keeps me busy.'

'Yet you haven't had the role yet to make you a star. You're well known, of course, in your profession, but you've never had a task that really tested your mettle.'

'Perhaps not, but . . .'

'Don't interrupt. I think I've found it.'

'Is this another film?' she queried, confused.

'Not exactly. It's a little more taxing than that. Though it's still technically a performance and perfectly within your abilities. In fact, this could be your moment. I've often thought that what distinguishes a real star is the ability to seize the chance when it presents itself. That's a lesson I've learned in politics, but it applies in all areas of life. In some respects you're still a rough diamond, Clara Vine, but I intend to polish you into a jewel. I've always had you down as someone who would be good at guarding a confidence. There's something reserved about you – I would say sly, but I don't want to sound rude, so let's just say you seem like you might be good at keeping secrets.'

'I am.'

'I thought as much. So I've chosen you for a little mission. I hope you won't let me down.'

He stood up and limped over to the window, staring out at the Bogensee beyond. The drizzle was getting heavier, pattering through the damp trees, darkening the terrace in the fading light. A cloud of rain was rolling over the surface of the lake. The absolute solitude was disturbed only by the harsh call of a goose rising precipitously from the reeds.

The interval gave Clara a moment to compose herself and she stood up. When Goebbels turned, she was regarding him with equanimity. She didn't even flinch when he came right up close and examined her. At five foot six they were the same height and their faces were directly level.

'Look at you! Your reaction tells me everything I need to know.'

Inside she felt the twist of her intestines and the clutch of fear.

'You haven't turned a hair. I ask you to undertake a confidential mission and you behave as though you've had an invitation to a garden party. My instincts are always right.'

'And what do your instincts tell you, Herr Doktor?'

'They tell me you will be perfectly suited to our little arrangement. Nothing formal, of course, but I would like there to be an understanding between us. I may have future tasks for you if you are successful this time.'

'Could you explain what this mission will involve?'

He threw himself back into his chair and fixed her, eyes glittering.

'You will make a trip to Paris. The Führer wants nothing more than the most civilized of occupations and therefore he has asked me to ensure that the French people have a taste of German culture free of charge.'

'What kind of German culture does he have in mind?'

'Symphonies, plays, that sort of thing. The Reich Chamber of Culture is holding concerts in the parks and a couple of the theatres will be staging work by German authors. Reuber's performing too, though his task is to entertain the troops. You will be visiting Paris as a singer. You do sing, don't you?'

'Not really. I mean I *can* sing, but . . .'

Goebbels waved a dismissive hand at Clara's objections, as if brushing away a small but irritating fly.

'Doesn't matter. No one's expecting Marlene Dietrich. Your main task is to befriend Reuber. How you do it, I don't mind – he's a vain man and he loves a pretty face so you'll be pushing at an open door, but the moment you have any evidence of his treachery, I want you to report your findings. Reuber will be dealt with accordingly.'

'But . . .' Clara tried to absorb the instructions Goebbels was delivering. It seemed he was asking her to lay a honey trap for a fellow performer, a hypnotist at that, and one who had every reason to be on his guard.

'Surely Reuber would be suspicious to encounter a German actress in Paris.'

'Not at all. You've heard of the Frontbühne, it's my new association for the entertainment of German troops abroad. We have a division performing in Paris right now. You'll be joining them for a couple of days.'

'Just a couple of days? How will I explain that?'

'I'll leave the details to you. You'll come up with

something. You'll need to because I've booked you a spot on the Request Show in a few weeks' time to discuss it.'

The *Wunschkonzert für die Wehrmacht*, the Request Concert for the Wehrmacht, was Germany's new favourite show, a weekly *mélange* of light music and personal requests for soldiers at the front that drew half the population to their radio sets. *'For every request two marks to the Winterhilfswerk!'* was the programme's slogan, repeated with bracing regularity. The musical numbers alternated between marching songs and love ballads – parents tended to request uplifting military music for their sons whereas girlfriends and wives chose love songs. Every celebrity, from Hans Albers and Willy Fritsch, to Marika Rökk and Werner Krauss, was desperate to be part of it.

'You're going to talk about your work for the Frontbühne. The challenges, rewards, your pleasure at serving the Reich. The usual script. I'm sure you're capable of that kind of thing. Anyway, the train tickets and the Reisepass will be delivered to your apartment and you will leave in forty-eight hours.'

It seemed he had thought of everything.

Following him as he made his way briskly to the door, Clara suddenly realized that this request was not a disaster but an opportunity. Leaving the Reich was almost impossible for German citizens, yet in France it was different. From Paris it might be possible to find an escape route to England. If that was what she wanted.

Goebbels paused, one hand on the door handle, and gave a smile as fake as the cream cakes in Schiller's Konditorei.

'How's that lad of yours? Helga Schmidt's child, isn't he? I hear you take care of him.'

He had caught her off guard. Clara had no idea that Goebbels had ever heard of Erich.

'He's doing well. He's a very promising student.'

Goebbels smiled pleasantly, but there was ice in his eyes.

'It's good of you to look after the boy. I suppose he has no one else to take care of him. What would he do without you? It would be sad if anything befell him.'

The smile dropped like a stone.

It was not until she was crossing the gravel drive towards the official Mercedes that would transport her back to Berlin that the full import of Goebbels' audacity dawned on her. Erich was his hostage. If she didn't return to Germany, Goebbels would ensure that her beloved godson came to some harm.

He really had thought of everything.

Chapter Five

Katerina was sitting at the front upstairs window of the children's home, looking out at the latest arrivals. The word 'home' was somewhat misleading to describe the forbidding Gothic block in Lichterfelde, southwest Berlin, where the NSV orphans lived. Beyond an iron fence, a stretch of gravel and an honour guard of rose bushes gave way to a red brickwork entrance edged with pale, triangular inserts like the jagged teeth of an opened jaw. With its blank face and five imposing floors it looked more like a factory than a children's home, which, in a way, it was. A factory that took in orphans, drilled and processed them and turned out useful members of society, ideal adornments to any family and perfect citizens, to be relocated through the Reich Adoption Service. And on account of the war, there was now a never-ending supply. They came in their best clothes, with a knapsack and either a single favourite toy, provided that it met the ideological requirements, or a book, so long as it was in German. Looking through the flaky iron bars that filled half the window frame, Katerina heard the gates close with a metallic clang and was reminded of the children who followed the Pied Piper of Hamlyn, the great rocky doors of the mountain groaning shut behind them.

Inside the home the Gothic gloom theme continued, with floors covered in ugly linoleum, walls painted an institutional brown and high narrow windows through which a listless light penetrated, illuminating by way of decoration a series of instructive posters pinned to cork boards. Most of the posters had messages like *Girls! Do Your Duty!* and *Collect for Youth Hostels!* and *Save Bones for Aircraft Production!* but others depicted happy, flaxen-haired families clustered around a hearth, or gazing at a swastika-lit sunset, or hiking through Alpine fields on a Strength Through Joy holiday, though whether these were deliberately designed to remind the orphans what they were missing, or merely insensitive, was not entirely clear.

The orphanage was close to the military barracks that trained the Führer's bodyguard and frequently lessons and meals were interrupted by the sound of gunfire. The children gossiped that the barracks were where people were assassinated and there was supposed to be a wall spattered with bloody flesh, but the teachers cracked down harshly on talk like that. Outside, soldiers marched past day and night, and inside, with equally military precision, the female officials of the NSV, called the Brown Sisters, held sway.

The Brown Sisters were nurses who were committed to National Socialism and had taken an oath of loyalty to Hitler. Unlike nuns, who had been responsible for a lot of government childcare in the past, the Brown Sisters had no difficulty with modern practices like sterilizing idiots that the more old-fashioned nurses shunned. They were sticklers for regime and as if they were not controlling enough, they received a steady stream of memos from SS-Reichsführer Himmler on subjects ranging from the correct way to steam vegetables to the amount of porridge to serve orphans at breakfast each morning and the importance of administering cod liver oil. There was a bath once a week and a daily cold-water wash. The Brown Sisters were also responsible for sorting their charges into one of four classes. First- and second-class orphans would go to the best SS families and receive support from the government. Third-class children frequently remained at the orphanage, or were sent to families of lower social status. No one knew what happened to fourth-class children.

Until last December, Katerina had never known any children who had no parents. Even now, she didn't think of herself as an orphan. Orphans were like something out of the books she used to read, always being abandoned, or abused or left on a doorstep or a mountainside. They cropped up everywhere from Greek myths to Cinderella, and fairy tales were full of them. Generally orphans were plucky and resourceful characters who ultimately came good, whether it be finding the parents who had mislaid them, turning into princesses or inheriting kingdoms. Indeed, sometimes, having no parents seemed like a precondition of making an adventure of your life, but the NSV home was nothing like an adventure. It wasn't even like a home. The only privacy was a small box beneath the beds in the dormitory, where orphans stored their meagre clothes and their sole permitted possession. Most of them chose stuffed toys that would be taken out and hugged at night, their eyes blank and beady, their fur wet with tears, but Katerina had selected a much-thumbed magazine about dogs.

Probably the worst thing that had happened after Papi died was having to say goodbye to Anka. Papi had found Anka in a sack tossed into the Landwehr Canal, a shivering, curly-haired puppy who cringed when anyone stroked her. She grew into a glossy creature of boundless energy, racing across the Tiergarten at dawn, sniffing and chasing and leaping into Katerina's lap at inappropriate moments with a little yelp of joy. She could still feel the way Anka would push her nose into the crook of her leg, or reach up to lick a hand in a demonstration of unconditional love. When Papi died, the same committee of relatives who had ordained that Katerina live in the orphanage had arranged for Anka to be rehomed. Katerina had not known a thing about it until she came home from school to discover her dog gone and Sonja smoking irritably in the kitchen, charged with delivering the news. It was perhaps the only occasion Sonja had been properly tender towards her. She explained that she had not known about the plan, but that Anka was now in the countryside, loving her life on a farm, able to run off the leash and with plenty of fresh meat to eat. She had no details of where this farm might be, but she was firm that there was no chance Anka would return. In the meantime, to help her get over it, she had bought Katerina a copy of *HundeWelt*, Dog World. Katerina had read the magazine so many times she knew it by heart.

Nearly 1,600 boxers, Dobermann pinschers and German Shepherds have joined the Wehrmacht. Her favourite picture was a photograph of the Führer reaching out to pet a stray dog on a French battlefield. The Führer loved animals, almost as much as he loved children, and enjoyed feeding wild deer that came to his hand at the Berghof.

There were no animals at the NSV home, unless you counted the bees that drifted through the air to the old wooden hive at the end of the orchard, and it was hard to form much of an attachment to them. They had studied bees in Nature lessons at the BDM. Never run away from bees, there was no point – the swarm would capture you if you angered them. A single person had no chance against thousands of stinging insects. Much better to make the swarm feel that you were no threat. Bees were utterly disciplined, each with their own task and purpose, all working for the good of the hive and the figure at the centre, their queen. Some of them were workers, others drones, condemned to fulfil their allocated functions.

Bees were a good model, they were told, for girls of the BDM.

When the letter had dropped onto the mat on Katerina's tenth birthday, informing her that she must buy a uniform and report to the Jungmädel group nearest to their home, she had been overjoyed. From that group she had graduated nine months ago to the BDM, along with all her friends, and acquired the leather knot, ID card and special emblem to be stitched onto her clothes. Being a solitary child, with only a father who spent most of his time at work, the idea of a

ready-made group of friends to see every week was delight-
ful, though Sonja was unimpressed.

'What do you do at that place anyway?'

'We play games. We bake cookies and sing songs and tell
fairy stories.'

Sonja set a lot of store by reading. There had been a time
when she would even read to Katerina. *The best stories have a
little piece of glass in them. It might prick you and make you bleed
inside, but it also reflects a bit of your own life back at you.* She must
have changed her mind, though, because now she shrugged.

'I can get all the fairy stories I want listening to Goebbels
on the wireless.'

Katerina tried to think of something more impressive.

'We're always collecting for charity.'

When she was issued with her first WHW collecting tin
she brought it home and placed it proudly on the mantelpiece, but one day, entering the room unexpectedly, she
came across Sonja raiding it for cigarette money. Her sister
had merely looked askance and said, *What are you going to do,
call the police?*

Now Katerina wondered if she *should* call the police.

Every time she thought about her sister, she had a sick feeling of dread. Despite her other failings – and even at her age
Katerina realized that those failings were many – Sonja had
always been reliable about telling her younger sister where
she would be.

So long. Be good, kid.

Her thoughts were interrupted by a single finger on her
shoulder, causing her to startle and jump to her feet, trying

to stand as straight as possible, pulling herself to her full five foot nothing and holding her damaged leg as stiff as she could bear. Fortunately it was only Fräulein Koppel, the kindest of the Brown Sisters. Unlike most of them, who had faces like the gargoyles on Berlin Cathedral, Fräulein Koppel was extremely pretty and even managed to make the shapeless brown serge of the nurses' uniform look chic. She had curls of coppery hair peeping out from under the starched white cap, a confetti of freckles and frank, grey eyes that were now looking at Katerina in speculative fashion.

'You are a *proper* orphan, aren't you?'

'I have a sister.'

'No parents, though?'

'No.'

'Well, I've given it some thought, and I think you will be suited to a very special task.'

'Thank you, Fräulein Koppel. Can I ask – I mean, what is it?'

She leaned forward with a sweet, confidential smile and whispered in Katerina's ear.

'I can't explain right now, but come to the nurses' office at eight p.m. All I can say is, it's a very great honour.'

Chapter Six

Since the war, Berlin had gone grey overnight. Luxury was the scarcest of commodities. The grand hotels – the Kaiserhof, the Esplanade, the Adlon and the Excelsior – were doing their best to retain the glamour of their pre-war days but beneath the gloss, there were unavoidable signs that the gilt was wearing thin. Five o'clock Tea Dances had been banned, both because dancing was disrespectful to the troops, and because tea itself carried distasteful connotations of Englishness. The scented wealth of pre-war days was long gone and with all young men conscripted, a shuffle of ageing waiters, shirt fronts whitened with talcum powder, promoted an air of decrepitude. The furnishings were down-at-heel. Although the restaurant menu still advertised a number of meat dishes, shortly before lunch waiters would circulate with pencils, striking all but one dish from the menu, leaving only floury potatoes and canned vegetables. What else could guests expect at a time when everyone, even farm animals, had their own ration cards?

The monumental Hotel Eden, across the street from the

zoo, was once the most stylish of all Berlin rendezvous. Rising with staid grandeur from Budapester Strasse, it boasted a pavilion, a ballroom and an American grill. From its rooftop café diners could enjoy dazzling views from Charlottenburg to the far stretches of the Tiergarten as they consumed their *Kalbsbraten* and champagne. Now, however, its pocked marble lobby and reek of cleaning fluid had an air of the public convenience. Past the reception desk with its mandatory silver-framed placard announcing, *We Don't Deal With Jews*, Clara entered the brass elevator and rode six floors, stepping out onto the roof where once all Berlin society went to tango. Between two potted palm trees a banner had been strung.

Ein Volk Hilft Sich Selbst.
A People Helps Itself. The motto of the NSV.

The NSV was in charge of all welfare activity in the Reich. Its aim was to secure the health of the German people, though obviously only those of desirable political, racial and biological stock, and despite reports that its funds were squandered on luxury, the nation's favourite charity had gone from strength to strength since the government decided to dock a compulsory donation from every worker's pay packet. Yet with the advent of war even this master stroke was not enough to meet the nation's welfare needs so it was now deemed essential that every citizen make some kind of a personal contribution. In Clara's case this meant being conscripted onto a committee organizing a series of high-profile fundraising events. At least, she thought as she pushed into the throng, it would take her mind off Paris and the impossible task facing her there.

Trays of *Sekt* and soda water were circulating among a cluster of glossy women dressed in hats and chiffon tea dresses. While most of Berlin's citizens looked increasingly shabby, the glorious expansion of the Reich had brought some welcome souvenirs for the lucky few: silver fox from Norway, shoes and hats and silk dresses from Paris. The miasma of French perfumes in the air made the upmarket parts of Berlin smell like a beautician's salon. Clara had rescued from her cupboard a pale green Chanel-style suit that had been run up by her seamstress friend Steffi a few seasons ago. Although no hotel, restaurant or café was allowed to sell cigarettes to women, most of those present toted Moslems and Aristons between their jewelled fingers, and their glinting eyes and angular, observant features gave them the appearance of intelligent birds.

Clara made a quick automatic scan of the crowd. This reception was to launch a fundraising evening for orphans to be held in August and while it was hard to imagine any group in Germany having less in common with underprivileged children, the scheme was the brainchild of Emmy Goering, which meant attendance was pretty much compulsory. The female ranks of the Nazi regime were out in force. A cast of A-list actresses, including Marika Rökk and Jenny Jugo, as well as a panoply of politicians' wives, had fallen into line. Only Magda Goebbels was a conscientious objector. There had to be some upside to being pregnant for a sixth time.

'Clara Vine!'

Emmy Goering came barrelling towards her, the white enamel gold cross of the Badge of Honour for Caring for the German People bouncing on her corsage.

'I hope you realize it was me who got you elected onto this committee. There's only a small number of us. Frau Doktor Goebbels has not seen fit to attend despite the fact that she is the NSV's official patron.'

'I think she must be indisposed. I heard she was expecting another child.'

'Hmm. One might think she had the hang of it by now. Anyway, we're unveiling plans for our cabaret evening at the Hitler Youth building. It's in aid of orphans of the Reich. The announcement will be made here and carried in tomorrow's papers. The committee is just me and a few of the senior women and you. It *is* rather an honour.'

'I realize that. Thank you.'

'I said to Hermann, this fundraiser is all about children and as poor Clara Vine doesn't have any little ones of her own the least she can do is work with needy families.'

A sympathetic frown creased her features.

'Don't you sometimes wish for a child, Clara?'

'I'm not married, Frau Goering.'

'That doesn't matter so much at times like these. Lots of women are raising children single-handed. And didn't you tell me you had a godson you looked after? Motherhood is the most rewarding calling. Can you believe our little Edda just celebrated her second birthday?'

Edda Goering was, by any reckoning, the most important child in the Reich. A tiny replica of her father with the same wide cheekbones and broad mouth, she was commonly known as the Crown Princess and treated with appropriate reverence. Not for Edda the humble wooden toys and dolls in dirndls; her playthings included a complete replica of Sans Souci Palace erected in the ministerial garden.

'If you had a child you'd be no different from any other widow who's lost her man in the fighting.'

'I suppose. But to tell the truth, I'm too busy to even think about it.'

'Yes, you *do* look a little tired.'

'Aren't we all tired?'

Fatigue was everyone's favourite subject, what with disrupted nights and extended working hours that meant factory workers had their shifts lengthened to twelve hours a day, seven days a week, and even actresses were being required to work overtime. At every canteen, bread queue or tram stop encounter, the same topic would surface. People never got tired of how tired they were.

'I can see it round the eyes. Look at you.'

Even if she could, Clara didn't need to look at herself. Outwardly she knew she was little changed; still poised, though thinner than she had been, and while her eyes were a little shadowed, her complexion was mostly unlined, yet inside she had transformed entirely. It was as though all the years in Berlin and the hammer blow of Leo's death had carved their way into the marble of her being. Experience had chiselled her into someone sharper and more distinct.

'You need to get yourself a doctor's appointment. I'll see if I can fix you up with Theo Morell.'

Doktor Morell worked out of a fancy slice of wedding-cake baroque in the Kurfürstendamm, whose stucco entrance was garnished by nude sandstone caryatids in far better shape than his most famous clients. Saggy jawlines and irregular features were a lucrative part of Doktor Morell's business, his marriage to the actress Hannelore Moller having brought him plenty of custom at the Ufa studios where he had long been the first choice for adjusting noses and removing unsightly blemishes. But his real star patient was one whose stubby nose, bulging eyes and ugly features were never going to be fixed. Morell had got lucky in 1936 treating the Führer's perennial stomach cramps with a concoction of vitamins, and thereafter Hitler appointed him his own personal doctor. All the senior Nazis followed suit, despite the rumour that Morell did not set too much store by patient confidentiality.

'I'm fine, really.'

'If you're sure. But we all need to be fighting fit if we're to help others.' Emmy Goering glanced impatiently away. 'Now the Hitler Jugend has organized a consignment of orphans to be photographed for *Sonne ins Haus* . . .'

The Sun in the House was a leading Nazi family magazine, much given to True Life stories, beautiful baby competitions, recipes for fat-free cake and all types of heart-warming senti-mentality. Fundraising events for orphans was its bread and butter.

'The children should be here any moment, so if you see one you like, just say the word . . .'

Fortunately, this train of thought was derailed by the spectacle of the statuesque Zarah Leander passing through the throng, standing out from the crowd by a good head. Her neck was circled by a serpentine diamond collar and the pale gleam of her Swedish skin was set off by gems that dazzled like a lighthouse beam whenever she turned. Emmy Goering's mouth twitched.

'Wouldn't it make sense to have a fully *German* actress as the Diva of the Third Reich? I know Goebbels thinks it's helpful to have a Scandinavian since the Reich occupied Denmark because it enhances our reputation there, but really, I would have thought a pure-blooded German woman . . .' Possibly recalling Clara's mixed heritage, she stopped herself, reached for a passing ham sandwich, ate it and collected a spare. Clara helped herself too, marvelling at the quality.

'Mmm. I haven't tasted Black Forest ham for a year.'

'One has to eat when one can. Given we're living in permanent Lent.'

Frau Goering dabbed at her mouth.

'Anyhow, it will be over when the British see sense. That's what my husband's always saying.'

'How is the Herr Reich Marshal?'

A theatrical sigh.

'It's been so difficult. The Belgium incident. You may have heard.'

That January, Goering had suffered a serious political setback when a Luftwaffe plane carrying secret plans for the invasion of France crashed in Belgium. The pilot swore that he had burned the documents himself and there was no chance that anyone could have pieced together the charred remains, but all the same the debacle cast a cloud over Goering's reputation.

'Hermann consulted my clairvoyant who assured him the papers were destroyed, but the Führer was angry and my poor darling has suffered terribly. His glands are playing up. He's heavier than ever and his war wound is inflamed. He's in constant pain.'

Clara had heard that Goering kept a dish of codeine pills on his desk and ate them like sweets.

'He's absolutely exhausted. Do you know he had a stag imported from France – a little victory present to himself – and sent up to Carinhall last weekend? But when he went out with his gun he fell asleep on the stand before he could shoot it.'

She passed a hand across her eyes.

'Please God all this can be over soon. The Führer says the British are a reasonable people. They're not going to reject an offer of peace. Of course, *you* should know, you're half English. I so often forget.' She paused pensively. 'Other people keep mentioning it, but whenever they do I say, Clara Vine is one of us!'

Clara smiled. 'Do they keep mentioning it?'

'My dear, you mustn't worry. I'm not one to listen to unkind talk. If you want to gossip about someone, I'm the last person you should come to. Rumour and speculation are so damaging. If you have nothing nice to say about a person, don't sit next to me, that's my motto.'

She was distracted by a guffaw of laughter from across the floor. A bleached blonde in a tight-fitting plum silk dress with a shrill, fizzy laugh, like a champagne glass overfilled, was drawing fascinated looks.

Frau Goering raised her eyebrows.

'You haven't met our other committee member. Irene Schönepauck.'

'I don't know her, I'm afraid.'

'You wouldn't. She's only just arrived on the scene. She's landed a very high-ranking fiancé.'

Clara looked again. The young woman could not have appeared less like the standard Party spouse, firstly because she was attractive, secondly, because she was defying all the basic rules for Nazi women by wearing vivid orange lipstick, thirdly because she was poured into a body-hugging silk dress, and then a whole lot more reasons to do with her Slavic cheekbones, liberally applied eye make-up and tumbling platinum curls.

'I'm not supposed to say anything about it because the man in question has only just divorced his last wife.'

Clara waited. Whenever Emmy Goering mentioned a secret, a disclosure was sure to follow. For her, morsels of gossip were like canapés; no party was complete without them.

'But just between you and me, his name is Walter Schellenberg.'

The breath caught in Clara's throat.

'Schellenberg!'

'I know. It's a surprise, isn't it? Everyone was astonished. Frankly, we all assumed that, if anything, Schellenberg was more interested in the boss's wife. Frau Heydrich. Everyone thought they were having an affair. Apparently Heydrich believed it too because he took Schellenberg out for a walk and threatened to poison him if the rumours were true.'

Even as Emmy Goering dispensed her news, Clara's mind was busily calculating. Walter Schellenberg was the man whose suspicions had led to her new role as a honey trap. An opportunity to meet his new fiancée, and find out more about the man himself, was too good to miss.

'Schellenberg is a devil, though,' whispered Emmy Goering. 'A brute, and a ruthless one. You heard all the talk about Coco Chanel? I wonder if this girl knows what she's getting into.' She broke off because the blonde woman was sashaying towards them, in a strut more suited to a Parisian catwalk than a Party meeting. The eyes of the crowd stuck to her like burrs.

'Mind you, she looks like the type who knows what she's doing. Let me introduce you.'

'So pleased to meet you, Fräulein Vine.' Irene Schönepauck's voice was a soft coo, straight out of a perfume commercial. 'I recognize you from the piece in *Neues Volk*.'

Emmy Goering had already placed a piece in the newspaper announcing the members of the committee. Alongside the panoply of top-ranking wives, including Annelies von Ribbentrop, Marga Himmler and Margarete Hess, Clara was an exception, being neither a wife, nor having any expectation of matrimony.

Irene rested a cool hand in Clara's and lowered her voice as if in confidence.

'Apart from you I don't know a soul here.'

'I'm sure Fräulein Vine will fill you in,' said Emmy Goering tartly, melting away.

Schellenberg's fiancée looked around restlessly before hooking an ancient waiter by the elbow and tipping her empty glass towards him. Once it was replenished, she swallowed its contents in one, as if downing cyanide, and shuddered visibly.

'*Scheisse*. I thought at least here there might be something worth drinking. I'm sorry, you're probably wondering why I'm here, aren't you? Everyone else is. Even I am.'

'Not at all.'

'There's no point pretending. I was only asked because I'm engaged to Walter Schellenberg.'

'Congratulations.'

'Thanks. Not to say I'm not interested. It's a good cause and all that, those poor little kids. But I know all the Party wives are talking about me behind my back.'

There seemed little point in denying the obvious, so Clara said, 'They talk about everyone. But I'm not any-one's wife and I don't even belong to the Party. I'm just an actress.'

'Does that mean you don't know Walter?'

'I've never even met him.'

Her eyes widened in delight. 'Wonderful! That means we girls can chat without me having to watch every word I say! I can, can't I?'

'Of course. I promise nothing you say to me will get back to the Party. And do call me Clara.'

'You must call me Irene.' The name issued like a sigh

through her lips and Clara understood what a man like Schellenberg would see in her.

'Can I ask when the wedding will be?'

The lips puckered in a sulky grimace. 'I only wish I knew. I've had the physical examination, I've got the certificate to say I'm racially perfect and Walter says he wants us to get married as soon as possible, but he keeps putting off the date. Partly because that old baggage, his first wife, dragged out the divorce, and partly because of work. I say it's not easy for me making all these arrangements and then cancelling them, not at a time like this, but he claims he's up to his neck in counter-security problems.'

'I'm sure that's true.'

'Perhaps,' she shrugged. 'It would be better if he could discuss things with me, but when he gets to my apartment he just sits brooding, getting more and more drunk. It's easy for you actresses. You have your work to take your mind off things. But I'm a dress designer, at least I was until I met Walter, and now I'm not working at all. I just stay in the apartment all day, drinking coffee.'

'Coffee!' No one in Berlin could find coffee any more. 'How do you get that?'

'My little secret. My doctor gives it to me. If you can persuade your doctor that coffee is necessary to your health, he'll put it on prescription and then it's provided for you. I'll get you an appointment with him if you like.'

Clara shrugged. If people were going to keep recommending doctors to her, she may as well take the one handing out free coffee.

'Thank you.'

Irene hooked a curl from her face with a single fingernail and sighed.

'I know what you're thinking. Lucky girl with all those connections. But Walter being so senior works both ways. You've got no idea of the evenings I have to sit through. The other night we had dinner at Horcher's, which would have been lovely except that it was with Heinrich Himmler and his wife. I can't tell you how scared I was. I knew Himmler had complained to Walter about me wearing lipstick – he sent Walter some pictures of me covered with critical remarks in green ink and the way he looks at me is so acid it would burn through a Panzer – but frankly God forbid I ever end up in the same boat as his wife. Marga Himmler – what that woman has to put up with! She was on about her husband's new plans for marriage. He's decided that all healthy SS men should have two wives. The first one will be called Domina to show that she's older. I thought, that's not going to work. Who wants to be known as the older wife?'

'I hope you told him.'

'Oh, I couldn't. Walter would have gone crazy if I'd interrupted SS-Reichsführer Himmler, so I just kept shtumm, nodding and pretending to look interested. Unfortunately that only encouraged him. He started telling me about how if a German soldier is prepared to die then he must also have the freedom to love unconditionally, with many different women. The sight of that funny little man with no chin talking about sex, I tell you, I was dying to laugh. I was kicking Walter beneath the table, but he didn't move a muscle. I don't think he felt it through his jackboots. Then Himmler got on to the subject of *Menschmaterial*.'

'Remind me?'

'Oh you know, human material. The birth rate. All that business about *Dem Führer ein Kind schenken*.'

The slogan *Give the Führer a Child* was plastered everywhere.

'That's a big topic for him, isn't it?' reflected Clara. 'Having babies.'

Her sole encounter with Heinrich Himmler had involved a lecture on the subject of breeding racially superior children.

'Apparently the attempts to raise the birth rate aren't going as well as he planned. The idea is that all SS families should have at least four children, but a lot of them aren't managing more than one. I hope nobody's expecting me to take up the slack.'

At this point their conversation was interrupted by a burst of applause and they turned to see a gaggle of children being ushered out of the elevators and herded into a group. The photographer was fiddling with his equipment, assembling the legs of the tripod and the camera with its lens on top like a soldier clicking together his gun. Frau Goering was orchestrating proceedings, positioning VIPs behind the small figures.

Irene grimaced. 'I thought they were supposed to be evacuating children, not bringing them to parties.'

The orphans were outfitted in standard Hitler Youth uniform – white blouse, belted blue skirt and ankle socks for the girls, shorts for the boys – but what marked them out was their unusual attractiveness. All the children had clear skin, shining hair and even teeth. They had almost certainly been selected for their looks. No VIP wanted their picture taken with an ugly child. The children hesitated wide-eyed as the celebrities clustered around, arranging their features into appropriate expressions of concern.

'They like kids, don't they, your actress friends,' observed Irene shrewdly.

Clara looked across at Jenny Jugo, crouching cinematically beside the most photogenic child, her sleek brunette coiffure pressed unnaturally close to the young girl's head in a pose which seemed guaranteed to appear on the front pages of the following day's newspapers. The girl had big eyes, blue-green like jade, and tightly braided hair. She stood stiffly, plainly unused to such close contact, one leg slightly bent. There was something wild and shy about her, as though she was only temporarily tamed, like one of the lion cubs Goering kept as pets in his home. When she caught Clara's eyes on her, she met her gaze and returned it with a penetrating stare.

'I suppose we should join in,' said Irene, grimly. 'I'm standing at the back, though. I don't want any kids getting jammy fingers on this dress.'

It was late afternoon by the time Clara escaped from the reception. The conversation with Emmy Goering had unsettled her. So her English heritage was once more prompting gossip and rumour. That was to be expected, and yet, it was important that she discovered in what quarters this speculation was rumbling. The routine chatter of actresses was one thing, but if the unease issued from Frau von Ribbentrop or her friend Lina Heydrich, wife of the SD chief, it was far more disturbing. For months, ever since she had cut her ties with the British secret services, she had told herself she was safe. Since the outbreak of war she had had no communication with any foreign agent. She had gone from home to work to home again with the stupefying regularity of a metronome. S–Bahn to studio to shop to S–Bahn. Sleep, work, eat. And cinema or meals with Erich at weekends. So precise was her routine that no agent shadowing her would have need of a watch, and so immaculate her cover that Joseph Goebbels himself had entrusted her with a mission of his own. Yet still the old worry rose up to haunt her with a rush of dread. Could it really be that her seven years of spying and informing and watching every move of the Nazi elite had gone entirely undetected? She might have the confidence of Goebbels, but he was only one cog in the extensive apparatus of this police state. She thought of the vast databank of Gestapo files that stretched beneath Berlin like the labyrinthine coils of a human brain, the thousands of human informers its neurons and synapses. What was the chance that within it some glint of knowledge existed, waiting to come to the surface? Or that some zealous functionary had decided to increase targeted surveillance against foreign-born citizens? Was it crazy to hope that she could continue undetected in a Germany at war?

Reflexively she looked around. Following a target on foot was a challenge for anyone; the absence of traffic in the streets made it harder to hide a lone tail and Clara liked to think she could detect a shadow's sensory fingerprint. They tended to conceal themselves behind clumps of pedestrians, switching from one side of the street to the other, easing into shop doors, making ample use of windows to mirror their target. They might work singly or in pairs, covering their suspect, intensely focused behind bland, professional exteriors. Now, in the early evening, the crowds were lighter and Clara felt sure that if any kind of shadow was around, she could spot them.

Her eyes passed over a Hausfrau pushing a gas-resistant pram with a curved brown lid, like a turtle on wheels. A man in a café watching her legs. A newspaper seller with a portable paper rack strapped to his body like some strange mediaeval instrument of torture, a burst of headlines running down his front. The *BZ am Mittag* said the S-Bahn attacker had struck again, stabbing a woman near Rummelsburg S-Bahn. The *Völkischer Beobachter* declared Britain would be foolish to reject any offers of peace. The *Berliner Morgenpost* had a photograph of Polish Jews, bewildered old men and children who were being dragged by the hand, still young enough to be fascinated by everything, even the camera that so coldly recorded their fate.

But nothing out of the ordinary. No tail.

She quickened her step, feeling her surge of panic subside through the meticulous inspection of her environment.

A pair of factory girls, hair still up in turbans, jostled past and, looking further along the street, she saw a long queue forming outside the cinema.

In May an early closing order had been imposed on cafés, and dancing was banned throughout the Reich. Such trivial pursuits were unsuitable in wartime, Joseph Goebbels decreed. In response cinema audiences had spiralled, with droves of citizens making several visits a week. Some establishments extended their screenings to ten shows a day to cope with the demand, yet it was not adventure movies or romantic feature films that the citizens of Berlin were seeking out, but news.

There was plenty of news on the radio, of course, but listening to Goebbels every evening had the power to drive you mad. Cinema newsreels were another matter. Until recently, the Ufa Tonwoche had been a mild diversion, a dutiful propaganda checklist to sit through before the main feature, a short trot through a week's worth of international events, taking in the odd visiting dignitary or celebrity promoting their latest venture. But no longer. Now the newsreels had been extended to forty minutes, and when they ended there was an interval inserted before the main feature began to give audiences a chance to calm down. Instead some people simply got up and left, having had their fill of drama for one evening. Who needed an action movie when you could watch the fall of France?

The climax came on the 14th of June when the Germans entered Paris, marching down the Champs-Élysées, just as Bismarck had done after his victory over the French in 1871. In Berlin, a fanfare of trumpets had come over the public loudspeakers and people everywhere had jumped to their feet. Those in cafés and restaurants had even stood on chairs in most unPrussian fashion, raising their arms and cheering. Bells rang for a week and official flags were flown.

Clara had watched the newsreels with mounting dread. The reporters breathlessly delivering their bulletins, rockets flaming into the air, machine guns providing a background soundtrack. Then the cameras panning along the troop lines, tilted up into the soldiers' faces to display their angular battle-hardened features to better effect. Dramatic music playing behind the reportage. *'We see new German tanks ready for attack, ready for a mighty push forward. They are the new romance of fighting. They are the knights of the Middle Ages.'* Alongside the troops were the faces of conquered civilians – old men at the farm gates staring with terrible calm at the encroaching troops, peasant women straight out of a seventeenth-century Flemish portrait feeding pigs while their children played oblivious in the yard. Then Paris, and the troops in clean lines beneath the Arc de Triomphe.

This time tomorrow she would be there. Clara felt a throb of alarm at what she was being asked to accomplish. What were the chances that she would be able to get Hans Reuber on his own, and even if she did, how could she possibly discover if he was indeed a foreign agent? If she warned him of Schellenberg's distrust and Reuber was a loyal German patriot, then suspicion would in turn fall on her.

In the hallway of the apartment block a dull-eyed Polish girl, a forced labourer recently acquired by her neighbour Frau Ritter, was mopping the hall. She wore a filthy yellow headscarf and a threadbare apron. Not for the first time Clara wondered where she had come from. Everyone employed foreign workers. They moved through the streets and dwellings of Berlin like an invisible army, an undercurrent of misery no one ever thought about. Numerous Polish women had been seized after the invasion and brought to Berlin to live in large camps on the outskirts of the city. They were mostly employed in factories but some, like this one, were made available for work in private residences. Clara realized she didn't even know her name.

The girl glanced sourly up at Clara then bent her head back to the task, sending a rank perfume of ammonia up the stairwell to mingle with the old cooking and washing smells that issued from closed doors. Halfway up the stairs the faint wail of a child pierced the clash of raised voices. From Frau Ritter's apartment came a metallic voice on the radio giving '*Tips For The Housewife*' and as she passed the door opened a crack and the woman herself, in a dressing gown, peered out, surveying Clara with pursed lips and a wordless glance, before retreating. On the fifth floor the light was broken, and Clara had to fumble for her key in the dark. Her neighbour, Doktor Franz Engel, was listening to a concert from the Berlin Philharmonic at full blast – his private signal that Clara could, if she chose, turn on her shortwave set without detection – yet that evening she had no desire for distraction. She needed to pack a bag and focus on the task ahead.

She began to sort through her dwindling selection of clothes, picking out a velvet hat and an anonymous grey serge jacket, and choosing her best gown, a plunging halter-neck of Prussian blue silk from the couture house of Madame Grès, for her stage appearances. A single pair of stockings, darned many times. Ferragamo shoes wearing perilously thin in the sole. A crêpe de Chine blouse. A rare tube of Kolynos toothpaste, sent in by a fan. An indigo bottle of Soir de Paris.

Catching its fragrance, memories of Leo tumbled through Clara's mind like a heap of glinting shards and this time she didn't try to distract herself. There was no point resisting it. Leo was forever part of her. He was there physically, ingrained in the memory of her muscles, and his spirit, too, remained here, in the last place they had loved before his existence had emptied out of the world and vanished like footsteps in the dew. She breathed in and held her breath, as though she was inhaling the last traces of him.

Increasingly, she realized, it was not just grief she was feeling but guilt. That she had lived and Leo hadn't. If she had accepted the place he offered in the car leaving Germany that night, it would have been her lying dead in a pool of blood on the border, and not him.

And then, confusingly, the anger came. That he had entered her life and changed it, then disappeared, with her still standing. That their love should have been so cruelly sundered. That he had robbed her of any hope of finding happiness again.

How bitterly she wished that she had a photograph of him. Anything to shake the terror of forgetting his face. Abandoning the packing, she went over and pulled a book of Rilke's poems from the shelf, thumbing through to Leo's favourite, *Exposed on the Cliffs of the Heart*, in which the poet talked of the raw landscape of the heart and his sense of isolation.

Exposèd on the cliffs of the heart.
See, how small down there,
see: the last hamlet of words, and higher,
and yet so small, a last
homestead of feeling.

Was it some prophetic gift that made Leo love this short poem shot through with a desolate sense of loss? He had read it to her time and again, and whenever her eyes moved across the page, she heard the intonations and inflections of his voice, which was why she read it often, just to bring him back to her. She loved it too, and could not ignore how, even at a time of grief, Rilke managed to see beauty in the stony ground.

Even here, though,
something can bloom; on a silent cliff-edge
an unknowing plant blooms, singing, into the air.

Clara replaced the book, made herself a *Leberwurst* sandwich and ate it ravenously, then went over to the basin and washed. The only soap available now was uniform soap, thin, with no lather, but abstractedly she washed herself over and over, rubbing the flesh as if she was trying to rub away the whole of Berlin, and the Nazis, her loneliness and everything that had happened in her life.

Chapter Seven

'The hot water, Mademoiselle, is available from seven in the evening.' The bellboy coughed nervously and corrected himself. 'That is, the new seven o'clock.'

Times had speeded up. Clocks in France now ran on Greater Reich time, and in this new future everyone was obliged to live one hour ahead.

'And breakfast is from seven in the morning until nine.'

Clara nodded, surveying the hotel room. It was archetypal of the kind of modest residence in which a travelling actress might stay. A small basin in the corner, with its delicate blue and white china bowl, a white armoire and a faded frieze of flowers on the walls. A high, narrow bed that was certain to be rock hard, sheets thick and coarse, though clean. The window, with a crust of mildew at the rim, and a spotted mirror. Her eyes went to the latch, working out whether it would be possible to climb onto the rusty balcony in a hurry, down into the brick-paved courtyard. Searching for ways of escape had become second nature in the years since she had first taken on her secret role. Her first thought in any space was to find the way out, to calculate the method of rapid exit and how to extricate herself in a hurry should circumstances require it. It took a second to remind herself that there would be no call for an escape in Paris. She was here, after all, on Goebbels' orders, and Erich was his hostage to ensure she returned to Berlin.

'Will there be anything else?'

'I'm performing at the Théâtre de Montmartre so please ensure the concierge knows that I won't be back until late.'

'Certainly, Mademoiselle. Fräulein.' He shuffled, uncertain whether tips were part of the new regime, and Clara reassured him with fifty centimes that were still, as far as she knew, legal tender.

She walked out of the front door and turned into the Avenue Foch. The chestnut trees were bursting with summer green, and in the houses of Paris's smartest arrondissement lilac, laburnum and clematis were tumbling over the high walls. The buildings, in the morning sun, were pale and golden, the colour of fresh bread. Outside one of the grander edifices two lorries covered in tarpaulins had drawn up and Chinese jars, paintings, rolled carpets and tapestries were being ferried out under the direction of a German officer.

It was ten days since the Germans entered Paris. The wide boulevards, designed by Baron Haussmann to allow the broad passage of civilization, had instead allowed German troops in shining boots and well-cut uniforms to march, several ranks abreast, up to the Arc de Triomphe unopposed. Like a field-grey spear lancing into the city, the column of soldiers, tanks, armoured cars and anti-aircraft guns had stretched for miles, while the houses each side closed their shutters against the sight. Vehicles fitted with loudspeakers trundled through the streets – *'Parisians stay home. No demonstrations will be allowed'* – promising the death penalty for disobedience. Planes roared overhead. As tanks crunched over the cobbles, French police with white batons lined the sidewalks and the population watched, frozen with astonishment and fear. Veterans of the first war, their medals pinned to their chests, had tears streaming down their faces while some small boys, unable to contain themselves at the sight of the gleaming machines, waved and cheered as the parade made its way across the Pont Alexandre III to the Esplanade des Invalides, where the gilded tomb of Napoleon sketched its famous shape on the skyline. A fleet of sedans led the way to the Hôtel de Crillon, which had been singled out as the new HQ for the high command.

And yet, less than two weeks after this dramatic parade, a sense of normality, or at least the new normality, had returned. Schools, restaurants, theatres and bars were back in operation. The women on the sidewalks, in slender-waisted dresses, retained their understated Parisian chic. Outside the cafés, cane-bottomed chairs were still lined three deep on the pavement. If this had been an Ufa newsreel, as it surely would soon be, audiences in Germany would be unable to discern the uncanny changes that had descended. Yet to Parisians they were all too painfully obvious. For a start, the city *sounded* different. There were no motorcars; vehicles had been requisitioned and bicycles rigged up with trailers to serve as taxis. Push carts were everywhere. Those buses that still existed had been equipped with charcoal burners on the roof, giving them the appearance of exotic monsters. Thin strains of Beethoven drifted over from the free concerts in parks and squares and everywhere the German language splintered the air.

There were other changes too. Signs were now in German, with French in smaller type beneath, and news-paper kiosks had been requisitioned to sell only German papers and magazines. Scaffolding had been erected for the camera crews to record military marches and along the Rue de Rivoli the familiar blood-coloured banners billowed like a row of carpets ready to be beaten. *If you want to earn more, go and work in Germany* advised the advertising hoardings, and *Give your labour to save Europe from Bolshevism*. One poster portrayed a Nazi trooper holding a fair-haired child with the slogan *Populations abandonnées, faites confiance au soldat allemand!* You have been abandoned, put your trust in the German soldier.

There was also a deeper, more telling difference. For some weeks Parisians had been holding their collective breath, but now their faces were beaten and downcast. Not even a spark of rebellion lit their dejected air. A pall hung over the city like a leaden sigh.

Midway down the Rue de Rivoli Clara paused at a café called Angelina. Her appointment was not for another two hours, so she might as well eat while she could. Entering, she marvelled at the way light streamed through the windows and shimmered on the gilded mirrors, the chequered floor and murals, and the glass cases at the counter where piles of croissants and choux buns and macarons gave an impression of careless plenty. The place was, she remembered, a favourite of Coco Chanel, where the designer took a demitasse of *chocolat chaud* every morning accompanied by a dish of whipped cream. Confident chatter bounced from the mirrored walls and for a moment, as Clara sat down, her mind blanked and she couldn't think what to order. Months of deprivation had diminished her imagination so much that she could barely conjure anything but coarse bread, padded sausage and bitter root vegetables. In Berlin cafés you had nothing more than a grainy slice of rye bread and a smear of margarine accompanied by a cup of watery tea and Immergut Milch, a milk substitute that never went off. In the end she asked for a boiled egg, accompanied by a *café crème* and a tartine spread with real butter, sweet and silky pale, rather than the sharp yellow chemical back home with its rime of grease. This meal she consumed like a fairy-tale feast.

Opening her copy of *L'Illustration,* she turned to read what it had to say about the invasion.

Under the headline *Tourists in Uniform*, the editorial confirmed her worst expectations. It oozed fascination with the invaders and their rosy complexions and blond hair, their confidence and clicking heels. The Germans were 'handsome boys, decent, helpful, above all correct'. Perhaps, after the fears of mayhem and the unspoken terror that troops might rape any women they encountered, the sheer orderliness of the occupation came as a relief. These Germans seemed so perfectly assembled, like the tanks and cars they drove, their hair precision-parted, their boots polished to a high shine;

why, even their uniforms choreographed harmoniously with their surroundings, the Wehrmacht field grey matching exactly Paris's weathered domes and spires. To Clara, however, the picture of the Wehrmacht against the elegant backdrop of Paris was a glaring horror. They were robots marching through a daydream, Expressionist figures on an Impressionist canvas.

Finishing her coffee she headed north. Outside a little Basque restaurant off the Opéra she saw a German officer brandishing a Baedeker guide and discussing sites of special historical interest with his men. A busload of soldiers on a guided tour sailed by, photographing everything they passed. Compared to Albert Speer's gleaming, monumental blocks in Berlin, Paris's stately buildings must seem dramatically different, covered with a calcified crust of soot, their musty grape-skin domes dissolving into the skyline. Further on, a soldier had erected an easel and was painting a church. Everywhere, Germans were wide-eyed at the beauty of Paris and already a blitzkrieg of shopping was underway. Food, stockings, cosmetics for their girlfriends. At the Place Vendôme Clara saw a soldier staggering under a pile of boxes and recognized the interlaced black-on-white C of Chanel.

This looked not so much like war as tourism.

She walked on. Although outwardly she observed everything she passed, it was as though an invisible membrane existed between herself and the rest of humanity. It took scarcely anything – a vague silhouette, a strain of music, the register of a voice – to recall Leo's face and bring images of their time together rising from the depths of her mind. His touch setting her senses alight, his hands roving hungrily across her body, his heart banging against his ribcage as their limbs entwined. The ache in her was almost overwhelming and even as she dug her fingers into red crescents in her palms to end it, Clara couldn't stop thinking how different things might have been. If she had left Germany last year at his bidding would they be together now in his London flat, high above the plane trees of a Bloomsbury square? Would they take walks through the dusk and spend their evenings cooking and sitting peacefully, Leo doing his translations or writing his poetry and her content to read at his side? Or would the war have driven them apart again? What would her life be now? How slender the split-second decisions were on which existence hinged, and that opened doors to such different lives.

For a moment Clara felt a shaft of grief so profound, her heart contracted.

Her rumination was so deep that she stepped off the kerb and was almost knocked down by a leather-coated motorcyclist with a sidecar.

'*Achtung!*'

A young German soldier appeared from behind and grabbed her arm, hauling her out of danger.

'Be careful, please, Fräulein.'

'Thank you.'

'Not at all. It's easy to forget, but these motorbikes are very fast, you know. You ladies must watch out.'

He clicked his heels and smiled at her startled face, but

Clara's shock was more the result of his own behaviour than the accident so closely averted. This degree of good manners was rarely extended by troops in Berlin. Back home, stone-faced soldiers marched in lines or progressed in pairs along the pavement, expecting ordinary citizens to get out of their way. Their conduct was brisk at best and brutish at worst, yet in Paris the same soldiers were transformed. Could it be because the Germans planned to occupy the city with a relatively small army, and so had instructed troops to place an emphasis on civility? Or was it simply Paris itself that had cast its spell? Either way, with two million Frenchmen already taken prisoner, Clara guessed some women would find such courteous strangers hard to resist.

She stopped by a shop with lemon soap for sale and bought two bars, then passed a boutique selling silk underwear and retraced her steps with amazement. Such items were impossible to find in Germany, where the only brassieres available were scratchy contraptions of coarse cotton. Inside the shop, French knickers with little frills of chambray lace, crêpe de Chine slips, satin basques and delicate peach silk camisoles hung on gilt rails. Clara's mind raced ahead to the purpose of her mission here, the honey trap for Hans Reuber, and she was surprised to find her reaction was not revulsion but indifference at the idea of the proposed seduction. She wondered exactly how far Goebbels expected her to go. Did he assume she would go to bed with this man in order to gain his confidence? She imagined another man moving above her, his alien scent, and his unfamiliar hands ranging over her naked body as she tried not to flinch. She pictured herself succumbing. What would it matter if she did? Erich was all she minded about and if it kept him safe then who cared? Leo was gone. What point was there in preserving some fidelity beyond death? She didn't believe in any shining hereafter where Leo would be waiting for her. All she believed was that her love for him should be cherished, burnished by memory, like the precious thing it was.

She tried on an apricot-coloured camisole and a lace-edged matching bra. They weren't cheap but Goebbels had provided her with an allowance and what was underwear if not a justifiable expense? She noted the treacherous, sensuous caress of silk against the skin, and studied her reflection in the changing-room mirror with grim resolve. She would need to gain Reuber's confidence by any means possible. If he was a traitor to his Fatherland, then she had to find out. Not to warn Goebbels, but Reuber himself.

Montmartre, in the northwest of Paris, had for centuries been the traditional haunt of artists, its narrow streets crammed with cinemas, cabarets and bars. Reaching the theatre, Clara saw the original sign now obscured by a giant banner reading *Deutsches Soldaten Theater*, crowned by the imperial Eagle. Beside it a poster had been pasted up advertising that night's attractions and, even though she had expected it, she was still taken aback to see her name prominently displayed on the bill. The repertoire looked identical to the kind of variety evening that could have been found at any Berlin theatre in the past five years – light-hearted sketches spiced with senti-mental tunes, magicians and dancing girls, and the whole performance interspersed with some Schubert Lieder. It was entirely familiar and, as she walked through the brass doors and crossed the foyer, she heard the bars of a song so distinct that no German, and no Frenchman either, could fail to hear it without a shudder.

Auf der Heide blüht ein kleines Blümelein . . .

On the heath a little flower blooms . . .

Erika. The marching song of the SS.

Pushing past a musty velvet curtain, she stood in shadow at the back of the stalls. Hans Reuber was on stage, supervising a dwarf and a female contortionist whose face peered incongruously from between her clasped knees. The woman wore a flesh-coloured leotard that made her look, from a distance, as though she was entirely naked, and the dwarf stood by, ready to spring onto her turned back. An acrobat was finishing a backflip, coming to a halt with a stormtrooper's precision. Clara caught a flavour of something she had not scented for years, the shimmering, decadent air of the old Berlin cabaret, brimming with subversive sexuality.

Reuber was dressed with artistic flair, with a spotted cravat at his neck, secured by a swastika tiepin, and a smart, well-cut suit. His shirt was expensive-looking and his hair a decadent inch or so longer than was *de rigueur* among German men. His eyes were as brown as polished chestnuts. As she made her way through the stalls he turned and spread his arms in a stagey welcome.

'Fräulein Vine! Our guest star. Forgive me for not coming to meet you but we are working against the clock to get the concert ready. I was so pleased to hear that you could join us.'

Clara stood at the stage edge and smiled up at him. 'I wouldn't have missed it for the world. Any of us would leap at the chance to be in Paris right now.'

'You're right.' He jumped down and came to stand beside her, rubbing his hands. 'Have you had any briefing of what we'd like you to do?'

'Doktor Goebbels told me it would involve singing.'

'Precisely. Perhaps we should take a break and find somewhere to discuss it. Tell me, have you had lunch? Or coffee?'

'I can't get enough coffee here.'

'That was my reaction.' He checked his watch and turned to the actors on stage.

'Ladies and gentlemen, we break for an hour.'

The contortionist uncoiled herself, and stood, hands on hips, glancing between Reuber and Clara with a scowl that suggested that her relationship with her producer went beyond the merely professional. The pianist began chatting to the dwarf and Reuber and Clara made their way through the streets to the picturesque Place du Tertre.

The square was almost a pastiche of a perfect Parisian scene. The air was mild, and artists stood behind their easels in the plane trees' dappled shade, making and remaking the weathered façades while ignoring the uniformed interlopers who strolled before them, picturing a city that existed only in memory and whose charm was now as shallow as a stage set. Paris, the eternal city, determined to regard defeat as a temporary distraction. All around, cafés and bistros were doing a busy trade, exuding the smell of roast chicken and the tang of garlic. The yells of flower women and souvenir sellers mingled with the clatter of bicycles over the cobbles. It was so picturesque that Clara had to remind herself that she was only in this holiday setting on Goebbels' orders.

On one side of the square a restaurant called La Mère Catherine stood, with a dark wooden façade and traditional navy canopy sheltering the pavement tables. A sign had been freshly fixed in the window announcing *Man spricht Deutsch* – though it scarcely needed spelling out. Lounging and chatting at the tables prettily clad with pink gingham, groups of Wehrmacht officers were savouring glasses of beer, their harsh babble of German drowning out the treacly croon of Maurice Chevalier issuing from the gramophone. Skirting them, Reuber chose a table at the far end of the gloomy interior and handed Clara a menu. Just as before, she registered an initial shock of plenty. The carte boasted a 'dozen egg omelette'. There was a terrine of foie gras and the *plat du jour* was *Filet de sole au vin du Rhin*, the inclusion of German wine no doubt designed to make the occupiers feel at home.

He touched her arm. 'Eat well. We have a long day ahead.'

It was clear why the idea of seduction had occurred to Goebbels. In the dim light of the café table, Hans Reuber was even more handsome than he appeared on his posters. He was more bronzed than the usual German, with dark curly hair, a sleepy smile and a look in his soulful brown eyes which seemed to say that the woman he was speaking to was the only one who would ever understand him. He projected an air of immediate intimacy, as though the two of them were privy to some special secret, despite the fact that they had only just met. Clara wondered if, under different circumstances, she might have found that easy charm attractive, even though she knew that it was more about Reuber himself than the girl on the receiving end. Yet now, she felt nothing.

'Fräulein Vine. Or can I call you Clara . . .? You must call me Hans.'

Reuber propped one ankle across his leg and curled a hand round his glass of beer.

'Can I say how flattered and surprised we were to have you visit our company.'

'I was a bit surprised myself, actually. But it'll be an honour to contribute.'

'Indeed. Here's to your good health.' He raised his glass, and tipped a little down his throat. 'Where are you staying?'

'Just off the Avenue Foch.'

'Very nice. I'm at the Crillon. They've given me a fabulous room. It looks out over the Place de la Concorde. Here.' He hauled a booklet from his top pocket and Clara saw the familiar stationery of the Ministry of Propaganda. 'Before we go any further you might want to take a look at our briefing. These are the guidelines for our performances.'

Clara scanned the first page, recognizing in the dreary official bullet points the familiar mix of hectoring and bureaucracy that was copyright of Joseph Goebbels.

Pieces in foxtrot rhythm are not to exceed twenty per cent of the repertoire.

Musical pace must not exceed the degree of allegro commensurate with the Aryan sense of discipline and moderation.

Music of the barbarian races conducive to dark instincts is banned.

'Dark instincts?'

'Ah yes. On that subject Herr Doktor Goebbels is most particular.'

'That much I do know.'

Reuber spooned a dollop of foie gras onto a square of toasted brioche and shrugged complicitly. 'It wouldn't be so bad if it weren't for the fact that we have such formidable competition. Most of the cabarets have reopened. The Don Juan, Eve, Chez Elle, the Tabarin, the Lido – they're all going strong. Not to mention the Moulin Rouge and the floor show at the Sheherazade. Every soldier in the Reich has heard of the Moulin Rouge and you know what young men are. The girls here are nothing like the ones you see in Berlin.'

Most of the girls appearing in Berlin's theatres now resembled statues by Arno Breker, the Führer's favourite sculptor – hefty nudes with sleek flanks and the blank docility of Friesian cows.

'So how can you compete?' said Clara. 'Without invoking "dark instincts"?'

'A question that has been at the forefront of my mind and the only answer I've come up with is to offer them a little of everything – starting with my own humble performance,' he grinned with transparently false modesty, 'followed by a magician, a chorus act, a few musical numbers and at the end a song from you to bring the whole show together. With luck it should remind them of the *Request Concert* back home. Nobody could call that a dark instinct.'

'You're not saying the audience can request any song?'

'Don't panic. I decide the songs. And I'll make sure you know the request in advance. Tonight, I'm thinking of *Schön ist die Nacht*. You know it, of course?'

How could she not know the most popular song of the past year? Back in Berlin you could not set foot in a nightclub without hearing its wistful strains. It mingled nostalgia with a joyful love of the old Berlin.

Reuber winked and tipped the beer down his throat.

'Truth is, and don't tell Herr Doktor Goebbels, I *have* made the smallest concession to the dark instincts. I've had a consignment of girls sent from the Folies-Bergère to satisfy the more basic of appetites. Young men expect that kind of thing and we wouldn't want to disappoint them, especially in Paris. But their lasting impression,' his voice lowered to a seductive whisper, 'will be of you. And if your voice evokes any man's dark instincts, as I fear it may, then I can't be held responsible.'

With this blatant flirtation, his eyes bored into hers and momentarily Clara wondered if, perhaps, Reuber might be covertly exercising his hypnotic powers. Then she reassured herself that she would not easily be susceptible to hypnosis; her need for control was too great, and the idea of relaxing her grip and letting anyone else command her thoughts was a kind of horror. You got enough practice at that in Berlin, where a torrent of heavy-handed government propaganda issued day and night from radios and public loudspeakers, edging its way into every corner of the soul. Yet it wouldn't do to be complacent. There was obviously far more to Hans Reuber than his silky demeanour might suggest. Otherwise she wouldn't be here in Paris, trying to discover if he was a spy.

Breaking eye contact she focused on the square outside, where a photographer with a Leica and an official armband was taking pictures of a flower seller. The old woman, planted behind a cart of tulips more riotous and scarlet than the swastika banner draped on the building behind them, was gnarled and impassive like an ancient stump. As the German photographer crouched and snapped around her she remained unsmiling, hands crossed on the head of a stick, and only the slight droop at the edges of her mouth suggesting apprehension of what was to come.

'Everywhere you look, someone's taking a picture.'

'Goebbels has promised that Paris will be a recreational city for the Reich,' said Reuber, following her gaze. 'Apparently people at home are desperate for pictures and that sort of thing can't be left to chance. The city must look attractive, whatever his private feelings about it.'

His meaning was plain. Goebbels hated France, Germany's historic enemy, yet this was to be a model occupation and it was important to project the image of a thriving city whose citizens were happily coexisting with their conquerors. Courting lovers in the parks, busy cafés lining the boulevards, beautiful girls, old men playing the accordion. All the clichés. Clara recalled the busload of German soldiers, their faces alight with excitement, and one soldier throwing a bar of chocolate to a group of pretty girls. Paris was to be one big tourist brochure saturated with colour; the soaring blue of the sky, the pulsing pinks and yellows in the shop windows, the stately jade of the Tuileries. So much more vivid than the indomitable buildings of Berlin, with their leaden façades rising starkly against a bone-bleached sky.

'It would be hard to take a bad photo of such a beautiful city.'

Reuber smiled.

'And we Germans are especially susceptible to beauty.'

It was only a whisper, the subtlest of intimations, and in other circumstances Clara would have chosen to ignore it, but the seductive fire of Reuber's eyes encouraged her. She had barely two days to ensnare this man and discover if he was, as Schellenberg suspected, a foreign agent. After which she needed to decide what to do with that information.

'Perhaps, Hans . . .' She met his smouldering gaze full on, then lowered her eyes and stroked a finger down the side of her glass. 'You could show me around.'

He paused, drained his beer and wiped his mouth with satisfaction.

'I can think of nothing I would like more. Shall we say tonight, after the performance?'

That evening the theatre was packed. A sea of grey-green uniforms. Cigarette smoke, mingled with cosmetic powder, twirled up through the arc lights. Row upon row of young faces, the undisputed masters of Europe, sat glorying in their easy conquest. Reuber's decision to hire girls from the Folies-Bergère was inspired. Many of the troops were too young to remember the time of Weimar Germany, when their own country's cabarets were the most risqué in the world, so they greeted the high-kicking French girls, in their feathers and tutus, with a raucous glee that would have had Goebbels slamming his desk in rage. At the end, Clara's song provided just the right touch of nostalgia to send them home with a glow in their hearts.

Clara had dressed carefully, with her new silk underclothes beneath the Prussian blue Madame Grès evening dress and a single strand of pearls. She wondered if she would end the evening in Reuber's room at the Crillon and, if so, whether it would be possible to be drunk enough to get that far, yet remain sufficiently sober to persuade him to reveal his hand.

He met her backstage, still in his costume of evening dress with a tideline of orange make-up around the edge of his face. He undid his bow tie and tucked it in his top pocket.

'Why don't we walk up to the Basilique du Sacré-Coeur? You can see the whole of the city from there. If you're not here for long, it's a sight you shouldn't miss.'

They made their way uphill through Montmartre's tilting, cobble-stoned streets, beneath the mottled trees of the Place du Tertre, towards the basilica's bone-white domes. In the moonlight their design seemed fiddly and intricate, like an outsized ivory trinket on the skyline. Even at this hour, the area was humming with life. Clara glanced through the door of a smoke-filled salon to see women in brightly coloured silk dining with German officers, and a pile of caps, with glinting silver badges, stacked precipitously above the coat rack. These Parisiennes had no competition from the female German auxiliary workers, the secretaries and telephone operators who had arrived to service the command posts in their drab uniforms and no make-up, and they knew it. The excitement showed on their faces. A snatch of song travelled on the breeze. Edith Piaf, the little sparrow, singing *Embrasse-moi*.

Negotiating the flight of vertiginous steps leading down from the basilica, Reuber offered Clara his arm and she took it, pressing deliberately close. When they reached the semi-circular terrace below he did not detach himself. She sensed the pulse of male attraction and his understanding that she was making him an offer. An offer that he would surely not decline.

Before them was a vista as astonishing as anything to be found on the walls of the Louvre. A tapestry of lead roofs, domes and spires, a panorama of the city in all its grandeur, bisected by the glint of the Seine. This was the spot where Paris presented herself voluptuously for tourists' eyes in full knowledge of her mythical beauty, even if the city was observing a blackout, and only the faint blue gleam of painted street lights punctuated the gloom. The *ville lumière* had become the *ville éteinte* – the extinguished city.

'That song you sang was perfect tonight. It must have made those men feel quite at home.'

'I doubt any of them were homesick.'

'Why would they be, when they have this city to explore? As we do. It's a shame that the Frontbühne should only have you for two nights.'

Reuber was testing her, she recognized. Suspicious.

'I know it's not long but I'm afraid I had other commitments. I wanted to do my bit for the troops though.'

'Of course.'

'And I'm sure my real motivation for being in France is the same as yours.'

He lifted an enquiring eyebrow.

'Which is?'

She gestured at the view before them.

'To see this, of course. Paris!'

'Oh. Naturally.'

On the shadowed gravel a few pigeons still strutted and bowed. Reuber leaned his arms on the parapet, took a cigarette out of his pocket and struck a match against the stone of the balustrade.

'So tell me. Why you are really here?'

A rush of alarm prickled her skin.

'I thought I'd explained.'

He scrutinized her as carefully as a card player watching for a tell on his opponent's face, searching for some tic or involuntary twitch that would give the truth away.

'Forgive me, my dear Fräulein, if I speak frankly. But a surprise guest, brought in for just two performances? And a lady who, although you gave a very good performance, is not widely known for her voice? That might be understandable if you were – with due respect – a big star. An Olga Chekhova, perhaps. Paris is a popular posting and I'm sure there are any number of celebrity names who would like a break here, so when I was informed of your arrival, I asked myself some questions. Why is this beautiful woman being sent to Paris?'

'Because I requested it?'

'Sure. I thought of that. I said to myself maybe this is one of those young women whose whims Doktor Goebbels is keen to satisfy. That was eminently possible. But for only two nights? Even the most loyal citizen of the Reich would want to leave Berlin for more than two nights. I began to think that your visit had less to do with Paris, and more to do with me.'

Though outwardly she remained unruffled, Clara was alarmed at the speed with which Reuber had come to this conclusion. Had she been careless? How was it possible that she had allowed some fracture in her façade of a guileless actress, dazzled by Paris and all too happy to succumb to a celebrity's charms?

At that moment a shriek echoed from the steps of the basilica behind them. A group of soldiers were entertaining three local girls and one man had just delivered a playful slap on the black satin rear of his new girlfriend, who responded with a shout of laughter as she brushed him playfully off and pushed a curl of fair hair behind her ear.

Reuber's face darkened.

'The papers here say the French look forward to being welcomed into the National Socialist adventure. But I've heard the locals have already coined a name for this awkward situation. *Le temps des autruches.* The time of ostriches. The Parisians will ignore our occupation so long as we Germans behave in a civilized fashion. At least, I *think* that's the term they use. Civilized. I've always wondered at the French definition of that word.'

Something in his tone, an acid mix of disdain and subversion, put Clara on alert. It was like a pheromone in the air, a high-frequency vibration just on the edge of hearing. A signal, transmitting itself more carefully and enigmatically than any military code. Goebbels said there were concerns that Reuber was a traitor, and given that those suspicions stemmed from Reinhard Heydrich's security empire, the Sicherheitsdienst, whose reach and power could scarcely be overestimated, they were more than likely to be true. So what was Reuber signalling – and how should Clara respond?

To show her entire hand so soon and with no evidence was a dangerous step. Disclosing her own allegiance would be lethal if Reuber was merely a patriotic German, intent on nothing more than giving everything he had to the war effort. Yet if she revealed that she had been sent to check his own loyalty, well – that need say nothing more than that she had succumbed to his seductive charm.

She cast an involuntary glance around, trying to calibrate the situation. An old woman, a concierge from the basilica, approached and passed them, with a hard, bony face like a bird, but the look she cast was one of hatred rather than suspicion. It said only that they were Germans, and she wished them dead.

'If I had to guess I would say you were here to report on me.'

Clara decided to act on instinct. After all, there was no time to lose.

'I suppose I should be honest with you. I'm not just here to entertain the troops. My presence here has to do with Walter Schellenberg.'

'Schellenberg?'

'He has questions about your allegiance to the Fatherland.'

The silence seemed to last for ever before he said, 'I guessed as much.'

'How?'

The hypnotist looked ahead grimly. Despite the exquisite skyline spread out before him like a seductive woman show-casing her charms, the beauty of the scene was lost on him. Reuber was, in his mind, pacing the gaunt grey streets of his home city.

'Herr Schellenberg has long been suspicious of me.'

'What makes you say that?'

Another silence. Then suddenly his sombre expression was lit by a shaft of jollity.

'All right. I'll tell you how I found out. It makes an amus-ing tale.'

'There's not much amusing about the SD.'

'Oh, I think you'll find this entertaining. It came about last year. Heydrich was worried about high-level leaks that were making their way to the French and the British about plans for the invasion of France so he asked Schellenberg to investigate. The man's famously lucky and in no time at all he had a break. A lady called Kitty Schmidt was arrested crossing the Dutch border and this lady happened to own a brothel called Salon Kitty. It's in Giesebrechtstrasse in Charlottenburg and quite a place by all accounts, frequented by a lot of foreign diplomats. Anyhow Frau Schmidt had amassed a small fortune in a British bank account and decided it was time to cut loose and make her way to retirement. Unfortunately for her she was caught, and there were any amount of charges she was facing – false documents, currency smuggling, you name it – but when Schellenberg got wind of it he dropped all the charges on condition that she go back to the brothel and take up where she left off. Only before it reopened, it was fitted out with cameras and double walls constructed with concealed microphones so that every word spoken would be recorded by Gestapo agents in the basement. That way he would have plenty of material for blackmail and entrapment.'

'How ingenious he is.' Yet again the thoroughness of Schellenberg chilled her.

'And cunning. Never underestimate his cunning. That's exactly why he's been made head of Germany's entire counter-espionage department at such a young age. He's brilliantly clever and pays enormous attention to detail. He never cuts corners. He hand-picked twenty special girls and had them assessed by psychiatrists to weed out the emotionally weak and unreliable, then sent them for two months to some hotel in the Bavarian Alps to learn a whole routine – codes, how to identify military insignia, current affairs, foreign languages – and now they've been put to work in the brothel. And you know the funny thing?'

Reuber gave a bitter grin and ground out his cigarette on the stone in front of him.

'The only serious transgression they've uncovered so far is that Mussolini likes to make fun of Hitler in private. He does comic imitations of our Führer to entertain his dinner guests. That information comes straight from the mouth of the Duce's own son-in-law. Once the transcript was shown to the Führer, relations between Germany and Italy have never been the same.'

Clara stalled. The account itself seemed perfectly credible, yet how did a stage celebrity like Hans Reuber come to know it?

'When did you hear this story? Do you visit the brothel yourself?'

'Fräulein Vine! I can't imagine what you must think of me!' Reuber grinned, but she sensed an underlying scorn at the suggestion that a man like himself would need to pay for the attentions of women.

'Don't answer that. I know what they say about me. A philanderer. An incurable womanizer. But I flatter myself that I am a little more discriminating than the clients of Salon Kitty. Even if they do include Heydrich himself.'

Even while he said this, Clara's mind was calculating rapidly, trying to work out why Reuber was confiding in her.

'You have a lot of detail.'

'And from an impeccable source.'

'So you got it from another client?'

'No.' He hesitated. 'Not at all. In fact, it came from a British agent. He's posing as a press attaché at the Romanian Embassy.'

There was a hiatus as he glanced sideways at her from beneath the brim of his hat, his keen eyes probing her reaction. Such an admission was devastatingly dangerous. To voice such information – to go so far as to identify an agent of a foreign power – was to put himself at immense risk. If Clara was not what he took her for, then his knowledge of British spies effectively sealed his fate.

'Every day this man's morning walk takes him past the brothel and one day he happened to notice that there was some cable work going on in the pavement outside. Yet curiously, all the workmen had clean overalls. When he probed a little deeper he discovered that the cable workers were SS employees rerouting an extension to SD headquarters. After that, all the British had to do was get a technical expert into the brothel and tap the interior wiring and all the secrets of Salon Kitty were available to them too. Including the fact that they had doubts about me. So you see,' Reuber stroked his moustache ruminatively, 'it would be foolish of me – or anyone else – to underestimate Herr Walter Schellenberg.'

His voice dropped further and the easy smile that danced on his lips vanished again, to be replaced with a deadly seriousness.

'What made you tell me, Clara? That you were here to check up on me?'

'Perhaps I like you.'

'And I like you. But that's not enough to take such a risk. So I ask again. What brings you here? What makes you do it?'

Clara knew what his question meant. He was convinced that she herself was working for another power. He had laid himself bare, and in return he required that she be absolutely level with him. Yet still she was reluctant to give away any more of herself than she needed to.

'I could ask the same of you.'

'That's easy. I'm married, you know.'

'I do.'

'My wife Cici is a performer too.'

'I think I knew that.' Clara tried to summon the picture of the rangy, dark–eyed beauty who had appeared in publicity shots of Reuber's home life before the Reich Chamber of Culture had deemed a wife and family inconvenient accessories for one of their A–list stars.

'Most people don't. Cici's French actually. She has family here in Paris. That was one of the reasons I wanted to come. To check that they're all right. They're Jewish, you see, so you can imagine how that complicates things.'

'I certainly can.' The fact of Clara's own Jewish heritage was something she had kept even from her closest friends. She knew that Hans Reuber would have no idea.

'Cici has some protection being married to me, but there's no way she can perform in public. She hasn't worked for years. And there's no doubt she affected my career too. Until a few years ago, I flatter myself I was a favourite of Doktor Goebbels. I received chocolates and flowers by the cartload, as many as any of those women he chases. He would call me regularly to remind me how valuable I was to the Reich. But after a while the calls and the gifts began drying up, and so did the film roles. It's been an age since I had a contract to top the bill at the Wintergarten. All I've had in the past six months is a provincial tour. Then came a piece in that SS newspaper, *Das Schwarze Korps*, saying I was married to a "full-blown Jewess". The message couldn't be clearer if Goebbels broadcast it on the nightly news.'

'What message?'

'Divorce Cici, of course. Or lose my career.'

'What can you do?'

'I've tried everything I can think of.' He grinned ruefully. 'You imagine me a lothario. A lot of people do, and perhaps there's some truth to it. I'm a vain man and I'm getting older. The smiles of pretty women are a powerful drug for me, though that doesn't mean I don't love my wife. But it also suits my purposes. I do my damnedest to make people forget that I'm married at all. I only wish Joachim Gottschalk would do the same.'

Gottschalk was a fellow actor who had come under intense scrutiny from the Propaganda Ministry for refusing to divorce his Jewish wife, a proposition the uxorious star refused to countenance. So far his high profile and popularity had kept him safe, but who knew how long that would continue? Already the roles had vanished for him in a war of attrition that would only end when the actor finally buckled and agreed to a divorce.

'So for the moment Cici stays home with our children and I tread the stages hypnotizing young women.'

Reuber's mouth curdled in disdain.

'A hypnotist. What kind of profession is that? Blinding people to the reality of what's around them.'

Suddenly he looked from left to right and focused on the spot, a hundred yards away, where the balustrade ended and a winding path, shaded by a dense clump of laurel shrubbery, led down to the next level of the terrace. Clara sensed him stiffen, then he took her arm and strolled languidly in the opposite direction, back up the steps.

'A watcher,' he murmured, once they had crossed into one

of the narrow streets leading away from the basilica. 'I should have guessed.'

'Are you sure? Even here?'

His grip on her arm was painfully tight.

'I'm a German with a French wife, whose family are not, you might say, overjoyed at the prospect of a Nazi occupation. No secret service worth its name could ignore a person like me. I already guessed I was being watched. I knew about Schellenberg's suspicions, and though I'm amazed that they would follow me here, what you told me tonight only makes me more certain.'

As if in confirmation, footsteps crunched purposefully on the cobbles behind them. Against all her instincts, Clara glanced behind and saw a squat blond man with a fleshy face half hidden beneath the brim of his hat, coat belted and collar upturned, and eyes trained on the ground in front of him.

Reuber slid his arm round her waist and drew her towards him, like a man hoping to accelerate the romantic promise of his date.

'Every day I've been here I've expected to open the newspaper and discover I've been stripped of my German citizenship. To be honest, it will almost certainly happen, but in the meantime, a cloak is as good as a dagger. And performance is the best cloak that I can think of for my current enterprise.'

'You haven't explained. What exactly is that?'

His hand dropped down and took hers and she felt him push something into her palm. Instinctively she plunged her hand deep into the recesses of her jacket.

'After the show tomorrow evening, come to this address. There's someone I want you to meet.'

There was no chance of a taxi at that late hour, but it didn't matter because Clara wanted to walk and walk. She needed to assimilate the information Reuber had relayed. So Schellenberg's suspicions were right. Reuber disdained the Nazi Party, plainly despised Joseph Goebbels and was indeed in touch with agents of an enemy country. But what exactly was he engaged in? And what was the meaning of the meeting he proposed for the following night? It might be foolish to consider agreeing to such an encounter, especially now that she knew Reuber was being shadowed, yet she also knew that she would go. After all, Goebbels had ordained this honey trap and a late-night assignation was no more than he would expect.

As she reached the Avenue Foch she passed number 84, a stern-faced building, its windows shuttered and the biscuit-coloured stone tiered with wrought-iron balconies. Despite the lateness of the hour a door was open, giving a glimpse of high chandeliered ceilings and a bevy of black uniforms coming and going, like malevolent bees into the darkness of a hive.

She waited until she had returned to the hotel and closed the door behind her before she took the card from her pocket, unfurled it where it had been clenched in her fist, and looked at it.

Cartier
13, Rue de la Paix, Paris

Chapter Eight

It was an extraordinary thing to see your own face staring out at you from a ten-foot hoarding opposite your home, but it was the experience Katerina Klimpel had when she woke up and made her way to the breakfast room that Monday, and it was not a nice one. A poster of herself with the famous actress Jenny Jugo, heads pressed together and matching smiles, above the legend *Freude durch das WHW*, Joy through the Winterhilfswerk, had been pasted up all round Berlin, including the spot directly across the street from the NSV home. As Katerina queued for her porridge she realized that every child in the home had seen it, not to mention all the supervisors. The children in line elbowed each other and giggled. The smallest ones looked at her with awe. Reactions ranged from envy to hilarity and outright dislike but the one sentiment the poster did not inspire was joy.

It made a change from looking at the Führer, though. Every child was handed a picture of him when they arrived at the NSV home. *To hang above your bed so you can see him whenever you want.* A line of Hitlers scowled down into the girls' dormitory and when they woke and stretched out in the scratchy sheets his face was the first they saw. It was a bit like the crucifix that had hung on the wall at home with its little Jesus, his kindly face dripping minuscule drops of crimson paint – only religion, Katerina now knew, was Jewish and unGermanic, whereas it was quite all right to kiss your Führer picture reverently every night and most girls did.

Except for Heidi. Heidi was the sole friend Katerina had made at the NSV home and going on fifteen she was almost too old to be there. She was large-boned and well developed, with milk-white hair and eyes pale as water. She spent most of her time talking about boys. Although she worshipped Hitler as much as anyone else, Heidi reserved a special adoration for Heinrich Himmler because she had been born on his birthday, which meant, when she entered the NSV home, that the SS-Reichsführer became her official godfather and gave her a silver cup with his name on. It was also why her mother had given Heidi a name with the initial H in the first place, though she got off lightly, Katerina pointed out, because girls born on Hitler's birthday were often named Adolfine. But after the pride of producing a child on Himmler's birthday, disaster had followed. The next baby had been born imperfect, and the hospital had not allowed Heidi's mother to keep it. They had strongly suggested she be sterilized as soon as possible so as not to risk any further mistakes. Shortly afterwards Heidi's mother was found stone cold with a bottle of pills by her side. The father went to pieces and Heidi was sent to the NSV home because he could not look after her, though she insisted this situation was only temporary. It was not like she was an orphan or anything.

Despite the banter and jokes resulting from the poster outside, the picture was not uppermost in Katerina's mind that morning. Monday was the night of her weekly BDM meeting, and it was what might come after that occupied all her thoughts.

The day seemed to last for ever. It was a struggle to concentrate. In maths her head was swimming.

An aeroplane flies at a rate of 240 km an hour to a place at a distance of 210 km to drop bombs. When may it be expected to return if the bomb dropping takes seven and a half minutes?

The construction of a lunatic asylum costs six million marks. How many houses at 15,000 marks each could have been built for that amount?

The numbers on the page twirled and drifted in her head like fragments of ash. Maths was her worst subject; a monochrome world where everything was either wrong or right and there was an answer for everything if you looked hard enough. She ploughed along, her hand aching. Naturally, Katerina was left-handed and wrote very fast, her pen racing along with her fingers crabbed around it, but any child here attempting to write with their left hand got it rapped with a stick. The teacher, Herr Rauch, would patrol the rows of desks, eyes fixed on their papers, and if he caught a child out would summon them to the front of the class and allow them to choose the cane that would punish them. This he brought down on the offending hand with a couple of sharp cracks, so if the child tried again, the wrong hand would be too sore to write with. Katerina knew why — left-handedness meant deviance or idiocy and left-handers would never get a job. 'What employer is going to employ someone who uses their left hand?' Herr Rauch would demand, yet in truth it was neither the pain nor the job prospects that kept her careful. Using her right hand was all part of creating a new identity for herself. It might be effortful and fraudulent, but it meant that she would no longer stand out any more than she did already.

By five o'clock, she was knotting her Jugend scarf and tugging her hair into tight plaits, calculating furiously. The BDM meeting usually lasted an hour, but there was to be a careers talk that evening so she could quite easily explain that the session had lasted far longer than normal. That would give her time to slip away to the apartment on Fischerstrasse. It would mean making her way through the darkened streets and coming back late on the S-Bahn, which frightened her. The carriages were so dark, and you needed to be absolutely sure to find your way in the blackout. But it was the perfect opportunity and besides, she needed to find Sonja, didn't she? Without Sonja, there was the danger of being adopted and that didn't bear thinking about.

'It's time to consider what you will do when you come of age.'

Frau Hofmann, the Reichsfrauenschaft leader giving the careers talk, had a navy suit, matching fedora, red triangular badge identifying her rank and eyes like a prison searchlight.

They travelled over the assembled girls, freezing them to their seats and drilling down into the soul.

'What does a young woman do if she has no husband and no ambitions for an office or a shop?'

The girls swapped uncertain glances. The problem with questions from officials was that you needed to give the right response, but what was the right answer in this case? Frau Hofmann couldn't be genuinely interested in their ambitions, could she?

Fortunately the question turned out to be rhetorical.

'If when you come to choosing a future, you cannot think what to do . . .' Here Frau Hofmann paused, and an expression of inspired delight spread across her features as though the ideal solution had only that moment occurred to her. 'Why not consider giving a child to the Führer?'

This suggestion met with blank looks and knitted brows.

It was so simple, Frau Hofmann explained. An organization called the Fount of Life Foundation had been established to support racially valuable families. The enterprise was directly overseen by SS-Reichsführer Himmler himself, who had been kind enough to take care of every detail. He had ensured that food for expectant mothers was plentiful and every residential home had a programme of lectures and entertainments.

'What better way could there be of serving the Reich?'

Having a child for Hitler had never been Katerina's idea of a career choice, but she noticed that several of the girls perked up with interest and raised their hands with questions.

'What kind of girls are required?'

'How do you qualify for the Foundation?'

'Can I keep the baby myself?'

Frau Hofmann smiled broadly. It was a pleasant surprise to find this level of interest from a BDM Mädelschaft in Berlin. Country areas tended to be more fruitful recruiting grounds for the Foundation of Life. The girls there were simpler and expected less from lives that would be dominated by strenuous and unrewarding farm work, whereas city girls had education and expectations. They wanted to be secretaries or at the very least work in a factory. In some districts the very suggestion that young women might become breeding partners for SS officers met with incredulity and frank distaste. But Frau Hofmann was not in this job for nothing. She had dealt with enough young women to know the way their minds worked and had evolved the perfect skill set for this recruitment exercise. It was all about presenting the concept in the right way.

'We are only interested in the very best young women. The finest Aryan girls. And we like to preserve total anonymity. Not even your family need know you are undertaking this valuable service. Anyone who is interested will be given a series of medical tests and have their background investigated and if all of that goes smoothly, will be introduced to SS officers at one of our residential places. You might be surprised at the quality of our premises. One of them is a real castle! The only proviso is that the girl should choose a man whose hair and eye colour correspond to their own.'

Katerina had already lost interest. This enterprise was suspiciously likely to involve sex and for all her intelligence, she knew very little about that. The book they had been issued with, *Mädel von Heute, Mütter von Morgen*, Girls of Today, Mothers of Tomorrow, tended towards generalities. There was a lot about keeping your body pure and holy for the Führer, but little precise information about the alternative. Everyone knew that the BDM was nicknamed the Bald Deutsche Mütter – soon to be German mothers – but Katerina still had little idea how the state of motherhood came about. She thought of the physical pleasure provided by everyday sensations: soft air buffeting the skin, the aroma of baking bread, the sweet, pungent fragrance of the linden blossom pervading the city, and imagined that sex must be a hundred times as intense. Sex was just another subject she had been relying on Sonja to explain.

After the session ended Katerina made her way to Fischerstrasse and took the clanking elevator to the top floor, peering through the tiny diamonds of its iron gates at she rose up through the unlit hallways to the apartment that her sister shared with Bettina Beyer. When she opened the apartment door Bettina's face fell, as though she had been expecting someone else. Bettina was dressed in a shift of frothy silk that barely reached the tops of her stockings, with slightly grubby lace embroidery around the bust area. Her dyed orange bob had a tigerish stripe of darker hair at the roots and she smelled of tobacco and the musky scent of old bedsheets.

'Oh. It's you. What do you want?'

'I wondered if you'd heard anything from Sonja?'

'Sorry. No.'

Bettina closed the door a fraction, as though to forestall any further conversation.

'I'm afraid I don't have much time. I've got a dentist's appointment.'

If Katerina had been older she might have wondered what kind of dentist worked at eight o'clock at night, but instead she said, 'Could I come in? Just for a few minutes. You said to call if there was anything I need.'

'What do you need?'

'Just a chat. You could get dressed while we talk.'

Bettina said nothing, but moved her body fractionally to one side, allowing Katerina to squeeze past, then came and threw herself with disgruntlement on a chair and crossed her legs. She didn't seem inclined to get dressed but took out a packet of cigarettes and lit one.

'You'll have to be quick.'

'I suppose you haven't heard from her?'

'Not a thing. Sorry.' Bettina traced a finger over one eyebrow, which was thin and plucked into a high arch.

'So you've no idea where she could be?'

'How could I if I haven't heard from her?'

'Do you think she's still abroad?'

'What am I? A mind reader?'

'But there are ways you could find out,' persisted Katerina.

'Oh? Like what?'

'How many clothes did she take? Did she pack for hot weather or cold? Did she take all her jewellery? Her perfume?'

'For God's sake, Katerina! If I wanted the Berlin police department I'd have called them.'

Immediately regretting her sharpness Bettina looked at her pensively, then seemed to make a decision.

'I didn't want to tell you this, sweetheart. It won't help you. But there's nothing to lose now and I don't like to see you like this. Fact is, your sister had a boyfriend.'

'A boyfriend?' Katerina repeated stupidly.

'She's been seeing him for some time. But she kept it quiet, especially from you. There's no telling what a kid might blab.'

'Why would I blab? She's allowed a boyfriend, isn't she?'

'Perhaps,' said Bettina, springing up and going over to the mirror, which was propped against the mantelpiece. 'But not if he's a Jew.'

Katerina blanched. Romantic liaisons between Jews and Gentiles were forbidden – against the law, as far as she knew, and besides, why would anyone want to have a liaison with a Jew? Her BDM group had been taken to see an exhibition called *The Eternal Jew* the previous year and Katerina still flinched as she recalled the images of rats scurrying through cellars and sewers intercut with scenes of Jews emigrating from Palestine and spreading throughout the world. *Where rats turn up, they spread diseases and carry extermination into the land. They are cunning, cowardly and cruel, they travel in large packs, exactly the way the Jews infect the races of the world.*

'Sonja didn't want your father to know,' said Bettina, sliding a cherry red lipstick from its tube and outlining her mouth with the focused concentration of a Renaissance artist painting a titled lady.

'But Papi's dead. She could have told me.'

141

Bettina rubbed her lips together and pursed them provocatively at her own reflection.

'Yeah. I suppose she might have got round to telling you, but then this guy went and disappeared. Just after Christmas. Sonja said some men came to his house at six o'clock in the morning.'

Even Katerina knew that no one good ever came to a house at six o'clock in the morning. The Gestapo always called at dawn.

'They said they just wanted to ask some questions and they'd bring him back in a few hours.'

This was a standard tactic to avoid panic. Berliners were given to obedience, in everything from stepping on the grass to crossing the road, and if someone in official clothes with a piece of paper in his hand told them something, they were liable to believe it.

'Sonja said he left out the back and gave them the slip, but she hadn't seen him since. I think she might have gone looking for him.'

'But you said she went abroad for a singing engagement.'

'I'm sure she did, darling. Sonja sings everywhere she goes.'

'Where abroad?'

'Sweetie, if I knew that, I'd tell you, wouldn't I?'

The doorbell sounded and Bettina swivelled round, smoothing down the shift that even at its fullest extent reached only to the top of her thighs.

'Is that the dentist?'

'That's right. He's making a home visit. So you'll need to leave.'

The dentist was a plump man of around forty in army uniform with a sweating, meaty face. He seemed put out to see Katerina.

'It's all right, *Liebling*. She's leaving.'

He grunted and helped himself to a bottle of beer on the table. Then he sat on the sofa, legs spread, fingering his belt and eyeing Katerina with a curiosity that made her feel uneasy.

'I'll just see her out.'

Bettina squeezed round the door and closed it, detaining Katerina in the dark hallway with an arm on her shoulder.

'I've got something for you.'

She brought out a wallet – an old thing of garish orange leather with a broken zip that Katerina recognized immediately. *Sonja's wallet*. Her heart leapt.

'You *have* seen her!'

'Of course I haven't. I'd have told you straight off, wouldn't I? I just found this in the apartment and I thought you should have it. Just until your sister gets back. There's money in it.'

As Katerina seized the wallet and held it tightly against her chest, Bettina looked at her gravely.

'It's best you stop asking questions, sweetheart.'

'I only want to find my sister.'

'It doesn't matter what you want. You're a kid. There's nothing you can do. No one's going to tell you anything.'

'Doesn't stop me asking.'

'Questions won't help. Poking around and trying to find things out will only cause more trouble. Just keep quiet and if I hear anything I'll let you know.'

143

'Will you?'

'Course I will, sweetie. Now let me get back to my guest.'

Katerina went down in the lift, left the block and limped back up Fischerstrasse, but she knew that if she did nothing, there was little chance that anyone else would. Certainly not Bettina. Sonja was all she had left in the world and whatever trouble her questions might cause was nothing to the trouble Sonja must be in.

Chapter Nine

The Rue de la Paix was a chic street of luxury jewellery and fashion boutiques leading from the Opéra to the Place Vendôme, lined with shiny Citroëns and Renaults that due to the petrol rationing were going nowhere. Number 13 had a striking façade of dark marble, studded with elaborate gilding that gleamed in the moonlight. The long frontage was set with ebony window frames, faced in gold like some sumptuous treasure chest, and royal crests flanked the arched entrance beneath a snow-white awning.

Cartier. The most famous jeweller in Paris. Patronized by royalty and celebrity.

Clara had never owned anything made by Cartier, though Angela had a watch from there as a wedding present from her husband and several of the more senior Nazi wives were walking showcases for the French jeweller's work.

She knocked on the door and after a short wait heard the sound of locks being unfastened and a lozenge of light fell onto the pavement, revealing a slender woman in a rose pink turban, with a long rope of pearls round her neck. She stood aside with a frown, scanned the street, then ushered Clara into a cavernous showroom. A chandelier dripping crystal tear-drops revealed a place of hushed magnificence, like a glittering temple to some savage oriental god.

Hans Reuber was already there. He must have come straight from the show.

'Is this the lady you were talking about?'

The woman was subjecting Clara to a cold, appraising stare.

'Clara, I would like you to meet Mademoiselle Toussaint. Jeanne, meet Clara Vine.'

Jeanne Toussaint was small and birdlike, with startling blue eyes like shards of coloured glass. She must have been in her fifties, yet her complexion was smooth and white as an egg. Despite the hour, she was dressed as if about to leave for some grand event, in a vivid jacket of so many colours she was like a piece of jewellery herself.

'Jeanne's a legend,' continued Reuber, with his habitual grandiose flourish. 'Director of Fine Jewellery. A great artist and the soul of Cartier.'

'*Enchantée.*'

Jeanne Toussaint allowed her slender hand to rest in Clara's for a moment, then the froideur melted slightly and she said, 'Perhaps you'll join me in a glass of champagne? It's only Lanson, I'm afraid.'

As she opened the bottle, Clara stared at the opulence around her. The showroom was walled in blond wood, the floor was chequered marble and the surfaces furnished with lavish displays of roses. Against the walls stood cabinets of silverware, cutlery and candlesticks and, most of all, jewellery, shimmeringly multiplied by mirrors. Diamond-studded neck-laces, multicoloured jewels, sapphires, amethysts and garnets, wrought into brooches, clusters, earrings and filigree chains. Some with large stones and others set with gems so tiny they resembled a type of pointillism. Objects that if you needed to ask their price, you almost certainly could not afford.

Above the display cases the walls were hung with a series of sketches portraying birds and animals. Parrots, flamingos and birds of paradise, fantastical creatures with exuberant, iridescent feathers. Leopards, tigers, and coiled panthers. As Jeanne busied herself with glasses and a tray, Reuber pointed to one of the panthers and whispered, 'Jeanne adores big cats. They call her La Panthère.'

'Who does?'

'Everyone. And she's known everybody. Proust, Cocteau, Hemingway, Scott Fitzgerald. She and Coco Chanel are inseparable.'

Jeanne handed around the glasses and raised hers in a toast.

'To better times.'

'Clara Vine is half English, Jeanne.'

The cool eyes turned on Clara curiously.

'I knew there was something about you I liked. Apart from that dress. It's Alix Grès, isn't it?'

Clara glanced down at the fluid blue gown she had worn for her performance.

'I'm impressed you can tell. It's the only one of its kind.'

'I have a good eye.'

'On the subject of good eyes,' said Reuber, 'Jeanne was

just telling me about an excitement. The best stone she has ever seen.'

For a moment, it was as if he had spoken out of turn. A shaft of fury crossed the jeweller's face and then it dissolved as fast as it appeared. Plainly Reuber was underlining the fact that Clara could be trusted. No matter what.

'It's true.' A nonchalant flutter of the hands. 'I haven't decided what to make of it yet. All I know is, it is the most precious diamond I have ever worked with.'

'Would you show us?'

Jeanne pulled open a drawer, produced a tube of crimson velvet wrap and unrolled it on the table in front of them. In the middle was a stone the size of a damson, exuding from its depths a hard, cold fire.

She placed it in Clara's palm where it rested trembling, like the trace of a kiss.

'It's blue!'

'It's called the Blue Heart. Diamonds can be any colour – yellow, orange, pink, even black – but blue diamonds are the most sought-after. There are so few of them. This is one of the loveliest in the world. It was owned by Louis XIV.'

'What makes it . . . the way it is?' asked Clara, mesmerized.

Reuber leaned in. 'The diamond is crystallized deep in the earth's mantel under intense heat and pressure. In some cases, a minute trace of boron gets trapped in the crystal lattice when the gem is forming. This then absorbs red light and . . . well, it turns the diamond blue.'

Jeanne plucked it back and balanced it between her fingers and thumb.

'But this one is not only blue, it's special. It's the highest grade of colour and its clarity is almost perfect. If it belonged to anyone else I would use it as a solitaire.'

'A solitaire? For a stone that size?' objected Reuber.

'Sure. It deserves to be seen and appreciated without the distraction of other stones. Nothing else can touch it. But . . .' Jeanne sighed. 'Sadly, simplicity is not what my client likes.'

'Who is your client?' asked Clara.

'Ah. That I can't tell you. Only that it's a special diamond for a very special client. Someone I'm not at liberty to discuss. Unfortunately, though, I'm worried. My client was unable to collect it before they had to leave. It might be that this stone will never be set. Perhaps it's destined to remain in a safe for ever.' Jeanne wrapped the stone up and replaced it in the drawer with resolution. 'Still. There is a silver lining. It's given me the opportunity to concentrate on another design. It may not seem much, but it's the work of which I am most proud. Perhaps the one by which I will be remembered. My legacy.'

Feeling in another drawer beneath the display case she brought out the piece.

It was unassumingly small to be anyone's legacy, no more than an inch across, a tiny brooch glinting on a satin bed. It was in the shape of a golden cage, enclosing a minute bird fashioned in coral, with lapis lazuli wings and a diamond-set head. Red, white and blue, the colours of France.

Jeanne Toussaint looked on it lovingly.

'My songbird. La belle France in her cage. She has sad eyes, does she not? And even though she's a songbird, her beak is closed. She no longer knows how to sing. What do you think? She will go on display in our front window from tomorrow.'

'Jeanne!' Reuber's voice was hushed with horror. 'You can't mean it. They'll arrest you. You know what their interrogations are like.'

'I'll say I had the idea long before they arrived. And it's true. I made one of these little birds some years ago for a very wealthy lady who was unhappy in her marriage. The husband paid for it but he never got the hint.'

'The Nazis *will* get the hint, though, Jeanne. They're no fools. They'll take your imprisoned bird as a sign of resistance and treat you accordingly. They make no special favours, not even for legends.'

For a moment it seemed Jeanne Toussaint's icy composure might falter, then she switched on a smile as brilliant as her diamonds and said, 'We'll just have to see. Perhaps one day I'll make another one with the cage door open. Anyway, to business. Wait here while I fetch what you came for.'

She returned with a brown leather pouch and, reaching for the jeweller's tray, tipped out a small rubble of stones – irregular lumps of grey and yellow from which even the desk lamp could only coax a stubborn gleam.

Reuber poked at them.

'Do you know what these are?' he asked Clara.

She squinted at the dull nuggets.

'You might find it hard to believe. They're weapons.'

Clara shook her head uncomprehendingly.

'The most important weapons of war. More valuable than

Panzers or guns or twenty thousand troops on the march. These are what will make the difference between Hitler winning everything he dreams of, or failing utterly.'

Clara looked down at the litter of stones on the tray. She could not begin to imagine what Reuber was talking about.

'I don't understand. They look like ordinary stones.'

'There's nothing ordinary about these. They're diamonds.'

His fingers curled protectively, as if mere observation could injure them.

'Industrial diamonds. The kind of diamonds you're familiar with, my dear, come in the shape of necklaces or earrings given to you by besotted admirers' – he waved a hand at her objections – 'forgive me for presuming. The kind you see in Cartier's window. Diamonds that have already been cut and sawn and polished. But these stones, though they have no physical beauty, are far more important. In wartime, they have a vital strategic function. They control the production of every bullet and battleship.'

Clara was aware of Jeanne Toussaint regarding them intently.

'How can that be possible?'

'Because diamond is the hardest substance known to man. Only diamonds are hard enough to stamp out the precision parts for mass-producing aeroplane engines, torpedoes, tanks, artillery – any other weapon of war you care to think of. Only diamonds can provide the jewelled bearings for guidance systems in submarines and planes. It's safe to say that without industrial diamonds no war can be won. And Germany has no access to diamond mines.'

Clara's mind was racing ahead, trying to take in the implications of Reuber's revelation.

'So you're saying without these gems Hitler could not win the war?'

'I'm saying that obtaining diamonds is his paramount objective. Without them his war machine will rapidly slow to a halt. For at least a year, Germany has been offering far in excess of normal market prices to tempt Continental dealers. A river of diamonds has flooded into Germany, but a steady stream has also been flowing in the opposite direction. A number of German jewellers have been smuggling their diamonds into France, desperate that the Nazis should not get their hands on their stocks. Those in Paris assumed their own diamonds were safe – they have at least twenty thousand carats stowed away in private vaults and offices – but now they're not so sure.'

Reuber cast a sober glance at Jeanne, who said, 'When the Nazis arrived in Holland their first action was to check on the diamond stocks. Fortunately the British had sent a destroyer and managed to evacuate the stocks just hours before the city fell. There is no chance of that here. The Germans are searching the city. It's only a matter of time before they uncover most of our stones. We're doing everything we can to get the diamonds out of the city, but we need people brave enough to transport them. The penalties are, if you're caught, severe.'

For a second Jeanne's eyes filmed over, as though imagining the horrors that might lie in store in the interrogation rooms now being set up across Paris, in requisitioned buildings and the basements of grand hotels. Then, briskly, she said, 'So, Hans. Let me find something for you to carry them in.'

As she disappeared to a room at the back Clara whispered, 'Why is she giving them to *you*?'

'Louis Cartier is, it's safe to say, no sympathizer of the Nazis. He's a strong supporter of the Free French – in fact he's given over the upper floors of the Cartier building in London to General de Gaulle. He and Jeanne are exploring ways to get French diamonds out of the country. At the moment their only hope is a network of human couriers to take them down through Spain to the coast.'

'And you're one of these couriers?'

'Not exactly. We're passing the stones to men who have volunteered to carry them.'

'Who's we?'

'You remember that my wife's family is French? They're part of a network here in Paris, trying to organize some resistance in the city. It's very hard. The Gestapo are already making arrests. They've had spies here for years, making notes of residents and addresses, working out who to pick up when the time comes. On which subject, you mentioned you're staying off the Avenue Foch. Be careful. The Gestapo have set up their interrogation headquarters there.'

He looked down at her with a peculiar intensity.

'Not that it matters where they have their HQ. They always get the results they want in the end. With their methods, anyone will confess to anything. All we ask of our agents is that they endure for forty-eight hours. If you can hold out that long before you start spilling names then it gives other people a chance.'

Something about his demeanour alarmed her.

'Why are you telling *me* all this?'

'Because it affects you. Now that I know I'm being followed, I can't afford to be found with these diamonds on me, but you're under no such suspicion. Quite the opposite. You are on the Nazis' business. You have a minister to vouch for you. So I'm asking *you* to deliver them.'

A heartbeat's hesitation. Too short, she hoped, for him to notice, but he did.

'It's all I'm asking, Clara. One trip across town. It will take less than an hour.'

'What would it involve?'

'There's a safe place. A room above Café Jacques in the Rue Vavin. We've found that the Latin Quarter is the best place to meet right now because the streets are narrower and there are fewer Germans there. They seem to prefer big houses on the Right Bank.'

'Is this a regular meeting place?'

'No such thing. We don't have anything regular. Nor do we meet in groups and we only send messages by word of mouth. It's far too dangerous any other way. They're expecting someone tomorrow morning. First thing.'

'What shall I say?'

'Tell them you've come about a delivery.'

'Tell who?'

'A man called Martin.'

Jeanne Toussaint reappeared and placed two objects on

the showroom table. A golden-crusted baguette, wrapped in boulangerie paper, and a matchbox. Peeling off the brightly patterned paper, she set the loaf lengthways and with a knife made a deft incision midway, lifting the crust and carefully excising a hunk of dough. Then she scooped the industrial diamonds in one hand, funnelled them into the matchbox and squeezed the box into the vacant space, before replacing the lid of crust, firmly rewrapping the baguette and tying it with string.

'Here,' she said brightly, presenting it to Clara like a priceless necklace packaged in satin ribbons. 'Most baguettes in my showroom come in the form of rings, so I'm sorry I can't oblige you tonight. Perhaps if you come back one day.'

Clara took the loaf and tucked it under one arm and Jeanne Toussaint reached to give her a kiss on both cheeks in the French fashion.

'Thank you. Each little consignment is a help, though there are many more stones we need to keep from Nazi hands. We have a plan, quite an audacious plan, but I fear very much that it will never come off now. We've left it too late.'

She enfolded Reuber in an embrace then led the way to the door.

'Remember, my dear friends, there's a curfew in place. It's nearly midnight already and one thing I know about you Germans, you just can't help obeying orders.'

Chapter Ten

Clara woke before dawn. The first streaks of light were beginning to pierce the sky, and pure notes of birdsong quivered like arrows in the air. It was a good hour's walk from the Right Bank to the location that Reuber had identified for her assignation, but although she was tense with anticipation, she welcomed the exercise. The day-old baguette was dry and stale, but she carried it purposefully, as if she had not positioned and repositioned the red and blue striped boulangerie paper numerous times and adjusted the piece of crust so that it was entirely invisible beneath its jaunty wrapping. She might be any other Parisienne, fetching the daily bread for her breakfast tartine before she headed off to an office or a shop. Who was to know it contained a cache of gems, a cluster of small drops in the invisible river of diamonds that was now flowing out of France under the Nazis' noses?

At the Pont Alexandre III she crossed the rippling quilt of the Seine, along the Quai d'Orsay, then down the Boulevard Raspail. It was still quiet, and in the glimmering moment before daybreak there were glimpses of the city that visitors rarely saw. Street sweepers, barely raising their eyes to a lone passer-by, supplies of food being trundled into the kitchens of the grand hotels that had already been requisitioned by the Germans, crates of seafood and oysters and Pouilly Fuissé. A priest hurrying to Mass. In the gloaming Clara saw a young woman in an alleyway with a pigeon hanging from her hand, feathers upended like a speckled bouquet.

Everything was normal, in this most abnormal of times.

Nonetheless, true to her training, she diverted sharply, and walked through the black gates of the Jardin du Luxembourg. Nowhere was better to spot a tail than the open spaces of a park.

At first glance, everything about the loveliest park in Paris was the same as it had always been. Mist gathered in veils beneath the trees. The rigid formality of the garden, with its chestnut tree-lined avenues, parterres and geometric paths, the sparkling glass orangerie and statues of goddesses and French queens, still presented to the world an impression of serenity, as if nothing had happened to disturb its tran-quillity since it was created three hundred years ago. As if Paris was still a city of elegance and order, rather than the distant playground of a brutal dictator. But at closer sight, one important constituent of the picture was missing. Until last month this spot so beloved of Parisians would have been full of small dogs on their morning constitutional, beautifully groomed and weaving their way on leather leashes around the octagonal basin. Yet now those beloved, pampered pets were absent, shot and dumped on the street corners like so much rubbish. Dogs were no different from the china, linen, paintings and everything else that people could not take with them in their desperate flight.

Clara made a complete circuit of the park, and when she had satisfied herself that she was genuinely alone, she slipped out of the back gate closest to the Rue Vavin.

At this hour it was hard to imagine anyone visiting the Café Jacques for a convivial drink. It was a narrow space, whose crepuscular mood was made gloomier by dark blinds installed for the blackout. There was a sign advertising Coca-Cola in the window and the floor was sticky with spilled beer. A lone flypaper flapped listlessly beneath a central fan. A middle-aged bartender was already installed, making desultory swipes at the glasses with a grubby cloth. He hesitated for a second when he saw her, then in reply to her expression of enquiry he gestured with a faint nod of his head towards a door at the back, leading to a steep set of pocked linoleum stairs.

The door at the top was opened by a young man in a herringbone tweed suit and round horn-rimmed glasses, smelling of cologne and tobacco. Despite his stylish dress and faintly dandyish air, his face was pasty with fatigue and a blue shadow of stubble. He looked terrified to see her.

'I'm looking for Martin. It's about a delivery.'

'Why is the other man not here himself? Where is he?'

'I was with him last night. He noticed that he was being followed so he asked me to come instead. My name is . . .'

'Yes. I know who you are.'

Clara was startled. In Germany she was used to being

recognized but she was hardly well known in France where, unsurprisingly, no one had much of an appetite for German films.

The man must be Martin. Yet even if he was, it would only have been a *nom de guerre*. He gave her a moment's further scrutiny before making room for her to enter and muttering, 'In here.'

The shutters were closed, rendering the room in shades of charcoal. In the dim light, its contents seemed like something from a still life – a sketch of chairs and table, with a couple of bottles of beer and a jug and stove to one side. It took a moment for Clara to notice that they were not alone. In the far corner, a solitary figure was sitting smoking. He was well built, with a shock of dark hair that he rubbed reflexively out of his eyes and an anxious expression. In the dim light filtering through the shutters his face was slatted with shadow, poised between light and shade like a monochrome photograph by Lee Miller. At Clara's approach he half-rose, but Martin waved and said, 'Please sit down, Captain Russell. There's no need to worry. It's just a bit of business.'

Clara stared. The man addressed as Captain Russell was in his thirties, wearing an ill-fitting jacket too short in the arms, and a pair of bluish sagging trousers that could never have belonged to him. An open-necked white shirt, stained and frayed at the collar, displayed a wedge of skin, heavily tanned.

'Hello,' she said in English.

'Captain Russell was wounded after escaping the Germans. He has had quite a journey but he's fortunate. We've been able to give him shelter and we will arrange him safe passage. You can talk in front of him,' said Martin, adding tersely, 'I take it you have the delivery?'

Clara produced the baguette, placed it on the table and slid a finger beneath the crust to reveal the matchbox.

'They're in here.'

'Excellent.' Martin opened the matchbox and inspected its contents. 'Thank you for coming so promptly. I'm afraid I have business elsewhere now, so I will say au revoir.'

'Wait . . .'

The Englishman had risen to his feet and was standing up with difficulty. Clara noticed that he instinctively clamped a hand to one side. The toe of his shoe was open and his bare foot poked through.

'I wonder . . .' There was a note of urgency in his voice. 'If the lady might like to take a cup of coffee with me? If you're not too pressed for time?'

Clara was. She had a ticket for a train heading back to Berlin that afternoon, leaving her only a few hours to collect up her clothes and make her way to the station. Besides, her every instinct told her to leave the Rue Vavin as fast as possible in case anyone had witnessed her arrival. It would be foolhardy to linger at a safe house that might already be under Nazi surveillance. Yet the urge to stay and talk to this quiet Englishman surprised her. Was it loneliness, or a yearning for home? In that split second she quelled her fears and said, 'Why not?'

Martin looked from one to the other, shrugged and gave a curt nod before heading out of the door.

Once they were alone Captain Russell shook his head. His high brow and angular cheekbones reminded her of a warrior on the face of an old coin, yet the strong features were mitigated by a warm, sensitive mouth that turned slightly down at the edges and eyes as soft as an English sky.

'Please forgive me if I'm detaining you unduly. I'm sorry to sound desperate but the prospect of human company was just too enticing to pass up, especially when I heard you spoke English.'

He was tall, but with a stoop that shortened him. His grip was firm and his hand rough against the smoothness of her palm.

'I'm afraid we weren't introduced properly. I do hate to neglect basic courtesies.'

'I'm Clara.' Something about the man – perhaps his remark about 'basic courtesies', the kind of thing that her own father might say – reassured her that she need not disguise her Christian name. Yet still she would not risk identifying herself any more than that.

'And please call me Ned. Would you like a cigarette?'

'Thank you.'

She lowered her face to his lighter then sat at the table opposite.

'Have you been here long?'

'In this room? Three days. In France, it seems like for ever.'

His face was grubby, and grime had settled into the lines, so his eyes formed a net of wrinkles when he smiled. 'It seems a long way from Yorkshire.'

'That's where you're from?'

'Originally. My family owns a farm in west Yorkshire. A village called Oxenhope.'

The single word, and the way he said it, conjured a picture of the place itself. The twinned images, at once ancient and uplifting, of slow-moving cattle and sheer human endurance. The deep, northern edge to his voice was like the unyielding flint of some desolate moor.

'Not to say I stayed there. I moved down to London some years ago. I was living in St John's Wood until last year, teaching a rabble of little boys how to read English literature.'

'Didn't they miss you on the farm?'

'Not one bit. Once they realized I could spout history and poetry my family thought I was too good for farming. They assumed school-mastering was a higher calling. I'm not sure they're right but at any rate, as soon as war broke out I couldn't wait to take myself off to the recruiting office.'

'How did you end up here?'

'You really want to know?' He cocked an enquiring glance to distinguish genuine interest from mere politeness.

'Very much.'

'In that case, I'd better give you that coffee I promised.'

He rose and took from the stove a battered iron coffee pot and poured out a thick aromatic trickle into two cups. The movement seemed to cause him some effort and she watched pain flash across his face as he gripped the side of the table. Then he sat down again and passed a hand across his brow.

'You heard what happened in Dunkirk?'

She nodded.

In recent weeks the British Expeditionary Force had been hemmed in by German troops and pushed back to the coastal town of Dunkirk. It was a devastating retreat and for a few days it appeared that the core of the British army was about to perish, when a flotilla of eight hundred small ships, fishing boats, lifeboats, merchant vessels and pleasure steamers set sail from England to retrieve them, saving more than three hundred thousand lives.

'We'd been in northern France for months. Sitting on one side of the Maginot Line waiting, the Germans on the other. We were so close we could hear the Germans communicate with each other by hooting, just like owls. Did you ever learn to do that? When you were a kid?'

He cupped his palms together and blew into the gap between his thumbs. A low, cooing sound issued from his pursed lips and instantly it was as if the bird appeared, with a swoop of tawny feathers.

'It was their call sign.'

Clara stared transfixed at his large, rough hands, as the fluting notes issued from them. She pictured those hands farming, cutting hay, heaving sheep from the hillsides, delivering lambs. How his clothes would smell of loam and wood smoke.

'Then suddenly in May, the blitzkrieg began. It was terrifying. Bullets flying, people you knew getting killed all around you. Stukas above, incinerating everything, even the Red Cross vans. Ammunition slamming into the ground. Body parts everywhere. You could taste the cordite in your mouth. We were driven back towards the coast.

'Our lot was divided from the main army and pushed south into Normandy. We held the Germans briefly at the Somme but finally we retreated and were surrounded at the port of St-Valéry-en-Caux. The German artillery were in the hills above, pounding us, and we all of us could see defeat was coming. There was one British ship, the HMS *Broke*, that made a landing, but the bombardment was too intense. Men were climbing down the cliffs, falling to their deaths on the rocks. You could see them lying there still alive, crying out. In places the earth was sodden with blood.'

From the street outside a few ragged yells arose, the early morning calls of delivery boys, and a ringing of bicycle bells, but in that room, the two of them were inviolate. Russell kept his eyes fixed on the enamel cup in front of him, his pupils dilated with the darkness of suffering.

'Eventually the Germans breached our defences. Some lucky beggars were found by a crew for the Red Cross who disguised them as French soldiers and took them off to hospital. The rest of us had to survive as best we could. My group hid in a cellar but the Germans found us. There was a debate about whether to shoot us straight off – they did actually line us up against a wall – but after a while the Krauts changed their minds and forced us to march through the town and then across the fields.'

He hesitated and dragged a hand across his face.

'I can't describe what it was like. The ground was littered with bodies, men with their tin hats still on. Young lads ripped from their lives. Flesh rotting in the sun, dead cows and horses too, everything bloated and flyblown. Dogs whining, running about. Some of the poor animals had been left tied up and howled at us as we passed but we could do nothing. We had no idea where we were headed. We were walking sixteen miles a day on nothing more than acorn coffee. They told us that anyone who stepped out of line would be shot, and, to tell the truth, at that moment I didn't care. We slept in the open, or in ditches, and some of the men took greatcoats off the bodies of dead men. In the morning, farmers would put down pails of milk by the side of the road, but the Germans kicked them over before we could touch it. After a few days, they let us know where we were headed. We were marching all the way to Nuremberg.'

As he paused to stub out his cigarette the pain of these memories seemed to pass viscerally across his face.

'Funny thing, Clara, it wasn't the totality of it, it was the little things that stuck in you like thorns. At one point we got a rest because they decided to transport us some of the way by train. It was a cattle truck and on its side was a sign saying *Hommes quarante, Bêtes huit*. Know what that means? Forty men or eight cattle.'

He stalled, seemingly exhausted at the weight of it, and looked around the room. His lips were beaded with sweat and she realized he was in pain.

'You were injured.'

'Shot in the side. I was lucky.'

'How's that lucky?'

'The muscle was torn but it missed anything important so I could still walk. I'd been patched up pretty well when it happened, though I'd lost a lot of blood.'

She imagined the jagged scarlet wound beneath his shirt, the flimsy dressings failing to stave off infection.

'How did you escape?'

'Ah, that. Quite suddenly, as it happens. We were approaching a narrow bridge and from the other side a cart was coming, piled high with a family's possessions, so our guards ran up front to manage the jam. There was a ditch running alongside the road, covered with weeds and brambles. I took the chance to duck down and roll myself to the bottom. I couldn't believe they hadn't missed me. I crouched there for hours. Eventually I got the courage to make my way to the river and took a drink and when I looked up there was a corpse in a tree, staring back at me.'

His jaw trembled, and Clara felt an echoing shiver on her skin.

'Full in the face. Just a lad. He looked surprised more than anything. He was halfway up the branches. Must have got himself shot as he tried to hide.'

'But you were shot too. You must have been in pain.'

'Sure. In fact, I was certain I would die too. You know, Clara, losing a lot of blood induces a kind of serenity in you. You feel yourself quite ready to let go. But even while I was lying there, feeling my life leaking away into the mud, there was still a part of me thinking of all the things I'd never do. All the books I'd never read. Forgive me if I embarrass you, but I had the thought that I'd never again hold a woman in my arms. Feel the softness of a woman's skin, or the scent of her. That tormented me.'

Clara was quite still, watching the words form on his lips,

the images of his memories passing in her mind as though they were her own.

'A couple of days later I had the good luck to be found by a farmer. I was covered in earth, every inch and crevice of me, but he took me in and laid me on his sofa. It was a lovely old velvet thing, like an heirloom, and even though I was in pain, I kept thinking, how will they explain away these bloodstains? The wife tore up her nightgown to make bandages.'

'They must have been risking a lot. Rescuing a British soldier.'

'Their lives. And they knew it. All over the region the Germans had put up posters, warning people not to help – the penalty's death for men, or a camp for the women. But they're heroes. The risk doesn't stop them. There are hundreds of men like me trapped in France, shut away in barns and attics and bedrooms, and these people are putting themselves in danger, and their families in danger, to help us. From what I can gather, some are liaising with authorities back home to find us documents, ID cards, currency, clothes.'

'Who are these people?'

'Can't say. It's a network, but they don't want to give it any kind of name, not even describe it as an organization. I suppose names or any formal identification makes it more likely they'll be targeted by infiltrators.'

'So do you have your ID?'

'Not yet. Two days ago I came south, first in a cart, then in a cargo carriage, and they passed me on to the chap who brought me here. As soon as I have my papers, the plan is to get me out of Paris any way they can.'

'What will you do then?'

'With luck I'll make my way down through the unoccupied zone. Then to Perpignan and through Spain to the coast. From there I can sail for England. I'm just waiting for the word. Until then,' he gestured with a dry smile to a pack on the table in front of him, 'it's cards.'

'Are you frightened?'

Why did she say that? What a question to ask anyone in a war. Yet still, he paused to reflect on it.

'Of course. Not of pain or death. But frightened of never seeing the people back home. Of my life ending before it's really begun. There's a poet I think of called Chidiock Tichborne – I used to teach him to my schoolboys. This fellow was consigned to the Tower of London back in Queen Elizabeth's day and he lamented the fact that he would be dead before his time. He wrote:

> My tale was heard, and yet it was not told,
> My fruit is fallen, and yet my leaves are green,
> My youth is spent, and yet I am not old,
> I saw the world, and yet I was not seen.

'My lads liked that poem because it rhymes. Makes it easy to learn, you see. I like it because I still think I'm young.'

He rubbed the bulge of bandage on his flank.

'Despite feeling like a crock.'

His eyes flitted to the door.

'I'd like to do something to thank these people, but what can I do? It seems sacrilege to complain about boredom. It helps having a window to look out of but I wish I'd paid more attention to the French lessons I had at school. I can't tell you how good it is to speak to another person in English. What about you, Clara? Do you live in Paris?'

'I live in Berlin.'

She saw the shock widen his eyes.

'It's not what you think. I've lived in Germany for seven years. I can be useful there.'

Understanding passed between them, swift and silent as electricity. The previous two months had opened Ned's eyes to a world of networks and secret connections and he knew to probe no further.

'Married?' She sensed him glance at her hand.

'The man I would have married was killed last year.'

Speaking it aloud – the truth that she had never declared to anyone – sent pain lancing through her. The fact was that war had left her no space to heal. It was as though the body of Leo still lay unburied on that blood-soaked tarmac, covered only with the slightest scattering of earth.

Ned blanched visibly. It was hard to gauge his reaction, but it seemed like genuine sorrow. Despite the fact that he knew nothing of the man she had mentioned, or how he met his death.

'I'm sorry. Are you getting through it?'

What could she say? Some days were harsh with jagged edges, sharp with memory. Other days were numbed and sedated. Nothing was normal. There was no guidebook for grief. No manual, like Goebbels' instruction leaflet, with its bullet points of advice for guarding against dark instincts. How was it supposed to feel when you lost the love of your life?

'I think so.'

Ned didn't respond. He simply looked at her.

'Anyway.' She made a hesitant move to depart. 'My train leaves at two o'clock from the Gare de l'Est.'

She saw the instant flicker of dismay.

'You should go then.'

He was smiling, but those eyes were trained intensely on her, asking her to stay. The weariness she had felt earlier from her late night, and then the early start, vanished and she sat down again.

'No. Not yet.'

On the narrow windowsill a bird alighted, the colour of wet leaves, with a dull sprinkling of speckles on its wing. Ned glanced up.

'There's some interesting ones here. Different birds, they have. I've been trying to remember the names.'

'Do you know about birds then?'

Clara recalled Leo telling her how much he had learned from birdwatching. How he had schooled himself to observe the minutest detail, not just of the bird, but the environment around it and its interactions with others. How sometimes it was important to ignore a brasher or more colourful creature so as to keep focus on a bird that melted into the background. How that ability had trained him for espionage and endowed in him the skill of a professional watcher.

'Right from a boy. I've always loved observing them, even the ones that seemed dull to other people. Up on our moors we get curlews and golden plovers, peregrines, merlins. You see them making their nests in the heather and raising their chicks.'

She saw the harsh moorland, where gaunt trees stretched their branches beneath a slanting north wind. While they might be in the heart of Paris, the soldier in front of her seemed rooted in another place, a place of safety, far away.

'One of those nights when I was lying in that French field I distracted myself trying to identify a bird from its call. It was a kind of churring sound, almost mechanical. Took me hours to get it.'

He beamed.

'A nightjar.'

She laughed at his boyish delight and he gave a deprecatory swipe at his lock of hair.

'Enough of me. You're too good a listener, Clara. I want to know more about you.'

So she began. Talking about herself, her acting, and her youth back in England. Pacing the difficult path back to her own childhood. A rambling Edwardian building in a cleft of gentle hills with farmland sloping up towards the south. Inside, the fragrance of log fires and beeswax polish, and outside the long fields where horses grazed. A rust-coloured house that still came to her in her dreams, filled with cut flowers and unhappiness. Sitting in the powdery haven of her mother's room at her deathbed, scenting gardenia perfume, holding her frail hand. How her mother had been the connective tissue between the family and how her death had left them fractured and dislocated. Then came her own early days in the London theatre, trying to be pleased with the bit parts, the maids and servants and minor roles, and her all too frequently fruitless trips to her agent's cramped office in Soho. Her impetuous move to Berlin, escaping a disastrous love affair and finding a new career in film. Erich, and Mary Harker. Clara realized she was talking to this stranger in a way she had spoken to nobody since Leo's death, but when she apologized he only urged her to continue, fumbling in his pocket.

'My last one, I'm afraid. Care to share it?'

He took out the cigarette and struck a match. The flame leapt up like a tiny flower, illuminating all the planes and angles of his face and his eyes, which remained fixed on hers. She leaned over the flame, like a candle lit in church, and they shared the cigarette equally, passing it from one to the other, their eyes locked on each other's.

Somewhere, deep in the ashes of her life, an ember flared into life.

Chapter Eleven

The latest batch of orphans had arrived. Katerina looked up from her *Abendbrot* and scrutinized them carefully. They fell on the evening meal as if famished, tearing at the musty rye bread as though if they didn't bolt it, someone might take it away. There were six of them, ranging from around five to twelve years old, and a pair of twins so tiny that they needed an older child to help them cut their cheese. Shy as deer when you looked at them, as though they were poised to run away. At first glance, with their white-blond hair, pudding bowl haircuts and the same neat uniforms that everyone, even babies, wore here, they didn't seem too different, but there was something about their sharp features and the shifting anxiety in their eyes that marked them out. And when you heard them talk it became clear.

They couldn't speak. Or at least, they couldn't speak German.

'What's your name?' Katerina asked the girl next to her, a child of around eight with hair secured at the side with a clip, and ice blue eyes like a husky dog. It was Vegetarian Day, and supper was potato soup and bread spread with *Brotaufstrich*, a greasy new invention that was supposed to replace butter and margarine. The child was grappling with cutlery as if she had never used it before.

'Don't know,' she stumbled thickly, with an accent she could have cut with her own knife.

'You don't know your own name?'

'I know what my name used to be. Beata Sosnowska.'

'So I'll call you that then.'

'No.' Childish fear sparked in her eyes. 'I have a new name now.' She hesitated. 'Barbara. Barbara Sosemann, I think.'

'You think?'

'I'm sure,' she corrected herself.

'Why can't you speak properly?'

Silent tears slid down the child's cheeks as she abandoned the knife. She had an exceptionally sweet face, with a rose-bud mouth and a feather of near-invisible eyelashes.

'I miss my mother. I want to go back to her.'

'You don't have a mother. Hardly anyone does here. That's why it's an orphanage.'

'I do,' said the girl, stubbornly.

Katerina had barely any idea of her own mother, who had died just days after she was born. Having no recollection of her face, she sometimes thought of her from the inside, like the shell of a pink conch beneath which she herself had curled and divided, wholly perfect until the violent birth that left Katerina maimed and her mother dead.

'Where is she then?'

'At home.'

'You'd better not say that.'

The child's lip wobbled.

'The men who took us said we were going to a beautiful place with meadows of flowers and streams to swim in and woods with berries and mushrooms.'

'There is a garden,' said Katerina doubtfully, thinking of the parade ground of cabbage and asparagus laid out in tight formation behind the orchard.

'I miss my home.'

'Shhh. Be quiet. This is your home now.'

The child stared around as if seeing the place for the first time.

'Do you miss *your* home?'

Into Katerina's mind came the tall building in Wilmersdorf with its art nouveau entrance. The lift doors that opened like an accordion and took you three floors up to an apartment with a brass plaque inscribed *Herr Otto Klimpel*, behind which was a parquet-floored drawing room, whose mantelpiece was lined with Dresden china objects, alongside Papi's collection of pipes and his complete set of Goethe. The Bösendorfer piano that Sonja would play when she visited, and beyond, Papi's bedroom and the heavy Biedermeier dresser where he kept a nest of Chinese boxes with crimson lacquered dragons and silver orchids. There were seven of them, fitting into each other and getting smaller and smaller until you reached the tiniest one, where her mother's jewellery was. Then came Katerina's own room, with its miniature desk and bookshelf.

Now, by contrast, home was a hall where Brown Sisters

patrolled to stop older children stealing the younger ones' food. A draughty dormitory with ranks of beds and rough sheets, where nights were never still from coughing or snoring or the shudder of silent sobs. Lying awake thinking of stories from *HundeWelt* to distract yourself. *The army is harnessing the intelligence of dogs for the war effort! Dogs are being trained to communicate by tapping out words with their paws . . . The Tier-Sprechschule near Hanover led by Frau Margarethe Schmitt has trained an Airedale terrier to write poetry and sing.*

The truth was, she missed everything about her home. Papi, Anka, her bedroom, the Bösendorfer and the books, yet she kept it all folded tightly inside her, like a map, tucked away neatly for no one to see, and only occasionally would she get it out and allow herself to look at it.

'No,' she said. 'I hardly miss it at all.'

Across the room, above the scraping of china, some orphans were singing a nursery rhyme:

> *Corrupting our youth*
> *Stands the Jew in good stead.*
> *He wants all peoples dead.*
> *Stay away from every Jew,*
> *and happiness will come to you!*

The smallest of the new arrivals quickly picked up the tune and joined in, their faces wreathed in smiles. The younger they were, the more they resembled little rubber balls because they bounced back so quickly. They were like puppies, who could never be sad for more than a minute.

'I wish I could be a bird and fly back to my home,' said Beata, looking sideways at Katerina.

She liked that idea. She herself would be an eagle, soaring over Mitte, gliding on the updraughts of the air, floating on the warm currents of the breeze.

'I would fly into the kitchen and my mama would feed me *paczki*. With sugar on.'

'What's *paczki*?'

'It's . . . cakes?'

A fat tear formed at the corner of the child's eye and Katerina reached out a hand. Beata flinched, as though any form of touch was freighted with fear.

'You have to stop thinking about all that. You're here now.' Katerina summoned an expression of bright resolve she did not feel. 'Are you coming to lessons with us?'

If the children couldn't speak German properly, how were they going to manage?

'No. We have tests.'

'What tests?'

The child frowned, as if trying to summon the correct terminology, then gave up and poked a finger at her chest.

'Body tests.'

'What's that supposed to be?'

'With doctors.'

The thought of doctors was enough to remind Katerina that her leg was aching again. Indeed it had hurt increasingly ever since Sonja insisted the caliper be taken off, unbuckling the straps with impatient fingers.

These doctors don't know anything. Start walking with it and

177

you'll be fine. You'll build up the muscle. Like an acrobat, you know? Or a dancer. You want to be a dancer, don't you?

That had been calculated to please. Sonja knew there was nothing Katerina craved more dearly than to become a dancer. Whenever Sonja was singing, Katerina would watch the cabarets wide-eyed. One day she would be a dancer. That or a dog-trainer.

But now, without the caliper, the pain was getting worse. It hurt all the time. Indeed she began to wonder if Sonja had been telling the truth about making the leg stronger. The fact was, her limp was more noticeable than ever and it took an even greater effort to straighten the foot round to near normal. The terrible thought occurred to her that Sonja was actually ashamed of having a cripple for a sister. Was that why she wanted the caliper gone?

She got down from the table and followed the children into the hall for recreation. Just because lessons were over, didn't mean you could relax. In the evenings everyone was supposed to do something useful and for the girls that meant knitting.

Knitting is an Act of Patriotism! That was what the posters said and every female over the age of five in the Reich was supposed to engage in it. At the NSV home the production of socks was enforced with military rigour. The Brown Sisters checked the finished product ruthlessly, picking out clots of knotted yarn and ensuring that the toes had been grafted properly. Katerina remembered her grandmother knitting, her fingers a blur, the needles almost working themselves. It helped her think, Oma used to say, as though by descending into a trance of recollection the most elusive of memories could be trapped in her delicate nets of wool. Unlike the vivid colours in Oma's basket, the yarn here was a uniform rough beige, and although there was a swastika knitting pattern available for those who took a real pride in their work, Katerina merely produced the basics. How was a swastika sock going to make a soldier fight any harder?

That evening, however, knitting suited her. It meant she could concentrate on her plans without anyone interrupting, or asking what she was thinking. It had taken a while to work out what to do, but the visit to Sonja's apartment had provided her with an unexpected new direction. A fresh plan that might – just might – yield more clues to her elder sister's disappearance.

She would go one night this week. She had already studied the S–Bahn timetable and had the money in her pocket for a seven-station round-trip ticket. If she was too late back she had instructed Heidi to tell Fräulein Koppel that she was visiting her sister's friend Bettina. It was an infraction of the rules, but it would buy her time, and a family visit was far less *verboten* than calling on a complete stranger. She had memorized the route, too. Either because of his work at the Post Office, or maybe because he thought it would strengthen her leg, Papi had enjoyed trekking around the city with her on Saturday mornings. He took a lunch-tin and a map, and they made regular hikes, exploring the way the city connected up from Pankow to Neukölln, Charlottenburg to Prenzlauer Berg. Once she had learnt the routes, Papi kept the map folded up in his pocket, and insisted that she tell him the way from memory instead. She had adored playing that game. It made her feel like the boy in the story *Emil and the Detectives*, navigating the unfamiliar streets of Berlin, an adventure round every corner.

Now she reached into her pocket and glanced again at the piece of paper she had found in Sonja's wallet, squinting at the wavelike swells of soft black ink in the signature.

Clara Vine.

She pictured the actress she had seen at the charity reception. The pale-green suit that emphasized her slim outline, and the smudge of shadow under her eyes. She looked like the kind of woman who might wear perfume, the scent of grass and figs and white flowers enfolding her like a second skin. She had seen Clara Vine on screen once, in *The Pilot's Wife*, where she played a plucky resourceful woman determined to rescue her husband from behind enemy lines. Katerina knew it was only a film and people were entirely different in real life, yet when she caught a glimpse of the actress that afternoon at the Hotel Eden she had detected a kindness in her eyes. She had no idea what would happen when they met, but Clara Vine's face filled her with confidence and besides, she thought as she stuffed the piece of paper back in her pocket, it was not as if she had any other plan.

Chapter Twelve

The sultry heat had returned to Berlin. The air in the trams was unwashed and the rank smell of stale sweat hung in the S-Bahn. The sun hung in a sky of burnished steel and the asphalt sank like pudding beneath the heels. Past images of summer, of ice-cream carts in the Tiergarten, of women in bright print dresses and men in short sleeves that showed off a tan, were like a mockery when so many were sweltering away in uniform and milk was rationed. This summer was the warmest anyone could remember, but most people were too hot even to think about it.

Yet out west, beyond the sticky centre of the city, in the upmarket district of Berlin-Schlachtensee, a refreshing waft of pine straight from the heart of the Grunewald pierced the air. The Schlachtensee was the southernmost of Berlin's lakes, famed for the silkiness of its water and its green depths tangled with weed. The grand mansions in the surrounding roads were screened by high fences and shaded by graceful lines of trees, their gardens furnished with wooden swing seats and tasteful statuary. The spacious whitewashed villa in

Augustastrasse with its sloping red roof and privet-trimmed gravel path was no exception. It was a picture of bourgeois serenity – or it would have been, had it not been the home of SS-Gruppenführer and chief of security police Reinhard Heydrich and his wife Lina.

The tumult of events that had engulfed Clara in recent weeks meant that Goebbels' mention of the bridge circle to which his wife Magda belonged had barely registered in her mind. Returning to Winterfeldtstrasse and finding a letter with the official purple stamp of the Ministry of Propaganda in her pigeonhole was a shock, and opening the envelope to discover an invitation to a game of bridge the following day a heart-sinking surprise. But when she checked the address on the invitation, she was filled with genuine alarm.

It had been seven years since Clara first entered the close circle of the Nazi wives, during which time she had been privy to all kinds of feuds and conspiracies deep within the Nazi regime. Magda Goebbels had confided her marital miseries and Eva Braun had laid bare the pitiful state of her life as Hitler's secret girlfriend. Yet it was quite another thing to visit the home of Reinhard Heydrich, whose merciless devotion to duty was unparalleled in the Nazi regime and whose narrow face, sharp as an executioner's axe, seemed to embody all the sadism he perpetrated in prisons across Germany and the new eastern reaches of the Reich. The prospect of an afternoon with his wife, equally as fanatical a Nazi as her husband, was no less intimidating.

Outside the house a knot of drivers were chatting and lounging against the gleam of their official cars and as Clara passed they concealed their cigarettes behind their hands and straightened to attention, though not too stiffly, unsure of her precise rank. The door was opened on her first knock by a nervy young woman in a maid's outfit, who from her hesitant, heavily accented German was plainly a Zivilarbeiter, and the drawing room into which she showed Clara, panelled in light oak, richly carpeted, with cabinets of Meissen china, and stately mahogany furniture, bore all the appurtenances of long established wealth. Beneath the window there was a sofa in watered silk. Above the fireplace a painting of the *Dresden*, the World War battleship, and ranged along the piano a series of photographs of two boys wearing HJ outfits, playing the violin, visiting the zoo, both with the trademark close-set eyes and watchful expressions of their father. Beside them stood a silver-framed portrait of a figure clothed top to toe in full fencing kit that was, despite the headgear, unmistakably Reinhard Heydrich.

He looked a lot better in a mask.

'That's my husband as German fencing champion.'

Lina Heydrich had entered the room unobtrusively and was standing arms folded, raking the length of Clara with stony, basilisk eyes. Her dress was orange velvet with puffed sleeves and a frilly clutch of material at the bust. She had a thin, unpainted stripe of a smile, a pleat of wrinkles on the neck and her hair was restrained in twin muffs. The necklace she wore contained about as many diamonds as Clara had transported across Paris less than a week before.

'He won a gold medal.'

She extended a hand.

'I don't think we've met, Fräulein . . . Vine?'

The hesitation was a feint. Lina Heydrich knew perfectly well who she was. Indeed, Clara could see that this afternoon would be as carefully calibrated and as potentially deadly as any fencing joust. A shiver of nerves reminded her that she needed to be on her guard.

'This is Frau Doktor Goebbels' card circle, I hasten to add. I merely offered to host it. We take turns. The game's already started, I'm afraid.'

Lina Heydrich opened the double doors at the far end of the drawing room and led the way into an adjoining room, backing onto the garden and striped with sun like the bars of a gilded cage. Clara had prepared herself for anything, but even so she was startled to see, around a wide table covered in green baize, what amounted to a full hand, if not a royal flush, of Nazi wives.

Nearest was Inge Ley, wife of the alcoholic head of the German Labour Front, a woman as unhappy as she was beautiful. Her former life as a ballet dancer told in her bearing; she was straight-backed and graceful with a small nose, perfectly proportioned cheekbones and flaxen hair trained in waves, with two blonde commas tucked obediently to each side of her forehead. Beside her was Margarete Speer, the wife of Hitler's architect, dispensing coffee and cream into delicate Meissen cups decorated with sprays of indigo flowers, and next to them, heads bent over the pile of cards, the wives of two of the most senior ministers in the Nazi regime: Annelies von Ribbentrop, wife of the Foreign Minister, and Magda Goebbels herself.

Clara had known the Propaganda Minister's wife since her arrival in Germany seven years ago, when Magda co-opted her into modelling for the Reich Fashion Bureau, of which she was president. Then, Frau Doktor Goebbels was a chill, elegant woman, whose nerves were shot to pieces by the womanizing of her philandering husband. Now, several babies later, and having had her demand for a divorce refused by the Führer himself, she was in a far worse state. Tendons stood out on her neck like piano wires and she was dealing a round of cards as though someone's life depended on it.

She barely looked up as Clara approached.

'You've arrived. Forgive us if we've already begun.'

'It was kind of you to invite me,' said Clara, sitting down.

'I wasn't aware that I did. My husband informed me that you would be coming. I assume he wants to hear the gossip from the gaming tables. Though how he finds the time to concern himself with women's conversation when he's busy organizing the biggest parade the world had ever seen, I'm not entirely sure.'

Although this was delivered with an unmistakable tinge of sarcasm, the next day's Parade for the French Victory was certainly likely to be the largest rally Goebbels had ever orchestrated. It was to be the greatest standing ovation of Hitler's life. Like everyone else in her block, Clara had seen the poster pinned up by Rudi ordering citizens to 'greet Hitler with unparalleled enthusiasm'. Factories and shops were to be closed at midday, swimming pools shut and buses out of the city cancelled to discourage any members of the population planning to avoid the joyous occasion. Flowers had been ordered from the Berlin Allotment Association to carpet a kilometre of street from the Anhalter Bahnhof to the Reich Chancellery, and girls from the BDM had been drilled in throwing them spontaneously at the passing cars.

Magda collected up the cards and Clara sat beside her. She noticed a bottle of schnapps on a side table and guessed that Magda was adding occasional nips to her coffee. There was a moment's silence, broken only by the shuffle of the deck like the clipped flutter of a bird's wings.

'You do know how to play?'

'I've played a little, yes.'

Clara racked her brain for the card games they had played in the long, stultifying holidays of her youth. She had never been one for cards. It was Angela who was the expert, regularly enjoying a rubber of bridge with her smart set in Kensington. All Clara liked was the intellectual challenge of counting up the card values.

Magda pushed a pile of chips across the table.

'We only bet for buttons.'

'Though I'd guess Fräulein Vine is a person who likes to play for high stakes,' murmured Lina Heydrich.

'What makes you say that?'

'Just what I'd been led to understand.'

'Oh, that couldn't be more wrong! I'm not much of a player at all.'

'Aren't you?' murmured Annelies von Ribbentrop, looking up from her hand. 'Then you're different from the other British. From what I remember, they're obsessed with card games. When we were there you couldn't move for fear of being roped into a round of canasta or something called gin rummy. I played a lot with that girl you used to know, who was so infatuated with the Führer.'

'Unity Mitford?'

Unity was the most eccentric English girl Clara had ever met, with her pet white rat, Ratular, that lived in her handbag, and a grass snake, Enid, which she took to dances to intimidate the young men. 'If a party becomes dull,' she once told Clara, 'I allow my snake to escape.' The only thing Unity loved more than her animals was Adolf Hitler and her infatuation was so great that when war between England and Germany was declared, she could no longer bear to live.

'You heard she shot herself?' said Magda impassively. 'In the Englischer Garten in Munich. She used the pistol the Führer gave her, but it didn't finish her off. They found her twitching like a mangy rabbit. The Führer was so kind – he had her transported to England at his own expense.'

She paused for a deep sigh. 'I wish the women who moon after my husband would shoot themselves.'

Across the face of Frau von Ribbentrop a smile flickered, quick as the tongue of a snake.

'Seems a shame, when this girl wanted to die for love.'

Magda threw down a trick, her wedding ring flashing beneath a puffy knuckle.

'I've known people like that. Unfortunately they never do. They just poison everyone else with it.'

'Don't you adore cards?' said Inge Ley, with the valiant air of someone trying to change the subject. 'I always feel especially naughty at the card tables. I'm sure the Führer disapproves.'

'You're quite wrong,' said Lina Heydrich. 'The Führer's a keen supporter of gambling. He sees it as a good source of funds for the state. That's why he lifted the ban on casinos. He says casinos are marvellous institutions.'

'Well, I loathe casinos,' said Magda, thumbing through her hand as though her own fortune might be revealed in it. 'If you asked what my favourite game is, I'd say Solitaire.'

She left a heartbeat's pause for everyone in the room to make the connection. With a husband like Joseph Goebbels, a woman was going to be playing a lot of Solitaire.

'I'm never so relaxed as playing Solitaire in my own home.'

'Your home must look so lovely now. I heard you had some nice rugs and paintings brought from France.'

This remark, like most of Frau von Ribbentrop's utterances, was pointed. The removal of treasures from occupied France, while widespread, was officially disapproved of. Ignoring her, Magda took a swig of brandy-laced coffee and turned to Clara.

'*You've* been in France, haven't you? What were you up to?'

'Entertaining the troops.'

'How wonderful!' Margarete Speer looked at her with undisguised envy. 'My husband went with the Führer and he said the best moment was looking out on the city from Montmartre, right on the steps of the Sacré-Coeur. Did you go there? Did you see lovely things?'

'I did.' Clara flinched, thinking of how recently she too

had stood on those steps. 'I saw some amazing things in Paris.'

'I was longing to join them but Albert said I couldn't possibly.'

A pregnant pause revealed what everyone was thinking. The Speer marriage was said to be as empty as any of the echoing marble edifices the architect designed.

'Though I'm sure I'll get to see it before long. After all, the Führer has no plans to destroy Paris. He says the lesson is that it's a beautiful city, but that Berlin must become a hundred times more beautiful. There's no need to desecrate it.'

'Really?' Lina Heydrich cocked an enquiring eyebrow. 'When did he tell you that?'

'We were at the Obersalzberg a few weeks ago.' Frau Speer managed a modest shrug. The Bavarian mountain retreat where Hitler had his holiday home was the ultimate VIP destination and the Speers, like the Goering and Bormann families, were privileged to have their own home on the mountain compound within walking distance of the Berghof.

'It was glorious. Lunch at the Berghof and afternoon trips up to the Eagle's Nest. And we took our branches down into the salt mines.'

The salt mines that gave Obersalzberg its name formed a glistening labyrinth beneath the mountain surface. It was a tradition for local people to leave branches that they would retrieve at Christmas, covered in a deposit of scintillating crystals, as though they had been studded with diamonds.

'Lucky you. It sounds lovely,' said Frau Ley, enviously.

'It was. Except the Führer was in a terrible mood. He

had had to let one of his secretaries go. The SD turned up something in her papers – her origins couldn't be established and they found Jewish blood in the maternal line. Hitler explained he had no alternative but to dismiss her, but he promised to have Bormann Aryanize her family. Then it turned out that Bormann did the exact opposite and the woman's entire family lost their jobs.'

'That's Bormann for you,' said Magda.

'Baldur von Schirach spent ages trying to cheer the Führer up. They're writing an opera together. It's going to be a bit like Wagner, apparently.'

A sound like a snort issued from the direction of Annelies von Ribbentrop.

Boredly, Lina Heydrich looked round.

'Are we to expect anyone else?'

'Only one other,' said Magda, dropping a cylinder of ash in a cut-glass ashtray. 'Joseph asked me to befriend this woman. I have no idea why. Not the usual reasons, I feel certain of that.'

As if in response, the door was flung open and a waft of perfume and high heels clipped into the room. Walter Schellenberg's fiancée picked her way across the floor as though making her way through a minefield, which in some ways she was.

'I'm not late, am I?'

The frost in the air turned to ice.

'I'm afraid I've just dealt,' said Magda.

'What are we playing? Not *Führer Quartett*, I hope,' quipped Irene, in reference to the wildly popular schoolchild's game.

It was based on Snap and the cards were decorated with the faces of Nazi leaders, including the husbands of all of those present, as well as army generals, playwrights, musicians and other important Third Reich figures. One of them was Hitler's dog.

'I hardly think that would be appropriate,' said Frau Speer, quietly.

'Well, I'm absolutely parched so if you don't mind, I'll just wait out this round while you get on with your game.' Irene clicked her fingers at the maid hovering at the far reaches of the room, who hurried off to secure a coffee cup.

'In that case,' said Clara, jumping up, 'why don't I keep you company?'

'I can't tell you how much I didn't want to come. Here of all places.'

Although they were out of earshot, at the far end of the drawing room, Irene had an intimate way of speaking, at once hushed and secretive, as though through the curtains of a confessional. She flung herself on the watered silk sofa and Clara followed suit.

'Walter had to use every bit of persuasion to make me.'

The types of persuasion open to Sturmbannführer Schellenberg ran like a shudder through Clara's imagination.

'He said he wants me to keep in with these wives. It reflects well on him. I'm supposed to help him in his career. Nothing about *me* and how I'm going to feel with all these women bitching about me.'

'Surely not.'

Irene gave Clara a frank look.

'You have no idea. Frau von Ribbentrop has already been asking about my origins.'

That Clara could well believe. The Foreign Minister's wife had made the same apparently innocuous enquiries about her own background the previous year. In Nazi Germany, a question was as good as an accusation and an official inquiry was nine tenths of a denunciation.

'Himmler had a team put on my mother back in Poland and they discovered my aunt's married to a Jew. Walter says sit tight, but that kind of thing could be enough to stop our marriage. Added to which, Lina Heydrich over there has some absurd idea that Walter carries a torch for *her*. I mean my God, look at her.'

Clara didn't. It was well known that the Heydrich marriage, like so many in the senior Nazi circles, was in trouble. She recalled Hans Reuber's comment about Heydrich and his frequent appearances at Salon Kitty.

'All that velvet. She looks like a cushion. And she spends all her time feuding with Marga Himmler. Frau Himmler told me that when she began a coffee circle, Lina deliberately scheduled group callisthenics here instead and invited all the ladies to attend. Not that it's had much effect.'

She smoothed her own chiffon dress down over her slim hips, then sprang up and crossed to the photograph of Heydrich glowering into the camera like a wolf.

'Even if she *was* attractive I can't think she'd dare with this husband of hers. Walter says Heydrich's like an animal of prey. He's utterly ruthless. You've heard what Hitler calls him, haven't you? The Man with the Iron Heart. That's why Heydrich admires Walter. He sees him as a kindred spirit.'

Clara was struck by the accuracy of Heydrich's nickname. 'You don't think that, though, do you? I mean, you don't see Walter as heartless?'

'I don't know.' Irene's eyes clouded with hesitation in a way that Clara had noticed a lot recently. A refusal to see clearly what was staring you in the face was a common complaint in Berlin, and there was no obvious cure.

'He's brilliant, I know that . . .'

She sighed, and fiddled with a bracelet of chunky yellow gold.

'Trouble is, being brilliant brings its own problems. Walter's been given a new operation now and he's under tremendous stress. He's not sleeping a wink.'

'What's this new job then? No . . .' Clara laid a light hand on her arm. 'Forget I asked that. You shouldn't say. You've told me enough already.'

This approach was generally successful. No one wanted to be reminded that they were speaking out of turn, so they tended to compensate by filling in more detail. Irene, however, looked forlorn.

'I'd tell you if I knew. But he won't say a word. I tried to sneak a read of his reports, but frankly, they're so full of code letters they look like someone's fallen backwards on a typewriter. They're totally incomprehensible. When I ask Walter all he'll say is that it's a very important mission, something the old man – that's what he calls von Ribbentrop – has requested, and it's giving him nightmares.'

'I'd have thought he'd be used to it. Stress, I mean. A man in his position.'

'You'd think. I certainly am.'

Irene glanced in the mantel mirror, automatically checking powder, lipstick and rouge, then she threw back her shoulders, pushed forward her ample breasts and braced herself, as if the forthcoming card game was a testing military engagement all of its own.

'You want to know a secret? Walter's having a desk built for his office with two machine guns embedded in it, so if anyone tries to assassinate him he can press a button and spray the room with bullets. That's how careful he has to be. And he keeps a box of grenades behind a curtain. Whenever he goes abroad he wears a signet ring with a blue stone where he keeps his poison capsule.'

She drowned her cigarette stub in the coffee cup.

'But he'll manage. Walter's at the top of his game. That's what he told me. He never gets it wrong. He doesn't even need to hear them talking. He can smell a spy, he says.'

It was another hour and a half before Clara could excuse herself and head for the S–Bahn back into town. Looking out at the fluorescent glare of the shops and offices through the blurry train windows, she remembered that there was no food in the apartment. Food was a constant preoccupation now, requiring significant planning if one was to get enough to eat, and by this time in the afternoon the shops would be stripped bare, with only a few bones remaining at the butcher's and the odd crumb at the grocery store. Recent events had wiped her normal routine entirely from her mind and Clara realized she would have to stop on the way if she was to find anything to eat that night or the following morning.

At Nollendorfſplatz she entered a bakery. It was not her usual one and as she queued, she noted the air of tension among the other customers and a furtive jostling for the few remaining loaves of black rye bread with caraway seeds that remained behind the counter. The shoppers were shabbily dressed, their coats giving off a smell of damp wool and body odour, and Clara realized that they must be Jews, using their ration cards at the only time of day they were permitted, when most of the produce was gone. Everyone here must assume that she, too, was a Jew and they were right to assume it, of course, but they were not to know that. No one was.

When eventually she was served, she found she had no ration tokens and had to offer cash. The baker considered her a moment with a sullen countenance. It was not strictly allowed, but he quoted an exorbitant sum, that Clara, after a moment's hesitation, found in her purse.

The baker took the notes and handed her the loaf.

'I'll keep the change, shall I?' he said. 'For charity?'

Chapter Thirteen

If playing cards were now the indoor pastime of choice and cinema a regular treat, the Saturday races at Hoppegarten, a short train ride east of Berlin, were everyone's favourite day out. That included senior members of the regime, especially Goering and Goebbels, who could often be seen in the red-brick grandstand eyeing glamorous equine stars like Nereide, Alchimist and Ticino as eagerly as they would actresses on the red carpet. The only notable absentee was Hitler himself, who had proclaimed on many occasions that horse racing was the last remnant of a feudal society and would, as soon as he got round to it, be outlawed. Perhaps that was why people were making the most of it.

Erich and Clara made their way through the gates towards the viewing paddock. The air was filled with the oniony grease of the *Bratwurst* stalls and the path resounded to the clatter of wooden-soled shoes and the tinny music of an organ grinder whose wizened monkey surveyed the passing citizens with ancient, liquid eyes. Back in Neukölln Erich's grandmother was bedridden with emphysema and Clara reckoned it was good for the boy to get a break. Although he was devoted to her, Frau Schmidt had become imperious and demanding in old age and Erich's life at home was punctuated by her quavering voice, constantly summoning him on some small errand. Rather than be cooped up with an invalid in a stuffy three-room apartment, she decided, the boy needed fresh air.

And Clara needed Erich. Their tradition of Saturday outings, to the cinemas or the lakes or the swimming baths, was one that she guarded jealously. Erich was the single reason she had stayed in Berlin and her greatest respite from the anxieties that war brought. He had grown appreciably in the last year and now, at almost seventeen, he towered over her, his features sharpened, brows thicker and shoulders broader. His good looks attracted glances from the girls they passed and they were glances he returned. Erich was barely recognizable as the slight, nervous child Clara had met in her first month in Berlin, except that he remained the sole person for whom she would do anything.

'How's school?' she asked, cursing herself for uttering the dullest possible question.

Strolling along with his hands in the pockets of his Hitler Youth uniform, Erich shrugged.

'I know you don't like me saying this, Clara, but I've had enough of it. I like it, you know, but all my friends are the same. What's the point of studying maths and logic and Kant when we could be doing something useful?'

'Kant teaches you something useful. The moral law within you. Isn't that one of his?'

'Sure, I suppose. But the Categorical Imperative is pretty meaningless when your country's at war.'

'I would have thought it was more important than ever.'

Erich sighed and resisted the impulse to roll his eyes. Instead he focused on the betting boards that were tipping Schwarzgold as the favourite in the next race.

'Anyway,' Clara coaxed, 'you do your bit in the Hitler Jugend, don't you?'

'I suppose. But HJ work is pretty childish. It's just collecting scrap metal and delivering ration coupons and draft letters for other people, when actually it's us who should be joining up. It's crazy to be wasting time at school when my country needs me. You know how much I want to join the Luftwaffe. I've done pilot training and I can fly a glider. You're pleased about that, aren't you?'

Clara was, but only because the alternative was worse. The previous year Erich had been offered a position in the Hitler Youth Streifendienst – a corps of hand-picked boys charged with enforcing internal discipline in the organization. The position was pretty much a spying job, investigating misconduct and subversion, inspecting uniforms, and informing the police of unsuitable elements, but it was an honour to be approached and promised a short cut to SS officer training. Yet Erich had turned it down, preferring to focus all his dreams on the Luftwaffe.

'I hate thinking I won't get a chance to fly for at least another year.'

Clara hated to think of him flying at all, but if he did she prayed it would not be in the skies above England.

'You'll get your chance soon enough.'

For a while they ambled along, people-watching. It was a blisteringly hot day and all shades of Berlin society were out in force, from factory workers relaxing with picnics on blankets to elegantly dressed ladies perched in cane chairs with china cups of tea, all watching the jockeys parading round the paddock, their mounts stamping the turf and tossing shiny heads. Only close observers would have noticed that there were more and finer horses than usual. In the past few weeks hundreds of thoroughbreds had been seized from the stables of the top Paris racing families – the Rothschilds, Sterns, Wertheimers and Wildensteins – and transported to the Reich. It was probably for the best, Clara thought. Cropping alien grass was a small price to pay to avoid being bombed or eaten.

It was not until they reached the course barrier and secured themselves a good viewpoint, that Erich leaned on the railing and said, 'Actually, I wanted to ask you something.'

'Better not be about joining up.'

'No.'

'Or philosophy. I'm afraid I'd be no help there.'

'No. It's not that.'

From his top pocket he fished out a square of newspaper, folded and refolded so often that its creases were wearing thin, and angled his shoulder to shield it from prying eyes.

'The fact is, with Oma being ill, I have to go in her room sometimes. Anyhow, when I was there the other day she asked me to look for medicine in her drawer and although I wasn't searching for anything else, I found this.'

Even before he had uncreased it, the image lifted from

the ancient *BZ am Mittag* like the sepia glimpse of a ghost. For a moment it appeared to float before Clara's vision, the teasing smile and complexion Pan-Caked to perfection, the pert nose and high brows above sceptical dark eyes. It was a face freighted with memory and pain. The official Ufa studio portrait of Helga Schmidt.

Helga. The name ached within Clara like a cut that would never heal. Yet again she saw the blood on that Prenzlauer Berg pavement, and the beautiful leaking body that was broken but not quite dead. She saw the inquisitive crowd gathered around, and the open window five floors up from which Helga had fallen like a bird fledged too soon. Above the picture was a headline.

Helga Schmidt plunges to her death. Actress was suicidal, say friends.

For seven years Frau Schmidt had preserved this cutting of her only daughter, whose death, 'when the balance of her mind was disturbed', was the last newspaper write-up she was ever going to receive.

'When I was young,' Erich said sombrely as if such a time was irretrievably long ago, 'my friends used to laugh about her. At school I knocked a boy out for what he said about my Mutti.'

'I remember.'

Clara had been contacted by her godson's headmaster and was obliged to conjure all her charm – not to mention a school outing to the Ufa studios – to allay the man's suggestion that Erich was a violent and ungovernable pupil who deserved to be expelled.

'They said all sorts of things about her. And me.'

'I know.'

Mother's boy. Son of a whore. No better than a Jew.

'I didn't care what they said about me, but I'd fight them for insulting my mother. But the worst thing, Clara, they said about her was that she was an Enemy of National Socialism.'

So this was the heart of the matter. The ache that would not go away. Erich uttered the phrase like an obscenity, his eyes clouded with pain.

'It's a disgusting thing to say, but I have to know, Clara. Was it true? I can't ask Oma. But was she?'

What was Helga? A free spirit. By turns mordant, merry and vivacious. A girl who had taken plenty of hard knocks in pursuit of her acting dream but was not prepared to abandon it. A woman who looked National Socialism in the eye, understood it, and chose to laugh at it.

'She was a wonderful woman.'

'So why do people say bad things about her?'

'She made jokes. That was her only crime. To make fun of the Führer. And not much fun at that.'

Even as she said it, Clara could see how her words hurt Erich; loyalty to his mother and worship of the Führer colliding and cleaving inside him like some dreadful axe.

'What kind of jokes?'

Inappropriately a flood of jokes tumbled into her head. *What does WHW stand for?* Wir Hungern Weiter. *We're Still Hungry. Hitler and Goering are on the top of the Funkturm surveying the Reich. Hitler says he wants to do something to put a smile* on the sad faces of Berliners. Goering thinks for a moment then says, 'Why don't you jump off?'

'Just silly things that made people laugh.'

He frowned and corrected her automatically. 'Laughing at Hitler isn't silly.'

'It can be. As you say, I knew her. All your mother wanted was for people to see the lighter side of life. Not to take things too seriously. And she was right.'

For a second a maturity she had never witnessed in Erich seemed to pierce the boyish façade. Reality surfaced, like rocks revealed at low tide. He saw the awkward, jagged complexity of life that could not be labelled, categorized, or locked away. His face was sharp with love for a mother who had refused to fit someone else's idea of what a woman should be. Then the water returned, his shook his head, and the world was once more black and white.

'She wasn't right.' An angry flush had risen on his cheeks. 'If she was alive I would have told her. We're all lucky to live under the Führer. If you don't take things seriously, you get a decadent society. Everyone knows that. Only a weak nation disrespects its leaders.'

'And only a bad son disrespects his mother.' Clara's voice had an edge of steel. 'All that matters, Erich, is that Helga adored you. She thought the world of you. She wasn't some dangerous asocial, she just had a good sense of humour. Laughter was part of her. No one was going to get the better of her.'

'They did though, didn't they?'

This was the nearest they had ever come to discussing how

his mother had died. Clara had always thought that Erich had no idea of his mother's liaison with a brutal stormtrooper capable of volcanic violence. Or that the regime had considered Helga Schmidt better off dead. Yet now, it seemed, he knew more than she could have guessed.

'Whatever happened, you should be proud of her.'

He clenched his jaw. 'I am. But not that part of her.'

At that moment the ground trembled and a blur of glistening chestnut pelts thundered by, spittle flying from the bits in their mouths, and churned clods of turf bouncing into the air. Ragged cheers arose, making conversation impossible. Once the horses had passed Clara began to speak, but Erich interrupted.

'If you don't mind, Clara, I don't want to discuss it any more. Thanks for explaining.' He returned the newspaper clipping to his top pocket and produced the betting form.

'Who are you backing for the next race?'

There was no point arguing. Erich may quote Kant and his knowledge of logic might go back to the ancient Greeks, but to any boy of his age in Germany right then, the logic of the Führer was always going to prevail.

Chapter Fourteen

On the corner of Luisenstrasse fresh loudspeakers were being fixed to the walls. Whatever they broadcast, everyone knew they never told the truth. Hitler was like a disease that people suspected yet persisted in pretending didn't exist, as though by ignoring the symptoms the illness would go away of its own accord. But Hitler wasn't going anywhere.

His voice, with its ear-scraping screams of indignation, was like a soundtrack to Mary Harker's time in Berlin. It drilled right down, like a tinnitus of the soul. It vibrated in her bones and travelled into her brain. It permeated everything, like the tang of boiled flesh, cabbage and dust that hung in the air and made her feel, no matter how often she scrubbed herself, she would never be clean of it. As Mary sat waiting in Habel's restaurant, images of the time she had spent in this city and beyond flashed through her mind.

She remembered the hulking ruin of the main synagogue, burned down in 1938 as Brown Shirts unrolled the Torah and charged people a mark to trample the length of it. Trucks drawn up outside apartment buildings and soldiers with pistols jumping out. In Vienna, Jewish professors cleaning the gutters with toothbrushes, and last year in Poland, watching women boil weeds to stave off starvation. And now her beloved Paris, where she had lived briefly in 1932. Already the newsreels were running shots of Hitler on a visit so fleeting it looked almost furtive, driving past buildings that were ghostly as a stage set in the steely morning light, in a fleet of Mercedes sedans. Standing upright in his leather coat, gripping the windscreen, light bending towards him like a black hole. His face looked sullen, sulky almost, as though he was disappointed by the absence of cheering crowds. How different this must have seemed from his triumphant entry into Vienna two years ago, when carpets of flowers were thrown in his path. Could it be that the capture of Paris, the jewel of Europe, whose architecture he had so long pored over in maps and street plans, was proving an anticlimax?

Special to the New York Evening Post. That was Mary's byline, and if she was not so special to anyone else then she had learned to stop lamenting it. Leaving America and making a career for herself in Europe as a roving correspondent was the only destiny she had ever dreamed of, even if it had consigned her mother back in New Jersey to a state of perpetual disappointment. Playing golf with lucky friends whose daughters had chosen to be home-makers, Edith Harker's life was one long losing hand; not only had Mary failed to provide her with grandchildren, but she had elected to live thousands of miles away at a time of life when any widowed mother had a right to expect the attentions of a devoted daughter. Working, what was more, for a newspaper that neither Edith Harker, nor anyone in her country club, actually took. Perhaps though, Mary thought wistfully, that would change once her mother heard about her new opportunity. Not even the housewives of New Jersey could ignore a slot of regular broadcasts on CBS Radio.

Whether they would like what she said was another matter. Most of the ordinary Germans she knew regarded America as a wondrous land of automobiles and skyscrapers and dancing and fun and were theoretically happy to talk to a correspondent whose country was still on cordial terms with their own. Yet in reality, the risks they ran were considerable. Mary's phone was tapped, and the lives of her informants depended on her own vigilance. In a perverse reversal of hospitality, when she visited an apartment the owner would turn on the radio loud the moment she arrived.

The bell above the door chimed and Clara came in.

Mary watched her dearest friend from across the restaurant, before she had been spotted. She was wearing sunglasses and a belted black dress that set off her light golden tan, falling in neat pleats below the waist. There were fresh shadows in her face and some new lines, though time had not yet dragged its beauty down. It was a face Mary thought she knew, yet she was well aware how little she really understood. She marvelled at how much the cloak of familiarity could conceal. Clara had recently returned from France, ostensibly on a visit with the Frontbühne, though Mary felt certain that other business was involved. For both their sakes she never probed too deeply about Clara's work or any other part of her life. Officially she knew nothing of Clara's romantic relationships, yet she had never forgotten the stricken look that engulfed her friend that evening in the Press Club when she heard the report that two men had been shot in an illegal border crossing, one of them a suspected British agent.

By the time Clara had spotted Mary and was making her way over, she had returned to her copy of *NS Frauen-Warte*, whose cover girl that month was dressed in traditional peasant garb, ploughing a field.

'Not your usual reading matter,' said Clara, pulling off her sunglasses. 'I never had you down as a Nazi fashion fan.'

'I'm not. You could have more fun reading a headstone. Though I notice that you made *Neues Volk*.'

New People, the organ of the Party's racial office, was the stuff of Nazi dentists' waiting rooms, filled with opinion pieces on Aryan supremacy, the importance of Germanic names and the deficiencies of Jews and Poles. The news of Clara's appointment to the fundraising committee of the NSV had featured above an item on congenital disease accompanied by a lurid photograph. *This genetically ill person will cost our people's community 60,000 marks over his lifetime. Citizens, that is your money!*

Mary shrugged.

'But if you're really serious about campaigning for the importance of family life, Clara, you'll want to see this.'

She gestured to where a second magazine was sandwiched between the Nazi periodical's pages. It was a British magazine called *Look*.

'One of the other correspondents brought it back. I'm being careful no one sees me reading it, but you need this sort of thing every now and then if you're going to stay sane and I'm happy to say there's a piece in here that's got the Führer very upset.'

'I'm amazed he read it.'

'He wouldn't, only it's by his nephew, William, so Goebbels must have felt obliged to point it out. Apparently Hitler tried really hard for the boy, got him a job with Opel, invited him to all the best dinner parties, showed him around. And what thanks did he get? The lad only went off to England and moved into journalism.'

'What's the piece about?'

'Family matters mostly. It's called *Why I Hate my Uncle*.' Mary threw the magazine down as a waiter approached.

'You can read it later. Let's order.'

Habel's was an old favourite of theirs, both because its cosy wooden booths meant they could speak English undetected and also because it was a historic restaurant that prided itself on serving traditional German food in huge portions. Everything on the menu made the mouth water. Rich stews issuing savoury steam and glistening wurst on a bed of trans-lucent onions. Trout in a red wine sauce. Glossy sautéed potatoes. Asparagus swimming in butter. Schnitzels bigger than the plates they arrived on. In recent times, however, traditions had worn thin. The first tradition to be abandoned was the size of the portions and the second was the food itself. The only dishes on offer that day were *Schupfnudeln*, thick Bavarian potato noodles, and sawdust sausage.

From the loudspeakers outside the voice of Joseph Goebbels could now be heard, shrill with caffeine, saying something about *Lügen-Lord Churchill* and the *Jüdische Weltgefahr*. Lying Lord Churchill in league with the world-wide Jewish menace.

'When will he realize no one's listening?' said Clara.

'People are listening, though.'

Mary's expression darkened.

'Except it's the foreign stations they're listening to. We had proof the other day. The BBC reported the name of a young Berliner who's been arrested as a spy in England and put in prison. No less than eight people contacted the mother to say her son was safe. And how did she thank them? She reported them all to the police for listening to illegal broadcasts.'

The waiter brought their food. Clara looked down and sighed.

'Tell me something cheerful. I want to hear about CBS.'

'It's everything I hoped for! I have a regular slot – twenty minutes a week. This is my chance, Clara ...' Though she spoke softly, Mary reached over and gripped her friend's wrist with surprising strength. 'It's my *last* chance. We have to convince Americans that there's no alternative to military participation. Roosevelt's doing everything he can. There's an election coming up and he's called on the nation to make an effort, to build up our military defences, but the isolation-ists are strong. They want to keep out of Europe's problems. They blame everything on the Jews. You hear it from people at my mother's country club. Leave Europe to fight her own wars. Why should Americans die? People like Charles Lindbergh laugh at the idea that Germany could ever attack the United States. But Goebbels joins in that laughter.'

'What can you do?'

'It's difficult. We have to work out of the Haus des Rundfunks.' The Radio House, up in Berlin's Charlottenburg-Wilmersdorff, was the home of German State Radio. 'They censor our scripts and if they don't like a broadcast there'll be trouble. The fact that I'm on CBS makes it worse. It's an important platform, so they watch what I say much more closely. If they wanted to, they could concoct some story that I was slipping in military secrets by code words and put me up before a Nazi People's Court. They'd charge me with espionage and you know the penalty for that.'

'They wouldn't go that far.'

'Maybe not. Not yet. Not while they still care what Americans think. But time's running out. More and more correspondents are being thrown out because they displease Goebbels. It's all the more important that those of us who are left keep telling the truth. Finding the stories that reveal what's really going on – only I'm worried about the people who do speak to me. The Gestapo turn up at my apartment all the time, questioning me about my sources. I can't afford to be careless. The slightest slip and my informants could be arrested and charged with treason. Mind you, I had a story yesterday from a most unexpected source. My office is a few doors along from William Joyce. You know, Lord Haw Haw. The British guy.'

William Joyce was German Radio's prize possession. Born in America and Irish by heritage, he had the voice of an Englishman and the heart of a fascist. His programme, always beginning with the words 'Germany Calling', offered

British listeners advice on avoiding injury during forthcoming bombing raids, and tips on learning German and living under future Nazi occupation.

'Dreadful man,' said Clara, forking her meagre portion of noodles.

'I know. I can hardly bear to speak to him, but do you know what he told me when I passed him in the corridor? Goebbels has scored a major coup. P.G. Wodehouse has been taken prisoner in Le Touquet and he's being brought to Berlin to make propaganda broadcasts.'

Clara set down her cutlery in dismay. Her appetite vanished. Strange how such a trifling item, a mere arrest alongside the welter of daily deaths and deportations, should evoke such utter desolation. She had loved P.G. Wodehouse's novels since her teenage years and to her his characters, Jeeves, Bertie Wooster, Aunt Agatha, symbolized everything joyful about the land of her birth. His jokes, laughter, and butterfly wit that gave the impression nothing really terrible could happen.

Only now it had. She pictured the novelist in his tweeds and pipe, shambling out of his home under the escort of Nazi guards, fretting, perhaps, about his wife or his beloved dachshund. Trying to keep his spirits up with the kind of light-hearted quips that only his fellow countrymen would understand. No doubt, compared to the treatment inflicted on other prisoners of the Reich, Wodehouse would be treated with courtesy and all the special privileges Joseph Goebbels could devise. English breakfast tea, a gramophone, any banned book he might desire. She guessed he would regard flippant cheerfulness as an appropriate defiance of his dour Teutonic captors. Yet what use were jokes against the Wehrmacht? Humour and fun-poking glanced like toy arrows off the might of the Nazi machine.

'He'll *never* do it.'

'Won't he? Perhaps he agrees with the Duke of Windsor. Peace at any price. Anyhow, what about you? How was Paris?'

'Interesting.'

Mary raised an eyebrow. She was used to these gnomic remarks that said 'Don't probe any further'. Her own call-ing – if not her entire personality – was the polar opposite of Clara's. Mary wanted to talk, to expose, to bring the truth out into the open at every opportunity while Clara kept her thoughts private and her activities even more so. Yet Mary had no doubt that her friend's convictions were every bit as deep as her own.

'Meet anyone there?'

'I was only there two days.'

'A lot can happen in two days.'

She smiled, threw down her napkin and gave up.

'Well, remember what I said. If you come across anything that you think I should report on, you must let me know. Why don't we go somewhere else and find a drink? This coffee's so weak I can see through it.'

It was not until they had visited the bar of the Hotel Adlon and enjoyed several brandies with what remained of the American press corps that Clara made her way home and allowed herself to think properly about Paris and the man she had met there. Captain Russell. They had been together only a couple of hours, but there had been so much of him that she liked; his intelligence, his quiet intensity, the light in his eyes. The way he seemed to understand what she was saying with an instinctive sympathy. How he refrained from any questions when she threw off her layers of secrecy and laid herself bare. An Anglo-German woman living in Berlin. *I can be useful there.* How he had left so much of his story unspoken, as if to talk any more of the bodies he had seen, or the sadism he had witnessed being meted out to his fellow prisoners, might be hard for her to bear. As though she had not seen for herself the savagery that man could inflict on man. In a strange way Ned had reminded her of Leo, though physically the two couldn't be more different. Ned was a bear of a man, his body a heft of muscle carved from the very granite of his northern roots. Dark hair hanging down into one eye. Large hands made for hoisting logs rather than teaching English to a classroom of small boys. She wondered what had become of him and hoped with a fervency that surprised her that he had made his way out of Paris alive.

When she reached Winterfeldtstrasse the stray cat fell in with her, tail up, trotting in her wake. She bent down to stroke it but it held back, uncertain, its desire for companionship never entirely able to overcome its own unbreachable caution.

Chapter Fifteen

Irene had not forgotten her promise. She sent a note saying she had managed to queue-jump a slot for Clara with the doctor who had prescribed her coffee, despite a waiting list longer than the Maginot Line. The appointment would be at the Charité with a man called Professor Max de Crinis.

The Charité, Berlin's main hospital, was a great Gothic hulk of blood-red brick, whose arched windows and high concentration of research staff lent it the academic air of a dismal boarding school. The hospital had been established a few centuries earlier when plague was ravaging Berlin, and now that a different plague reigned in the capital, the Charité was busier than ever. Berliners were sick more often, their skin grey through lack of nutrients and their nerves shot, so an increasing stream of depression, alcoholism and anxiety trudged its way through the Charité's doors, alongside the routine chest pains and heart attacks.

The campus was divided into gloomy cloisters and quads that formed cubes of light and shade like some architectural chessboard. Clara walked through the main courtyard, passing chrome and white-tiled laboratories through whose murky windows she glimpsed weighing scales, blood pressure monitors, surgical instruments and stands with test tubes fixed in their jaws. Strange that this machinery of health should induce such a frisson of alarm. Maybe, for her, it went back to childhood. The smell of disinfectant evoked a lurching memory of the operating table in the local cottage hospital where she had had her tonsils out aged five and she was seized by a panicky urge to escape as fast as she could.

Under an arch from which a brace of Nazi banners hung rippling and flaming in the breeze, she turned left along a walk fenced by high railings to the block where Professor de Crinis had his office. To her surprise, the brass plaque on the door identified him as not merely a doctor but a psychiatrist, and no simple psychiatrist, but Director of Psychiatry, no less.

An assistant led her to the Professor's consulting room and left her alone. The place was furnished to resemble a comfortable bourgeois drawing room, carpeted and wood panelled and decorated with a couple of glossy pot plants. The shelves featured a row of academic textbooks and a number of photographs of a man in his forties wearing SS dress uniform with a saturnine complexion and a wing of hair slicked over one temple. His eyebrows arched like the gables of a Bavarian inn over a pair of coal-black eyes. Moments later the same man, now dressed in a tweed suit and bow tie, entered, rubbing his hands. He strolled over to his desk and consulted a diary with leisurely ease before greeting her.

215

'Fräulein Vine,' he announced with lordly confidence, as though the question of her identity had somehow been in doubt. He gestured to a buffed leather consulting bench. 'If you please.'

Clara settled herself onto the bench and he donned a pair of pince-nez that were hanging around his neck from a cord.

'Thank you for seeing me. I'm sure you must be very busy.'

'My pleasure,' he said, although his face told a different story. 'Lie back, please.'

Clara lay, trying not to flinch as the doctor bent over her with an astringent wash of cologne and his long, bony fingers prodded at her recumbent form. Behind the spectacles, deep-set eyes squinted in concentration and the lips were compressed tightly, as if reluctant to countenance the expenditure of any unnecessary words.

'If you would just relax.'

That was asking a lot in close proximity to Professor de Crinis. Clara's stomach muscles knotted reflexively and her skin prickled. She wondered how long it would be before she could request the free coffee and escape.

'It's not unusual to have abdominal problems at a time of war.'

As if in confirmation a portrait of the Führer, looking constipated, hung on the opposite wall.

'Digestive issues are extremely common in females suffering from generalized anxiety.'

Clara propped herself up on one elbow.

'I'm sorry for the confusion, but I don't have generalized anxiety. I'm not sure where you got that idea.'

De Crinis frowned and removed his spectacles.

'I was led to understand you were suffering from sleeping problems.'

'Isn't everyone? With the bombing raids?'

'Not necessarily. Insomnia is more likely to signal another kind of condition. Underlying stress. Some feeling of guilt or worry.'

Clara felt a warning pulse of alarm. This man was a top doctor, a leading authority, and as an SS member almost certainly familiar with the senior figures of the regime. Was it possible that he was obliged to report on patients suffering from secret stress? And if he did, would the notes he compiled end up in the safe that Reinhard Heydrich called his 'medicine cabinet', full of files of secret information about VIPs? Almost as soon as these thoughts went through her head she quelled them. They were wild suppositions. Simple paranoia. Just another product of her sleepless mind.

'Well, I'm not stressed. And I have no worries at all. At least, no more than anyone in wartime.'

'Are you not concerned for the fate of the Fatherland?'

'How could I be? With the Führer at the helm?'

De Crinis observed her silently for a moment, as though she were a laboratory animal about to receive a reward or an electric shock within its cage of glass. Then pulled over a leather swivel chair and sat a few feet from her, crossing his stork-like legs.

'I wonder. Have you ever considered undergoing psychotherapy?'

Clara summoned her actress smile. It was a soft and girlish

thing, a composite of all the light-hearted, insouciant parts she had ever played, and it conveyed a blithe disregard for the gloomier side of life.

'Do you know, I've always thought my job is a form of psychotherapy. We actresses have to put ourselves in other people's minds, you see, and when you inhabit different roles it makes you think about what motivates people to act the way they do.'

'Interesting.' De Crinis braced a pencil tightly between his fingers, as though hc might snap it, like a neck. 'I observe this response quite often. Many of my patients convince themselves that they hold the key to their own psyches. As if decades of professional training count for nothing. As if, forgive me, I might walk into the Ufa studios and take over from Emil Jannings this time next week.'

The tight lips wrestled themselves into a smile.

'Unfortunately, when the brain hides its truth, we need experts to seek it out.'

Clara had a vision of the doctor's bony fingers inside her head, probing the hidden wounds of her psyche. Parting the dark drapes of her mind for a glimpse of what lay within. She shrugged her shoulders helplessly.

'I can see I've said the wrong thing, Herr Professor. You must forgive me. I didn't mean any offence.'

'None taken.'

'I apologize if . . .'

'No need to apologize, my dear Fräulein.' The restless fingers were constantly busy, tapping a lip, plucking an ear, taming the sprouting hairs of an eyebrow. 'As far as psychotherapy goes, I understand your hesitation. Many people believe National Socialists should disapprove of psychotherapy – or view it as a Jewish conspiracy – but in fact nothing could be further from the truth. Analysing the workings of the mind is a science close to our hearts. After all, Reich Marshal Goering's own cousin, Mathias, runs the Goering Institute. Several of my staff are there at the moment, working on how we can contribute to the war effort. I would go so far as to say that psychological warfare does not just have the blessing of the regime, but it will be one of our most potent weapons.'

De Crinis rose and went to the shelves and returned with a finely worked wooden box from which he pulled two identical glass jars and stood them on his desk, side by side. It took a second for Clara to recognize what they contained and when she did, she had to suppress the gust of nausea that rose within her. In each quart of greenish viscous liquid a disembodied human brain hung suspended, a creamy walnut of matching hemispheres, their surfaces a furled maze of folds and convolutions. Whereas the empty chambers of a skull were redolent of death, these naked brains spoke of violation and dismemberment. Freed of their bony craniums they were at once vulnerable and sinister, and as de Crinis bent over them she could not help but be reminded of the hunched and staring figure of Doktor Caligari that she had seen on Joseph Goebbels' private cinema screen.

Each jar bore a paper label.

Male, 32 years, Nordic
Female, 24 years, Untermensch

'What an enigma the brain is.'

Picking up each jar alternately, de Crinis held them to the light, regarding them tenderly.

'Its coils are the fingerprint of the soul. Its cortex is a route map of the mind. Its minute electrical impulses govern our actions, emotions, apprehensions, affections. Entire regions are devoted to the sensations of pleasure, terror, excitement and what sentimentalists like to call "love". And yet what, apart from size, is the difference between this one that belonged to a Jewish female and that to a Nordic male? Can we tell if the owner was feeble-minded, or deranged, or a life unworthy of life? If they were human or subhuman? What can the naked eye tell from these brains about the people who once used them?'

'Nothing,' said Clara, trying not to look.

'Precisely.' The doctor replaced the brains with satisfaction, and Clara saw she had given the correct answer.

'I keep these specimens to remind myself that without psychotherapy, the brain is a closed book. It is the most complex machine in the universe, yet without the ability to unlock it, what is it? A slab of silence in a jar.'

He gave a vague wave at the tomes on the shelves behind him.

'I have dedicated my career to the understanding of the human mind. I've written extensively on it. And as it happens one of my personal interests is the psychological traits of Aryans. Aryan females in particular.'

His eyes were on her again, raking her soul. Clara braced herself and met his gaze steadily.

'In my experience Aryan females show a generally robust response to environmental stress. They have none of the nervous hysteria of other races. Yet you come to me complaining that bombing raids have caused you insomnia.'

She could not stop herself. She flinched.

'What is it? Have I touched a nerve?'

'Not at all.'

'We know that Aryan females are resilient in the face of environmental stress, but Fräulein Clara Vine cannot sleep at night. So what do we deduce from that?'

What did those fathomless eyes perceive? Could they see her Jewish blood? How deep was the perceptive power of his psychological training?

'We deduce that in your case something else is robbing you of sleep, and I suggest it is a buried guilt or shame or terror. Some powerful emotion that your own mind is attempting to hide from you. Some fear, perhaps, that is hidden even to yourself.'

De Crinis paused, and Clara realized instinctively that silence was one of his most effective weapons. He was not a man to make conversation just to cover an awkward pause. Pauses were where he did his work. Silence was eloquent. He was prepared to wait for her to offer something, anything, to break the silence.

'If it's hidden to myself, you couldn't expect me to know about it.'

'A good answer. Yet there *is* something.'

He waited, motionless as a hawk above hidden prey, then suddenly leaned closer, so near that she was able to observe the sharp indigo splinters in his iris, and said, 'What do you fear most?'

'The thing I feared most has already happened.'

'Then it is worse for you.'

'Why?'

'A person without fear is dangerous.'

The slam of a door in the outer office appeared to shatter his focus. He sprang up, checking his watch.

'But as you correctly observed earlier, Fräulein Vine, I'm a busy man. A fresh area of responsibility has recently been allotted to me and while it's always glorious to serve the Reich, it means I have to curtail some of my more interesting investigations. I'm not here to compel you to talk. If you don't want to talk, we'll have to seek other means.'

'Means? What means?'

Observing her alarm, he left a beat then gave a smile that seemed to surface from some deep crevasse in his soul.

'Medical means, my dear. What did you think I meant? Give me your hand.'

He reached for her wrist and held it.

'The pulse is fast. If it helps you, I can share a little secret. Just between you and me, the Führer is not immune to sleep problems himself. I know, it's distressing to hear, but we have discovered the ideal solution. A secret recipe. The Führer has an injection of it almost every day.'

Clara flinched. Hitler's arms were said to resemble pin cushions from the frequency of the jabs he received.

De Crinis went to a tray beside his desk, on which rested a number of surgical instruments. He began unfolding several small gold-foiled packages, dissolving them in a jar of water and taking up a hypodermic syringe from a steel kidney dish. Clara watched in dread fascination as he filled the syringe with a colourless solution, squeezed until a single tear welled at the tip, squinted at it and flicked the end.

'Just roll up that sleeve.'

'I'd rather not.'

'I assure you this is the thing. You'll feel like you're eighteen again. Even on a few hours' sleep you'll be fresh as an alpine flower.'

De Crinis grasped her sleeve and rolled it upwards, then rubbed a thumb across the bulging blue lattice of veins in the crook of her elbow.

'What exactly is in it?'

'This?' A theatrical pause. 'This, mein Fräulein, is gold dust. More than that, it's going to win us the war.'

'How on earth would it do that?'

'They're giving it to the soldiers in France. A single dose allows a tank driver to keep going all night. A soldier can stay marching for almost twenty-four hours without a break. The company that makes it, Temmler Werke, deserves an Iron Cross. The troops even have a name for it. They call it *Panzerschokolade.*'

Tank chocolate? Suddenly the prospect of what de Crinis might be about to inject in her veins made Clara jerk back in alarm just as the needle was about to penetrate her skin. The doctor remained very still, needle poised, voice deathly quiet.

'I have injected little children who show more courage.'

223

'I'm sorry, but I have a terrible fear of injections. I always have. Ever since I was very young.'

He tapped the syringe.

'Come. You want to be cured, don't you? It is important that we overcome mental barriers, especially those erected in childhood.'

He tightened his hold on her arm, aiming the needle for her vein. Absurdly, Clara's heart began to thud wildly and she pulled sharply away.

'Please don't! I'll probably faint.'

De Crinis sighed and replaced the syringe. For a second he looked supremely nettled, then he strode across the room and reached up to a cabinet.

'In that case, I can provide you with something very similar in tablet form. You've come just in time. The army has ordered three and a half million of these tablets. They're clearing out supplies as fast as the laboratories can make it. Soon no civilian anywhere will be able to get hold of this.'

He opened a glass door and removed a blue and red striped tube of tablets whose label bore the name *Pervitin*.

Advertisements for Pervitin were everywhere just then. On the U-Bahn, on the big advertising hoardings and in every glossy magazine, the drug was promoted to office workers and housewives alike as the ultimate pick-me-up. *Just one pill keeps you alert for hours. Self-confidence increases and doubts disappear.*

'You're telling me Pervitin is going to win the war?'

'Mark my words.'

She sat up quickly, accepted the tube of tablets and collected her jacket.

'How fascinating, Herr Professor. Thank you so much. And if you don't mind, there is one other thing. The fatigue does cause a problem with my acting in the mornings and I know that coffee would help. Real coffee, that is. I can't get hold of any, of course, but I understand that in special cases it can be made available. Just for medical reasons ...'

She was crossing the quad towards the front gate when she heard her name called and she was so anxious to leave that she almost didn't turn. When she did, it took a second before she recognized the scrawny man in a white coat and stethoscope as Franz Engel, her neighbour, who worked in the children's section of the Charité. War seemed to have washed all the colour from him, leaving his skin parchment and his eyes pale as rain.

'Clara?' His voice contained all the doctorly concern that the psychiatrist had so notably lacked. 'What brings you here?'

'I've just had a consultation with Professor de Crinis.'

'What circles you move in. I hope it's nothing serious?'

'Just a little insomnia.'

'Are you sure you're all right?'

'Of course! I didn't actually *want* to see a doctor. Someone thought they were doing me a favour.'

'I imagine the kind of favour that gets you an appointment with Max de Crinis is very difficult to refuse. But, in other ways ...'

Engel looked at her the way a doctor should look, at once tender and professionally probing, scanning the jumping pulse in her neck and the signs of fatigue around her eyes. He hesitated for a moment, as though debating with himself whether to go ahead, then he said, 'I have to tell you, there have been nights I heard you cry, and thought to come and comfort you, but I restrained myself.'

At his words a rush of misery came upon Clara and it was all she could do to prevent the tears swimming in her eyes. She could bear anything but sympathy. She had resisted the probing of Professor de Crinis with ease but the chance to confide her heartbreak to this kindly man was almost irresistible. It took all her will-power to restrain herself.

'Thank you, dear Franz, but please don't worry about me. Everyone cries in wartime, don't they?'

'That's true.' He plunged his hands into the pockets of his coat. 'So what did de Crinis recommend?'

'He tried to give me an injection and I was terrified so he gave me tablets instead.'

'What's in them, do you know?'

'Only Pervitin.'

'Only Pervitin! I hope you didn't touch it. There's nothing less likely to solve insomnia. If you take it you won't sleep a wink.'

'It's very popular, though. Isn't it?'

'Of course. It's a methamphetamine. Makes you feel invincible. Euphoric. It induces a heightened state of alert and increases self-confidence, concentration and the willingness to take risks.'

'So that's why the Wehrmacht like it. They're giving it to the army apparently.'

'God help us all then. We've done observations of patients who take it. It may work in the short term, but in the long term it makes you agitated and aggressive. If our troops are taking it, then I fear for them. Ultimately it brings on psychosis, heart failure and hallucinations. Dreadful stuff.' Engel ran a hand through his hair so that the sparse strands stood up rakishly then he looked away.

'Though if things go on like this for much longer, I might turn to Pervitin myself.'

'Is something wrong?'

'Just work. I'm drowning in it. I have a new job.'

'You're not leaving the Charité, surely?'

'No, but I've had a commission from on high. As a matter of fact it concerns the man you just saw. Professor Max de Crinis.'

'What is it?'

Engel's face was working with some suppressed emotion. He glanced around the quad, with its hundred overlooking windows, and bent closer. No one chatted in public places any more. Not unless they were discussing the performance of Union Berlin football club or what they thought of the latest war movie and even then there was the ever-present worry that the most desultory conversation might be mistaken for some kind of code.

'We can't talk here. Come with me.'

He led her through an arch, opened a door and turned sharply into a corridor lined with green-flecked linoleum and flanked by steel-framed doors. Through one of these they entered a laboratory, or some kind of teaching room, where serried ranks of tables were set out with microscopes, slides, test-tube ranks, Petri dishes and neatly arranged instruments.

Engel positioned himself at a table and bent over one of the microscopes, motioning for Clara to do the same, as though they were two medics, dissecting the origins of some dangerous and virulent pathogen.

'I'm not sure how much you know about him, but de Crinis is a very important man. An *éminence grise*. He's probably the biggest name in German psychiatric medicine today and more to the point he has impeccable government contacts. If he asks for your help, you don't refuse.'

'What does he want with you? Psychiatry isn't your specialism, is it?'

'No, but children are.' Engel hesitated. 'Ever heard of the Lebensborn?'

'A little.' In fact, Clara knew all too much. The Lebensborn was one of Himmler's organizations, a group of homes where unmarried mothers could give birth and surrender their babies to the Reich. Clara had visited one of these places once and the memory still haunted her.

'The Lebensborn has a new venture. It's to do with orphans of war. I've been commissioned to examine them. I have no choice.'

'You don't mind looking after sick children, surely.'

'No. Only these children aren't sick. And they're not even Germans – at least, not yet.'

'I don't understand.'

'They're from Poland. The SS rounded them up and the

Lebensborn brought them to Berlin. They want us doctors to determine if they're fit to be Germanized.'

'Germanized? You mean they're going to be turned into Germans?'

'Precisely.'

'Are their parents actually dead?'

A lift of the narrow shoulder blades.

'Who knows? It's not what the kids say, though we're not supposed to ask them any questions. Our orders are just to run the medical tests and the racial examination.'

'What do you examine? Whether they have Aryan features?'

'Oh, they have those of course. Blond hair, blue eyes, high brows. That was what got them here in the first place. But there are a host of other characteristics they need. We have a fresh batch brought here every day for observation.'

His gaze was still fixed on the microscope in front of him, his long nervous fingers restlessly twiddling the dial.

'We've been given a checklist of sixty-seven qualifications. History of illnesses, state of the teeth and vision, height and weight, precise eye and hair colour. We measure the seams in their skull and the shape of their calves. Their heart rate, earwax, fingerprints and blood group. We take full facial and frontal photographs to rule out Slavic traits. And they have to pass every single one of these tests.'

'What happens if they fail?'

At last he glanced sideways at her, his eyes behind their horn-rimmed spectacles impenetrable.

'That's the very question I've been asking myself. And the fact is, I just don't know.'

'Can you not enquire?'

He hesitated. Nervous tension was coming off him in waves.

'My colleague did. He was arrested last week for "unprofessional conduct". We've not been able to discover where he's being held. Another man – a distinguished paediatrician in my department – made a formal enquiry. The next day he was told he's being reassigned for the war effort and should report to the German weapons and munitions factory in Borsigwalde to make shells. The fellow's fifty-seven, for Christ's sake. My good friend Ernst Haber also put in a request for more information. Yesterday he was summoned for Gestapo interrogation and chose to jump out of a window instead.'

'My God, Franz.'

Clara paused, to steady herself.

'They really don't want people finding out.'

'Certainly seems so.'

'There must be some way. Someone has to ask questions.'

Engel stiffened, as though bracing something physical inside. It was the internal uniform that everyone in Germany wore, the straitjacket that kept the questions in and the knowledge out.

'Do they? There's nothing more dangerous than questions, Clara. Questions kill people. Take the advice of a doctor. Questions are dangerous for the health.'

'Wait a minute. Do you have any paper?'

Wordlessly he withdrew a prescription pad from his top pocket and Clara took it, wrote an address and pressed it into his hand.

'Read this. Remember it. Then destroy it. It's the address of a friend of mine, an American journalist. Meet her, and tell her what you've just told me. About the job you've been asked to do. About Max de Crinis and what has happened to your colleagues. If you can't ask questions, Mary can. Questions are what she lives by.'

Chapter Sixteen

The Ministry of Propaganda at the heart of Berlin was not the kind of place anyone dropped by for a casual chat. It may have been decked out in the finest walnut and oak veneer with sleek minimalist pillars of fawn stone and shimmering marble floors. The throne room and blue gallery of the old Leopold Palace may have been renovated and their original frescoes restored at great public expense, but no amount of redecoration could disguise the sullen menace that hung in its marble corridors, nor the batteries of anti-aircraft guns that festooned the government blocks outside. It was not a popular workplace. Joseph Goebbels believed in keeping his staff in a state of perpetual alertness, and to this end had recently reassigned some of his senior men to local factories where they were obliged to sign on as labourers in order to refresh their contact with the masses. As a result the Ministry had a high staff turnover and trouble hanging on to some of the more talented workers, as was evident to Clara when she arrived at five minutes to four o'clock that afternoon.

Inside his glass booth, a guard was manning the reception desk. He had cauliflower ears and the face of a bulldog stung by a wasp.

He stabbed a telephone and dialled, then grunted.

'The Minister's busy. You can wait outside his office.'

A functionary materialized and escorted her through the echoing hall, hung with heavy wrought-iron lamps. Clara marvelled at the fact that Mary Harker came to this place every day to hear Goebbels rage against the international liars and counterfeiters of the foreign press, and dispense his minute daily ration of genuine news. But Mary was an accredited foreign correspondent and an American, protected by her nationality and the Nazis' desire to keep the United States out of the war, and need never feel the German journalists' shudder of fear. The horror that they might ask the wrong question or file the wrong report.

'He'll be along shortly. Stay here.'

Clara stood in the corridor. A secretary clipped past, laden with files. In the distance a telephone rang. On a notice board instructions had been pinned concerning a couple of new crimes that had just been announced. There was a new criminal type called the *Wehrkraftzersetzer*, the citizen who undermined fighting morale, and another called the Enemy At Home, both of whom merited the death penalty. Harsher punishments had been introduced for women who engaged in sex with prisoners of war, deemed harmful to German womanhood and a betrayal of the Home Front. To distract herself, Clara picked up a paper, though it was too much to expect that she would find more cheerful news inside.

The *Völkischer Beobachter*, the Nazi Party paper, had more crime and punishment than a whole Russian novel and that week's edition was no exception. It being wartime, it carried a full page of death notices too. *In a hero's death for Führer, Volk and Vaterland my only son Rolf died in battle. In proud grief for our son Helmut who died for our beloved Führer.* Yet alongside battle casualties, there were plenty of other kinds of death to read about. One incident in particular was dominating that day's page three. A local prostitute, Ilsa Helton, had been found stabbed in the eastern suburb of Friedrichsfelde. Dead prostitutes did not generally make headlines, but under the standfirst *S-Bahn Attacker Kills?* the report revealed that police were exploring the connection between the assault on the woman and her proximity to the railway station. A man had been sighted near the tracks, with short black hair parted on the left and a pasty complexion. There was a photograph of the corpse. Looking at its raddled face, beaky nose and dull eyes, half hidden by strands of dyed blonde hair, Clara shuddered. The man on the train that night. The one who had subsequently accosted her in Potsdamer Strasse. It must be the same one. She knew for certain now that she had had a lucky escape.

Joseph Goebbels appeared, surrounded by a flea cloud of assistants and hangers-on. Signalling curtly for them to leave he led the way into his office and slammed the door.

'I'm surrounded by imbeciles,' he commented, tossing the files onto his desk. 'Dietrich. Not a brain in his head.'

From this Clara surmised that Goebbels had returned from the afternoon press conference, generally conducted by Otto Dietrich, the Reich Press Chief.

'He told me he has all his good ideas in the bath. I said in that case he needs to take a few more baths.'

Goebbels' office was large and well furnished. On the wall hung his latest acquisition – a Renoir head of a young girl that had recently decorated a Jewish-owned villa in Paris. There was a long mahogany desk containing more telephones than you would find in an entire apartment block, some of them connected directly to the Reich Chancellery, others to his home and country villa. Clara had heard there were microphones concealed in the lamps as well as a specially constructed Siemens switchboard with which Goebbels could plug into any conversation taking place anywhere in the building. She wondered if he knew about Schellenberg's plan to install machine guns inside his desk to spray unwanted visitors with bullets. If Goebbels hadn't heard of the idea yet, he surely would. He would probably do precisely the same and claim the copyright on it.

Without looking up he said, 'At least you're back promptly. How's that godson?'

'Good, thank you for asking.'

Their day at the races had ended happily, with Erich winning ten Reichsmarks and their dispute over his mother tacitly smoothed, if not forgotten.

'He's still at school, isn't he? A fine student with a promising future, I hear.'

She nodded. Goebbels couldn't make it any clearer.

'Let's hope that remains the case.'

He crossed his spindly legs, revealing Italian shoes polished like little mirrors, almost immaculate enough to obscure the fact that one was built up by several inches to match the other.

'Anyhow. More important matters. What did you make of Reuber?'

Clara gripped the arms of the leather chair, summoning a self-possession she did not feel.

'From everything I can see he's a loyal citizen if not a terrifically political one. The only kind of French resistance he was interested in was that offered by the ladies of the Folies-Bergère. And I shouldn't think he met much resistance there.'

A snuffle of agreement.

'When I got him drunk, I made some slighting remarks about the Führer – quite necessary, I'm sure you understand, Herr Doktor – but Reuber would only talk about his loyalty to Germany. He wants to serve the Fatherland to the best of his ability. He got quite sentimental.'

'So he's loyal?'

'Utterly loyal to his country. He feels deeply about it.'

'And did you . . .?'

Lascivious interest glimmered in Goebbels' eyes.

'As I said, Reuber was drunk, and you know what men are like when they've had one too many schnapps. His evening on the stage was the only performance he was going to be able to manage that night.'

Goebbels tapped his fingers on the desk.

'It's just as I thought. Schellenberg's neurotic, he sees spies everywhere. I've always kept a close eye on members of my Chamber of Culture. There's not much that escapes my gaze.'

He rose and crossed to a tall window disfigured by screeds of bombproof wire mesh. If he craned his neck he could glimpse the corner of the new Reich Chancellery, Hitler's vast behemoth that now occupied the whole of Voss Strasse. Just yards away was von Ribbentrop's Foreign Ministry and a few goosesteps down the street lay the monstrous bulk of Goering's Air Ministry. The inner circle of the Nazi regime was knit as tightly as a fist and as if these buildings were not physically close enough, all were linked below pavement level by a spider's web of tunnels and escape routes. Berlin's underground was porous with basements, shelters and torture cells, like a dark twin to the ceaseless architectural construction rising above.

But Goebbels was not thinking of this. A dyspeptic frown darkened his brow.

'I'm reassured by what you've found on Reuber but, unfortunately, this is not the end of the matter. Schellenberg has asked to see you personally.'

Shock ran through her like a shaft of ice and Clara had to fight to keep her composure. Had Goebbels not believed her account?

'Can I ask why? Isn't it enough that I give my assurance Hans Reuber is not a spy?'

'It is for me.'

She tried harder. 'Surely Herr Schellenberg would take the assurance of a minister of your stature? I mean, he wouldn't doubt the word of a senior minister?'

'Of course he wouldn't. He wouldn't dare. It's nothing to do with that. It's something else.'

'But what could Herr Schellenberg possibly want from me?' Clara tried, and failed, to keep the note of panic from her voice until suddenly she realized there was no need. Her reaction was utterly natural. Panic was the proper response to an audience with a man like Walter Schellenberg, the man who, above all others in the Reich, was trained to instil terror into the people brought before him.

'Don't ask me. I was too busy to discuss it.'

Plainly Schellenberg had refused to provide any further detail. Clara thought of Irene's comment the other day. *Walter never gets it wrong. He doesn't even need to hear them talking. He can smell a spy, he says.* Masquerading in front of Germany's pre-eminent spymaster, a professional at seeing through the strategies of spies, who could tell a lie at a hundred paces, was impossible. She could never pull it off.

'Is it really necessary? Just when I am being considered for this new film? Couldn't you explain?'

'Believe me, I'm not happy about it, either. I had half a mind to refuse him outright. Members of the Chamber of Culture are *my* domain, and they serve the Reich just as much as any member of the Wehrmacht.'

Goebbels was fighting his own territorial wars, Clara recognized. His irritation at this invasion of his personal empire was countered by the fact that Schellenberg was under Himmler's control and would thus be granted whatsoever he wished. For a moment, he remained surveying her with a kind of puzzlement, before striding to the door and opening it.

'I don't know why, but for some reason Schellenberg is

particularly interested in you. He's not to be thwarted. He's even arranged your transport.'

'To where?'

'Lisbon.'

'Lisbon?'

'Do you need an atlas, woman? It's the capital of Portugal. I assume you've heard of it. He's there on some business and he wants to see you without delay. It must be important because he's arranged for Hanna Reitsch to take you with her. She's expecting you at Tempelhof tomorrow morning.'

Back in the apartment Clara made toast and sank into her red velvet armchair, the words of Joseph Goebbels still ringing in her ears. *For some reason Schellenberg is particularly interested in you.* There could be nothing more alarming than that. Yet she attempted to console herself with the thought that Goebbels had seemed irritated, rather than suspicious, about the spy chief's request. Surely if she had been found out, she would have been sitting in Prinz-Albrecht-Strasse with a body full of broken bones, rather than being flown to Lisbon in relative comfort by the Führer's very own pilot. Or might it be that Schellenberg merely had suspicions of her activities rather than hard proof? Perhaps he wanted the pleasure of breaking her himself.

To distract herself, she took a screwdriver from its place in the drawer and rolled back the Turkish rug that covered the far end of her sitting room. The floorboards were old and worn in places and a couple of them bore especially long cracks, so it was understandable that she should have covered them. One floorboard, two from the wall, must have had a heavy jar or bronze weight dropped on it at some time, because it was cratered and badly splintered at the join. This one she now crouched over and unscrewed, retrieving from the dusty compartment beneath it the weathered cardboard rat poison box that contained her shortwave radio set.

That night there was no Mozart or Beethoven blasting from Franz Engel's apartment to drown out her transgression but she calculated that if she kept the sound very low, crouching close to the set, she would be safe. Frau Ritter, the woman who rented the apartment directly beneath her own, was stooped with fatigue and always complaining of the exhausting nature of her two small boys. Surely she must sleep like the dead.

Switching on the set, Clara turned the dial until the patrician tones of the BBC announcer resonated through the air. Compared to Goebbels' pronouncements, with their edge of hysterical frenzy, BBC voices were sombre, funereal even, tonight more than ever as the announcer told Europe what it was waiting with bated breath to hear. The Foreign Secretary Lord Halifax had broadcast from London rejecting the Führer's offer of peace. Hitler had announced that German troops of all arms now stood ready for the attack on Britain. The date of the invasion would be decided by the Führer alone.

The doorbell rang.

A shudder ran through Clara, transfixing her momentarily, and she dialled the volume to zero. What was she thinking of, using her set without Franz Engel's music as camouflage?

She had been far too complacent. Too trusting of the sour-faced Frau Ritter. Listening to a foreign station meant immediate arrest and if this was the police, then they would not hesitate to rip up the floorboards for further evidence of misdemeanours. She sat still as a hare, barely daring to blink. Half a minute passed until the doorbell rang again and adrenalin galvanized her to lift the set very softly and restore it to its hiding place, silently replacing the floorboard and tightening the screws. Then, using a small brush she kept for the purpose, she dusted them with a veneer of soot from the stove to hide any signs of recent disturbance. After all this, she finally opened the door.

The bulb in the hall was broken, but a slice of light from her apartment illuminated a girl of around fourteen. That in itself was not a surprise. Children turned up constantly at the door, rattling their collection tins, with a tray of badges or lapel pins for one of the Nazi charities. But never at this time of night.

'Fräulein Vine?'

'That's me.'

'Can I talk to you?'

In the dimness Clara made out that girl was about five foot tall, with a frank expression, milk-white hair and clear, wide-set eyes. She was wearing some kind of uniform but did not give the familiar Hitler salute, as a Jugend collector would, nor did she seem to have any collecting tin with her. She looked too young to be a fan, and nowhere near old enough to be out at this time of night.

'What's this about?'

'If you let me in, I'll tell you.'

'It's rather late. I'm afraid I was just off to bed.'

The girl didn't budge. She stood stolidly, as though she was prepared to remain outside Clara's door all night if necessary.

'Is this a collection?' said Clara, making for her bag.

'No.'

Automatically Clara scanned the hall, as though the answer to this child's presence would materialize behind her, but it was empty.

'Then . . . does anyone know you're here?'

'No.'

'I suppose you'd better come in.'

The girl stepped inside and looked curiously around. In the lamplight she was extraordinarily pretty, with the faintest blonde fuzz on her rosy cheeks like the skin of a sun-warmed peach. There was a fragility about her, and closer up it was clear that something about her was not quite right. She had slender legs, but one was thinner than the other — almost wasted — and the foot turned in. She seemed familiar, but Clara couldn't work out why.

The child settled herself in the armchair and looked around like a prospective buyer contemplating a rental. She carried nothing except a small satchel and her self-possession belonged to someone far older, though her face retained a childlike freshness, untainted by the hormonal ravages of adolescence.

'Would you like something to drink? Some water? Or coffee?'

'Water, please.'

Clara went into the kitchen. She had tipped the Pervitin in the bin, but she made a large pot of Melitta coffee that was no less delicious for being on prescription.

'What's your name?'

'Katerina Klimpel.'

Clara poured her a glass of water.

'You shouldn't be out alone at this time of night. Aren't your parents worried about you?'

'I don't have any parents. I'm an orphan.'

Of course. That was where she had seen the child before. At the NSV reception. She was the one whose face later appeared on a poster with Jenny Jugo. The one who had transfixed Clara with a particularly penetrating stare.

'Papi died in December. Mutti died when I was born.'

'I'm sorry.'

'That's all right. I don't need a mother. I miss Papi all the time but I don't even remember Mutti.'

Although she spoke quite matter-of-factly, the child could not have known how this remark lodged like a hook in Clara's heart. She knew that feeling so precisely. Sometimes she couldn't even recall her own mother's face – only an expression she had, of slight exasperation, and her voice, soft and low, lapsing into German at moments of humour or tenderness.

She came and sat opposite the girl and said, more gently, 'You were at that reception at the Hotel Eden, weren't you? Where do you live?'

'At the National Socialist Volkswohlfahrt home in Lichter-felde.'

'So why on earth are you here?'

'I thought you might know my sister. Sonja Klimpel. She's a singer.'

'I'm sorry.' Clara shook her head, bewildered. 'I don't think I do. What does she look like?'

'A lot like you. Very pretty.'

Clara looked in perplexity at the girl before her, sipping her water as delicately as a gin and tonic.

'Does she work at Babelsberg?'

'No. Nightclubs mostly, theatres sometimes. She was in *Sonnenschein für Alle* at the Admiralspalast.' *Sunshine for All* was a big hit of the previous year. 'And she sings at the Café Casanova.'

'If you have a sister, why are you in the orphanage? Could she not look after you?'

Clara's enquiry was mild but the riposte was sharp.

'Why on earth should she? She's extremely busy. She does have a career, you know.'

In the harshness of that protestation, Clara heard the echo of the older sister's voice.

'Besides, she isn't even my whole sister. My mother was Papi's second wife. I think that was why Sonja ... she ...'

The girl looked down at her neat brown shoes, to disguise the fact that her eyes were swimming. She sniffed slightly and Clara reached a hand towards her, uncertain how to proceed.

'I don't know Sonja, but perhaps you'd like to introduce me?'

'No. That is, I'd like to, but I can't. That's the whole point. She's gone missing. I haven't seen her for two months.'

'That's not so long. When people are busy.'

'She said she would only be gone two weeks.'

'Where did she go?'

'I don't know. Abroad, I think. That's what Bettina said.'

'Who's Bettina?'

'She shares an apartment with Sonja. 85, Fischerstrasse, top floor.'

'And is Bettina a singer too?'

Katerina frowned.

'I think. They met at the Casanova. Bettina has a flexible career, Sonja says. She turns her hand to anything.'

'Did Bettina have any idea where Sonja went exactly?'

'She just said it was work and Sonja would be back.'

'Things do get complicated with international travel. Now there's a war on.'

'If that was the case she could have written.'

The girl had a peculiar directness, as though she would say whatever was in her head without censorship or fear of the consequences. That kind of attitude was dangerous.

'If you're worried about your sister, you need to tell the authorities.' Clara spoke gently, but she needed to point this out. 'Your teachers will help you. Or your BDM leader.'

'I would. At least I would if I thought they would be able to do anything.'

'I'm sure they'd be able to do far more than me. I don't really know why you thought I might be able to help.'

'Because of this.'

Katerina reached into the satchel and drew out an orange leather wallet.

'When I went to Fischerstrasse, Bettina gave me Sonja's wallet. It had some money in it and Bettina thought I should have it. But I also found this.'

She pulled out a piece of paper and thrust it under Clara's nose, like someone requesting an autograph, yet in the same instant Clara saw that her autograph was already there. Her own looping signature, the 'C' curled protectively around the letters that followed it, cupping them like a palm, and the 'V' reaching high and sloping to one side, like a wayward tendril. Beneath it her address.

Apartment 5, Winterfeldtstrasse 35, Berlin-Schöneberg

'That's how I knew where to find you.'

Clara took the paper and turned it over. It was a store receipt, and on the other side was a fancy, navy blue heading.

Jaeger's of Berlin. Established 1859.

She recognized it at once.

Jaeger's was a jeweller's shop in the passage off Friedrich-strasse, a short alley crowded with upmarket cigar boutiques and luggage emporiums. It was a prestigious place that had been patronized by the smartest people in Berlin for generations.

Slowly Clara said, 'I visited Jaeger's some time ago. I wanted them to fix something for me.'

She remembered the jeweller, a handsome young man, bent over his work table at the back of the shop, monocular in his eye, peering down at his work – a butterfly made of rubies perhaps, or a cluster of yellow opals in the shape of a daisy. She had watched him for a moment, back straight, perched forward in his chair, pressing and polishing, the lines on his face knitted closer as he squinted, holding a gem up to the light between finger and thumb. Although he was big as a bear, his touch was one of extreme precision, so deft and delicate that it might have been a real insect he held in his palm, or a living flower whose petals might be bruised by a rougher hand. In the window there was a dazzling display of his work – pearl necklaces and sapphire bracelets, emerald and ruby rings, chokers and brooches and earrings. And diamonds, winking in the inky velvet of their settings like a hundred eyes.

'Was it something precious?' asked Katerina.

'It was certainly valuable.'

Not to Clara, though. It was a swastika brooch set with diamonds. A gift from Joseph Goebbels in 1933. So much had happened since then – most of her life had happened.

'It was a diamond brooch. The clasp was broken. Herr Jaeger took my address. He was going to contact me when the job was done.'

'And did he?' demanded the girl.

'No.'

'Why didn't you ask? You must have wanted to know how the repair was coming on?'

'I called. There was no answer. And then . . .'

Then there was nothing Clara could care less about than a swastika brooch. Of all the things she had lost, a brooch was the least of them. It suited her, actually, that the jeweller had not called back. Yet now she was puzzled.

'So why did Sonja have your jeweller's receipt in her wallet?' The girl had the cool persistence of a Gestapo interrogator.

'I might just as well ask you.'

'I don't know.'

'Did your sister take my brooch?'

'I never saw her with it.'

Clara studied the receipt, turned it over then put it down on her lap decisively.

'Well, it's easily solved. I'll go to Jaeger's and ask.'

'I went already. The shop has closed down.'

'Oh. I see.'

All through Berlin there were shops boarded up, with signs in the window informing respected customers that sadly this establishment was now closed for business. Once the prohibitions on Jewish trade were enacted, most shops in Jewish ownership had been Aryanized, with new owners and employees, but others, like Jaeger's, remained unoccupied, turning a vacant face to the world, their windows empty as dead eyes.

'There must be somewhere else you can ask,' coaxed the girl.

'I'm not promising anything, but I'll see what I can find out.'

Katerina's eyes lit up. 'Can we start tomorrow?'

'I have a rather important meeting tomorrow. But I'll look into it very soon.'

The hope died, to be replaced by dull despondency. Katerina looked like a child accustomed to having her requests denied.

'I'm sorry. I understand how worried you must be.'

'No you don't!' The blue-green eyes sparked with passionate fire. 'You don't understand at all! Sonja's the only family I have left and the Brown Sisters say if she doesn't get in touch then I'll be placed for adoption. I'll have to go and live with a family who don't really want me. Or just want me to work in their kitchen or clean their house, or make up family numbers because they're not *kinderreich*. And I can't bear the thought of that.'

There was a sheen in her eyes, and through that invisible film Clara saw herself and every unmothered moment since the day Helene Vine's coffin lurched into the yawning earth. She saw every adult face of awkward sympathy, every silent meal, every instance of solitary uncertainty that came from losing the central figure of her life. A mother was the universe from whose substance one was formed, and the gap she left would never be filled.

Impulsively she reached forward and gave Katerina a hug. The girl felt like a fledgling, a tense armful of bones, holding herself stiff as though a stronger embrace might break her.

'It's not just me. It's you too, Fräulein Vine. You must want to find your brooch.'

'Of course I do.'

Though in truth, Clara thought after Katerina had disappeared back into the night, complete with a torch and injunctions to walk swiftly, there was nothing on earth that she wanted less.

Chapter Seventeen

How did one ever get used to sitting in a tiny metal tube, suspended high in the air, deafened by the propeller and feeling the plane tilt and bank as it rose into the dazzling glare of the sun? Even if that plane was a Junkers Ju 52, fitted out for executive travel with black leather seating and walnut finish in the passenger cabin. Minute ferns of frost were feathering the window as Clara pressed her head against the pane and looked down at the Reich spread out below. Beneath the stately flocks of clouds was a vast patchwork of fields interspersed with a scatter of houses, the clotted darkness of forests and the occasional glint of an ink-black lake.

Ahead of her, hair coiled in a strict bun and keen eyes fixed on the dials, sat the rigid figure of Hanna Reitsch, the most famous aviatrix in the Reich. Famed for her skill as a test pilot, Flugkapitän Reitsch was a star of Nazi propaganda, her petite form and unscrubbed prettiness making her both the darling of the Luftwaffe and a pin-up among the women of the Frauenschaft. More importantly, however, Hitler was said to adore her and the feeling was mutual. Perhaps more than any woman in Germany, the unmarried Hanna Reitsch venerated the man she had sworn to serve. Every inch of her four foot eleven frame was pledged to his duty.

Clara had found Hanna in the appointed spot in the lobby of Tempelhof, beneath the windows depicting Paris, Rome and London in twenty-foot-high stained glass. The windows had been installed just a few years ago when these capitals were romantic destinations and flying was a luxurious adventure for modern citizens of the Reich, rather than the daunting prospect it had now become. The figures in the window with their chic clothing and pigskin luggage were a poignant reminder of what travellers were supposed to look like.

'I'm pleased to meet you,' said Hanna warmly, her tiny stature belying the strength of her handshake. 'I enjoyed that film you made with Ernst Udet, *The Pilot's Wife*. Udet is a great inspiration to me. It was he who gave me the honorary title of Flugkapitän.'

'You worked for Ufa too, at one point, didn't you? On *Rivals of the Air*?'

'Ach. I was only the stunt pilot. I couldn't act to save my life.'

That was almost certainly true. There was a simplicity about Hanna Reitsch, a frank directness, that suggested that she would never be able to dissemble sufficiently for any kind of performance.

She led the way briskly across the tarmac to the spot where a medium-sized Luftwaffe plane was being readied for the journey.

'Did you always want to fly?' asked Clara.

Hanna's eyes lit up.

'Since I was a child. I remember seeing the storks sailing over the fields in Silesia where I grew up and thinking how magnificent it would be to do the same. And you know what I discovered when I started flying? It's even better! Especially, like this morning, when I get to fly one of the Führer's own fleet. Not in your honour, I'm sorry to say, but because there may be some senior men who need transport from Portugal. All the same, I hope you'll find it comfortable.'

In the luxury of Hitler's leather seat, it was for a while. Until the plane bucked in a bout of turbulence that forced Clara to shut her eyes in a bid to control the wave of nausea threatening to engulf her. Yet even once the turbulence had passed and the plane was progressing steadily through the calm air, the dread in the pit of her stomach remained. It had nothing to do with the flight and everything to do with what, or rather who, awaited her in Lisbon. Walter Schellenberg.

During her time in Berlin Clara had encountered several of the most senior men in the Nazi regime. Goebbels she had met many times and Goering a few. Himmler had instructed her on his approach to breeding superior children and eliminating the weaker elements of the race. She had even been in the same room as Hitler himself. But nothing frightened her so much as the prospect of meeting the Reich's chief spymaster face to face.

Yet again she ran through the sparse selection of facts she knew about Schellenberg. He was the son of a piano maker from Saarbrücken, far more cultured and polished than his peers. He spoke several languages. He had studied law at the University of Bonn and was all set for a career in advocacy when someone had suggested it would help his career to join the Gestapo. From there he had risen rapidly through the ranks until he caught the eye of Reinhard Heydrich, head of the Gestapo's security service, who saw in Schellenberg's savage intelligence and ruthless lawyer's brain the right qualities to head the counter-espionage outfit for the entire German Reich. How could Clara, whose training went no further than a few terms at the London School of Acting and Musical Theatre in Waterloo, and the private tuition of Leo Quinn, hope to match him when they came face to face?

She tried to remember everything Leo had told her about interrogation techniques and the best way to comport herself under them. *Stay calm. Don't react instinctively.* That had helped her before, when she was grilled by a mid-ranking policeman in Barminstrasse prison in Berlin, but Schellenberg was no mid-ranker. His entire expertise lay in detecting foreign agents. His fiancée Irene had been almost proud of it. *He's at the top of his game. He never gets it wrong.* Clara shuddered at the thought of that blandly handsome face, and its priestly encouragement of her closest confidences. In the airless Gestapo cells the light was left burning at all times and prisoners were forced to face it. New arrivals would be marched past the inmates before interrogation to see the results of the beatings, the faces that were no longer faces, to encourage co-operation when they were questioned themselves. The screams and whimpers. Eventually these thoughts were drowned out by Hans Reuber's comment, resounding in her frightened mind like a leaden bell, with the bleak consolation of some extreme unction. *Forty-eight hours. That's all we ask for. If you can hold out that long before you start spilling names then it gives other people a chance.*

They flew down past Lyons and Marseilles to Barcelona, the bare rocks of the Spanish mountains like a lunar landscape, and the purple spine of hills stretching away. Looking down at the dwellings far below, Clara thought of all the lives there, each with its own loves and loyalties and secrets, and felt a painful surge of longing for the simple domesticity of normal family, of cooking meals, preparing for work, reading to children at bedtime. That normality could have been hers, too.

Eventually she nodded off, only to wake when, with a metal groan and a grunt of brakes, the plane landed and jolted forward, a shimmer of heat on the horizon.

'I'm sorry,' shouted Hanna, as they bumped their way along the runway. 'We had to approach from a greater height than normal.'

Clara peered out of the porthole window to see a swathe of tarmac bathed in dazzling sunlight. In the distance airport workers were driving trucks and unloading luggage and in the foreground, to her amazement, was the outline of a British plane. Next to that was a Junkers 90 and a little further along a Pan American Airways clipper onto which stacks of matching luggage were being loaded. Seeing her astonishment, Hanna Reitsch laughed.

'There are five airlines operating out of this airport. Portugal's the only country in Europe where a Luftwaffe plane can land next to a British one. And Lisbon is the only city in Europe that offers flights to both Berlin and London. It's a special place all right.' She climbed out of the cockpit, removed her flying cap and handed Clara an envelope.

'I have to leave you now, Fräulein Vine. There is some Portuguese currency here for your expenses. I've been asked to tell you that Herr Schellenberg has been called to Spain so you won't need to report to the German Embassy until Thursday. The telephone number of the embassy is here.'

'Thursday?' Clara had imagined that the summons was urgent, yet now she was being handed a reprieve. 'That's two days away.'

'It's not a problem, is it? Most Luftwaffe officers love having a stopover in Lisbon. They all visit the casino. And they like to spend the day at the beach at Estoril. Or shopping.' Hanna Reitsch winked. 'Perfume for their girlfriends. Silk scarves. And for us ladies there's a splendid little glove shop on the Rua do Carmo, Luvaria Ulisses, where they make the best gloves in the world. I recommend it.'

Taking the address of the embassy, Clara was engulfed by relief. So she was to have a stay of execution for forty-eight hours. Suddenly the prospect of two days outside the Reich was indescribably exciting.

'I'm sure I'll find something to occupy me. And thank you for the flight.'

'Don't mention it. Enjoy your trip. Good luck finding somewhere to stay. They say every hotel room in this place is booked at least twice over.'

*

Lisbon was a world of colour. Puce and magenta bougainvillea tumbled from the balconies, writhing against the delphinium-blue tiles that decorated every façade, and violet clematis, dark as ink, splayed against whitewashed walls. Squat-roofed houses, humped like camels up the hillside, were lit from tan to rose red in the sun's transit. The cobbled streets were fringed with jacaranda trees frothing with purple blossom, debouching suddenly into little squares where pigeons decorated the bronze statues of obscure statesmen and old men sipped bitter coffee beneath the midday sun. Everything about the architecture, the gardens and the ravishing light was exuberant and sensual. After the darkness of Berlin, Lisbon was a city at ease with itself, revelling in the luxury of neutrality.

Yet Hanna Reitsch's comment was all too accurate. Not one of those stately buildings or picturesque dwellings, it seemed, contained a free room. Requests for accommodation met with bored faces or simply laughter. Every boarding house was jammed, every pension block booked, every hotel had a waiting list. In the broad, leafy Avenida da Liberdade, Clara went from hotel to hotel, her leather bag making a red dent in her shoulder, until at last one proprietor took pity on her. 'German, yes?' he asked, after the standard shake of the head. 'Try my brother Pedro on the Costa do Castelo. Up by the castle. I heard he had a room come vacant quite recently. Who knows? It could still be free.'

Up a series of winding alleys and narrow streets decorated by Arabic-tiled façades, Clara found a palm-shaded court-yard leading to a tiny pension with egg-yolk-yellow walls and pitted parquet, where Pedro, a man with a tortoise face and small black eyes blinking from its folds, ushered her up a malodorous stairway into a back room.

'Last vacancy,' he commented briefly. 'It's probably the only one in the city too. I wouldn't have it but the occupant left in a hurry. That happens all the time now. They get lucky, their feet don't touch the ground.' He shrugged towards the closet. 'This one went so fast they left their clothes. Probably got a ticket on a clipper. Went without paying, what's more. I'm selling those clothes for recompense.'

The room was almost bare and its casement window more appropriate to a prison cell, but a flood of lemony light washed in through the shutters and the bed sheets looked clean, if shabby. The only other furniture was a closet, a cane-bottomed armchair, a chest of drawers and a rickety table bearing a lamp with a shade of garish stained glass and a tray with a knife and fork on it. And a cracked basin in which Clara took a quick all-over wash with one of the bars of soap she had bought in Paris. As the closet was full, she threw her clothes on the bed before opening the shutters and peering out of the window. A splash of blood-red blossom spilled from a gap in the wall opposite and by dint of craning her head she could see the distant outline of São Jorge castle, a hulking silhouette in the glare of the sun. A blast of heat funnelled up from the street and she had a sudden craving for a sea breeze and the sensation of sand beneath her toes.

Spend the day at the beach at Estoril. Why not?

Drawing the shutters again to keep the room cool, Clara pulled a single, chestnut hair from her head, then went over to the chest and placed the hair precisely in the aperture at the top of the first drawer. Closing the door behind her, she thought for a second then felt around in her bag and found at the bottom the Cartier card that Hans Reuber had given her in Paris. She wedged it into the door jamb, precisely two inches above the hinge, so deep that only its narrow edge was visible. As precautions went, it was basic, but effective. Then she went to the Cais do Sodré station and took a train along the coast.

Estoril was picture postcard perfect, a pretty eighteenth-century town and fishing harbour, with a parade of shops and cafés fringing the beach. Clara sat on the sand, sniffing the oysterish air and staring out to where the twin blues of sea and sky blurred into one horizon and the estuary of the Tagus River merged with the Atlantic Ocean. The tide stacked and shuffled over a lacy fringe of shingle and the gulls wheeled overhead, fighting over scraps left by the fishermen.

A few yards away, a group of German men sat in a bathing cabin, their loud, confident voices carrying out across the sand. To her other side a couple of dark-eyed, middle-aged women, trussed in black clothing, shot wary glances from beneath their umbrella. They were almost certainly refugees, nervous and incredulous that the international situation should have brought them just yards away on the same narrow strip of sand as the people whose country provoked their flight.

Clara adjusted her sunglasses, leaned back in her lounger and felt the tingle of her shoulders turning brown. What a contrast to the beaches of her childhood, the gritty stretches of Cornish sand where you cut your bare feet on the rock pools and huddled by a windbreak as your flesh turned blue. Here the tide sucked softly at the shingle and the air smelled of salt and honey. It was bliss.

Yet she couldn't settle.

Tension hummed through her body. Her senses were alive with an animal alertness, a heightened vigilance that crawled over her and kept her scanning the horizon for the unexpected. She told herself that it made perfect sense. In two days' time she would be reporting to the Reich's chief spymaster and she had no real idea what he wanted from her. That prospect would be enough to terrify anyone.

Taking a novel from her bag she attempted to read, but after a long time in which she had perused the same two pages over and over without absorbing a single sentence, she ditched it as a lost cause. It was impossible to concentrate. An hour later she abandoned the attempt at relaxation and headed to the station.

Back in Lisbon she killed time wandering the steep, cobbled streets, drinking in the food, the smells, the colours and the language. Here there were no troops marching on the street. Cafés spilled out onto the pavement beneath gaudy neon signs. Pedestrians wore well-fitting clothes and walked with their shoulders back and heads up, free of the watchful stoop one saw back home. The shops were full of local pottery and glassware, rather than the Hitler kitsch – the Führer cards and ashtrays and beer steins – that cluttered shop windows in Berlin. Every grocery shop was an assault on the senses. Clara entered a bakery simply to savour its mingled fragrance of yeast and hot sweet dough, and in an instant the scent transported her to the Bäckerei Balzer in Sophienstrasse where she used to take Erich to buy *Streuselschnecken*, sugar-glazed yeast buns, and gaze hungrily on squares of butter cake, apple fritters and cheesecake. Another place was selling spices, its interior a glimmering collection of amber and mahogany, sumptuous with odours of cinnamon and cardamom and ginger. At a fruit stall she ran a finger over the suede skin of a fig, then picked out a sun-warmed peach, feeling the sweet juice run into her mouth as she bit into its flesh.

Just as seductive was the Rua do Carmo, where she found a pretty, sprigged-cotton summer dress, printed with roses, and a sweet cream straw hat. In another shop silk stockings were on sale and remembering Mary Harker's lament she bought two pairs. But her most satisfying discovery was a chemist selling Elizabeth Arden lipstick in her favourite shade, Velvet Red. Such luxuries were thin on the ground in Berlin. Not only did the Propaganda Ministry issue sheaves of pamphlets on the evils of cosmetics, but the high-class brands had vanished from the shelves and women determined to beautify themselves were resorting to hard, waxy replacements that dragged at the lips or concoctions of home-made beetroot juice. Picking out one of the precious golden tubes, Clara delved happily into her purse. What better way to spend the money Goebbels had given her for expenses?

Halfway down the street she did a double-take when she read the name *Luvaria Ulisses* above a minute shop door squeezed between two baroque pillars and recognized it as the place Hanna Reitsch had mentioned. Through an art deco doorway no wider than an arm's span, beneath antique glass display cabinets, an old man was bent over a wooden counter. He broke off his work to take her hand and size up her shape and measurements, measuring each finger and the width of her palm.

'You're very precise.'

'But of course.' His gruff countenance lightened with a smile. 'We are all different. All unique. You must have heard the saying "to fit like a glove".'

She spent several minutes poring over the display before choosing a pair of white silk evening gloves fitted up to the elbow. He parcelled them up for her in brown paper and ribbon.

Muito obrigada.

Shopping was a welcome distraction. Yet gradually the shops, with their honey-scented candles, soap, hats and boots, began to blur before her eyes and she was forced to acknowledge the tension that was still running through her veins and along every nerve in her body. What was her instinct telling her? Reaching the street of her pension she conducted a forensic inspection of her surroundings: a man standing at an opened window in shirtsleeves smoking a cigarette, a couple playing chess at a street-side bar. An old woman, cheeks like a withered apple, leaning against a doorway. There was no one suspicious. No sign of any surveillance. Perhaps it was simply the fact of being in a strange place, surrounded by an alien language, that made her every sense alert. Or maybe she was merely hungry. Instead of going straight to her room she doubled back, entered the bar and ordered a sandwich.

At the pension, the hallway was as pungent as before, as if something had died and festered there. She peered into the ground-floor room occupied by the owner. It was grubbily panelled with a dirty glass cabinet stuffed with crockery and a portrait of Prime Minister Salazar on the wall. Pedro was sitting beneath a lamp, his tortoise neck sunk into a newspaper and a beer bottle open, his gnarled feet in their open sandals propped on a seat in front of him. He barely glanced up as she passed. As she progressed up stone steps that dipped in the middle where they had been trodden by a thousand feet, the nonchalance of that glance bothered her. Clara knew never to ignore the subtle signs that suggested an enhanced attention. Something to do with the man's studied indifference increased her unease and told her that something was wrong.

The door to her room was shut and the Cartier card she had slipped between the door and its frame was still there, just the edge protruding, two inches above the hinge. Pushing the door as silently as she could, she entered.

The room was in darkness, her clothes thrown over the bed exactly as she left them, the closet door half open. Her bottle of Soir de Paris glimmered on the chest of drawers. But in the air she scented faint traces of tobacco, something rich and alien. Moving towards the window to open the shutters, she saw two leather brogues crossed at the ankle, extending from the armchair, and then a shadow that rose suddenly and approached her, resolving itself into a man. In that split second she knew, because the Cartier card had been pushed back into the doorframe as precisely as she left it, that this man was no casual thief, or even a local policeman sent to check up on her, but someone who understood as much as she did about espionage. Someone who had been trained in the same arts and techniques that governed her own life and who lived by the same rules.

In the dim light he had a leonine demeanour, but what was most striking was his face. It was the kind of face you might find carved on a knight's tomb, inscribed in stone or brass. Thin-lipped and lofty, with a broken nose, twin cliffs of cheekbone and a mouth lifting into a sardonic smile.

'I don't think we've met.'

His voice was dark velvet. The kind of voice that wore a cloak and dagger and promised far, far more lay beneath the surface. He took two steps towards her and extended his hand.

'The name's Fleming. Ian Fleming.'

Chapter Eighteen

The first Saturday of the month was selection day at the NSV home. The officials from the Reich Adoption Service arrived, unburdening themselves of coats and hats and taking a swift cup of coffee with the supervisor while the orphans assembled in the great hall to receive instructions from one of the Brown Sisters. They were to stand with feet precisely four inches apart and face directly ahead as the potential adopters walked in. No whining. No talking. No fidgeting.

The would-be parents, all either childless families of good race, or those who had failed Himmler's injunction to be *kinderreich*, rich in children, would walk along the line, smiling and judging. Sometimes, they would even poke or prod a child, or reach forward to squeeze the flesh, like fruit in a marketplace, and if they did, the child should submit quietly, without complaint. They must not address the new parents, except to give an answer, and before answering they must give the Hitler salute. The adoption chief settled himself behind a desk in the corner of the hall and prepared his paperwork.

'Eyes forward!' said Frau Schneider, as though inspecting an honour guard.

The little ones always did best in selections. They tended to ignore instructions and make spontaneous physical gestures – one child even laid his head on a businessman's knee when he bent down to examine the face, and this proved a winning move; the child was picked immediately. Older children, though, had nothing to gain from physical contact. Any pubescent girl who held out her hand would meet with steely suspicion from potential mothers. A prod from a would-be father signalled something ominous for the future too.

Some of the orphans looked forward to selection day. It reminded them they still had a ticket in the lottery, a stake in the game, a chance to return to the Germanic ideal of a family. But others would cry, muffling their sniffs because it was forbidden, yet unable to stop the tell-tale shake of the shoulders.

Cars drew up on the drive outside, disgorging black-uniformed men and their wives, in varying states of excitement, resignation, suspicion or hostility. The visitors began to straggle in. Most of the potential applicants were from the SS.

'Why do they look so miserable when they're just about to get a new child?' Katerina whispered to Heidi. 'You'd think they'd be excited.'

Heidi rolled her eyes. 'It's obvious, isn't it? They don't really want any more children. The SS are supposed to have four kids each but most of them are nowhere near so they have to come here, see? Just as long as it's not us.'

'They won't pick us. We're almost grown-up. No one wants older girls,' said Katerina, as though by repeating this mantra she could console herself.

'The men do.'

'But the wives won't like it.'

'Depends how much they want a skivvy in their kitchen.'

'They have Polacks for that, don't they?'

Frau Schneider walked along the line. Noticing that one of the children was sucking his thumb she flicked it expertly from his mouth with her cane, provoking a sharp cry. Barbara Sosemann was chewing her plait, but Frau Schneider only plucked up the end and tucked it back over her shoulder.

At the end of the line Rose, one of the girls in Katerina's class, was crying silent tears. Her face was swollen like dough, her eyes swallowed up in creases. She had just heard that her brother, posted as an anti-aircraft gunner on the roof of a factory at Siemensstadt, had been killed. He was her last surviving relative. Most children at the orphanage never stopped talking about their siblings, as though to have brothers and sisters was defence against what was coming, and Katerina was no different. Siblings could throw a spanner in the works of adoption. Not only could you protest that you had some family, someone in the world who cared if you lived or died, but when a sibling came of age, they might adopt you themselves. So far Katerina had managed to conceal the fact of Sonja's disappearance from everyone. It was only discovering the jeweller's receipt that had prompted her to let Clara Vine into her secret. But what the future might hold if Sonja didn't return did not bear thinking about.

Surely Katerina's luck could not hold out much longer. To take her mind off it, she tried to think of something nice. Dogs, as usual, came to the rescue.

One of the loveliest things about dogs was that they were all a little bit different. You could get a purebreed and still there was an individual quality to how the animal stared at you, its eyes either curious or dull, some with noses wetter than others. What most distinguished dogs from each other was not their looks but their personality. It should be the same for people, shouldn't it? What could any potential parent tell about a child, just from looking at her eyes or teeth?

Katerina's reverie was interrupted by the approach of a couple. The woman was in her late forties, complexion the colour of sour milk, bulging out of a hairy green suit. The husband beside her was so fit and sleek in his SS uniform he might have been her son. Together they surveyed the orphans, checking the clarity of skin, the whites of the eyes, posture, strength of limbs. The man halted in front of Katerina and she felt his eyes travel down her body, as though he was trying to see what lay behind her frumpy blue NSV uniform or wondering how soft the skin might be beneath the rough texture of her smock. She clenched her fists and drew in her stomach as he reached forward a hand and tipped up her chin. Scenting his interest, Frau Schneider sped over.

'This is Katerina, Herr Sturmbannführer Hagan. A very intelligent girl.'

Hagan gave a snort of satisfaction, his gaze flickering greedily over Katerina's figure.

'A girl is what we are looking for, to complete our family.'

Frau Hagan had already passed on but now she returned, eyes narrowing as she scanned Katerina. She crossed her arms.

'She doesn't need to be intelligent. Any willing and obedient girl will suit us.'

'You have the right girl here then. Katerina is such a hard worker.'

'Is she teachable? I need a girl I can shape. We want one who can get accustomed to our ways, rather than a little Fräulein with ideas of her own.'

'Katerina has nothing of her own,' said Frau Schneider, encouragingly. 'She has been with us since December.'

'December?'

The implication hung in the air. Why had no one taken her in six months? Might there be some hidden depravity?

'How is her moral attitude?'

'Exemplary.' Frau Schneider hurried on. 'She was of good family before she was tragically orphaned.'

Katerina felt her cheeks bloom. She couldn't help herself.

'I still do have a family! I have a sister.'

'A sister? Is she here?' said the husband, his interest spiking, looking round.

'No, she's grown-up. Sonja is a singer. She's very well known.'

'Is she indeed? Would I know her?'

'You probably do. She's famous. They call her the Songbird.' Despite herself, Katerina couldn't help the swell of pride. 'Mostly she sings at the Café Casanova.'

If Sturmbannführer Hagen knew the Café Casanova, he was never going to admit it in front of his wife. The nightclub was not much more than a louche cellar, from which the degeneracy of the old days had not been entirely purged. The air was musky with sex and sweat, the tired banquettes stained with stale beer. The thought that this girl was the little sister of a nightclub singer may have interested Sturmbannführer Hagen, but it was the kiss of death for his wife. Frau Hagen winced as if physically soiled and turned away, her eyes focused down the line, towards the little blonde Poles.

'That one is more the age we were thinking of.'

Frau Schneider took the hint and hurried on to where Barbara Sosemann was quivering like a rabbit.

'This child was recently orphaned in the Greater Reich . . .'

Katerina allowed her limbs to relax. Another escape. But it was more obvious than ever that she needed to find Sonja. Sooner or later the NSV would start asking questions about this elusive sister of hers.

A face came into her mind. Cool elegance and luminous skin like the edge of a pearl, bisected by the faintest trace of crow's feet at the eyes. The cloud of scent called Soir de Paris that must have come from the semi-circular blue glass bottle on the mantelpiece. Katerina wondered if Clara Vine would really do anything to help, or if she was just like all those other adults who promised the earth so long as they never had to deliver.

Chapter Nineteen

'Two dirty Martinis. A splash of olive brine. And stirred, please, not shaken. Shaking bruises the gin.'

The bar of the Hotel Avenida was heavy with mahogany and scarlet leather. The walls were hung with crimson silk wallpaper, the marble tables dotted with fancy gilt lamps and brass-potted ferns and the entire décor was as blood red and busy as a butcher's shop. Ian Fleming returned from the bar and established himself on the scratched chesterfield sofa with a sigh of satisfaction.

'Isn't this the most extraordinary place? Like a gypsy's funeral parlour.'

He glanced around him. The Portuguese love of excess, which decreed that no single mirror was enough where two would do, meant that every surface glimmered with infinite reflection. A whole bevy of Ian Flemings, an entire cocktail party's worth, sipped Martinis around them.

'Did you know that this hotel has a tunnel that runs under the road directly to the station?'

'How extraordinary,' said Clara, shifting in her seat at the thought. 'Why would that be needed?'

'So people can come and go without being noticed. It was installed by the Germans, so presumably they're planning on staying. This is their place. We're very diplomatic about our watering holes here. The Germans like the Avenida and the Café Chiado in the Rua Garrett and Gambrinus restaurant, which they've tricked out as a Bavarian beer cellar, whereas the Hotel Aviz belongs to us.'

He gestured to the copies of the London *Times*, the *Daily Mail*, the *New York Times* and the *Deutsche Allgemeine Zeitung* lying side by side on the table beside them. 'Some people think that's Lisbon all over. Every nationality under the sun rubbing along together. But it won't last. This city will be under Nazi rule in no time.'

With his single-breasted suit of dark blue worsted, Old Etonian tie, and crowded, nicotine-stained teeth, Fleming's own nationality could not have been more evident if he had hung a large Union Jack round his neck. His jacket, Clara noticed as he leaned forward, bore the label *Benson, Perry & Whitley of Cork Street*. Shirtsleeves were double folded with Cartier cufflinks. Whereas many of the Englishmen she knew back home wore suits their father had owned, she reckoned that Fleming, in his impeccable tailoring, was entirely his own invention. He appeared supremely, almost superciliously, relaxed. His craggy features, with the help of a broken nose, had the angular quality of a Cubist portrait.

'You seem very sure.'

'I give it months.'

If this was a Nazi place, why had he brought her here, unless he was so brazenly self-confident that he assumed he could outwit any surveillance? Yes, she realized as he passed her a glass, deliberately brushing her fingertips, that's exactly what it was. Ian Fleming loved the idea of speaking English in a bar that had been co-opted by the Germans. For him drinking Martinis was war by other means.

The cocktail was as sharp as a knife, briny as a sip of seawater, with an after-kick of alcohol that would go straight to her head. It was folly to drink when she needed her wits about her, but there was no way Clara would let this man know that.

'Too strong for you?'

'Not at all. It's perfect.'

'Didn't think you looked like a sweet sherry girl, but in my experience most ladies find these a bit hard to handle. Three measures of Gordon's, one of vermouth, large slice of lemon peel. This is the only place in Europe you can get a Martini made with English gin.'

'So refreshing.'

'Isn't it? I always imagine I'll create my own cocktail one day, but the trouble is, I require perfection. And perfection is so hard to find, in drinks as much as in women.'

He winked and Clara put her glass down. The gin was already entering her bloodstream and she needed to end this flirtation right now before her senses were blunted in a pleasant alcoholic haze. She had been far too curious to refuse Fleming's suggestion of a drink, but despite the small talk they had exchanged on the way here, she still had no idea exactly who he was or why he had staked her out. She did not know how he had entered her hotel room, whether he was who he claimed to be or, most importantly of all, who he was working for. All she knew was that her instincts that she was being followed that day were justified.

'Why were you tailing me, Mr Fleming?'

A wolfish grin.

'What a suggestion! I wasn't. At least not to begin with. I was out in Estoril because I was planning an evening at the casino. I had just enjoyed a long lunch at the Hotel Palacio. Gulls' eggs, quenelle of sole, crêpes Suzette and half a bottle of Chablis as a matter of fact. Just about my ideal meal. I went along the promenade to walk it off and almost as soon as I saw you I knew I was going to have to forgo my evening's cards.'

'Not on my account, I hope.'

'It's probably for the best. My long-term plan is to strike a blow against the Germans by winning as much money from them as possible, but the casino here can be pretty dull. On weekdays there's usually no one but a few fat Nazis and low-level Portuguese and the stakes are dismally low. Even in the *salle privée*. And the smoke and the sweat can be quite nauseating. However, it's worth keeping one's hand in. You can learn a lot from cards. The whole trick is to work your way into somebody's head and then think fast to get yourself out of trouble. It's not the hand you're dealt, it's how you play it.'

'I take it you're not in Lisbon to improve your gaming technique. Did you come here specifically to find me?'

He gave a laugh drier than the Martini he had just drained.

'Forgive me if it sounds ungallant, but as I say, running into you was the last thing on my mind. It was more of a happy accident. Discovering a pretty girl at a loose end is always a boon, but to find someone of my own persuasion was sheer serendipity. I followed you as far as your pension, and when you diverted into a bar, I walked up to your room.'

Clara crossed her legs and took a swift look around her. The place was empty, apart from a fat man with a fine sheen of perspiration ordering a double in decelerated German. She cupped her chin in her hand to avoid any risk of lip-reading.

'And what makes you think I'm of your persuasion, as you put it?'

'A million things. That card, for instance. The one you left in your door. That was how I knew it was your room. Strictly you should have torn that card into pieces and burned it in an ashtray. It says too much about you.'

Clara shifted in her seat, annoyed at herself. He was right and she knew it. She had trained herself never to keep any tickets or receipts – they were valuable little sources of information that enabled anyone to pinpoint your move-ments – but the Cartier card had slipped the net of her own scrutiny.

'Not to mention your other little burglar alarm – the hair in the chest drawer. It's a standard precaution. No trace of talcum powder on the closet handle, but then you'd not bothered to shut the closet.'

'I hope your curiosity was satisfied.'

'I wasn't particularly curious, as it happens. I already knew you were no ordinary little tourist. I could tell what you were about within about ten minutes of watching you.'

'Is that so? What could you tell?'

'What kind of woman spends an afternoon at a beach alone?'

'Hard though it may be for you to imagine, there are some women who are capable of enjoying their own company.'

'You were reading *Gone with the Wind*.'

'Where I live, in Berlin, it's a bestseller. The Führer himself recommends it because he admires the racial hierarchies of the American South.'

'Your copy was in English.'

'Ah.'

In Berlin Clara was exceptionally careful never to be seen with a book in anything but German. She had removed almost all the English novels from her apartment and deposited them in the empty home of a friend out in Griebnitzsee. But she missed reading in her mother tongue and in Lisbon, she had calculated, an English novel would raise no eyebrows. In Lisbon no one would judge you by your reading matter. How foolish she had been to let down her guard.

'What else?'

'Where shall I start? You were nervous. You looked around every time someone came near. You asked about the train times at the station so I knew you weren't local. It was obvious you were English.'

'Perhaps I was American.'

'Do me the credit of being able to tell an Englishwoman from an American girl. From someone who has known plenty of both.' He stretched his arms behind his head and flexed his entire body in a gesture that reminded Clara suddenly of a cat she had owned as a child, a powerful, half-feral creature, who made up for his solitary and unfriendly nature with his unrivalled predatory prowess.

'An English girl is painted in watercolour, whereas an American is always in Technicolor.'

Clara had tried, even harder since war broke out, to Germanize herself. To overlay the pastel wash of Englishness with the oils of her German ancestry. With every gesture and move and meal, she buried the English half of herself deeper. She joked in German, thought in German, even dreamt in German. At home she never spoke a word of English, except to Mary Harker, and even then only out of earshot. Yet, perhaps, Fleming was right. No matter how you tried to whitewash it, nationality could not be erased; its traits would still protrude like stubborn Braille, its instincts as ingrained as deeply as the urge to use the right or the left hand.

Fleming raised his glass and signalled to the bartender for another.

'Why were you nervous? Has there been someone on your tail?'

'No.' She twirled the lock of hair at the side of her head.

'You should watch that. Habits are an agent's enemy. Being distinctive is what you need to avoid.'

'So this is what you believe then. That I'm an agent of some kind?'

'Precisely.' He cocked an amused eyebrow. 'But as with cards, a little foreknowledge is always helpful. I did have a perfectly good guess who you are. We have an acquaintance in common.'

He took a long draw on his cigarette, paused to exhale, then grinned like a poker player who has just laid down a winning hand.

'Your sister. Angela.'

Angela. Her beguiling, glamorous elder sister. Who had posed as a Nazi sympathizer among the British upper classes, while covertly informing on them to British intelligence. Who, long before that, had acted as a substitute mother to Clara, coaching her in the ways of English society – how to tip a maid, which neighbour to converse with at dinner, how to pass the port. The effortlessly elegant Angela, golden hair pushed back from a flawless brow, hair that had in childhood been brushed fifty strokes every night with a Mason Pearson brush until it gleamed. As glamorous in a Barbour with a pair of Labradors as in a Hardy Amies evening gown. How would Angela have adapted to wartime strictures? Certainly not by wearing clothes refashioned from a blanket or run up from a magazine sewing pattern the way everyone else did. Clara pictured her sister in a belted gabardine jacket with wide lapels, teamed with a velvet pillbox hat, full skirt and unexpectedly high heels.

The image seemed so real that she could barely restrain herself from a rapid glance around the bar, as though Angela might be about to materialize from behind one of the potted palms.

'You know my sister? Where is she?'

'In London, as far as I know. Helping that husband of hers fight plans to turn his golf club into a cabbage patch.'

Gerald Mortimer was a Conservative MP whose right-wing views seemed closely aligned to their father's. He had a bluff manner which he liked to call direct, but was in fact merely rude.

'The tennis courts in Kensington have already been ploughed up for an allotment by the Dig for Victory people. They have rows of carrots there now. Apparently your brother-in-law has written a letter about it to *The Times*.'

Although that would be entirely typical, anyone could see a letter in *The Times*. It was no proof that Fleming knew Angela at all.

'Did she tell you I was here?'

Angela would have no idea that Clara was in Portugal.

'She never mentions you at all. I wouldn't have known Angela even had a sister if I hadn't seen the photograph of you in an Asprey's frame on the grand piano in her drawing room.'

A little glance of triumph. He was aware that he finally had her trust.

'I knew I'd seen you before. It only took a few moments to place that face of yours in context. And when I did, I'll confess it did set my imagination running.'

A barrage of questions rose in Clara's mind. What was Angela really doing? Since war broke out, it had been impossible to receive letters or calls from England, yet even if they had communicated, Angela would never have discussed her true activities except face to face.

'Is she happy? What's she up to? Do you know?'

'Probably missing the job I fixed up for her with Noël.'

'Noël Coward?' Clara remembered the playwright from Angela's parties. An elegant figure in his smoking jacket, always equipped with an acid rejoinder, sharp as Angostura Bitters in a pink gin.

'He's a good friend of mine. Last September he was desperate to do something for the war effort so they gave him a job running the British Bureau of Propaganda in Paris, liaising with the French. I suppose they thought a man like Noël would be good at getting on with people, and he was. He got an apartment in the Place Vendôme and held quite riotous dinner parties, all sorts of writers, actors, journalists, personalities. Claimed he was dining for England. I suggested Angela might like a spell as his secretary but she only had a couple of weeks there before Noël got fed up with it. He said the British idea of propaganda seemed to go no further than dropping copies of entire speeches by Neville Chamberlain over Germany.' A languid chuckle. 'He said if the British plan was to bore the Germans to death, we didn't have quite enough time. So Angela went back to London and Noël sailed off to America. The idea was that he should persuade the Americans to come into the war. Noël's terribly popular there, only he can't explain the real reason for his presence of course so everyone thinks he's just like Auden and Isherwood.'

The two men had emigrated from Britain to the United States the previous year, to the disdain of their fellow countrymen.

'Everyone assumes he's gone to have a lovely time. Must be

damned frustrating for him. Still, we all have our crosses to bear, some of them more arduous than others. And Angela's talents clearly run in the family.'

Fleming withdrew a slim silver case from his inside pocket, extracted two handmade cigarettes and a Dunhill lighter and lit first one for her, then himself.

'You'll like these. They're a mixture of Balkan and Turkish tobacco. They hand-roll them for me at Morland's in Grosvenor Street.'

The remark made Clara smile. Ian Fleming was an odd mixture of a sophisticate and a schoolboy trying to impress. As if she'd care what cigarettes he smoked or which address they were rolled at. Yet she did relish the unfamiliar, rich tobacco and as she inhaled she could feel his eyes drilling into her, assessing her reaction, trying to probe her thoughts. Actually, she was thinking of Angela at the age of twelve in an Aertex shirt and cotton shorts, parting the laurel branches in the shrubbery in a game of hide and seek.

Oh Clara. Is that the best you can do?

Deception, like modelling and tennis, was just another skill at which Angela beat her hands down.

'Do you know, I had no idea, until last year, that my sister was anything other than a Nazi sympathizer. She had me completely fooled. She is so much better at it than I am.'

'Don't do yourself down, Miss Vine. One thing I can tell about you is that you're a listener. That's a quality they look for. Someone who will sit back and watch, ask the right questions. A person who can lose themselves in a crowd.'

She took another glance around the deserted bar.

'Does Angela work in . . . wherever it is you work?'

'Hardly.' A throaty chuckle. 'I suppose I should explain. I'm Lieutenant Fleming, as it happens. I was a humble stock-broker until I was invited to lunch at the Carlton Grill by a brace of admirals and conscripted into the Naval Intelligence Division.'

'What's that?'

'We call it the NID. It's a glorious place. Based at the Admiralty. Full of tweedy types working out how to freeze clouds and build fortified icebergs in the north Atlantic. The department of daydreams and dirty tricks. They're all going to blow up the iron gates of the Danube, parachute into Berlin and assassinate Hitler. I love it, but I'm not a desk man. I was desperate to escape and get some fresh air so they sent me out to help the British evacuation of Bordeaux. There were a large amount of aero engines and spare parts we needed to keep out of the hands of Goering and his merry men and as it happens, I was in the right spot to help King Zog of Albania board the last ship out. After that success with royalty, they sent me down here to do a spot of babysitting.'

'If you don't mind me saying, you don't look the type.'

'I'm very good at it actually. Though my charges run rings around me.'

'Who are your charges exactly?'

'A couple of our own. The Duke and Duchess of Windsor.'

Clara started, recalling what Mary Harker had told her about the Duke and Duchess. *Churchill is begging them to come home but word is they're having a very enjoyable time in Europe.*

The Duchess is digging in her heels. She's refusing to get dragged into the war.

'So they're *here?*'

'Unfortunately. And they're not behaving themselves.'

'That seems an extraordinary way to talk about members of the Royal Family.'

'Not sure I hold with all that royal business. In my mind, the only people I call sir are God and the King. Certainly not ex-Kings.'

'So how are they not behaving?'

'They won't obey orders. They came down here in a hurry when the Germans took Paris and now the Prime Minister urgently wants them to leave. The prospect of the Duke and Duchess being here if Portugal falls to the Nazis is pretty grim. There's an American Export Lines passenger ship called the *Excalibur* waiting for them in the harbour right now and all they have to do is pack up their things and get on it like good royals, but they're not budging.'

'Are they going back to London?'

''Fraid the Queen would take a very dim view of that. She'd rather not be in the same continent as them, let along the same city. No, they're being sent to the Bahamas. They feel rather sorry for themselves, but I feel sorry for the Bahamas.'

Clara couldn't help smiling.

'They're probably the only refugees in the whole of Lisbon who have the opportunity to leave and won't.'

'Precisely. Or at least, if they do intend to leave they're in no hurry about it. It's almost as if they're waiting for something.'

Fleming frowned and leaned forward, elbows on knees, as if trying to puzzle out a problem.

'He's a tricky devil, the Duke. He's a man who was born with three aces in his hand and spends most of his time complaining about not being given a fourth. Can't say I warm to him one bit. He's dangerously sympathetic to Herr Hitler. Practically a Fifth Columnist. And he seems to bear a deep grudge against his brother.'

'Bitterness runs deep. Anyone who's ever had a family knows that.'

'Perhaps. He insists he'll only accept this Bahamas posting if his wife is given the title HRH and treated the same as other members of his family. She must be received at Buckingham Palace and paid by the civil list. And that's never going to happen.'

'You're saying he won't go just because of his wife's title?'

'Could be. But it's my sense that it's something else that's keeping him. And I'm damned if I know what it is. In the meantime, they're at the casino until four in the morning, and they require a whole team of watchers to protect them.'

'Protect them from who?'

He arched an eyebrow at her. 'I'm surprised you could even ask that. Have you not noticed there are Gestapo everywhere? The street outside the Duke's residence is crawling with them. Not to mention the swarms of informers. They've bugged the Foreign Ministry, they bribe all the officials, and they have an extensive network of spies. They've bought up everyone we couldn't get to first – bartenders, policemen, waiters. They probably have listening devices in the Duke's bedside table. Fortunately we do have some valuable people – I've cultivated a man at the casino, a German by heritage, name of Hertz. He manages the *salle privée* where the Duke likes to play. Pretty silent sort of fellow with a wonky eye, but utterly trustworthy.'

'Surely the Windsors . . .?'

'Unfortunately, the happy couple won't believe a word we say. They take everything the British tell them as lies. It doesn't help that the Nazis have informed them that Churchill wants them murdered.'

'They can't believe that.'

'The bitterness, as you said, goes very deep.' Fleming exhaled a jet of cigarette fume and studied its upward drift abstractedly, like a smoke signal. 'But their behaviour is *odd*. It's not just a case of spending too much at the casino, or drinking too much, though they're guilty of both of those sins. But frankly, aren't we all . . .'

He glanced at Clara's single Martini lined up against his own three empty glasses and corrected himself.

'Well, perhaps not all of us. But I'm convinced there's something else keeping them here and I'm damned if I know what it is. In the meantime, I'm devoting myself to keeping tabs on the enemy. Only the other day I noticed a new character keeping an eye on them.'

'Gestapo?'

'Not entirely sure. It's a girl. I saw her at the casino the other night. A long way from your standard-issue shifty-eyed

German goon in a raincoat. She was distinctly attractive. Practically radioactive. I realized I'd seen her before in one of the nightclubs here, singing a rather catchy song. Something about a woman under a lamp post. Ever heard it?'

'You must mean *Lili Marlene*.' Clara had first heard the song the previous year at the Kabarett der Komiker in Berlin and it had transfixed her. The girl's voice, half choked with emotion, had lingered in her mind long after the last notes had died away. 'But seeing a nightclub singer at the casino is hardly unusual.'

'Except that she was shadowing the Duke, I'm sure of it. And it wouldn't be the first time they've used a nightclub singer to spy. I know for a fact that Joey Goebbels keeps a file of all the artists he can use as agents in foreign countries and there are plenty of little cabaret artistes in second-rate bars who fit the bill. Only a few months ago three cabaret singers were arrested in Antwerp for transmitting information to the Germans. When I saw this young lady, sheathed in satin and nervous as a cat on a hot tin roof, I guessed she was more of the same so I tipped off a couple of Portuguese policemen and they rounded her up. If she is working for the Nazis, as I suspect, they'll let her go soon enough. But I like to keep them on their toes.'

A couple of German businessmen entered the bar and Fleming offered them a beaming smile.

'Shall we walk?'

They moved outside and continued along to the Rossio, the city's grandest square with its lush, colourful vegetation, ornate façades, bronze fountains and intricate Portuguese paving. At this hour it was thronged with people spilling out from the bars, relaxing in the way they had for centuries with a stroll in the cool of the evening. All the cafés and bars were open, and the nightlife was peppered with the language of every imaginable nationality. French, Dutch and German tangled in the air, intersected by the occasional strident American voice, loudly demanding service with the assurance that money, and an American passport, were enough to secure any conceivable object in life. Lisbon was like one long party whose guests might intend to leave but showed absolutely no signs of departing. Yet in the side alleys and along the steps of the National Theatre shadowy forms were congregating and laying out their bags. The first rough sleepers were settling down for the night.

Fleming led the way and they strolled for a while, as comfortably as all the citizens around. Clara breathed the balmy, blossom-scented air and tried to imagine, for one futile moment, that she was on holiday. It was a pleasant experience to walk through a city at a gentle pace alongside a companionable Englishman. She wished she could properly relax and enjoy the novelty of the situation, but like the little stray cat at home, her desire for companionship was always overcome by her instinctive caution.

'So, as they say in nightclubs, what's a girl like you doing in a place like this?'

She paused for a heartbeat, then said, 'I've been summoned to the German Embassy.'

She had, at last, succeeded in surprising him. The

expression of urbane irony remained intact, but a flicker of the muscle in Fleming's cheek told her that this information took him aback.

'Can I ask why?'

'Have you heard of a man called Walter Schellenberg?'

'Course I've heard of him. Head of counter-espionage. Iron Cross first class.'

'He's asked to see me. He has suspicions about an actor. A man called Hans Reuber. He wants me to report on him.'

Even as she spoke Clara was still turning the problem over in her head, trying to probe her own instincts, dreading what lay ahead.

'If you live in Berlin, why not get you to call in on him there? Why drag you all the way here?'

'That's what I don't understand.'

'You can't imagine Germany's chief spymaster invited you here for a seaside holiday.'

'Lieutenant Fleming, do you really think I'd have survived as long as I have in Nazi Germany if I didn't ask myself questions like this? If Schellenberg wanted to arrest me, it would be much more convenient to do it in Berlin. He has plenty of cells at his disposal at Gestapo headquarters. No. I think it's something else, but I honestly don't know what.'

Fleming's face was set, calculating.

'He's an interesting character, Schellenberg. He has us all puzzled. He's had a brilliant career, he's climbed the Nazi ladder and he's Heydrich's man all right, but he's far more cultured than most of them. Loves travel, art, literature, music. He must know what swine those SD brutes are – he could hardly be a soulmate of a man like Heinrich Himmler – and he's clever enough to keep his distance. It's significant that he's taken an office in Dahlem, well away from Gestapo HQ. I often wonder if he keeps a locker at the Hauptbahnhof with a complete change of clothes in case he needs a quick getaway when the music stops.'

'You seem to know a lot about him.'

'It's my job.' He turned to her purposefully.

'A session with him won't be easy. Do you understand what you're up against? Do you have any idea how to withstand interrogation?'

'I've done it before.'

'Do you have a gun?'

Clara laughed.

'I don't think you understand. Walter Schellenberg is accompanied at all times by a squad of armed men. If he's intending to arrest me, there'll be no shortage of guards to help him.'

Fleming had steered her into a dimly lit alley, leading away from the square to the maze of winding streets beyond. He leaned back against a wall, an arrow of shadow bisecting his face.

'Nonetheless, he's extremely cunning. It doesn't do to underestimate Herr Schellenberg.'

'You think I don't realize that? Knowing how clever he is is hardly reassuring. If you want the truth, the idea of meeting him terrifies me.'

'Oh come!' Fleming wheeled round, his face suddenly alight. 'You're looking forward to it! It's a challenge. This world of ours suits a certain type. Those of us who are good at keeping our feelings under control. Who know how to keep our lives in compartments.'

'That's not me.'

'Of course it's you. You're quick-witted, and most of all you're alone. You actually *like* being solitary.'

'What on earth qualifies you to say that?'

'It takes one loner to know another. And believe me, it's useful in our line of work. Married people are security risks. If you're single it means you can't be manipulated. You're your own person. We have a lot in common, you and I. We're both alone.'

There was a flare of attraction in his eyes, as though Narcissus had glimpsed his reflection in the mirrored lake, and liked what he saw.

'Perhaps,' he placed a hand on her waist and drew her towards him, 'you'd like to see my apartment. It's above Amigos bar in the old fishermen's quarter. The embassy keeps it as a safe house so suffice to say that no one's splashed out on décor, but it's comfortable enough.'

He obviously expected her to agree. Clara sensed that Fleming was accustomed to women finding him attractive. Maybe he was the kind of man who seduced women because he had no idea how else to get on with them.

'As far as discretion goes, you needn't worry. Officially, I don't exist.'

In the half-light of the alleyway he did for a moment

resemble some kind of phantom, an Englishman conjured up from her own exhausted imagination. A man whose background matched hers, who was as familiar as Clara with the streets and squares of her own childhood. Who knew her sister and her secrets. A man with whom she could feel momentarily secure. The comfort of the known and understood ran deep within Clara and, added to Ian Fleming's animal magnetism, it was a combination almost impossible to resist.

But she had already made enough rash decisions for one day and had no intention of making another.

'Sometimes even loners like us can offer a little comfort to each other,' he murmured. He was close enough for her to smell a spicy Jermyn Street cologne, vetiver and sandalwood, mingled with sweat and warm skin.

'I'm rather tired.'

Fleming leaned closer, and stroked a single finger down the length of her neck, ending at the swell of her cleavage.

'I'm sure we could wake you up a little.'

Suddenly her back was against the wall and his hands were on her arms, infinitely soft and caressing.

'Wouldn't it be nice to slip out of these clothes and into another cocktail?'

His mouth moved to kiss her but she turned her face away. Did he really imagine she would come with him after so short an acquaintance and allow him to peel the dress from her like an orange? Almost certainly he did. War had that effect on people. And she felt herself respond. War had that effect on people too.

'It's a bad idea.'

'Why? Am I too English for you? Have your tastes changed after all your years away?'

'No.'

'Some chap back in Germany?'

'There's no one. I'm just not interested.'

With surprising pressure he pushed her harder against the wall, pressing his entire six foot two inches against her, his breath hot on her cheek. He was kissing her roughly now, and the weight of him on her was almost suffocating. She could not tear her mouth away to breathe.

'I'm not sure I believe you. You're a spy, after all, so you like pretending.'

She stiffened and yanked her head back. The wild idea went through her that this was some kind of test.

'I'm not pretending.'

His thigh wedged between her legs.

'Aren't you? In my experience all girls prefer the door to be forced.'

She couldn't risk crying out; it would compromise both of them and any attention they attracted was sure to be unwelcome. What was the point of landing them both in a Portuguese prison? As Fleming's arm moved down to caress her hip, she raised a knee and found his groin.

He recoiled, bent over for a second, before straightening up.

'Well *this* girl prefers a more civilized approach.'

'Really? Where's the pleasure in that?'

Fleming adjusted his suit and shot his cuffs with a suave grin, his demeanour undented.

'Another time, then.'

At first, she was astonished at his reaction. It was as though she had turned down the offer of a cigarette, or a polite request for another cup of tea. As if his suggestion of forcible sex was entirely normal and her refusal had caused no offence. She guessed this was how men of his type operated. Maybe, to them, sex really was nothing personal. He turned and offered his arm and she took it.

'I wouldn't want to keep you from your beauty sleep.'

Then he laughed, as if the entire thing had been one enormous joke, and in that moment he was transformed again into the prank-playing schoolboy, straining for sophistication, and Clara couldn't help smiling too. He smoothed his hair and lit up again as they walked, then as if struck by an afterthought he said, 'As a matter of fact I have another proposition for you.'

'I'm not sure I like your propositions.'

'Oh, this one's rather brilliant actually. It occurred to me the moment I saw you sitting on that beach turning a pretty shade of brown. Ever been to a royal garden party?'

'Once. My parents took me to one at Buckingham Palace. It rained, there were a lot of queues and piles of cucumber sandwiches. And I met Queen Mary.'

She remembered the elderly Queen, as upholstered as a horsehair sofa, touring the guests, white-gloved hand extended, a servant beside her proffering an umbrella against the damp.

'Well, I shouldn't mention *her* at this particular party. Wallis Simpson is not her greatest fan.'

'Wallis Simpson? So this is the Duchess's party?'

'She's taken to hosting little get-togethers, just local ladies. It dispels the boredom, I suppose. She's having one of her dos tomorrow afternoon and I'm sure she'd adore to meet you. She can't stand the English but she loves Germans and Germany. She spent some of her honeymoon there, after all. I'll have you put on the guest list as staying at the German Embassy. It'd be awfully useful if you could get any clue as to what's keeping them here.'

'And how on earth would you get me on this list?'

'One of the maids is in our pay. She'll sort you out.'

'It sounds the most unlikely plan.'

Fleming sighed, as if her objections were as tiresome as a badly made Martini.

'Look, Clara, if you're half as intelligent as you appear, you'll stop trying to assert your authority and agree with me. Go to this party and see if you can find out what's keeping them from sailing.'

'How will I let you know?'

'There's a dead letter box at the grave of Henry Fielding in the English Cemetery. Novelist chap. Came for a few months, hated the place, and promptly died here. It's a stone tomb with an urn on it, looks like a soup tureen. Stick a message under the left pediment. It's checked every couple of days. If it's urgent, though, I noticed a clothesline outside the window of your pension. Hang a handkerchief on it.'

'Must it be a handkerchief?'

'Private lingo. H for help, if you see what I mean.'

He tilted his head to one side. 'I suppose you wouldn't reconsider a nightcap?'

This time she laughed and shook her head, and while he returned the smile, a melancholy swam in his eyes. Perhaps it was a knowledge that he would never find what he was searching for, neither the perfect Martini nor the perfectly compliant woman.

'You didn't tell me. Where do they live? The Duke and Duchess.'

'I'll write it down.'

He pulled out a fountain pen and scrawled the address, then handed her both the scrap of paper and the pen itself.

'As you won't have a gun when you see Schellenberg, you should take this.'

She held it up to the light. It was a heavy black and white enamelled fountain pen with a chic silver trim. It looked expensive but there was no maker's mark.

'Thank you. Though I'm not sure how this is going to help, unless he wants my autograph.'

'It's one of my little toys. I had it made up by some chaps in the department and it comes in very useful in emergencies. But be careful how you handle it. If you press the clip . . . here . . . it emits a large amount of tear gas. It takes a cyanide cartridge too, but I don't use those except on really danger-ous outings. Which I trust this will not be.'

She looked down at the address.

'So where is this place?'

'It's a curious spot. Place called Cascais, out beyond Estoril.

The house itself belongs to Ricardo Espirito Santo Silva, a friend of the German Ambassador to Portugal, and it's set on a rather dramatic landscape. A kind of rocky headland. The magician Aleister Crowley staged a suicide there a few years ago; pretended to throw himself off the cliff. Rather appropriate really. It's called the Jaws of Hell.'

Chapter Twenty

Grandiose titles – in places as much as people – frequently fail to live up to expectations, and the spot known as the Boca do Inferno, or the Jaws of Hell, was no exception. Set on an isolated promontory jutting into the Atlantic, the local attraction was a steep gulley formed by an erosion of lime- stone in the cliff face where seawater trapped in a narrow cleft of rocks seethed and boiled as it searched for an escape. Sightseers climbing down a rocky ledge would peer over a railing to see the natural archway in the cavernous cliffs lashed by roaring water of deep cobalt blue. The sight was impressive, and in the swell of a westerly gale even spec- tacular, but infinitely less fearsome than the Reichenbach Falls Clara had seen on a recent visit to Switzerland, and far from being hellish, the ozone-rich air engendered a bracing vitality. Watching the water frustrated by its rocky trap into a fine arching spray, people came away awed by the energy of Nature. When Clara gazed down into the raging foam, however, it was a different kind of trap she was pondering.

*

Lieutenant Fleming had been nonchalantly confident that he could secure her entrance to the Duchess's tea party, but what would happen if the maid in question had not turned up for work that day, or she had not succeeded in adding Clara's name to the guest list? And even if she got through the door, how likely was it that the Duchess would welcome a total stranger taking tea with her, let alone confide just what issue was preventing the royal couple making an urgent escape from the continent? If the royal couple distrusted her, no doubt there were plenty of both Portuguese and German officers on hand who could be summoned. It took some time, the breeze whipping her hair into her face, before she was able to summon the resolve to go through with Fleming's plan. Eventually, she fortified herself with a deep breath of the bracing air, clambered back up the rocky steps and turned inland towards the last house along the isolated coast.

The rambling, rose pink stucco villa, with gabled roof and colonnade, looked precisely what it was: the comfortable country refuge of a wealthy local family. In common with much of the architecture in Lisbon there was a gimcrack quality to its roughly painted walls, stippled with pebbledash, and the faded, fraying awning that shaded the terrace. Nothing about the place suggested that it was, at that moment, serving as the last sanctuary in Europe for an exiled British king and his American wife.

Clara's version of garden party attire was the sprigged rose-print dress that she had bought the day before and white leather T-bar shoes, all finished off with her glorious

Elizabeth Arden lipstick. Smoothing her hair with a diamanté clip and replacing her new straw panama, she pushed open the high black gates to see three Cairn terriers chasing each other in joyous abandon across a parched lawn. The garden was bordered by umbrella pines and monkey puzzle trees and decorated at its centre by a circle of scrubby rose bushes and a stone fountain. In front of the house, in the shade of lemon trees, cane chairs were set out alongside tables draped in white linen and a group of svelte ladies in tea dresses and sunglasses were already established, sipping punch. Fluent Portuguese and heavily accented English clashed in the air, surmounted by a deep Baltimore drawl which came floating imperiously across the rose bushes.

'Oh, it's a pathetic little job in a ghastly backwater. We feel like Napoleon being exiled to St Helena.'

The speaker was standing on the terrace next to her husband, the pair of them dapper as matching china figurines: the ex-King of England and his wife, Wallis Simpson.

The Duke was wearing a well-cut white linen summer suit and a red tie in a Windsor knot. His eyes were pouched with shadow and he had a cigarette on the go. Beside him the Duchess held herself very straight, as if a steel bar ran up her spine, with the cold, ivory composure of a chess piece. The same rigour could be observed in the parting of her hair, blue-black as a bird's wing, and the severe fitting of her diaphanous blue spotted tea dress, cinched at the waist with a crimson leather belt, and falling in filmy pleats below her knee. The Duchess was not quite perfect – the angle of her jaw was too wide and her lips too thin – but she had a bold elegance that seemed to defy suggestions that she was not as beautiful as the clothes she wore. Something about her porcelain complexion alongside the Duke's bleached linen figure brought back to Clara a memory of a tomb she had once seen in a church in Oxfordshire; a fourteenth-century knight and his wife carved in smooth alabaster and exquisitely detailed, down to the wisps of hair, the coils of chainmail, and the fur of the small dog crouched beneath the lady's feet. A petrified pairing, frozen in stone. United in eternity.

'Good afternoon! And you are?'

Wallis detached herself and approached, extending a hand as thin as a bunch of twigs threaded with veins and garnished with an enormous engagement ring. A large flower was pinned to her lapel, made entirely from sapphires, with an emerald stalk and diamonds at its heart. Her smile was wide, but her eyes were as hard and as crystalline as the jewels she wore.

'Fräulein Clara Vine,' Clara replied, adding for good measure, 'Your Royal Highness.' If Wallis desired that title so dearly, who was Clara to deny her?

'Ah yes. Have you come far?'

'The German Embassy,' replied Clara smoothly,

A maid approached with a tray of Pimm's and Clara selected a tumbler decorated with a sprig of mint. The maid had a blank, greasy face with an impassive expression and Clara wondered if this was the woman in British pay who had so obligingly tampered with the guest list.

'We've met once before, in fact. At Carinhall, when you visited the Goerings.'

The Windsors' visit to Goering's baronial home had been a highlight of the Berlin section of their honeymoon tour in 1937. Luftwaffe officers and Nazi Party elite had turned out in force for a candlelit dinner served by waiters in silken breeches and girls whose cleavage was barely restrained by ruffles of dirndled lace. The hall was hung with hunting trophies and the air thick with excitable gossip. While Clara had not actually been introduced to the royal couple, she felt sure the Duchess would not remember a detail like that and she was right. Wallis Simpson's eyes lit up like a child reminded of Christmas.

'Carinhall! I dream of Carinhall! The gymnasium! That massage machine! All that glorious art. It brings back such happy memories.'

Excitedly she wheeled round to her husband.

'David! Fräulein Vine here is a friend of the Goerings! Oh, do give them our love when you see them! If I could just go back to that time . . .'

The Duke of Windsor came over, a bobbing tide of Cairn terriers at his feet. Close up his petulant mouth, pert nose and diminutive stature gave him the boyish air of a Peter Pan who has landed in an uncomfortably adult predicament but is unable to fly away.

'Very good to meet you, Fräulein Vine.'

Clara gambled on a curtsey. She didn't want to emphasize her English origins, but she guessed that in this particular royal garden party, with its scrubby grass and assorted foreign strangers, any form of deference would be welcome.

'Your Royal Highness.'

'Awfully good English,' he observed. His eyes were as yellow and bloodshot as oysters in Tabasco.

'My father is English.'

This revelation aroused almost no reaction in the Duke. Clara realized he was one of those men so self-absorbed that the details of other people's lives registered no more than the brush of midges in the afternoon air.

'Indeed. Can't someone control these creatures?'

The terriers were weaving in and out of his legs, their high yipping cries fracturing the air.

'Pookie, Detto, Prisie!' exclaimed Wallis, bending to caress them. 'Do you love dogs, Fräulein Vine? We got these from a woman in Surrey. A terrifically nice lady, and you know what? She supplies David's family with corgis, and she gives their cousins to von Ribbentrop. Don't you think that's the most splendid form of Anglo-German alliance? She should be in the diplomatic service.'

'It's a wonderful idea.'

'She provided two chows for Goering and his secretary. If you know the Goerings you must have seen them.'

'I think I must have,' lied Clara. 'Though I'm more of a cat person myself.'

'Don't know about cats. It's the lions I remember,' muttered the Duke.

Hermann Goering's predilection for having lion cubs running freely around his home always left a strong impression on visiting dignitaries.

'Damned creatures gave me the fright of my life. He's jolly lucky someone doesn't shoot them.'

'Goering may be frightfully keen on hunting, but I don't think he'd forgive that in a hurry,' said the Duchess, reaching to caress her husband's cheek. It was a curiously intimate gesture in the midst of strangers, yet, Clara realized, for the Windsors there was no such thing as privacy. The most personal details of their lives had so long been played out for public consumption that any border between their private and public lives had already been utterly breached. Their lives had solidified into history and it was history that had left them beached here in unknown territory, on a distant shore.

'I understand you're shortly to leave for the Bahamas?'

Wallis's mouth wrinkled sourly, like someone with too much lime in her margarita.

'They've made my husband governor. We'll be three thousand miles away from the war. David wanted a far more active role but that family of his back on the island won't consider it.'

The island? Was that how she referred to Britain?

'So what brings you to Lisbon, Fräulein Vine?' enquired the Duke, with no perceptible interest in the answer.

'Just a short engagement. I won't even have time to catch any sun. I'll be going back to Berlin in a few days.'

'Lucky you,' sighed Wallis. 'I wish *we* were. We're bored to sobs here. All we have are these endless dinners with local dignitaries, most of whom have only the barest comprehension of who we are, and the occasional tea party. This afternoon we have several wives of Portuguese worthies and a lady from the Red Cross and they have scarcely a dozen

English words between them. Just *How d'you do* and *Thank you*. I try my best, I really do, but Portuguese is such a tricky language, don't you think, and they *won't* try Spanish. I can't tell you how lovely it is to have a guest who shares one's mother tongue. If it wasn't for the golf course and the casino we'd go quite mad. David adores the casino – he's there almost every night, aren't you, darling?'

The ex-King grunted assent and moved off. Once he was out of earshot Wallis's bright façade faded and she wrapped her arms round her skinny frame, gloomily surveying the house behind her with its fringe of orange rose bushes. Even the roses looked different here – blown and gaudy, their petals garishly bright.

'What do you think of this place? It's a little scrubby, isn't it? Not a patch on our villa, La Croë.' A long sigh. 'We left on my birthday. The staff were all in floods. I *so* miss France. I wonder if we'll ever see it again.'

'How long do you think you'll be staying here?'

'Oh that's what everyone keeps asking. I only wish I knew. It was my fault at first. Winston sent a ship to collect us but I said I was not going to budge an inch until someone had fetched my swimming costume for me.'

This remark prompted Clara to inhale a little of her Pimm's, prompting a coughing fit.

'Your swimming costume? Where did you leave it?'

'The south of France. It got abandoned at La Croë. We had to leave in a rush and it was not packed, but I said, if I'm going to be heading for the Bahamas I *simply* can't be without it. It's a beautiful Nile green and my absolute favourite. Even if one's lying in the sun one wants to look one's best, don't you think? Any woman would understand that, surely.'

'The south of France is rather a long way away, isn't it? I mean, there's no hope of actually getting it back.'

'What defeatist talk! As it happens the very sweet American consul in Nice went to collect it and brought it down here.'

'That's quite an achievement.'

'In what way?'

'Given the roads and the refugees and so on.'

'Oh, I suppose.' Wallis looked suddenly disconsolate, as if the return of the swimming costume had not been quite the joyous reunion she'd anticipated.

'So now you're ready to leave?'

'If only it were that simple.' She rolled her eyes. 'But there are other problems. Firstly the British are messing us about disgracefully. They've refused to allow us to stop off in New York on the way to the Bahamas, which my husband is furious about. But what's really preventing us from going is . . .'

A call sounded from the terrace and she broke off.

'Ah. They're serving tea inside. Won't you come in? I'm going to have to mingle with these ladies but perhaps you might like a little tour, Fräulein Vine. Though I warn you, there's precious little to look at.'

When she opened the doors to her new living quarters, Wallis Simpson might have been Howard Carter lifting the door to Tutankhamen's tomb. The plethora of gilded furniture, porcelain, antique vases and bronze figures crowding the small drawing room suggested the opulent jumble of a Pharaoh's antechamber, containing all the necessary treasure for the afterlife. The couple had clearly brought as much as they could carry in their headlong rush from the advancing Nazis, loading up several cars with oriental plates, Chinese screens, jade clocks and spindly-legged Louis XVI side tables. There were numerous photographs of Wallis herself, posing with one arm slung over a chair-back and gazing haughtily into the distance, as if the exercise of extreme dignity might counter the torrent of indignities that life had brought her. There were also pictures of the couple themselves and beside them, on the mantelpiece, an autographed photograph of Joachim von Ribbentrop – plainly if the Duke had heard the rumours of Wallis Simpson's affair with the German Foreign Minister, then he had chosen to ignore them. Yet it was the image above, hanging in a sleek ebony frame, that stopped Clara in her tracks. It was a pencil sketch of a panther, coiled around its own spangled pelt, its body a picture of lithe precision and its eyes sparking cold fire. Clara recognized it at once. It was identical to the one she had seen in Cartier's showroom in Paris.

So this was the special client Jeanne Toussaint had talked of. The one who could not be mentioned.

'That's a design my husband made. For a piece,' said Wallis, following her gaze.

'It's Cartier, isn't it?'

'Clever you! I like a woman who knows her jewellery. Is it a passion of yours?'

'I was in Cartier's last month, actually. Just by chance.'

At once Wallis's bland countenance was suffused with interest.

'Were you now? Isn't that showroom positively the most glorious place in the world? Jeanne Toussaint and I are firm friends. I think she's an artistic genius, as great as any Picasso or Monet. She told me her life's work is to take my dreams and turn them to stone.' A little laugh. 'I said I'd rather she turned them into platinum and gold and diamonds.'

'I thought her designs were wonderful. Especially her latest.'

'Oh, yes?' Wallis's eyes were alive with interest. 'What was that?'

'It was quite spectacular. She thinks it will prove her legacy. It's the piece that means more to her than any other. She plans to display it in the front window.'

Immediately Wallis's entire frame was animated by curiosity. Gone was the brittle politesse and in its place a barely concealed shudder of excitement. The thought that Clara Vine had seen Cartier's most precious piece, a legacy item that would tantalize collectors across Europe, was almost unbearable. Like anyone with an obsession, be it birdwatching or baccarat, Wallis wanted to stay ahead. Still, though, she contained herself. She was desperate to know, but she wouldn't ask about it, not yet.

'If you were in Cartier's showroom I imagine you must collect yourself.'

'I have a few pieces,' said Clara, thinking exactly how few that was – a single silver locket, a row of pearls and a pair of diamond earrings in a scarlet box with the maker's name in faded gold, nestling on a satin bed.

'You're teasing. I'd guess you're a person of great discrimination.'

Wallis was plainly mystified. Her eyes roved over Clara's form, probing and assessing, trying to work out what it was that allowed her access to Cartier's most precious piece. She touched Clara's arm lightly.

'I've an idea. As you're a fellow aficionado and talking to these local ladies bores me rigid I'm going to show you my children.'

Her children?

She crossed the room and threw open a pair of double doors to reveal a dressing room. The shutters were closed against the sun, but in the corners glimmering sheaths of dresses in silk, satin and taffeta could be discerned, jostling for space on a temporary rail with Chanel jackets and Mainbocher frocks. Another rail held lingerie, boudoir jackets, negligees and ivory crêpe de Chine nightgowns. Satin gloves, clutch bags, capes and beaded boleros. Beneath them an army of handmade shoes, Vivier, Ferragamo and Anglisano, stood braced to attention, awaiting glittering occasions to come. Many of the accessories bore Wallis's initials, or those of the royal pair entwined, as if the reality of their marriage required perpetual reinforcement. In a flash of insight, Clara realized that nowhere was Wallis's spirit more evident than here, in her wardrobe. Elegance was her weapon and in a life of constant reinvention, she had made a subtle armour out of labels and styles. Everything about her, from the flower brooch in her lapel to the dress that matched the precise sapphire of her eyes, was a carefully calculated construction. It was only in her present circumstances that such elaborate planning had gone awry.

At the far end of the room stood a tall cabinet and from it Wallis took a square Louis Vuitton travelling case, patterned in mulberry and old gold, inscribed with the title *The Duchess Of Windsor*. She laid it on a table, lit the desk lamp and opened the lid.

'I call them my children because they're all individuals to me. All of them are perfect, that's what people with children say, isn't it? They may have their flaws, but I know their pedigree and everything about them.'

Before them, on a series of velvet-covered drawers, lay row upon row of jewels. Necklaces, earrings, bracelets and brooches. A spray of flowers, a fat rose of rubies, iridescent butterflies. Trembling drops of colour that seemed to shimmer and move as they lay. Substitutes for, perhaps even improvements on, the flesh and blood children she would never have.

Wallis's fingers roved over them, fondling a bracelet of circular-cut sapphires, interspersed with diagonal rows of diamonds.

'I adore this. D'you know I have the sleeves of all my dresses shortened so the bracelets can be seen?'

She skimmed a pair of earrings in a matching sapphire *bombé* design and picked up a diamond and green peridot frog whose glowing stones seemed to warm a reciprocal light in her eyes. Her face was bathed in tenderness as, like a real mother, she stroked its tiny form.

'I love showing my little ones off but there's no one in this godforsaken place who has the slightest appreciation of fine jewellery.'

She held up a crystalline scorpion, its claws two rubies like drops of blood, and placed it against her cheek, pale and smooth as a hard-boiled egg.

'Don't you find, when you wear your jewels, that they tremble on your skin? Whenever I wear this one I feel it on my neck like a kiss.'

She fondled a necklace whose diamonds refracted the ambient light in a glittering cascade.

'You know, Hitler told me he has a personal collection of diamonds. I always wanted a look at them. They call them the Tears of the Wolf.' She darted a quick, curious look at Clara, still trying to make her out. Assessing her level of access.

'I suppose he hasn't shown you?'

'Not yet. But if I see him I'll tell him you mentioned them.'

'Oh, do! Diamonds are my favourite. They're the strongest of stones. They're supposed to have magical properties, warding off evil and so on. In fact I could do with some more of them. But then I adore all gems, except opals. Opals mean bad luck and I've had all the bad luck I can handle for now.'

'This one's magnificent.'

Clara was studying a brooch in the shape of a flamingo, a spectacular thing made of platinum and gold, brilliant-cut diamonds, emeralds, and rubies, with sapphires for feathers and citrines for its yellow beak. Although she knew very little about gems, she could tell that the creation in front of her was a virtuoso example of the jeweller's art. The stones caught the warm glow of the lamp and flashed it back like the light from a thousand stars.

'The Duke designed that. My husband has such a good eye. He goes off to Cartier with little sketches he's done and they reproduce them. He's going to design me a whole menagerie – birds, leopards, cats, panthers. Though frogs are his favourite.'

Her eye flickered towards Clara's left hand.

'How about you, Fräulein Vine. Is there a fiancé on the horizon?'

'I'm afraid not.'

'Oh dear. I do recommend marriage. However doubtful one feels about going into it. And after all my experience, I should know.'

The fact that she had married three times hovered unspoken between them.

'It's the pair of you together, for better or worse. *A tower of strength in the face of their enemies.* It actually says that in the wedding service, you know. You'd never think getting married would mean making enemies, would you, but I've gained a whole army of them. If the British Royal Family spent half as much time hating Mr Hitler as they do hating me, perhaps we wouldn't all be in this fix.'

Close up, the Duchess looked tired, her skin as soft as cigarette paper and one eyelid twitching. Although they were alone, she lowered her voice.

'Now *you're* English, but you choose to live in Germany . . .'

'At the moment.'

Almost beneath her breath she said, 'I understand.'

Clara tilted her head and waited. She sensed that the Duchess would not require much of an invitation to open up about her problems, even to a virtual stranger. Clara had rejected her British heritage by choosing to live abroad. That was enough. Wallis picked up a string of coloured gems, rubbing them absently like a pagan rosary.

'I of all people know about divided loyalties. I do miss England sometimes, at least I miss Fort Belvedere and bridge and golf and the flat I used to have in Bryanston Court where all our set would drop in for cocktails. We had such a terrifically gay time, but David's family were determined to make things difficult. It was them that started the war.'

'The war? I'm not sure I understand.'

'The war with *us*. All my husband wants is for me to have the title HRH and to be received properly by his family. You would think he was asking for the moon, but the King has issued instructions to the Foreign Office that anyone using that term for me will be officially reprimanded. So petty! David says all he wants is an assurance that simple courtesies will be forthcoming. It needs to be the two of us together in the same position. Both HRH. People might say it's a trifle, with the war on, but I don't think it's a trifle at all.'

She was caressing another piece, a sumptuous yellow gold brooch sculpted into a luscious panther, but her thoughts were miles away. There was, Clara realized, something pantherish about Wallis herself; the tense, arrested muscles, the extreme rigour, as she paced the confines of this ramshackle villa like a lithe cat behind bars.

'When we returned to England in September the family wouldn't put us up. They wouldn't even have him met. Everywhere we saw rigid, turned backs. It's the Queen, you know. She bears a terrible grudge. It's impossible to imagine so much anger inside such a *small* person.'

Small. She picked out the word as if with sugar tongs. The adjective, delivered with biting Baltimore scorn, was made to encompass everything about England's new queen, from her background, intellect and outlook to her apparent lack of style. Beside the tiny, curvy Queen Elizabeth the Duchess stood slim as a Sobranie cigarette.

'The fact is, the Queen simply couldn't bear to have my husband back in England. He offered his services in any capacity and he was given a job working with the British Military Mission at Vincennes while I had to join a French relief organization knitting socks. I did everything I could. David's so angry, it smoulders away in him.'

She picked out a ring, slid it onto her finger and held it out reflexively. She had large hands, somehow too big for her body, but she turned it this way and that almost defiantly, as if to say this was the hand that her husband had chosen. This hand above an empire.

'Stanley Baldwin called me a whore, did you know?'

There was a glint in her eye, a tear that trembled but refused to fall.

'Surely not.'

'Oh yes. As far as David's family and the Court are concerned I might as well not exist. I feel like a bird in a cage. I'm ragged with nerves. You've no idea.'

Clara laid a light hand on her arm.

'It'll be better in the Bahamas. All that sun.'

'That's if we make it. Our Spanish friends are saying we'll never get there alive. Once we set foot on that boat we'll be murdered en route.'

'You don't honestly believe your husband's family would have you murdered? Now, when you're not even living in England any more?'

There was a wildness in Wallis's eyes. The tension was maddening her. If she had been told that Queen Elizabeth supplied the knife herself she would have believed it.

'I suppose I don't. Not really. The Germans tell us one thing, the English tell us another. I don't know what to believe. All I know is, I hate that country. I shall hate it to my grave.'

Suddenly, the frenzy left her and her shoulders drooped.

'Do you know what the worst thing is? Really the worst?'

Clara hesitated. In a time of war, the worst could be so many things. The loss of relatives, the death of children. The Duke himself must be haunted above all by the prospect of his own country being conquered by a merciless Nazi regime.

'It's different for everyone, I suppose.'

'My husband says the worst thing is having to leave all our possessions behind in Paris. We had no choice. They're sitting in boxes in our villa in the Boulevard Suchet and I don't know if I'll ever see them again. All our linen and china and antique glassware and silver. And our Meissen tableware. A friend brought our lovely George II silver salt cellars down to the south of France in his pockets, but it's getting so hard to retrieve one's valuables. For myself, I wouldn't mind so much, but David asks why should we disappear to some fly-blown island without them? If we're to do any entertaining at all in the godforsaken Bahamas then we'll need all our tableware. My husband was a king until very recently and there are standards to be kept, but the authorities here seem to have no conception of how important these things are when one entertains regularly. They have eventually agreed to allow our maid to be sent back to Paris to collect as much as she can, but it's taking an age and we've not heard a thing. I've no idea why.'

Clara thought of the river of refugees pushing through France and Spain, the routes choked for miles with abandoned trucks, carts and cars with mattresses tied to the roof. The roads blooming white with dust. How long would it take for one maid to make her way through two countries, with a car full of china?

'You could be waiting for weeks. Months even. With respect, I would advise you to sail as soon as possible.'

'You know what?' Wallis's face had regained its spritely humour. 'I entirely agree. The fact is, I'm sick to death of all this. I'm desperate to leave. But my husband is adamant. Mostly I can persuade him about anything to do with the household, but in this matter he's simply put his foot down. It's just like he was over the abdication. He can be unbelievably stubborn when he wants. I've spent hours arguing, but he won't step on that boat until our things arrive.'

Could it be true? That the real reason that the Duke of Windsor would not leave Portugal, despite their perilous position and the urgency of the hour, despite the relentless march of an advancing Nazi army and the prospect of England itself under siege, was because he was awaiting a delivery of household goods? What would Ian Fleming make of that?

Chapter Twenty-one

Clara telephoned the German Embassy on Thursday morning as instructed from a café near her pension where she had gone to find breakfast. The café was barely more than a couple of tables squeezed onto a pavement in one of the twisting lanes that led down from the Castelo. It had peeling wallpaper inside and a fan wheezing asthmatically overhead, but it also had a call box at the back and the number Hanna Reitsch had given her connected her to a switchboard where a precise Prussian voice informed Clara that she should report to the Sturmbannführer's office at precisely four o'clock that afternoon. The thought made her stomach churn and when she returned to her table she looked at the *pastel de nata* on her plate, its custard spiced with cinnamon and vanilla, thick and creamy with a glossy crust, and realized she could not possibly eat it. Apprehension had strangled her appetite and it was all she could do to choke down a glass of water as she wondered how to pass the hours until the confrontation.

She wandered up to the fortifications of the castle and

looked out at the jumbled roofs in ochre and rose pink like a patchwork of different textures stitched by a rough and inaccurate hand. Far below, the city glittered with an azure purity, and on the walls around her peacocks strutted, fanning jewelled tails of a hundred eyes. How ironic that this castle should be dedicated to the patron saint of England. What protection could Saint George possibly provide when, any day now, Goering unleashed his air attack on England? Clara imagined the lights of London extinguishing in the darkness, one by one, as the massed fleet of Luftwaffe came over, raining bombs. Afterwards the same houses with doors like mouths and windows like broken eyes, under a blanket of ash. The picture was so vivid that her stomach twisted and she shivered, despite the warmth of the sun.

Leaving the Castelo behind she wandered down the dramatically sloping cobbled streets towards the Tagus River. The Alfama was the oldest district in Lisbon, the only area untouched by the famous earthquake, and still a mediaeval maze of alleys and tiny squares. Barefoot children and cats ran between huddled, whitewashed houses whose balconies were hung with birdcages and washing. A dog lay asleep on a step, a spill of scarlet geraniums dotting the wall behind him like the blood-spattered residue of a passing fight. Fisherwomen passed with baskets on their heads, as they must have for centuries. Clara followed the labyrinth of streets, ducking under small archways, until she came to a sun-warmed square where from the steps of the church a group of women in ecclesiastical black were watching their children play. Even as they talked, the mothers' eyes dwelt fondly on their infants, at once alert and absent, and something about that protective gaze brought Clara's own mother unexpectedly to mind.

How often, caught off guard in a shop window or in the mirror, had Clara seen her own features moulding and settling themselves into her mother's familiar lines? Helene Vine had been an unhappy woman, she realized that now. Beyond the dazzling veil of her beauty was a kind of absence, as if part of her would always exist in the Germany of her birth rather than with the craggy, tweed-jacketed husband, ten years her elder, possessed of a puritanical rigour in his bearing and a chill in his pale eyes. Clara had a photograph of her standing on a windswept hill on one of their walking holidays, head averted and eyes looking into the distance, far across a continent perhaps, to where her life might have been. Now, watching these women, with their mixture of negligence and indulgence, Clara wondered if her mother had ever regarded her in that way. Or if her own eyes would ever follow a child with the same fond devotion. The image came to her of Katerina, the young girl from the orphanage, and her solemn assurance. *I don't need a mother.* The child was wrong, of course. Everyone needed a mother. Quite apart from the fact that this sister of hers seemed to have disappeared without a backward glance.

We have a lot in common, you and I. We're both alone.

Even if it was how she appeared to the world, Clara had never chosen to be alone. Although solitude might be her habitat now, and it may be the only way she could keep herself safe, it would never be her natural state. Yet it was vital not to dwell on her loss. Wasn't that what they told you? Live in the moment. And there could scarcely be a more terrifying moment than the one she was facing now.

The first thing that was obvious, as she was shown into Walter Schellenberg's office, was that he was in far greater need of Pervitin pills than she was. His muscular physique was evident, but he looked much older than he was, the skin on his wide cheekbones waxen, his eyes bruised from lack of sleep, the face full of haggard shadows. He was dressed as a civilian in a dark grey, double-breasted suit and Hermès tie, as though he knew his reputation was fearsome enough without the help of an SS tunic and cap. She thought of what Fleming had said about his background, how he tried to keep a distance from his more brutish colleagues, and involuntarily glanced at his well-manicured hands – hands that played the violin in Heydrich's string quartet. Yet hands that also wore a signet ring with a large blue stone, the one that according to his fiancée Irene contained a capsule of deadly cyanide.

He was standing beside a pair of lofty windows giving a view of the harbour, flipping through a file, and as Clara entered he went to a safe positioned behind his desk and stowed the file away, spinning the dial to lock it before turning to greet her.

'So this is the famous Clara Vine I've heard so much about.'

There was a flirtatious edge to his tone, calculated, Clara guessed, to soften her up and catch her off guard, but the face was full of intricate intelligence and the gaze was razor-sharp.

These eyes had watched people in interrogation rooms, torture cells and execution grounds. They studied twitches, tells and body language, the way a scholar studies an ancient manuscript. She must not drop her guard for a second.

'Please sit down. We have coffee, unless you'd like something stronger?'

He waved a bottle of Portuguese Macieira brandy at her and removed the stopper with a practised flick.

'It's early, I know, but, when in Rome . . .'

She sat, smoothing her skirt, readying herself. She had dressed plainly, with no jewellery, in a belted cotton dress of cornflower blue and low heels, attempting to project the image of a professional who had performed an intelligence mission and was there to report back.

'I'll just have coffee, please.'

'Certainly. Black with one sugar?'

Schellenberg ran a hand across his thick brush of hair, already flattened with brilliantine into a crisp side parting, and poured a cup from a trolley waiting beside him, alongside a glass of brandy for himself. Then, shuffling through the files on his desk, he extracted one and withdrew it. It was a standard item of Nazi bureaucracy, a plain manila file with the RHSA logo at the top, stamped *geheime Reichssache* – top secret state document – the second highest classification. It was accompanied by the stamp of a purple eagle and swastika emblem, but the aspect of the file that triggered Clara's alarm, and sent a violent tremble through her body, was the fact that along the bottom, in black Gothic script, were the words *Clara Vine* and the stencilled number *6732*.

He leafed through, then picked out a paper, to which two photographs were attached at the side and the top left-hand corner, the same ones that appeared on her identity card, and skimmed them, showily flicking his gaze between the pictures and Clara herself.

'If you ask me, you're prettier in person than on screen. It's usually the opposite with actresses. One falls in love with a silver image, only to find when one meets the lady in question that the truth is all too unvarnished.' He gave a deprecating shrug. 'Or perhaps I'm just too practised at seeing behind the mask. Something of an occupational hazard, I suppose.'

If this was a reference to his famed interrogation skills, then it was not lost on Clara. Schellenberg's suave wit was barbed, like a feathered fishing lure with a hook inside.

'I was thinking about your profession only this morning. Some VIP back home gave me a list of movies to pick up out here. Those that the good Doktor Goebbels sees fit to ban in the Reich can be taken in through the diplomatic pouch.' He winked. 'It's highly irregular but that doesn't stop them asking.'

The confidence was transparently intended to disarm her, so Clara smiled and took the initiative.

'I hope the Minister told you my findings about Hans Reuber . . .?'

'Yes, yes.' To judge by his reaction, she might have been asking if Schellenberg had enjoyed good weather during his stay. 'Thanks for your investigative work. It's a relief to be able to set my mind at rest about the man, but to be honest with you, Fräulein Vine, the activities of Hans Reuber weren't the sole reason for my asking you here today.'

He rubbed his chin lightly.

'You come highly recommended. Doktor Goebbels assures me you are totally reliable and utterly discreet.'

'I hope so.'

'So do I . . . because it is impossible to ignore the fact that you are, by birth, half English.'

The smile dropped. His flirtation was over as suddenly as it had begun.

'What does this file tell us?' He resumed leafing through her papers. 'You were born in 1907 in London, England. Your father is Ronald Vine, your late mother, Helene Vine, was born Helene Neumann in Hamburg. You have a sister, Angela, and a brother Kenneth. Your German's flawless. I imagine you spoke it as a child, though there is a slight accent.'

This took her by surprise. No one had commented on her accent for years. Generally, the softer, rounder trace of vowels passed undetected as the English edge migrated deep into the ether of her speech. She was beginning to understand exactly how little escaped Schellenberg's forensic attention.

'My accent may be flawed, but my loyalties aren't. Even as a child. My father was always a keen supporter of the National Socialist Party.'

That much was the truth.

'You were how old when you came to Germany? Remind me.'

'Twenty-six.'

'It was,' he made a show of consulting the file again, 'April 1933. To be precise.'

'I have lived in Berlin for seven years. I became a full citizen of the Reich and renounced my British passport.'

'All the same. Despite the passport and the papers and all those bureaucratic ... trifles ... these must be difficult times.'

'As they are for any citizen of the Fatherland.'

'Your two countries are at war.'

'As I said, Herr Schellenberg, I have only one country.'

'Of course. That much we would never doubt.'

He flicked a paper and regarded her ruminatively.

'You became friends with an actress, Helga Schmidt, who later killed herself. You remain in contact with her son and his grandmother, is that right?'

'It's right.'

'You have since become friendly with certain well-placed women – Frau Doktor Goebbels and Frau Goering among them. You have enjoyed a few – what shall we call them? – liaisons – with Party members, yet you have never been tempted to settle down. Would that be accurate?'

'If you put it like that.' Not with a Party member.

'You have enjoyed a number of male friendships. Klaus Müller, Arno Strauss, Max Brandt, Conrad Adler.'

She was aware that her body was stiff from sitting still, yet to shift would be a comment in itself, semaphoring weakness or guilt. She steeled herself to remain immobile.

'All these relationships have been short-lived. One, indeed, particularly so. I see Obersturmbannführer Adler was killed

323

in an incident last year, in an unauthorized attempt to leave the Reich.'

Clara's eyes were on him, yet at the same time they were looking through him, to the patch of unknown ground where Leo Quinn lay alongside Conrad Adler, their mingled rivulets of blood blackening the dust. Just hours before, she had refused Leo's urging to take the place in Adler's car, and promised to follow them. Leo assumed it was her who was in danger, but instead it was his own life he gave for that last contact with Clara. In the months that followed, that image she had concocted of the two sprawled bodies imposed itself on her. She had no real idea what had happened, yet in her worst moments she returned to it and embellished it with detail, curated it and burnished it, adding fresh brushstrokes of pain to the picture she kept so fiercely hidden.

Her eyes focused on Schellenberg again. How long did he intend to run through his history of her personal life, all correct and also the opposite of correct? How far did he intend to rehearse her story, and for what purpose? Was he waiting for a snag in the narrative, some non sequitur that would prise apart the contradictions he sensed within her, or had those same informers who noted her 'liaisons' with other men and confided them to the Gestapo also discovered the truth about her life?

'I wonder . . .'

He stood rigidly, staring down at her. Despite the fatigue, there was a priest–like stillness in his demeanour, a kind of patience that suggested he was prepared to wait as long as it took for his opponent to condemn themself.

'Do you enjoy espionage, Fräulein Vine?'

'I'm sorry?'

'Your recent task, I mean. Checking up on Hans Reuber.'

What game was he playing? She remembered Ian Fleming's remark. *The whole trick is to work your way into somebody's head and then think fast to get yourself out of trouble. It's not the hand you're dealt, it's how you play it.* The only cards in Clara's hand were her reputation as an actress who had managed to survive in Berlin without asking too many questions. That was the role she needed to play.

'Not really.' A disarming smile. 'It's hardly my forte. I'm afraid filming a spy movie at Babelsberg is about my limit.'

'No matter.'

At last he sat down and leaned back in the leather desk chair, steepling his hands together as if in prayer. His tone shifted abruptly. Suddenly he was discursive, reasonable, confiding. A man with the leisure for a friendly conversation.

'Myself, I have to confess, I *do* enjoy the challenge. Sniffing out spies is so different from all that Jew-hunting business.' His handsome mouth twisted in distaste. 'The Gestapo's work is very crude, for the most part. Searching for hidden people, false doors and compartments at the back of cupboards and so on. Usually when they go in the Jews come pouring out straight away like termites. It's no effort whatsoever to pick them up.'

He trickled some brandy into his glass. The Macieira was liquid amber, as though the Mediterranean sun itself had been distilled and bottled.

'Finding spies and conducting interrogations are quite a

different art. Or perhaps they're not an art at all. Your work is Art. Mine is more like Science.'

'How so?'

'Because it requires a deep and scientific knowledge of the human condition. In fact, the heart of my work is psychology.'

Schellenberg stretched out his legs before him, sipping at his brandy. He had a somewhat portentous delivery, like someone who has been invited to lecture on his favourite topic – car engines, or Prussian history, or famous wines – and is determined to take his time.

'I was talking about it at dinner the other day to SS-Reichsführer Himmler. You won't know this, but Himmler recently took possession of a very beautiful holiday home in Schönau overlooking the Königssee. It's on the Obersalzberg, very close to the Berghof. Convenient for when he's working with the Führer, just a few minutes away in the car, but far enough that the family can enjoy all that alpine air and really feel they're on vacation. Anyhow, this was all very well until Himmler discovered that the previous owner of the house was Doktor Sigmund Freud. You know, the Jewish psychiatrist. And once Herr Himmler had got over his outrage, I was able to point out that they did, in fact, have some qualities in common.'

Clara was impressed. Suggesting to Himmler that he had anything at all in common with the notorious Jew Sigmund Freud was daring, if not downright foolhardy.

'Our line of work can't be done without a sophisticated understanding of the human mind. Just like the unfortunate Doktor Freud advises, that mind, its attachments, likes and dislikes, phobias even, are formed early. But once formed, they are there for life, and that makes us all vulnerable. Dig deep enough, find the thing a man cares about most, and you will find his weakness. And once you have that, he will be ready to talk, whether he's on the couch, as in Doktor Freud's case, or sitting in front of me. A psychologist can tell you how men under pressure will behave. How to spot when they're lying. How to spot if they are the *type* to betray – which as it turns out is almost every type.'

'Every type?'

An urbane shrug. 'You seem surprised, but betrayal is natural to human beings. A man will betray the most loving wife in the space of time it takes to order a beer. He will betray her day after day, for years at a time, as easily as he washes his hands, or changes his clothes. If he will betray his wife like that, how much more will he be ready to betray his country?'

He shook his head and Clara caught the slight, enticing fragrance of his hair oil.

'You see, people will talk about how they cherish integrity, democracy, freedom, decency, et cetera.' How terrible was that casual *et cetera*. How languid the dismissal of all the values she tried to defend and live by. 'But none of that will keep a man from betraying another when it comes to it. Or a woman, either, for that matter.'

Clara imagined Schellenberg interrogating his prisoners, probing the tell-tale signs of weakness, wooing his victim with the subtle attention of a lover, the light veneer of charm silvering over the threat of pain or death.

'Don't think it gives me pleasure when they break. God, I'm not that kind of man. It's the intellectual aspect I enjoy. Like bridge. Do you play bridge?'

'Badly.' She smiled, deprecatingly. 'I can't really cope with all that counting cards and keeping a record in your head. And having to bluff that you don't have good cards, or convince the other players that you have a winning hand when it's no more than a few clubs. It's not that I don't enjoy playing . . .' Had his fiancée Irene mentioned their recent encounter at Magda Goebbels' card party? 'It's just that I'm hopeless at it.'

'You're too hard on yourself. I find it difficult to believe you're hopeless at anything.'

It was time to deflect attention from her own abilities.

'If you don't mind me asking, Herr Schellenberg, what brings you to Lisbon?'

Such a direct and guileless question was typical of an actress.

'I don't mind at all. Since you ask, I have a little business with your Duke of Windsor. He's staying here, as it happens. I have to say the British lost a great leader when they decided to get rid of him. And on such flimsy grounds. Objecting to the fact that his wife had been previously married.'

This remark exuded all the disdain of a man going through a bitter and truncated divorce, as indeed Schellenberg was.

'The Duke's a man dedicated to peace. Perhaps, who knows, there might come a day when he can help Britain in that great cause. In fact ...' He reached for a piece of paper on his desk. 'On the subject of your Englishness, that reminds me. There was a speech the other day by Winston Churchill. Let me read you a bit.'

He began to read aloud in a drunken slur. That was how Churchill was always portrayed in sketches and on state radio, conforming to the popular view that the British Prime Minister was perpetually intoxicated. As Schellenberg recited the transcript, he waved a cigarette in hammy parody of Churchill's own cigar.

'*Even though large tracts of Europe and many old and famous States have fallen or may fall into the grip of the Gestapo and all the odious apparatus of Nazi rule, we shall not flag or fail. We shall go on to the end. We shall fight in France, we shall fight on the seas and oceans, we shall fight with growing confidence and growing strength in the air, we shall defend our island, whatever the cost may be. We shall fight on the beaches, we shall fight on the landing grounds, we shall fight in the fields and in the streets, we shall fight in the hills; we shall never surrender.*

'And so on. You get the idea. He writes it all himself, apparently. There's more.

'*Even if, which I do not for a moment believe, this island or a large part of it were subjugated and starving, then our Empire beyond the seas, armed and guarded by the British Fleet, would carry on the struggle until, in God's good time, the New World, with all its power and might, steps forth to the rescue and the liberation of the old.*

'Tell me, does it stir your soul to hear such flowery stuff from one of your compatriots?'

A deep stillness took hold of Clara as the speech reverber-ated through her. Even when delivered in the mocking tones of Walter Schellenberg, Winston Churchill's words reached to the marrow of her bones. She thought of her country, of Angela and Kenneth taking up arms as Nazi soldiers marched through the city streets and country lanes, and further on through the farmland and wheat fields soon to be raped by the Reich. The population fighting, or worse, as in Paris, standing in abject misery as invincible columns of Germans filed past. The roar of planes overhead and the taste of fire and metal in the air.

It took an almost inhuman effort to prevent the tears coming to her eyes.

Quietly she said, 'It does. How could it not?'

Schellenberg jumped up from his seat, beaming.

'That was exactly what I wanted to hear.'

She looked at him dumbfounded. Surely she had betrayed herself. How could this skilled interrogator not observe her blood rising to Churchill's words like a magnet turning to north?

Schellenberg was waving his brandy glass with satisfaction.

'You would need to be a stone, a clod, to hear that speech and remain unmoved. It's a speech designed to make the heart beat faster. Words like that could raise the dead, let alone the English. If you had no reaction to this speech, you would lack all sensitivity to language and that, as it happens, is what I brought you here to talk about.'

Clara strove to read the twists of his mind. What could he possibly want of her?

'It's true,' she conceded. 'English was my mother tongue. I love the language.'

'Tell me, have you heard of P.G. Wodehouse? Another fine writer, though perhaps not in Churchill's league.'

'He's one of my favourite authors.'

'Is he? Well, as it happens, he was recently apprehended by our troops in France and he's on his way to Berlin, where he'll be giving some broadcasts under the guidance of Doktor Goebbels. Goebbels wants a few speeches from him about life in Germany to reassure our American friends. The future of Europe under National Socialism. Food in the shops, happy people in the cinemas. That sort of thing. I'm looking forward to meeting Wodehouse, but until he arrives, Fräulein Vine, I was thinking of *you*.'

'But . . .'

Was it possible that Schellenberg was asking her to broadcast to Americans, or worse to her fellow Britons? To urge them to lay down arms and accept a Nazi occupation in the interests of peace? It would make perfect sense. What better use for an English actress who had turned her back on the land of her birth and embraced the Fatherland? Clara Vine would be the female Lord Haw Haw, preaching treachery in honeyed tones. Her entire soul revolted at the thought.

'I wouldn't be the right person to broadcast. I'm barely known outside Germany.'

Schellenberg frowned quizzically, head on one side.

'That wasn't what I was thinking. Though now you mention it, I shall bear it in mind. But my first plan revolves around another issue. Correct me if I'm wrong but Herr

Wodehouse has an encyclopaedic knowledge of the English ruling classes?'

'I can't think of anyone who knows the upper classes better.'

'Precisely. And until he arrives, it was in the field of etiquette I wanted your help.'

Etiquette?

Clara's mind filled with Angela's strictures on addressing bishops, on the difference between signing letters *Yours sincerely* and *Yours faithfully*, never *Yours truly*, of the serried ranks of dinner table cutlery, soup spoons and fruit forks and fish knives, that existed to catch you out. The invisible fault-lines dividing everyday language. Looking glass, never mirror. Napkin, never serviette. Writing paper, never notepaper. Etiquette was a complex theology. A dinner table was a minefield where errors lurked like unexploded ordnance. The words you used and the way you held a teacup were unerring tests of authenticity. But how could all this possibly concern Walter Schellenberg?

He noted her confusion and smiled.

'Let me explain. It's no secret that in the event that Churchill does not change his mind, and I think we can guess that he won't, Germany will soon be advancing operations towards England. Reich Marshal Goering is stepping up air attacks and the invasion should be fairly swift and simple. But before then, a few measures are in place. The Propaganda Ministry has been rewriting the prophecies of Nostradamus to predict that England will fall and getting the pamphlets circulated in Great Britain. Psychological warfare, it's called. But my own initiative is somewhat more complicated. I'm putting together something of an advance party. Do you understand what I mean by that?'

'You want to put some agents into Britain.'

'Precisely. And the fact is, despite the many similarities between our two nations, there are certain idiosyncrasies about the English that a German can never understand. The language itself, for a start. English is a good language for spies. It takes so much decoding. It's never simple for us Germans. Apparently innocuous words conceal so many meanings, so many ways to catch one out. Let alone the conventions. Take a tennis match, for example. What do you call the man who sits on the high seat and calls the points?'

'The umpire?'

'Whereas a German might call him a referee. What's silly mid on?'

'A fielding position in cricket. On the leg side, very near the batsman. My brother taught it to me.'

Schellenberg reached forward and tapped the manila file with Clara's name on it.

'This file tells me all that the SD knows about Fräulein Clara Vine. Everything the security service has collected on you for a number of years. Every role you have played. Every apartment, every associate, every handsome officer who has caught your eye. Yet it makes no mention of the most important thing about you. The very essence of your being.'

'And what would you say that was?'

'Your deep knowledge of English life. You know every little detail that makes a man English – how much to tip the taxi driver, how to order a gin and tonic in a tavern . . .'

'A pub.'

'Thank you. How to . . .'

The door opened a crack and an assistant peered in.

'Herr Schellenberg?'

He shook a hand, like someone repelling a rabid dog.

'I'm busy.'

'It's the Foreign Minister's office calling from Berlin.'

'They'll have to wait.'

His eyes remained fixed on Clara.

'We were talking about psychology earlier and the fact is, different nations do have different psychologies. It's a racial thing. I may speak French like a native but the psychology of the French is almost incomprehensible to me. The British, perhaps, I feel a little closer to. They are a proud and warlike race. I have had the Goering Institute prepare psychological profiles of enemy nations and I put all my people through courses in race science, biology, the customs of other countries, language, character, geo-politics, and so on. By the time I've finished with them they know as much about their target country as if they'd been born there. They think in their new language, they even dream in it. But you, Fräulein Vine, have no need of that. You already understand how the British behave.'

Clara strove to keep her calm, but relief, compounded with astonishment, was pounding through her. She had survived the interrogation. Her true loyalties had not been found out. Nor, as far as she could tell, was she to be used as a pawn in Germany's propaganda war by being made to broadcast to Britain. Instead, Germany's counter-espionage chief wanted her services to train Nazi spies. He was enlisting Clara's expertise to spy on her own country.

'If you agree to our proposition,' here a courtesy nod to the hypothetical possibility that she might be able to decline, 'you will require an extensive briefing. You would work under the guidance of the counter-espionage headquarters in the Berkaerstrasse in Dahlem, and you would make regular reports to . . .'

The secretary's head reappeared unwillingly around the door, a flustered bloom on her cheeks.

'My apologies, mein Herr.'

'I said no interruptions, woman.'

'Herr von Ribbentrop says to tell you that it's urgent.'

Schellenberg suppressed a sigh and rose.

'We'll continue this conversation shortly. Wait here. Help yourself to more coffee.'

Picking up the file with Clara's name on it, he rammed it in the safe, turned, and stalked wordlessly from the room.

Clara did as he had ordered and helped herself to coffee then sat again, a single observation throbbing through her head. She was possessed of an intense clarity that came to her at moments of extreme tension. Although Schellenberg had shut the door of the safe he had not, as before, spun the dial. Was it possible that the safe was still open? And if it was, might she, without knowing the combination, be able to retrieve her file in Schellenberg's absence and discover precisely what the SD's counter-espionage department really thought of her?

She remained still for a second, glancing upwards at the

light fittings for evidence of recording equipment, as though her very thoughts might be detected, before rising and crossing swiftly to the safe. She grasped the dial and, as she had guessed, the door clicked open. It was a small space, less than a foot in width, perhaps a foot and a half in length, and it contained a thick stack of files rammed one on top of the other. Some were worn, others new and a couple tied with ribbon. Her own was right at the top. As Schellenberg had intimated, it contained just two pages of closely typed script. Shakily she read it through.

Clara Helene Vine, born in London, 1907. Shape of face: oval. Colour of eyes: blue. Colour of hair: brown. Distinguishing features: mole on left shoulder. Her address. A list of all the films she had made. Details and dates of the two separate incidents when she had been arrested and questioned by the Gestapo. Names of various men she had been seen with. The address of her godson, Erich Schmidt. But nothing to suggest that the SD had any suspicion of her as an enemy agent.

Nothing alarming at all.

By now the caffeine had entered her veins, spiking her nerves. Emboldened by relief, she returned her own file to the safe and contemplated the remaining stack. What point was there in looking? The comment of Schellenberg's fiancée, Irene, sneaking a read of his secret reports, rang in her ears.

Frankly, they're so full of code letters they look like someone's fallen backwards on a typewriter.

Nonetheless, she reached for the next file. It was a long list of names, alphabetized, alongside addresses and itemized payments. Local agents who had been bribed to inform.

Alberto Estacio, waiter, Rua do Crucifixo. Reports French Jews discussing sabotage of German car.

Anabela Cruz. Laundress. Monitors English guests at the Hotel Aviz.

She strained her ears for the sound of approaching footsteps but the air was empty except for the distant clack of typewriters in the secretaries' office and the insistent trill of a telephone. She ran her fingers over the spines of the remaining files. There must be something more than this.

Another file. Photographs of various public buildings and private houses. With shaky fingers she shuffled through police mug shots of ill-shaven men. Then Clara recognized the file that Schellenberg had been reading as she came in.

This one had the same stamp as her own, with the added classification of *Top Secret* marked in red across the top and alongside, in the dense Gothic font used by the SS, the title:

Operation Willi

Inside was a far thicker sheaf of papers than in her own file, some of it in code. Her eyes skimmed through telegrams from the Reich Main Security Office, the Foreign Ministry and the Reich Chancellery itself. It was clear, on a rapid scan of the material, that the subjects of the file were the Duke and Duchess of Windsor. That made sense. Schellenberg had told her he had private business concerning the Duke. One of the papers was a report from a Spanish diplomat who had dined privately with the couple a few days before.

The Duke is known to be in favour of a peaceful compromise with

Germany and is convinced that if he had stayed on the throne things would have been different. He is extremely annoyed at the attentions of the British security service and he does not one bit like the idea of becoming Governor of the Bahamas. He says Britain should beware, Germany will bomb their industrial centres out of existence.

Another read:

The Duke is convinced that if he had been King it would never have come to war. He agrees to cooperate at a suitable time in the establishment of peace. He has agreed a code word, on the receiving of which he will immediately come back over.

More recent was a carbon copy of a letter sent by von Ribbentrop from on board his special train in Fuschl, Austria, detailing a conversation he had had with Adolf Hitler.

'*The Führer has ordered that fifty million francs will be deposited in a Swiss bank for the Duke's personal use if he makes some official gesture dissociating himself from the Royal Family. The Führer's preference is for him to live in Switzerland, though he could choose another neutral country if it was under the influence of the Reich.*'

It appeared that the Germans had an entire plan for the future of the Duke and Duchess of Windsor. But what say would the couple themselves have in it?

A clatter in the corridor outside alerted her to advancing steps. She froze, analysing the footfall with the intent precision of a gazelle. They were heels, swift and purposeful, signifying a female secretary coming to check on her perhaps, or to enquire if she needed more coffee. Turning to face the door, Clara pushed the file back and the safe door to. There was no time to sit down. She would be caught red-handed. She could imagine the startled face, the expression of polite enquiry turning to suspicion, and then all the rest that would follow – the furore, the cell, the questions. The heels were almost upon her, clacking on the parquet, each one going through her like a gunshot.

'Hansi!'

A voice floated along the corridor. The steps halted.

'Where have you put my stamps?'

'They're in the place they always are.'

'If that's the case, why can't I find them?'

A heartbeat passed and Clara almost heard the slight exasperated sigh that issued from Hansi's lips before the heels swivelled and retreated, their clicks gradually dying into the distance.

Come on!

Steeling herself to continue she retrieved the file and turned to the next page.

The Führer has asked to be updated daily. The preferred title will be 'President of the Great British Republic' and the Duke's first act should be to make a public statement asking his people to lay down arms for peace. The Führer advises using the Duchess of Windsor to persuade her husband. She has great influence over the Duke.

Her eyes flicked swiftly down, until they reached the final sentence.

If the Duke should prove hesitant, the Fuhrer will have no objection to him being brought to the correct decision by coercion, or even force.

The only other paper was a telegram from the Foreign Ministry, dated that morning. It stated simply:

The abduction is to take place tomorrow night, on the Führer's orders.

So the Duke and Duchess of Windsor were being brought to Germany. Whether they liked it or not.

By the time Schellenberg re-entered the room, Clara was sitting in her chair, her hands on her knees to prevent them trembling. His eyes flicked to the safe, but only for a microsecond.

'Hmm.' He eased a finger around his shirt collar. 'Looks like we'll have to halt our conversation, I'm afraid. That was urgent business from Wilhelmstrasse. They want a project I'm working on brought forward, so it seems we'll have to discuss the details of our little plan later.' He summoned a grin he was clearly not feeling and held out a hand.

'We'll pick up where we left off in Berlin, I hope? Time is of the essence, you understand. I'll brief Hanna Reitsch to fly you back to Tempelhof, if that suits you, the day after tomorrow? Jot down here the address of the place you're staying, and if you call when you're ready to leave I'll have my car take you to the airport.'

Did he trust her? Although his mouth was smiling, his eyes didn't match. Clara wrote down the address of the pension and hoped that his mind would be too busy with the problem of the Duke of Windsor to worry about her.

As she rose he seemed to remember something and felt in his pocket.

'Ah! Before you go, I have a little puzzle that you might

find entertaining. The Portuguese police came to me the other day with a problem. They arrested a young lady, around twenty years old, acting suspiciously. She was hanging around the Palacio casino at Estoril and they assumed she was attempting to pickpocket customers. There's been a spate of petty criminals targeting the clientele and the Palacio requested firm action. Anyhow, turns out the girl's from Berlin. At least she says she is. She has no papers with her, she wasn't even carrying a bag, but she speaks German and hardly a phrase of Portuguese, so I assume she's a Reich citizen. The trouble is she won't say another word, despite our most strenuous encouragements. The only thing she has produced is this.'

From his pocket he withdrew a blue leather pouch and tipped the contents out onto the table.

'Interesting, don't you think? She seems to think it will protect her. You're probably wondering why she would have thought that.'

Clara looked down. It was a brooch set in white gold, sparkling with sixteen exquisitely cut diamonds and a ruby at the heart. Wrought in the shape of a swastika. Schellenberg chuckled.

'Let me solve the puzzle for you. Heinrich Himmler believes that the swastika carries magic powers. Apparently it's an ancient Sanskrit symbol of light, been around for thousands of years, bringing luck to anyone who carries it, et cetera. But somehow I don't think it was that kind of magic the girl was counting on. No, it's something far more basic, I'm afraid. Base, even.'

Clara reached out to touch the brooch at the spot where its clasp was a little loose. Liable to fall off at any time.

'The reason, my dear, is very simple. This brooch is one that our minister Joseph Goebbels likes to hand out to attractive young women with whom he is . . . shall we say . . . particularly pleased. He gives the same brooch made in exactly the same design. It's his trademark. Everyone recognizes it. Even his wife has one, poor woman. They're made by Jaeger's, his favourite jeweller's.'

'I've heard of them.'

'I'm sure you have. A lady like yourself. God knows what this girl had to do to get one, but she must have regarded it as some kind of talisman. The ultimate protection. What does that American novel say? *Diamonds are a girl's best friend.* Something like that. It was obviously what this young lady was relying on. She asked the Portuguese police to pass it to me, knowing that I would understand its significance. Which of course I did and we took her in straight away.'

Clara picked up the brooch, as if to scrutinize it more closely. It was her own brooch, the one that Joseph Goebbels had given her in 1933. The same brooch whose receipt had been brought to her by Katerina Klimpel, in her desperate search for her elder sister.

Schellenberg watched the blood suffuse her cheeks.

'Pretty, isn't it? You like it, I can tell. I have yet to meet the woman who doesn't love diamonds. But this brooch is especially interesting. See the little mark on the back?'

He turned it over and showed her three vertical scratches. Clara had always wondered what they represented.

'These marks signify that this is the thirtieth brooch issued. This lucky lady came somewhere in a long line, though I daresay Jaeger's have made many more since then.'

He smiled pleasantly, his air of menace held lightly in check.

'Now what shall we do? This girl is currently languishing in one of our cells and I'm in two minds whether to hand her back to the Portuguese or make an example of her in a People's Court. There are any number of charges we can apply. Engaging in criminal activity, consorting with foreigners, degrading the name of the Reich. All quite serious and meriting a long corrective prison stretch. I think I'll allow *you* to choose. If we're to work together, I'm going to have to trust your judgement. Let this be our first project.'

Clara allowed herself a moment's reflection.

'It would be tempting either to punish this girl or to keep her in custody. She was almost certainly up to something, as you say, and the likelihood is that she will talk before long, but if you want to know what I think, my advice would be to send her back to Berlin and release her without charge.'

He frowned, puzzled.

'Explain.'

'You mention she's a favourite of Goebbels. In my view, there's absolutely no advantage in tangling with that particular minister. Not over something as trivial as this.'

The frown lingered for a moment, then softened into an indulgent grin.

'I see that as well as an expert operative I've found a diplomat too! In that case, for your sake, let's do as you recommend.

I'll have the young lady returned to Berlin and I'll order my agents to stop all action against her. Though if she should prove to be trouble, proceedings could begin again at any time.'

He sighed and drew a hand across his brow.

'Besides, believe me I have far greater problems on my plate than one of Doktor Goebbels' young fancies attempting to pickpocket customers outside a casino.'

Chapter Twenty-two

The tram from the Germany Embassy to Lisbon's Alfama district was dirty yellow and the lacquer on its wooden seats cracked and blistered. It climbed the vertiginous streets with alarming speed, rattling round the sharp corners, weaving its way up towards the pension, echoing the twists and turns of Clara's mind.

The brooch. The one that Goebbels had given her in 1933 and she had not expected to see again.

Was the girl who had been apprehended outside the casino at Estoril actually Sonja Klimpel? All Schellenberg had managed to establish was that she was German, yet she must have understood the significance of the brooch because she had clearly gambled that it would protect her if she came face to face with the authorities. But what was Sonja Klimpel doing that would require protection? Was she genuinely attempting to rob the casino customers, or did she have some other business?

She has no papers with her. Wasn't even carrying a bag. And she won't say another word, despite our most strenuous encouragements.

If Sonja was refusing the encouragements of Schellenberg's men, hers must be a pretty big secret. As Clara disembarked from the tram in the street where her pension was situated, something else came to her. The remark of Pedro, the patron, when she arrived.

The occupant left in a hurry. Left their clothes.

The street was deserted. She opened the heavy wooden door to the pension, crossed the small courtyard and passed quickly up the steps. Shutting the door of her room behind her, she closed the shutters, then looked for the fork she had seen on the tray. She placed it in the latch-hole, took it out again and bent the prongs halfway in an angle of ninety degrees, before snapping the handle off. Then she inserted the prongs of the fork in the latch-hole and threaded the handle of the fork through the prongs. The door was locked and the handle could not be turned.

It was only then that she turned to the closet and inspected its contents.

They were not the kind of clothes one would lightly abandon. A soft purple woollen jacket, of a quality one rarely saw any more, finely stitched, with the Adefa label in the collar certifying that it had only been made by Aryan hands. A printed summer dress and a chiffon blouse. A good maroon leather belt. And behind these clothes, hanging on a peg at the back of the closet, the bulge of something else – a distinctly upmarket knitting bag. She took it out and laid it on the floor. It was well-made and fashioned from soft ivory leather, with a chunky brass clasp and fake tortoiseshell handles. The leather was slightly scuffed and pleated at the sides and inside were knitting needles and several balls of wool of varying colours and thicknesses. Clara picked out the needles – no different from any of those one saw every day in Germany – and the wool was unremarkable too. Experimentally she picked up one of the balls and rolled it around in her palm. There was something strange about it. It felt heavy – heavier than it should. Grasping the end of the wool she tugged, unwinding the yarn with increasing urgency, until from the centre a small package tumbled. A chamois bag. She poured the contents into her hand and surveyed them in the sunlight that slid through the shutters' cracks.

They were diamonds. Dozens of them, flaring in the light. Some with a buttery tinge, others with a pure, crystalline fire. Flashing prisms that captured a rainbow in their sleek faceted sides. The ultimate weapon of war.

She picked up the next ball of wool and found the same. Then another and another, until twenty bags lay on the floor in front of her with hundreds of carats between them.

The audacity of it almost made her laugh aloud. What better place to conceal valuables than a knitting bag? Every German woman carried their knitting with them now. Everywhere you looked women were knitting feverishly away as if socks and scarves and vests were some kind of talisman that might protect their sons and husbands against the iron and fire of war. At a time when every bus and train passenger found themselves searched, when policemen would run expert hands down the seams of coats feeling for hidden

347

valuables, or pluck the hat from your head to finger the lining, which official would interrupt a young woman in the virtuous act of knitting for the Reich? What better way to transport a cache of diamonds?

As she stood in the darkened room, cradling the glinting grit in her hand, Clara thought of Jeanne Toussaint in the Cartier showroom in Paris.

We have a plan, quite an audacious plan, but I fear very much that it will never come off now. We've left it too late.

Jeanne loathed the Nazis and would do everything possible to keep her diamonds out of their hands. She was also a close associate of the Duke of Windsor. What had Wallis Simpson said, frustration vying with annoyance in her eyes?

He won't step on that boat until our things arrive.

The answer came to Clara even before she was able to give it thought. The Duke of Windsor had decided to serve his country in the currency he uniquely understood. Sonja Klimpel had intended to pass these diamonds to the Duke so that he could transport them out of Europe, and she had gone to the casino to arrange a meeting. Only she had been arrested before she had the chance.

And now there were plans to abduct the Duke of Windsor. It was imperative that someone get to him as soon as possible, but it was far too late to make her way to the English Cemetery and hunt out the grave of Henry Fielding. No time to leave a note for British intelligence operatives. Instead she opened the window and taking a handkerchief from her pocket attached it to the clothesline. *H for help.*

As she did she realized that even if Ian Fleming did

respond to her urgent message, he had already told her that the Germans had a ring of agents around the Windsors' villa. Anyone approaching Cascais would surely be noted. How else could the Duke be warned?

Then she remembered what the Duchess had told her about the boredom of their Lisbon life.

If it wasn't for the golf course and the casino we'd go quite mad. David adores the casino – he's there almost every night.

She would wait until nightfall. Thank goodness she had an evening dress and a pair of white silk gloves.

Pedro was sitting by the door with his newspaper as she came down the stairs. The heat of the evening had encouraged him to shed his shirt, and he was wearing only a string vest, his torso glistening with a chequered sheen of sweat. He lowered the paper and raised an eye.

'Off somewhere nice?'

'Everyone tells me you can't come to Lisbon without spending an evening at the casino.'

The sky was clear and the first stars were burning as Clara made her way out of the station at Estoril. The moon was white as a knuckle in the sky. Shadows had swallowed most of the buildings around the square but the broad boulevard was well lit and from sheer habit she skirted the pools of light, crossing into the gardens, where she felt the slither of her thin-soled shoes against the gravelled paths.

As she approached the casino, she knelt to buckle her shoe and gave an automatic scan of her surroundings.

There was a pair of men on the corner, dressed in dark suits, who looked as though they were waiting for a tram, except that there was no stop. A couple standing on the steps of the hotel opposite, chatting softly. A gardener, washing down the cobbled path with a hose. From a bar on the far side of the square issued the muffled blare of conversation and the clink of bottles. But nothing else. Why would there be?

She turned in the direction of the thick stripe of golden light that spilled out of the casino doors and down the wide marble steps.

She had almost reached it when she felt a hand on her arm and turned with a start.

'You've discovered my secret.'

It was a fair-haired figure, with brilliant blue eyes, dressed in a satin gown of vivid rose pink, with matching elbow gloves and a pearl choker. A fox stole coiled around her shoulders. For a second, Clara didn't recognize her until she realized that the slight woman in incongruous evening dress was the off-duty version of Hitler's favourite pilot, Flugkapitän Hanna Reitsch.

'I misjudged you, Fräulein Vine. I thought you'd be more interested in shopping – that's what most ladies love about Lisbon.'

The evening gown looked wrong on her, like a child dressing up. The dress, which met in a burst of frills at her bosom, and the pearls with their gentle lustre, were far too soft and frivolous for a woman as steely and unadorned as the aeroplanes she flew.

'I'd never have guessed you shared my love of the card tables. Are you a fellow addict?'

'I can't keep away,' Clara smiled.

'Me too, though I have to keep it very quiet.'

'Why should you? There's nothing unladylike about cards.'

'Oh, it's not that! It's just that nobody wants a pilot who's a gambler. Would you? Who wants to take their chances in the air with someone who likes to play for high stakes?'

'The Führer, for one.'

'Oh, the Führer's an exceptional man. He's not a natural flyer – in fact, between you and me he gets very nervous when it's time to board the plane, but he knows his destiny is written in the stars. Whenever he climbs aboard he reminds me that all of us are fated to give our lives for the Fatherland.'

'That's comforting.'

'Isn't it? I always associate the Führer with stressful situations.'

'As a matter of fact, so do I.'

'Do you? I'm glad it's not just me!' Delighted at this shared insight, Hanna gripped Clara's arm. There was a schoolgirlish quality to her hero-worship that sat at odds with the technical brilliance of her flying skill.

'What I mean is, whenever I'm in a difficult spot Hitler always comes to mind and he calms me. It's as though he's right alongside me. And I remember that if I'm serving my Führer and my Fatherland, nothing else matters.'

'And that's enough, is it? To calm your nerves?'

'That and gambling. I've been longing for an evening at the casino. I've been testing a flying petrol tanker over the

351

last few days and I tell you, compared with that no amount of losses at the card tables can scare me.'

The casino was full. Within its claret walls, the rank, alcoholic tang of sweat mingled with perfume and the choke of cigar smoke. The murmur of laughter and the click of gambling chips, the muffled comfort of deep carpets and thick wads of money. The glint of the chandeliers was reflected in glasses of cheap champagne. Among the mahogany tables and studded leather chairs sat German businessmen, French executives and refugees spending the last of their fortunes in the hope of raising a bribe to pay for a visa. Nonchalant women in diamond wristwatches and men in evening dress with silk scarves. American consular officials and Spanish traders chatting to Portuguese good-time girls. But there was no sign, in any of that international throng, of either the Duke or Duchess.

Clara and Hanna Reitsch settled themselves on barstools and ordered drinks.

'Now what do you like to play? Backgammon's my weakness.'

'Give me a game of roulette any day,' said Clara, pulling off her gloves.

'What do you have in that bag? It's not knitting, is it? How funny! I sincerely hope we won't have time for that!'

Glancing up the marble staircase Clara saw a door, one half concealed by the drapes of a velvet curtain, and the other half obstructed by a mountainous man with a heavy jaw and an eye-patch. What had Ian Fleming said about the man in British pay? *He's a German by heritage, name of Hertz.*

He manages the salle privée *where the Duke likes to play. Pretty silent sort of fellow with a wonky eye, but utterly trustworthy.* The man mountain had to be Hertz.

'In fact,' she turned to Hanna confidingly, 'you know what I'd really like? A game in the *salle privée*.'

'Oh, they won't let you in there. They're awfully stuffy about allowing ladies in. And besides, it's so much more fun down here.'

Already a couple of Casanovas along the bar were attempting to make eye contact, leering and tipping their glasses in what they must have assumed was an inviting manner. No doubt they thought Clara and Hanna, like so many of the other unaccompanied women, were out for a good time, allowing the pressures of wartime to loosen their manners and their morals. Clara amused herself wondering what they would have done if Flugkapitän Reitsch had chosen to wear her Luftwaffe uniform that evening. They would probably have had a stroke.

'I'd like to try,' said Clara, but Hanna was returning the men's glances with an enticing smile. Compared with the Führer and his doomy prognostications, even the lamest barfly must make sparkling company.

'Go ahead then.' She crossed her legs, revealing a pair of stockings that were another benefit of her travels. 'I'll take my chances down here.'

Clara mounted the staircase and approached the *salle privée*, but a few feet from the door she dropped one of her gloves. Immediately the man with the eye-patch moved to pick it up and when he stooped down she whispered, 'Ian Fleming sends his regards.'

Without a word Hertz straightened, focused his one good eye on her, smoothly drew the velvet curtain and pushed open the swing doors.

The Palacio *salle privée* was a cavernous space with gilt and dove-grey walls, dominated by a grand chandelier and to one side a kiosk where the cashier was flipping through piles of notes and exchanging them for plaques of red, yellow and white. The air was heavy with muttered concentration. Around the tables a mostly male cast was playing *chemin de fer*, blackjack and backgammon, and in the centre, at the top table, the diminutive figure of the Duke of Windsor was seated, fiddling with a jumbled pile of plaques as the croupier raked away his chips. Through the fug of cigar smoke Clara saw he had the despondent expression of someone who has been losing all evening and is clinging valiantly to the mood-enhancing qualities of alcohol.

As she approached, a casino official made to restrain her, but the Duke glanced up and a momentary puzzlement pierced his official demeanour, before he said, 'It's Fräulein Vine, isn't it? I'm losing my shirt tonight, Fräulein Vine. D'you have any clever theories?'

The Duke's delivery was a curious mix of standard upper-class English with a twang of something like cockney and a hint of American. That comment, *I'm losing my shirt tonight,* was like something he might have copied from a film. It was as though his voice, like everything else about him, had lost its identity and was searching for a new one.

'I'm not sure I do, sir.'

'Come now.' He cast a glance round the table, openly relieved at the distraction. 'Great thing about roulette is the novice knows just as much as the seasoned player. Sure you don't have a pet system? Everyone else here seems to.'

'Well . . .'

Clara had always loved mathematics. She adored feeling the numbers twist and turn, warp and evolve in her mind until they fell into place. She liked puzzles too, all kinds of crosswords, codes and patterns. She understood that patterns governed everything in the universe, from predicting the weather to the petals in a daisy, and she enjoyed how they made the brain fizz with possibility, like a motor clicking into higher gear. When she was a child her formidable father had recognized his younger daughter's talent and began setting her problems to be solved. It might have been a natural extension of his general approach towards her, because she was herself a puzzle to him, the only one of his offspring he did not entirely comprehend. So he resorted to drilling her in mathematics, teaching her theories, showing her the beauty and precision of numbers and how they interlocked like the facets of a perfectly cut jewel. Risk assessment, pattern identification, number games. She recalled a holiday in Cornwall when the three of them, Angela, Kenneth and herself, were buying ice cream and their father took the opportunity to teach her probability theory.

If two girls go into a shop selling vanilla, strawberry and chocolate ices, what is the probability that at least one of them will choose vanilla?

Roulette was even simpler than that. There were thirty-seven slots on the wheel, eighteen of them red, eighteen black and one zero. In terms of probability, each roll there would be an 18/37 chance of red or black. Not much of a winning strategy there. But then Clara remembered another theory her father had told her.

'I do know a strategy, sir, but I wouldn't want everyone hearing it.'

The croupier was calling for bets, spinning the wheel in one direction and preparing to spin the ball in the other. All eyes were on the Duke, willing Clara to disappear and allow him to continue his losing streak. He rose decisively.

'Right you are, then. Don't want to give the game away, do we? Better come over here and tell me quick.'

They moved over to a tall window that gave onto the square of Estoril. In the distance, through the palm trees, the implacable tide could be glimpsed, dragging up the shingle like a heavy cape.

Lines of worry were carved deep on the Duke's face. His fair hair was threaded with grey and the movie-star looks that once made him the heart-throb of a thousand young women had faded, like a magazine left open in the sun. As he fixed a cigarette in his holder, Clara noticed that his gold cufflinks still bore the cipher *EVIII*. It was as though having given up his kingdom and country he could not quite bear to give up his regnal title.

'So. Let's hear this strategy you have then.'

'It's called the doubling-up strategy and it goes like this. If I put a pound on red and it goes to black, then I double up with a two-pound bet on red the next roll. So if it goes red, I have cancelled out my pound loss and I'm still a pound up. If it goes to black again I double up again with a four-pound bet on red. So that way I will still be a pound up. If it's black again I double-up to a stake of eight pounds on red. The theory is that I will always win because eventually it will land on red and I will end up with a one-pound profit.'

'You think this will save my bacon?'

'It could. But there's a problem with that theory. It doesn't ask how far you are prepared to go. If black wins a certain number of times in a row, your stake must eventually rise to a million. It's very unlikely that you would ever lose as much as a million, but the most likely event is that all you will win is a pound. It's what's called False Thinking. So you have to ask yourself, sir: how much are you prepared to lose?'

'How much am I prepared to lose, eh?' The Duke's expression darkened and he took a swift, savage swipe at his cigarette.

'I rather think that's the question of my life, wouldn't you say? Same thing Baldwin and Churchill and the damned Archbishop of Canterbury and every other Tom, Dick and Harry has been firing at me for years. I would have thought my answer was plain to see.'

His gaze strayed out of the window, towards the inexorable ocean beyond, but Clara could tell that he was gazing much further than that. He was gazing out to the cold lawns of Windsor Castle and the London streets where newspaper vendors shouted the scandal of Mrs Simpson to an eager crowd. To the years of agony and indecision, the shuttered faces of royal officials, the fury of his family, the disdain of the English establishment. To a cocktail party past that had turned into a diplomatic disaster. To a life that had been maimed, marked and ultimately exiled by Love. It was Love that had beached him on this distant shore, cost him a crown and denied him any dignified way of escape.

'You think I haven't lost enough already?'

'I think perhaps you have. But you need to know what's at stake. And, sir, I didn't come here to play roulette.'

The Duke's face fell. Suspicion of others' motives came naturally to him now and here was yet another person trying to get him to do something he wouldn't want.

'What are you talking about, Fräulein Vine?'

'It's extremely important.'

He gave a jaded smile.

'More important than roulette? I'll need some convincing of that.'

'This afternoon I had a conversation with Walter Schellenberg. He's the chief of the counter-espionage wing of the Nazi intelligence service.'

'I know who he is.'

'I discovered that the Germans are working on plans to abduct you. When I was in his office I saw a telegram from the Foreign Office to that effect.'

'Seize us? Where on earth would they take us?'

'To Spain, first. Then Germany, I'd guess.'

The earlier jocularity had gone, to be replaced with ill-disguised hostility.

'What an extraordinary idea. Look, Fräulein Vine, I don't really know who you are, or who you speak for, but if I had a pound for every wild rumour that's brought to me, I wouldn't need to waste my time playing roulette.'

How could the man be so slow-witted! At last Clara understood the stubbornness that had the whole of the English establishment up in arms and Winston Churchill wringing his hands.

'Please, sir. You must take this seriously.'

'Must I indeed? Perhaps I should lodge an enquiry through official channels ...'

'No! There's no time. The abduction is already being planned.'

'And I'm to take your word for it, am I? That some madcap scheme is being hatched in Nazi headquarters to seize my wife and myself and carry us off to the German Reich.'

'Yes. It's not madcap. They're in deadly earnest.'

'And for what reason, pray?'

'So that you can serve as President of the Great British Republic after the conquest of Britain.'

There was a flicker in those faded eyes. A glimmer of recognition of that wording, as if he had heard this proposition before. Most likely just three years ago when he had visited the Führer's Berghof for a private conversation. When he had been the toast of Germany, a young Apollo on honeymoon with his attractive wife. How admiring Goebbels and the other Nazis had been of England's dashing ex-King, and how astonished that his own country was so quick to discard him. Perhaps, Clara realized, the Duke had agreed. Maybe the allegation in the Gestapo's file was true. *He agrees to cooperate at a suitable time in the establishment of peace. He has agreed a code word, on the receiving of which he will immediately come back over.*

Maybe he had signed that document the Nazis prepared for him, making him head of a British Republic in return for Britain's colonies. If so, that document was now safely stashed away, waiting for the moment that the Nazis needed to remind him of it.

'I'm sorry to disappoint you, but . . .'

His tone was terse, bordering on rude.

'You're being foolhardy!' Clara insisted.

Urgency lent her voice a strident note and immediately there was a warning flash from those washed-out eyes. A frown that said nobody spoke to an ex-King like that, not even if they were trying to save him from kidnap. The Duke was a vain man who had been destined for the throne and did not intend anyone to forget it. While he may have lost his crown, he had not abandoned his kingly airs and, Clara realized belatedly, she had not larded her message with sufficient deference.

'I'm sorry, sir.'

He glanced over at the nearest card table, where a losing hand had just been thrown down, a queen and a king lying like corpses on the green baize. Tapping the ash from his cigarette into a stand, the mouth a stubborn line, he said, 'I accept the apology, Fräulein Vine, but I'm afraid I can't leave just yet.'

'I know. You're waiting for something. The Duchess told

me. She said you were expecting a consignment of valuables from your villa in Paris. She had tried to persuade you to leave but you were adamant. But I think you were waiting for something else.'

Clara had tucked a packet of cigarettes into the leather bag and now she brought it up to rummage in it, as if searching for a smoke.

'In the pension where I'm staying I found this knitting bag. It belonged to a young woman who was arrested by Portuguese police outside the casino. She's currently in the cells, and refusing to speak, but I think she was trying to contact you. Perhaps she was trying to arrange a way of getting it to you.'

'A knitting bag?'

'It contains more than just knitting.'

The impassivity with which the Duke accepted the bag told Clara everything. He did not remark on its weight or question its contents. He barely even glanced at it.

'I shall have to speak to Her Royal Highness.'

'Please do. As fast as you can. You need to find her and leave.' She tried to recall precisely what Ian Fleming had told her. 'There's a ship in the harbour waiting for you. An American Export Lines passenger ship called *Excalibur*. It's been ready for days. With every hour you delay your freedom is at stake.'

Now that he had the bag, the Duke no longer seemed interested in her. He assumed the dismissive tone of one at a function or on a receiving line, edging away from some local dignitary.

'I appreciate the risks you have taken on my behalf. But now you'll have to excuse me. I have a losing streak to put right.'

Gambler that he was, he tucked the bag under his elbow, turned on his heel and walked back to the roulette table.

Mist had rolled in from the Tagus, enveloping the square and casting a milky halo over the streetlamps. Along the shore-line Lisbon was a distant necklace of bright lights. Stars like seed pearls pricked the violet sky. A sense of sheer nervous exhaustion came over Clara as she exited the casino. She had done what she could, and completed what must have been Sonja Klimpel's mission before she was arrested and thrown into a cell. All that mattered now was to return to the pension as quickly and unobtrusively as possible.

Around the square everything was shuttered, the last bar closed and the lawn in front of her a hushed lozenge of black. In the shrubs the cicadas hummed, and above her head the cones of the umbrella pines hung like bullets suspended in the dim light. A lush earthy scent rose from the watered grass and the waft of mimosa moved on the breeze.

Suddenly she felt a prickle in the air, a tingling sense of some human presence and, instinctive as a bird or animal, she looked around, searching for a suspicion of movement against her peripheral vision. Her stomach tightened in a knot.

Then the needles of the pines crunched underfoot and the shadows formed into a face.

Chapter Twenty-three

The disaster, when it struck, could not have seemed less alarming. Indeed Katerina did not at first recognize it as a disaster at all. It was Sunday afternoon and the orphans were crowded into the assembly hall watching a cine film called *Hitler at Home*, a short documentary of the kind that were regularly provided to NSV homes by the Youth Ministry for the purposes of entertainment and instruction. Hitler's main home was the Reich Chancellery in Berlin, but it was at the Berghof, the perfect, almost magical mountain house perched amid lush alpine scenery, that the Führer liked to rest from the cares of state. The film didn't have much of a story – mostly it involved Hitler conferring with his generals or frowning at maps in the Great Hall – but there were also scenes of him staring out at the majestic panorama with his dog by his side, and the jostling crocodile of pilgrims who climbed the road leading to the Berghof where, if there hadn't been a barrier preventing them plus a couple of guards, they would have been knocking at the front door. When the Führer emerged into the daylight, at precisely

the same time each day, the crowd surged forward screaming with delight and the guards would go into the throng
and pluck out an appealing child to meet him. Every child
wanted to be the one, of course. As the commentator said,
'*Thousands of people arrive at the Berghof each day to greet their
Führer yet he makes time for every child. Truly our Führer is the
Children's Friend.*'

Katerina's viewing was interrupted by Heidi, who yanked
her out of the hall, pulled her into a doorway in the corridor,
and hissed in her ear, 'They've taken your poster down.'

'Who cares? I didn't like it anyway.'

'It's because of your leg.'

'But Doktor Goebbels has a crippled foot.'

'Katerina! You can't say things like that.' Heidi's face was
tight with anxiety.

'It's true.'

Joseph Goebbels. If Heidi felt allied to Heinrich Himmler,
because she was born on his birthday, then Goebbels was
Katerina's own dark twin. It was knowledge she had buried
deep inside and had never articulated. She had seen him
once, when she was walking with Papi and they came upon
a military parade. The Minister was standing on a saluting
platform alongside Hermann Goering, like a stringy white
goat next to a hippo, and the tip of his built-up boot was just
visible beneath his trouser leg. Goebbels reminded Katerina
of Krampus, the Christmas demon, though without the beard
and horns, or the bundle of sticks to whip people. Krampus
had one normal foot and one deformed, and Katerina always
used to be given a chocolate figurine of the little devil on

Krampusnacht. You could get figurines of Goebbels too, but in plastic, not chocolate, and if Katerina had ever been given one she would have chucked it in the canal.

'I heard Frau Schneider tell Fräulein Koppel you should never have been put forward for the orphan scheme. She was quite angry. You're to be withdrawn from the adoption list immediately.'

'Are you sure?'

This was unexpected good news. Katerina recalled the kindliness in Fräulein Koppel's eyes when she had selected her for the photo-shoot. *Perhaps someone nice will see your picture.* As though she was hoping that advertising Katerina in a celebrity charity campaign might save her from the scrutiny of those steely SS wives. She could have no idea that Katerina never wanted to be adopted. That the thought of being taken into the family of some hatchet-faced woman like the one she had met the previous Saturday, to help with her housework and please her husband, was appalling.

'Yes, because Frau Schneider said you were a deviant.'

'A deviant?' The word grated like barbed wire on the skin. 'In what way?'

'I don't know.' On Heidi's face the struggle between friendship and orthodoxy was plain to see. She was grappling with the uncomfortable realization that Katerina was not the right kind of friend.

'Does it mean I have to stay here?'

'Perhaps.' Heidi was thinking hard. 'But then what happens to those children who don't get chosen at selection? Eventually they're sent away. Like Barbara Sosemann.'

It was true. In the last week little Beata had disappeared, along with two other Polish orphans.

'Perhaps you'll be sent wherever they go.'

Sent away. Already her initial optimism was clouding over with doubt. Her dog, Anka, had been sent away to a farm, but whenever Katerina thought of this farm she saw a dark door, with a long shadow behind it.

Heidi fell silent as someone appeared behind her. But it was only Fräulein Koppel, who smiled reassuringly and stooped so that their faces were level.

'Please don't worry Katerina about this, Heidi.'

'But I'm right, aren't I?'

You could talk this way with Fräulein Koppel. She was never going to report you.

'Heidi, I'm sure you have recreation to attend. Katerina, come with me.'

The film was finished and the new radio show, *The Voice of the Front*, was on. Katerina could hear the announcer's voice, breathlessly hectoring the nation, like an officer on a parade ground. '*The nation must draw together in the struggle and form a community of fate, which is tied together for life and for death . . .*' The show was supposed to be relaxing, a sentimental hiatus of entertainment before the working week began, full of heartwarming favourites like *Warum ist es am Rhein so schön?*, but the announcer's voice reminded Katerina of a dog barking endlessly in a locked room. It set her nerves on edge.

Fräulein Koppel led her down a long, tiled corridor, and into the nurses' office. It was more like a store room than an office, with manila files piled on shelves all up the wall, on top of gunmetal filing cabinets and in a tower against the murky, iron-framed windows that looked down into the yard. On the desk an Anglepoise lamp was switched on, illuminating a pile of papers that even from upside down, Katerina could see were Reichsführer-Fragebögen. These were hefty questionnaires to be maintained regularly on the orders of Himmler for every child under the care of the NSV. The nurses had innumerable boxes to check on behaviour and development, academic attainment, health, attitude and conformity to National Socialist ideals. No one questioned the need for it. Every citizen of the Reich was accustomed to being monitored and accounted for by the state. Nothing existed without being quantified. The Reichsführer-Fragebögen were no different from roll call, or having your rations weighed, or your height measured.

Fräulein Koppel pulled the door shut behind her and gestured to a chair.

'What Heidi told you is true. I had hoped that participating in the fundraiser would lead to something,' her voice tightened and she cleared her throat, 'but it's been decided you won't be put up for adoption any more.'

'I don't mind,' said Katerina automatically.

'You'll probably want to know why.'

Katerina cocked her head. Fräulein Koppel was fiddling with the paper in front of her. A little bloom of a blush spread across her freckled complexion, and for the first time Katerina realized that she was probably not much older than Sonja. Perhaps she had a family, and younger sisters to care for. Did she live nearby?

'We've had a letter concerning you from the office of the Propaganda Ministry.'

She picked up a sheet of thick, expensive notepaper with tentative fingers, as though it might explode if carelessly handled. Awed. Almost scared to touch it.

'The Minister says it has come to light that you have problems with your leg and only healthy and racially pure children are eligible for adoption. The facts of your case should have been made clear to us by your relative ... that's your sister Sonja, isn't it? ... and failure to disclose it was a breach of Reich regulations.'

'Sonja's away,' said Katerina stubbornly.

'All the same, the Ministry will want to speak to her about this.'

She could hardly get the words out of her mouth. Katerina could see the little gulp of her throat as she paused.

'Frau Schneider has discovered that you used to wear a caliper. Is that true?'

She nodded.

'If we had known that you might have been sent for treatment much earlier.'

The gravity of her circumstances was beginning to dawn on Katerina. She imagined the secretary at the Propaganda Ministry who had produced that missive, puncturing its expensive emptiness with a fusillade of letters, typing away with a machine-gun rattle. The signature in sharp black ink, as though the words were twisted from barbed wire. The letter, lying diagonally across the desk in front of her, was not so much an unexploded bomb as a piece of smoking shrapnel from the defect that had already detonated her life.

'But Sonja said . . .'

'We've tried to contact her with no success. We've even checked with the police. I'm afraid there's no sign of her.'

'I told you, she's away. She has singing engagements, abroad.'

'Well until she comes back you are the responsibility of the NSV and Frau Schneider has been empowered to decide on your future.'

Fräulein Koppel's kindly eyes were glassy with tears, but she breathed deeply and tucked an errant piece of hair behind her cap as if taming some irregular feeling.

She stood up, signalling the end of the interview, but Katerina sat immobile, as if lost in the sounds and sensations of the world around her – the harsh prickle of the uniform on her skin, a distant song on the radio, the mingled tang of that night's supper and disinfectant from the bathroom next door.

'What is my future then?'

It was a forlorn question; a query that would never be asked on a *Reichsführer-Fragebögen*, yet both knew it was the only question that mattered.

'She has arranged for you to be treated at a special hospital.'

Suddenly the nurse leaned forward, clasping Katerina close to her starched brown chest, before releasing her just as quickly. Her voice trembled with nervous urgency.

'God bless you, *Liebchen*. Keep your leg as straight as you can. And smile.'

Chapter Twenty-four

Even in the short time since Clara had seen Ned Russell, he had changed.

In the half-light he looked immense and solid, like one of the statues in the square around them, his face carved in marble, the eyes dark as peat. The clothes were no more likely than they had been before – patched flannel trousers, a workman's dusty blue tunic and soft cap and a scarlet scarf tied Spanish-style at his neck – but compared to the state of reflective calm in the Parisian attic room, his demeanour was now alert and nervous. Clara's astonishment could not be greater if he had been a ghost, but no ghost would grip her hand so tightly, or swing an arm round her shoulder, pulling her urgently towards him.

'Keep walking. Forgive me. You'll understand when I explain.'

His hand on her upper arm was firm. She had to hurry to keep up.

'You can't possibly go back to your pension.'

There was an authority in his voice that forestalled her

questions. He would have made a good schoolmaster, she saw.

'I don't have anywhere else to go.'

'There's a place down in the old fishermen's district.'

'Amigos bar?'

'I'm amazed you know it. It's a hole in the wall.'

'I only know it by reputation.'

The bar that Ian Fleming had mentioned was situated in a back street leading away from the docks, its sign, spelling out the word *Amigos* in guttering neon, hanging at an appropriately drunken tilt above the door. The place was deserted. Ned led the way through the darkened bar and pushed into a back room with a cracked tile floor and a single high barred window. He shut the door behind them and gestured to the lumpy bed covered with a thin, flowery cotton spread. There was nowhere else to sit. He poured beer into two enamel mugs and offered her one, then leaned against the wall looking down at her.

They had managed to commandeer a taxi to bring them along the coast from Estoril and Clara had taken the basic precaution of remaining silent in the presence of the driver, but now she said, 'Why can't I go back to the pension?'

'It's not safe.'

'How on earth would you know?'

'I've been there. I was looking for you. Peter sent me with a message.'

'I don't know anyone called Peter.'

His face was blank, impassive.

'Big chap, around thirty, curly hair?'

'I have no idea who that could be.'

'Forgive me. I was under the impression that he was your boyfriend.'

Clara shook her head, dumb with puzzlement.

'You're going to have to explain.'

'The day we met, a few hours after you'd gone, a couple of men arrived in that place in the Rue Vavin and told me it was time. They're part of an organization run from London – MI9 – who are devising escape routes for people like me, down through France and Spain. They brought documents and a change of clothes and took me out of Paris in a van.'

'That must have been dangerous.'

'It was chaos. The roads were solid with traffic, bumper to bumper, and in places nothing was moving at all because cars had run out of petrol and been abandoned. People were taking everything they could. There were grandparents being wheeled along in carts, and smart ladies carrying hat-boxes. Hatboxes! I thought have they no conception of what is coming behind them?

'It was dreadful out in the countryside. In some places the Germans had strafed the roads and there were bodies lying there, dead or dying. People starving at the roadside with no food, or water or shelter. You can't imagine the horror of it. It was worse even than when I was taken prisoner. Then it was just soldiers who were suffering. Now it's women, girls, old men, little children.'

He paused and Clara guessed that he would never be able

properly to articulate what had happened to him on that road, or how it had changed him. The damage in him went far deeper than the gash in his side. She reached out a hand and touched his arm lightly.

'Was Peter the man who drove you?'

'No, I only met Peter briefly, just before I left Paris. He told me the plan was to get me down to Portugal and he said that if I made it to Lisbon he wanted a favour from me. He wanted me to get a message to his girlfriend. He gave me the address of your pension and told me to look out for a woman with dark hair and blue eyes. About your height. He wasn't going to give me her name for her own safety. Anyhow, I got to Lisbon this evening, went straight there and the hotel owner told me that there was a pretty lady staying in that room, but she'd gone out. I could think of nothing else to do except wait. There was a bar a little way up the road so I settled down with a drink and kept an eye on the hotel entrance and very shortly a chap turned up, looked up at the window, then went straight in. He went into one of the upper rooms and pretty soon afterwards he was leaning out along the street, as though he was expecting someone. It wasn't hard to guess he hadn't called in for a cup of tea. Shortly afterwards he came dashing out and made off up the street. It was obvious the woman I was sent to find was under suspicion, so I strolled over and asked the owner where he thought his beautiful guest might have gone. Made out I was a disappointed beau who had been expecting to take this lady out to dinner and found himself stood up. Anyway, the fellow must have felt some solidarity because he winked and said the other chap had asked precisely the same thing, but he'd kept his mouth shut.'

'So why would he tell you?'

'Said he reckoned if you were the kind of girl who had two men in tow, you could probably look after yourself. Told me you'd gone off gambling to the casino.'

Ned shook his head in wonderment.

'I still had no idea who I was looking for. You can imagine my shock when I saw it was you.'

'Wait a minute. This man who came to my pension and looked out of the window. Describe him.'

'Tall fellow. Well-dressed, broken nose. Ran like the wind.'

A flood of relief came over Clara. Her cover had not been blown. Ian Fleming had seen the handkerchief and reacted accordingly. He was probably even now scouring the streets of Lisbon for any trace of her.

'Why are you laughing?'

'It's fine. He's friendly, Ned. He came to see if I was OK.'

He massaged his brow and vouchsafed her a puzzled glance.

'I hadn't realized, after what you told me about your fiancé, that there was anyone else. I had no idea that you and Peter . . .'

'We aren't. Of course not. I've never met him. I'm not the woman you were sent to meet.'

Into his grave eyes came a mixture of confusion and relief.

'In that case . . . If it's not you I was sent for then . . .'

'Peter's girlfriend *was* in my pension. She's been arrested.'

'Is she alive?'

'She's in prison, though I hope she might be released soon. I think she was picked up trying to contact the Duke of Windsor. I suspect she wanted to pass a package of diamonds to him.'

'To that man! He's a traitor to his country.'

'He might be. But whatever they say about him, and even if he is a traitor, he agreed to transport a cache of diamonds out of Europe.'

'Probably wanted to keep them for himself.'

'Whatever he intends to do with them, he's taking them out of Nazi hands.'

'How can you be so sure?'

'Because I've just given them to him. At the casino tonight.'

Clara paused.

'What was the message? That this Peter wanted you to pass on?'

'There was a break in the line. Someone was arrested in Paris and they may have given her name. So she needed to be careful. But it looks like it came too late. My efforts were in vain. And yet . . .'

He sat beside her on the cotton coverlet and his hand sought hers.

'I found you again.'

In the half-light, Clara looked across to him. Beneath the black curve of his eyelashes his eyes were steady and unblinking. She couldn't help but recall what he had said when he thought he was going to die in that field in France.

The thought that I'd never again hold a woman in my arms. Feel the softness of a woman's skin, or the scent of her. At the time, though she did not even admit it to herself, his words had sent a deep, sensual shiver through her. Now she felt acutely aware of his body close to hers, the heat coming off him, the fleeting touch of his knee against her own.

There was something secure and unflinching about Ned, like a rock on a moor. The feeling of not being alone, of having a brief respite from solitude, was so intense that a wave of exhaustion engulfed her and she had a deep urge to drop her guard and secrete herself against him. Before she could, with a sense of inevitability, like the deep blood returning to the heart, he leaned over and kissed her.

They spent the night talking. Clara's life, which had in recent months sped up and lost all direction, like a film flown free of its spool spiralling into a grainy blur, seemed to slow down and gain definition again. They spoke of their childhoods, of the books they had read, ambitions they cherished. Of their parents, his three brothers who had all, unlike himself, turned into farmers. Of Angela and Kenneth. The freezing bedsit he occupied in St John's Wood and the time he spent in the British Museum Reading Room, astonished to be in the same place that Marx, Lenin, Bram Stoker and Conan Doyle had frequented before him. How he had grown up in a church-going family, but that all the fighting and death he had seen had caused him to lose his own faith. Faith was dangerous, he believed, whatever guise it came in – ideologies like Communism and Fascism caused more misery than consolation. She liked the way he spoke – with deep, thoughtful pauses, his conversation leavened with laughter.

The future they didn't talk about at all.

At midday they walked up to the castle of São Jorge, through the pine-shaded courtyards towards the ramparts that looked westwards towards the harbour. Below them a vast liner could be seen, the *Excalibur*, faint gouts of steam emerging from its funnel and an American flag painted on its black and white prow. All around it a flotilla of small tugs milled, ferrying supplies, and on the dockside a small mountain of crates and luggage was piled.

The stone was warm beneath their hands, gossamer threads drifted through the air and Clara felt dissolved into everything around her, the scent of orange blossom, the ravishing clarity of the light, and the creeping wisteria cascading over the wall. High above them a flock of birds with long pointed wings and forked tails were hovering and calling in the dazzling morning light. They tilted in the air, balancing on the warm currents like a circle of snowflakes against the cobalt sky.

'Migrating terns. Soon they'll be off to winter in the Caribbean, just like our royal friends.'

'I always wonder how they know the way.'

'I'm glad you asked that. A little piece of crystal in their beaks helps them sense a magnetic field. I wrote a paper on it once. For an ornithology journal called *British Birds*.'

Ned turned to her, his mouth twitching with amusement.

'Eccentric chap. That's what you're thinking. With all his

talk about birds. I've always been that way. Right from when I was a boy on the farm. There was a lake close to where we lived, and every winter a pair of Bewick swans would appear regular as clockwork, all the way from Siberia. I'd look forward to them coming and think of all that distance they travelled. If they arrived early it meant we were in for a cold winter.'

'I don't think it's eccentric. It's just that I knew another birdwatcher once.'

She thought of Leo watching the starlings in the trees outside her apartment. The sun lighting the coppery tinge of his hair. She thought of Leo and then . . .

Ned Russell. *Edward Russell*. She had once asked Leo if he had ever told anyone about their relationship and he said there was only a single person in the world who knew. It was a man called Edward Russell; an old friend he had run into one day on the Strand during his long years in England without her. It had been a typically leaden winter's day and Leo was feeling hopeless. Over a drink together he poured out the story of his love for Clara, but even as he did he never doubted his friend's discretion.

Edward Russell was a common name. It must belong to thousands of men. It was a coincidence, no more.

'I wonder. I have something to ask you.'

The question danced in her mind. But even before she could frame the words he replied.

'You want to ask if I knew Leo Quinn.'

Clara nodded dumbly, electrified to hear the syllables of his name hanging in the air. To hear his name given breath and life again.

Ned's face was a mixture of recognition, and profound sadness.

'I sensed it was you when we met. You're right. Leo was a dear friend of mine. He once confided to me that he was in love with a woman – the only woman he had ever loved, he said. Her name was Clara. She was Anglo-German and lived in Berlin. When you told me you lived there and that the man you were engaged to had been killed, I hoped desperately that it wasn't him. But I feared it must be.'

Leo. Just hearing his name gave her the electric sense – the sense she had had many times since he died – that he was standing right beside her. As though his own voice was carried on the air, and now, through Ned Russell, a luminous thread connected her with him. It was both a searing comfort and almost too painful to bear.

Ned placed his arms around her and pulled her close.

'How long were you together?'

'It's hard to say. We met in April 1933.'

The days that they had spent together, even weeks on a few occasions, and the years that Leo had lived in her mind contracted together like the squeeze of a heart.

'He left again for London the same year. He had wanted us to marry but I stayed in Germany and I didn't see him again until 1938. Then we were together again for a short while until he went back to England to work ... In some ways we were scarcely together at all. He was always ...'

Always leaving, always receding into darkness.

'You miss him.'

'Very much.'

Training her eyes on the flotilla in the harbour Clara felt her words like paper boats, sinking under the weight of feeling they had to bear. Ned sensed her hesitation and stepped back.

'Do you mind this? Talking about him?'

'Of course not. It's just ...'

Just that for months Leo's memory had been hers to cherish and jealously guard. To argue with, nurse, reproach and lament. His memory was where she returned in her darkest moments, sustaining herself with the images of him and the cruelly brief time they had together. He was her first thought in the morning and her last at night and his memory had been hers alone. Now there was another who shared it.

'You want to talk about him, but you don't want that to change how you feel. It won't, Clara.'

She felt her heart lift towards him. The warmth of being with someone who remembered Leo, but who was himself, too. Ned's lips were moving softly.

'What did you say?'

'*Grief melts away.* It's a line from George Herbert. The poet. *Grief melts away, Like snow in May, as if there were no such cold thing.*'

Standing there with his arms around her, her body felt insubstantial, her sensations blurring into each other, sight and sound and taste and touch, as though there was no border between them.

'How long are you staying here?' he asked.

'I'm flying to Germany tomorrow morning. I have no other way of getting back to Berlin. Hanna Reitsch is meeting me at the airport.'

He unlocked their arms, took a step back and regarded her seriously.

'Surely not. Why go back to Berlin? Come with me. I can get you to England from here.'

To be in England. To forget Germany's iron skies and secrete herself in the soft folds of the Surrey countryside. To see the red buses sailing the arteries of London, and the Georgian terraces, as russet as a cup of tea. To walk the streets free of hypervigilance and the fear that every wall concealed a threat, every passer-by was a policeman. To escape the sense that numbed her to genuine experience, like a limb that has been anaesthetized. Her entire being yearned for it.

'I have to go back. There are people depending on me there.'

'It's suicide.'

'Not if I'm careful.'

Ned took her face in his hands and held her. His voice was thick with emotion.

'If you do get back, to England . . .'

She looked at him intently.

'You know you have someone to return to.'

They leaned over the parapet. Far below, a commotion on the dockside caused the miniature figures there to collect and scatter as a limousine, sun glancing from its polished roof, drew up, and two tiny people climbed out. The Duke was wearing a linen suit and sunglasses and the Duchess of Windsor had picked a chic, nautical jacket with navy braiding; an outfit that seemed to say, in her own sartorial semaphore, that having abandoned Europe, her home, her possessions and any hope of a crown, a sense of style was all Wallis Simpson had left.

As Portuguese police scurried around checking the couple's hand luggage, a cluster of officials from the British Embassy formed a rough guard of honour and the Duke and Duchess, barely acknowledging their heartfelt farewells, moved smartly past and up the gangplank. A lady-in-waiting followed with a flurry of dogs. On the deck a throng of passengers, impatient after the long delay, were angling for a sight of their fellow travellers, politely shoving and wielding cameras to record the moment for posterity, and Clara wondered if Walter Schellenberg might also be watching, through field glasses perhaps, from his room in the German Embassy, as his troublesome quarry made their escape. Mentally drafting his excuses for the fiasco that would, with luck, have banished the future of Clara Vine entirely from his mind.

Minutes later the ship sounded its horn, cast off and progressed down the broad mouth of the Tagus to where the sea, struck by the sun, had turned to luminous gold.

Chapter Twenty-five

The building housing the Berlin Philharmonic on the Bernburger Strasse in Kreuzberg had once been an ice rink and a lingering chill still pervaded its marmoreal halls. The drop in temperature was largely down to the tension between Joseph Goebbels and the orchestra's chief conductor, Wilhelm Furtwängler, who had not only refused to conduct in occupied France, but was also declining any involvement in Goebbels' latest venture, a propaganda movie to be called *Philharmoniker*. On top of this, Furtwängler had never joined the Party and insisted on championing Jewish musicians. Generally this level of uncooperative behaviour from a member of the Reich Chamber of Culture would warrant a one-way ticket to a camp, but Furtwängler's decision to stay in Berlin meant that he enjoyed Hitler's confidence and that was enough, for now, to keep him on stage before his adoring fans.

Watching the conductor's reedy, white-tied figure seized, if not actually transformed, by the *Allegro con brio* that swelled and died around him, Mary allowed her mind to drift. She was possibly the least musical person on earth and while she adored both jazz and swing, classical music was a foreign language to her and unlike all the other languages she had picked up around the Continent, this one she was never going to speak with confidence. Particularly not here in Germany, where even young children seemed to have a refined musical understanding and were as familiar with Wagner as kids back home were with Walt Disney. Besides, most of Mary's attention was reserved for the slender man with the particularly upright demeanour who was sitting next to her, apparently lost in the soaring beauty of the symphony. Doktor Franz Engel, of the Charité hospital.

The brown envelope containing a ticket to a performance of Beethoven's Third Symphony had been slipped under the door of her apartment the previous night. As soon as Mary noticed it she had thrown open the door, searched the stairwell and even run down into the square, but there was no one to be seen on the darkened streets other than a posse of French prisoners of war, working late into the evening digging an air-raid shelter. Whoever left the ticket had evaporated without trace. Instantly she wondered if it was a trap. All kinds of tricks were played on foreign reporters who had aroused the hostility of the regime and there was every possibility that this proposed meeting was a Gestapo ruse to associate Mary with a known subversive, or a way of ensuring that she was absent from her apartment for a guaranteed number of hours. These risks she contemplated for all of two minutes, before concluding what she had known all along: that she was far too curious not to turn up.

When she arrived in the stalls a fine-featured man in a

much-worn suit was waiting in the seat next to her. He was in his forties, she guessed, sitting with his hat on his knee, perusing a copy of that evening's programme. He glanced up and nodded politely when Mary sat down, as though they were two music lovers who found themselves in adjacent seats quite by chance, yet she knew from the minute inflection of his body and the widening of his eyes behind their horn-rimmed spectacles that this was the same person who had visited her apartment the previous day. They exchanged only courteous greetings until the interval, when Doktor Engel introduced himself casually and suggested a drink.

He had planned everything, Mary saw. The packed foyer was the perfect location to talk. Men in evening dress jostled alongside bosomy women in low-cut gowns and lorgnettes. No conversation could be heard above the excited babble of several hundred music lovers who were thrilled by the great conductor's interpretation and wanted to show off their knowledge at length. Exuberance filled the air, as though there was an ecstasy in being released, even for a few hours, from the ugliness and uncertainty around them. For these concert-goers music was a chance to re-immerse themselves in the beauty that had fled their daily lives. Mary, by contrast, was stunned at what Franz Engel had to tell her.

He found a spot out of the way behind a pillar and leaned casually against the wall.

'Thank you for coming. A mutual friend gave me your name. A neighbour of mine in Winterfeldtstrasse. She said you might be interested in my work with orphans of war.'

So this was Clara's doing. And yet, Clara had never

385

mentioned any doctor. Mary scrutinized him afresh. He was good-looking, but so skinny that she longed to give him a good meal.

'I'm sure I would be. Why don't you tell me?'

In a low, unhurried voice Engel explained his work with the orphans. The tests he was running and his anxiety about what might happen to those children who failed them.

'I told our mutual friend that I had no idea what happens to these children, but yesterday I discovered something that might explain it.'

His eyes closed momentarily, whether from emotion or fatigue Mary couldn't tell, then he carried on.

'I wonder, Miss Harker, if you might have seen those newsreels? The ones about euthanasia. How deformed children are a burden on the Reich.'

Mary shuddered. '*Lebensunwertes Leben*. Life Unworthy of Life.'

'Precisely. I don't know if you're aware but from last August the Interior Ministry began registering all children with disabilities, requiring us doctors to report all cases of severe malformations, especially of the limbs, head and spine, and paralysis, spasticity and so on. It's not about mental incapacity. It's about the degeneration of German genetic material. The cases go before a genetic health court, overseen by a judge and two doctors, and if necessary the children are sent to a special hospital.'

Engel's voice was pleasant and calm, as if, like everyone else, the pair of them were debating the virtues of the adagio or the precision of Furtwängler's interpretation.

'Yesterday, those of us who have been running these tests were told to redirect our results to a new office. It's run by Professor Max de Crinis and it's called the Charitable Foundation for Curative and Institutional Care.'

Mary raised a hand and he paused, understanding that she was memorizing the name although she was not going to risk writing anything down.

'I'm guessing you want me to ask some questions about this institutional care?'

'Our friend said you were good at asking questions.'

The bell rang and the crowd were finishing their drinks and shouldering their way back through the lobby to their seats.

'This office you mentioned . . .'

'Is at 4, Tiergartenstrasse. I'm not sure what questions you might be able to ask, but I feel certain the answers will lie in that building.'

In the second half of the concert Engel seemed to withdraw into himself, entirely lost in the slow movement, as though the music had the power to remove him completely from the world around him. Mary knew some artists said that that was their aim, to distract people from the war and all the sacrifices in their lives, but she felt exactly the opposite. Surely art should be about showing people the truth? Perhaps that was why she didn't have much of a cultural life any more.

Doktor Engel, though, she liked. When he shook hands and wished her good evening outside the concert hall, it was almost impossible to connect his gentle, courteous manner with the substance of their conversation.

'Did you enjoy it? The concert?' he asked.

'To tell the truth I found it hard to concentrate. But thank you for inviting me.'

'Furtwängler, though, is sublime, isn't he?'

'I guess.'

'He's an Inner Emigrant.'

'What does that mean?'

'It's what they call those artists who choose to stay in Germany and keep their heads down. There's a good argument for it. If you leave, what can you know close hand of what goes on? What good is simply watching the fate of your country from the stalls? Isn't it better to stay and bear witness?'

It was only after Engel had bid her farewell at the S–Bahn, insisted that she keep the programme and walked off into the gloom, that Mary realized he was talking about himself.

Chapter Twenty-six

The news was, she was to be sent away. To a facility outside the city where her disability would be properly treated, they would make her leg better and return her to health. The furthest Katerina had ever been from Berlin was on a holiday to Königsberg when she was eight, and that was fun. They had eaten fried fish at a pretty riverside restaurant and rowed boats on the castle lake. The doctors at this clinic were especially skilled, Fräulein Koppel said, and if she was lucky she might end up with true dancer's legs, twin tanned calves whose sleek muscles bulged when she walked. The leaving date was set for the following week. Frau Schneider had wanted her to go sooner, but Fräulein Koppel protested that Katerina was helpful in quieting younger children and a fresh batch of orphans was due to arrive the next day.

For a long time after the conversation in the nurses' office Katerina had sat on her small iron bed in the dormitory and thought about what might happen. She felt strangely dazed. When Fräulein Koppel had said they had tried to contact Sonja, and had even asked the police, her insides turned liquid with dread. If even the police had looked for her without success, what did that mean?

When she was a little child, her father had often given her sheets of paper covered with numbers. He made them himself. Once you worked out how to connect the numbers to each other a picture would emerge – a cat or a peacock or a flower – all you needed to do, Papi said, was to find the right pattern to connect the dots. That went for a lot of things in life, but with Sonja's disappearance it was impossible to connect the dots or to see through the confusion to get a true picture. For the first time Katerina allowed herself to imagine that her sister might genuinely not return. Perhaps she was dead. The worry clawed at her mind. Time was running out now and she needed to do everything she could.

It was hours before the solution came to her. And when it did, it seemed obvious. She didn't know why it hadn't occurred to her before.

She waited until the other children had gone into *Abendbrot*, then clambered across the iron railings at the far end of the garden, letting herself hang for a moment before dropping with a thud on the grass below. She miscalculated the fall slightly, landing more heavily than intended on her bad leg and causing an arrow of pain to lance up through the calf. Getting quickly up she made her way through the streets, along Finckensteinallee and the red-faced barrack block that housed Hitler's special guard, past the fancy high-gated villas with their Jugendstil decoration, and towards the station.

The S-Bahn station at Lichterfelde West was, like so many

of the stations in Berlin, disguised as something else – in this case the building had the arched windows and bell tower of a Tuscan villa. Katerina went down through the dirty yellow light of the tunnel and waited a few minutes until a train stopped with a sigh of brakes and the doors opened. There were only a few passengers, but being early evening the carriage was filled with the rank breath of a whole day's commuters threaded through the ashy tang of smoke. The train picked up speed, wheels clacking like knitting needles, looping softly through the late afternoon. It had rained, and an abacus of drops quivered along the outside of the window, until the jerk of movement made them shudder and chased them down. She took a seat, and thought about her sister's disappearance.

It didn't add up.

Where had Sonja gone, and what was she really doing? Her existence was like that nest of Chinese boxes Papi kept at home, with one inside the other inside the other, so that you never knew when you were reaching the centre. The first black lacquer box had a golden bridge and a weeping willow bending over, then inside was another, with a flock of cranes, and inside that a box painted with a tiny Chinese fisherman beside a ghostly lake. In the centre was the jewellery: strings of pearls that had lost their lustre, chunks of amber like dog's eyes and Mutti's ring, dull gold set with shiny topaz like a spoonful of honey. How often had Katerina slid that ring onto her finger in a vain attempt to conjure her mother before letting it slip heavily back into its silent box.

She wished she had tried harder to insinuate herself into

her elder sister's life. If she had, she might have a better idea where to search for her, but now the trail had gone dead. She wondered what Sonja's Jewish boyfriend looked like. It seemed impossible to imagine her with one of those sinister figures you saw on the newsreel, with their curved noses, tangled beards and dirty coats.

As Katerina mused, her hand dropped down and encountered something hard on the seat beside her. A postcard had been stuck between the slats as though someone had positively wanted it to be found. It was a standard tourist postcard of the Brandenburg Gate but on the reverse, where the message should be, there was a single line.

The Führer murders our sons.

What did that mean? Whose sons had been murdered? Even with her vivid imagination, Katerina found it impossible to envisage Adolf Hitler as a murderer, armed with a gun or a dagger, creeping into someone's home. The person who wrote it must be deranged. It reminded her of a joke that Sonja had told her once. '*The child is asked, who is your father? Adolf Hitler. Who is your mother? The German Reich. What do you want to be when you grow up? An orphan.*'

She had never understood how that was supposed to be funny. Surely it should be the precise opposite? After all, Hitler was *der Kinderfreund*, the Children's Friend.

By the time the train pulled into the station, Katerina's nerves were wound as tight as a music box. She had not dared bring her gas mask, in case it drew attention to her slipping out of the home, so she was praying no policeman would stop and interrogate her. She passed a chestnut seller with his tin cart and brazier trailing an aroma of nuts and burnt sugar, and her stomach clenched. That day had been a two-meal day, so no lunch, and breakfast seemed a long time ago. Reflexively she reached into her pocket. After their conversation the previous day Fräulein Koppel had sought her out, given her a cuddle and quite unexpectedly a bar of Sarotti Schokolade. Katerina couldn't remember the last time she had had chocolate, but retrieving it now she found the bar had melted in the heat of her pocket and only a sticky liquid remained, leaching out onto the jolly turbanned Moor on the wrapper.

Fortunately she had brought a few pfennigs so she stopped in a bakery to buy a roll, one of the day-old kind that could be bought without ration coupons. She noted that the shop-keeper did not make the Hitler salute when she came in. According to the book of instructions from the Propaganda Ministry, children were supposed to report any shopkeeper who didn't salute, but even if she had been inclined to, Katerina had other things on her mind.

After a fifteen-minute walk she arrived in a square she recognized as Wilhelmplatz, set with tall columns topped by great flat bowls filled with oil that were set on fire for the parades. This place, Papi told her, was the very heart of the German government. Looking around she tried to picture it as a heart, its walls the bleak façades of government buildings and its arteries the broad streets, down which a Mercedes like an ocean liner was just then sailing, two coal-black SS officers in the front seat and a dignitary in the back, trailing a leak of military music in its wake.

Her leg was hurting more than she could remember, pulsing like a fiery rod of pain, and she felt slightly feverish. Yet although her body was like lead, her mind was alive with images and impressions, darting like fish through the reefs and crannies of her brain. Around her the flowerbeds were planted with geraniums, aggressively red, their colour throbbing in the dusk. Katerina had seen a municipal gardener once, measuring out the spaces between the bedding plants with a ruler, as if even the flowers were a regiment. The League of German Flowers.

She sat on the pediment of a statue to rest and wondered what time it was. The day that Papi died, Sonja had given her his pocket watch. It was gold, with fancy filigree on the case, and Sonja said she had better take it quick before one of those thieving relations found it, so despite the strict prohibition on personal possessions at the NSV home, Katerina had managed to conceal it in her spare underwear, and now she took it out of her pocket and pressed it to her ear. It was still ticking, and she imagined she was listening to Papi's heart, still strong and beating.

At her feet she noticed a flicker of movement. She put the watch back in her pocket and reaching onto the dusty paving she saw it was a fledgling bird fallen from the tree above, its heart still visible through the transparent membrane of skin. She picked it up and felt a quiver of life pulsate in her hand even as the outsized beak jabbed blindly at her flesh. Where had it fallen from? Looking up at the light coming through the linden leaves, their veins like fingerprints against the sky, she realized that even if she found a nest in those forked branches it would be impossible to return the bird. It had fledged fatally soon.

She rubbed a tender finger across the spiky feathers and over the stippled skin. Papi used to rub a thumb down her cheek like this. '*You have skin like silk,*' he would say, '*skin like the petal of a flower.*' Sonja said love was like hypnotism, just a trick of the mind that could end with a snap of the fingers, but Katerina was sure love was more like this fledgling's quiver – the stubborn pulse that kept it alive. Love was her old dog Anka trembling at her feet.

She had written the letter carefully in private, first thing that morning. Crouching in the girls' lavatories, the seat down, the smell of sanitation fluid rising and the chipped tiles reflecting the glare of the naked bulb above. She wrote painstakingly, in her best handwriting, using her left hand because no one was looking, and it would surely be impossible for Herr Hitler to tell. She filled two pages because she needed to be entirely honest and she knew that Hitler would respect a person's integrity. Firstly she had explained all about her leg – how it had been deformed since childhood, and even the caliper would not help. It was a congenital condition – the same malformation that Doktor Goebbels suffered – so it would never be cured and going to any kind of special hospital would be useless. There was no point trying to treat her and she begged the Führer to intervene. Besides, the real difficulty about being sent away was that she was trying to find her sister. Sonja Klimpel. Sonja was a famous cabaret singer who had disappeared from Fischerstrasse, and it looked like her life was in danger. The Brown Sisters were talking of sending her away next week, so it was a matter of urgency.

Ending with the address of the NSV home where she could be reached, Katerina signed the letter and sealed it in an envelope she had stolen from the nurses' office, and addressed it.

Adolf Hitler,
The Reich Chancellery,
Voss Strasse,
Berlin-Mitte

Then, in the top right-hand corner, where a stamp would normally be, she had written in careful capitals *URGENT.*

You should never tell anyone what you're thinking, kid.

She had managed that perfectly well at the orphanage. She had been quite composed with Fräulein Koppel – Katerina wasn't the one who was crying. But there was one person you could tell anything. *Der Kinderfreund.* The Children's Friend.

Above her the statue of a Prussian soldier, his copper face blue with tears, stared out at the government buildings all around. Right to the Ministry of Enlightenment and Propaganda and across the square and up the length of Voss Strasse, to the Reich Chancellery, still draped with banners from the recent victory parade. It was even larger than it looked on film. A blank façade punctuated by a hundred windows and in the centre a pillared entrance surmounted by a carved eagle. An implacable cliff with gigantic bronze doors. In the street outside an SS driver was polishing his car, rubbing its sleek flanks as tenderly as if he were a mediaeval knight grooming a horse.

Before Katerina could help it, the story of the Pied Piper came into her mind. It was a tale that had ever since childhood festered quietly within her like a dreadful secret, a story she had always associated with profound embarrassment. Even thinking about it was enough to induce a hot flush of shame. In the story, all the town's children were able to dance their way out of Hamlyn to the magic tune of the Piper, except for one, the deformed child, who could not keep up. The child with the limp, who reached the mountain only to see its doors crash closed. That child was her, she knew, her leg always dragging away behind her like some harsh truth. Katerina had always hoped that one day it would be mended and she would dance along with all the others, yet now she knew she had been fooling herself. The leg would never be mended, no matter what any special hospital tried to do. Not all the medicine in the Reich could magic it. For the first time she properly understood what Sonja had told her.

The best stories have a little piece of glass in them. It might prick you and make you bleed inside, but it also reflects a bit of your own life back at you.

Inside her pocket, the letter burned. *A well-composed letter is the acme of communication.* That was what Papi had always said and it was why he was proud to work in the Reichspost. According to her father, the Führer received a thousand letters a month, most of it fan mail – poems and love letters and requests to marry him or bake cakes for him or have his baby – but no matter how trivial, he read them all. Every letter was filed and replied to. Every letter was stamped and numbered by his office and the appropriate action taken. That was why Katerina was so confident. Surely appropriate action would be taken in this case. She looked up confidently towards the great bronze doors.

In the event it was easier than expected. The sentry gestured towards a small glass cubicle just inside the door, where a uniformed officer accepted her letter with a wink and assured her that it would most certainly reach the Führer. She felt a lightening of her heart as she retreated. Everything now was in Hitler's hands.

Only one thing troubled her. On her way out of the home that evening, escaping down the corridor as the others filed into *Abendbrot*, she had run into Fräulein Koppel.

'Where are you going, Katerina?'

'My BDM meeting of course.'

Katerina was flustered. It was the first thing she could think of but Fräulein Koppel knew perfectly well which evenings her BDM meetings were on. She would know instinctively that the girl was lying and challenge her to tell the truth.

Except she didn't. She stooped down, her face pale as stone and nodded gravely.

'Good. I wanted to tell you. I've been trying very hard to contact your sister, but her friends might have a better idea of where she is. Perhaps they would be able to help. Do try to find Sonja, Katerina. Try as hard as you can.'

Chapter Twenty-seven

Number 11 Giesebrechtstrasse was a five-storey Wilhelmine edifice in Charlottenburg, painted the colour of faded lace. Its narrow balconies peered over the street like the pursed lips of a dowager, its pediments were decorated with stucco scrolls and everything about the stuffy gentility of its décor was at total odds with the louche nature of its current inhabitants. But that was, after all, the same with pretty much every other building in Berlin.

At first glance Salon Kitty was an impressively upmarket establishment. It had plenty in common with the exclusive Herrenklub, the fusty gentlemen's club in Voss Strasse that was patronized by Berlin's VIPs, and that was not only the clientele. There were clubby leather chairs surrounding low tables, crowded with cut-glass ashtrays, orange-shaded lamps, and brandy balloons. A marble-topped bar ran the length of the room and the walls were done out in burgundy wallpaper and hung with reassuringly dull oil paintings. This décor created a womb-like atmosphere intended to reassure the dignitaries, industrialists, high-ranking military officers, diplomats and foreign officials that this palace of pleasure was cut off from the rest of the world, with all its bourgeois morals, obligations and bureaucratic cares. In the corridors leading off from the reception room, thousands of Reichsmarks had been spent on beds that were ten times as comfortable as anything the clients had at home – not that anyone would be sleeping in them – as well as every conceivable modern convenience, including running hot water, chilled wine in ice buckets and state-of-the-art recording devices to relay every word of pillow talk to Heydrich's trained eavesdroppers in headphones, established in the basement of 10, Meinekestrasse, just a short distance away.

Bettina Beyer walked swiftly out of the front door and took a great gulp of fresh air. It was always a relief to leave Salon Kitty and fortunately it had been a quiet afternoon. Generally clients didn't start arriving until past nine o'clock in the evening, and before anything else could take place there would be a long, dull dalliance with a bottle of cheap *Sekt* listening to their woes or their triumphs. The girls were encouraged to chat: *Why are you finding your time at the embassy so frustrating? How much longer will this war be going on, do you think?* The men never wanted to hear Bettina's woes of course, which was just as well. If anyone asked her she might just be tempted to tell them.

First up was the fact that she was working at Salon Kitty at all. When she was a little girl growing up in a small town east of Berlin that had never been part of the plan. She had dreamed of being an actress, or in lieu of that a model, but in the event she had to settle for work as a leg model for a hosiery company. It went well to begin with. She still had the posters of herself, or at least her legs, lightly crossed and entwined around a sinuous black cat above the slogan: *The female leg enveloped by a fine, delicate stocking is one of the most powerful symbols of sensual desire.* But the war put paid to that. No one was advertising stockings any more. You couldn't get silk pairs for love nor money and the coarse grey woollen versions you found in the shops were not going to be any-one's powerful symbol of sensual desire. Shortly after the leg modelling dried up, she had run into a woman called Kitty Schmidt, a formidable bottle-blonde of indeterminate years who suggested a little moonlighting to make ends meet, and that was how it had started. Bettina knew immediately it was a dreadful mistake.

She hated everything about the work, and lived in terror that her modelling friends would find out. She had told her old parents she was engaged to an officer in the Wehrmacht and waiting for her man to return from France so they could marry. Mutti and Vati weren't to know any better and besides, Bettina wasn't sure how much longer she would be employed at Salon Kitty anyhow. In the past few weeks a troupe of hand-picked Bavarian girls with very superior airs had appeared – all kitted out in smart day dresses like Lufthansa air hostesses with single-strand pearls round their elegant necks. They spoke all kinds of languages and were assigned to the more important clients. There was the dis-tinct impression that freelancers like Bettina were no longer part of Kitty Schmidt's plan.

The tram arrived and Bettina climbed on and elbowed

her way gratefully towards a spare seat, from which she was swiftly ejected by a fat hausfrau with a Mother's Cross prominently pinned to her bosom. Hanging on to the strap, staring out of the bleary windows, her mind returned to the other problem. The visit she had received the previous night.

It was half past eight in the evening when young Katerina had come knocking, and it being Bettina's evening off, she had made the mistake of opening the door. God, it was like seeing a little ghost of Sonja – the same steady gaze, the same chin jutting out with determination, only with an unsettling innocence that her elder sister lacked.

Bettina couldn't help herself.

'What the hell are you doing here?'

She regretted her tone almost immediately and asked the kid inside – there wasn't much alternative and besides she showed no signs of budging. She gave the girl a cup of tea and some bread she had been saving for the morning and Katerina ate it all ravenously, in between bites explaining that she was still trying to find Sonja. Her sister would never have disappeared without a reason. Katerina needed to find her and she wasn't going to give up. That was all fine and Bettina was only listening with half an ear as she did her nails, until Katerina mentioned that she had enlisted an actress in her search.

'Clara Vine!' Bettina abandoned the nail varnish and sat up with a start. 'What are you talking about? You didn't give her this address?'

Not that it mattered. A few nights ago the police had visited and ransacked Sonja's room, presumably hoping they might find that Jewish boyfriend of hers hiding under the bed, and although Bettina had looked pretty and played dumb, inside she was fuming. She had no idea what Sonja was up to – God knows she was capable of anything – but one thing was for certain, she was on a suspect list now and if the police came back sniffing round Fischerstrasse, they would be wanting to know Bettina's business too, which could spell trouble.

'I didn't want to worry you, Bettina. I know you work hard. Fräulein Vine is on a committee assisting orphans so I asked her to help.'

'Why didn't you go the whole way and ask the Führer himself?'

The girl frowned, but Bettina was staring in the mirror, head tilted and lips pursed, posing for an imaginary photographer, so it didn't seem the right moment to answer.

Outside the stage door of the Haus des Rundfunks in Masurenallee a small crowd of autograph hunters had gathered. They were always there on the nights when the Werhmacht Request Show was broadcast, desperate to catch a glimpse of a celebrity, or even better to touch them, like mediaeval pilgrims grabbing the magical hem of a saint. A regulation pair of press photographers was usually present, by order of the Propaganda Ministry, lolling against the wall and stabbing out their cigarettes on the brickwork as they awaited any even half-recognizable celebrity who might make the next day's society pages.

When Bettina arrived and merged into the crowd, she

felt a miserable stab of envy. She had herself done a spot here once in the chorus of a concert – her one and only acting job as it happened, unless you counted what she did now as acting, as Bettina did. It helped to look at it that way and besides, with so many professional actresses now being assigned to factory work, making munitions and tanks, she was probably better off doing what she was. Drinking cocktails with diplomats and sleeping with them afterwards was her version of war work and frankly she deserved an Iron Cross for it.

A dazzle of flashbulbs, the stage door opened and she pressed forward.

'Fräulein Vine!'

'I always listen to the *Request Concert*. I never miss it. I liked your slot.'

'Thank you.'

The two women were ensconced in a scratched leatherette booth in a station *Kneipe* on the corner of Adolf-Hitler-Platz a few hundred yards from the Broadcasting House. Above them the steel Funkturm mast, like a mini Eiffel Tower, thrust into the violet sky, and directly below trains screeched and rattled through the U-Bahn. Clara brought a couple of bottles of Pilsner to the booth that Bettina had selected, in the far back corner of the bar. The air smelled of exhaust fumes and fried onions.

'I worked at the Haus des Rundfunks for a while. In the chorus.'

Clara squinted in puzzlement at the girl before her, with

her pretty, heart-shaped face, bee-stung lips and shameless scarlet lipstick, and tried to place her.

'So you're a singer. I'm sorry I didn't recognize you.'

'Singer, model, actress.' Bettina shrugged, airily. 'I'm an all-rounder really.'

After an hour on the *Request Concert*, Clara wanted nothing more than to head back to her apartment and try to sleep. Her mind was far away, back in Lisbon with Ned. She was still savouring the day they had spent together, treasuring it like a moment out of time. Something about war changed the natural progression of Time. War gave you grief that was leaden and slow, yet it also contracted the minutes so you had to seize pleasures while you could.

She forced herself to focus on the woman in front of her.

'You said you had something to tell me. Something I needed to hear.'

'It's to do with a kid I know. An orphan. You're interested in orphans, right? Well this one has a bad leg and she told me she's being sent to a special hospital for it. When she told me I thought, *special hospital*? What's that? Anything they call "special" these days usually means the opposite.'

Close acquaintance with Third Reich officials had developed in Bettina an acute ear for the weasel words of bureaucracy. The lies and evasions and downright monstrosities that cloaked themselves in the thickets of Nazi jargon.

'Anyhow,' she sipped her beer and coolly examined her nails, 'I don't think this kid should go, so I've decided she needs to be adopted.'

'And you're going to adopt her?'

Bettina realized she was going to have to ditch the actress fantasy and acquaint Clara Vine with her other occupation.

'Not exactly. Have you ever heard of Salon Kitty?'

A brief nod.

'Fact is, I may have ten generations of spotless ancestors behind me, but I've managed to blot my family record pretty well since then. I've spent a little time at the salon. Here and there. Which pretty much rules me out.'

'I don't see why.'

Bettina rewarded this with a sardonic stare.

'Can you honestly see me being approved as a new Reich Mother? Bettina Beyer, part-time actress and brothel worker? The only reason I get by is an army captain who's sweet on me. My ambition is to marry him some day soon and become a Reich widow, but I can't see that happening with a kid in tow. So no. It has to be you.'

'Me?' Clara put down her beer in surprise. 'Adopt a child? How could I?'

'You've seen that film, haven't you? *Hurra! Ich bin Papa!* with Heinz Rühmann?'

Hurrah! I'm a Father was a heart-warming comedy about a reluctant single parent who found himself unexpectedly bringing up a child on his own. It was yet another of Goebbels' projects to increase the birthrate.

'It would be like that.'

'I'm sorry, Bettina, but I really don't think . . .'

'Reason I'm telling you this, Fräulein Vine, it was this kid who mentioned you. Her name's Katerina Klimpel. You met her, didn't you?'

'The girl from the NSV home?' Clara frowned. 'Yes. She came to my apartment. But it wasn't anything to do with a hospital. She was looking for her sister.'

'That's right. Sonja. I share an apartment with her. At least I did, before Sonja disappeared. And God knows if she'll ever come back. Much better that she doesn't. A couple of days ago I had a visit from the police. We don't need an air raid on our place. Her room looks like a bomb already hit it.'

The shudder of a train running through the underground beneath them, causing the table to vibrate and the beer bottles to clink, provoked a momentary hiatus. Clara ruminated for a while then decided that there was no alternative to trusting the girl in front of her.

'I think I've found Sonja.'

Incredulity and suspicion collided in Bettina's face. 'You've seen her? Where?'

'I didn't say I'd seen her.'

'What then?'

'It was a few days ago. I was in Portugal. I heard the secret police had apprehended a woman from Berlin and were holding her in jail. This woman wouldn't give her name, but she did give them a brooch. And that brooch used to belong to me.'

'What brooch?'

'A diamond swastika. Sonja must have assumed that it would keep her safe, but I have no idea where she got it.'

Bettina took a cool, reflective draw on her cigarette.

'She'll have got it from Peter.'

'I heard about him. He was her boyfriend, wasn't he? But he's French. How would he have my brooch?'

'French? No. Peter's German. He comes from Berlin. Peter Jaeger his name is. A Jew, of course. He worked at his father's jeweller's before it was closed down. They came for his Vati one morning last year and arrested him, but Peter was tipped off and disappeared. He managed to take a lot of the stock with him, Sonja told me, but I have no idea where he went. So he ended up in France, did he? Yet you say Sonja went to Portugal.'

Clara was about to speak, but Bettina waved a hand.

'Actually. Stop there. I don't want to know. The less I know the better. If Sonja does come back she can tell me herself, it's the least I deserve. But if, like you say, she's in prison, then who knows if or when she's going to get out. Doesn't solve Katerina's problem. God knows what they've got planned for that kid at this special hospital. She used to wear a caliper but Sonja made her take it off. It doesn't look good to be a cripple in one of those NSV homes. It might work for Joey Goebbels, but it's a different rule for everyone else.'

'Sonja *will* come back. I'm certain of that. I just don't know when.'

'Not soon enough. Katerina's being sent away on Saturday.'

Three days. Clara swallowed.

'I'm so sorry, Bettina, but I couldn't just walk in and take her. These things take time and paperwork. And who says I would possibly be approved as an adoptive mother?'

'You must have connections. You people always do.'

'I just ... can't. It's my work, you see. I can't tie myself down. I have to travel.'

'Sure you do. Well it was worth asking.'

Bettina popped another of Clara's cigarettes in her pocket, collected her jacket, and rose from the table.

'Good to meet you anyway, Fräulein Vine. And if you see Sonja tell her she'd better start looking around for a new apartment. I've had all the excitement I can take for now.'

Later that night, just as Clara was about to go to bed, the siren sounded.

There were three levels of air-raid warning, L30, L15 and the last, L3, which meant there were an estimated three minutes before the danger of enemy bombs being dropped. Generally Clara left it until the last one before she moved, partly because most of the raids so far had been false alarms, and partly because her usual shelter was in a converted cellar that ran the length of several houses in Winterfeldtstrasse so there were only five flights of stairs to navigate and a short walk down the street in order to reach the door. Besides, the shelter was not a place you wanted to spend any more time than strictly necessary.

Designed for around thirty people, it had a whitewashed wall at one end that could be knocked through to the next building in case of collapse, and the air, filtered in from the street above, was stale and damp. The bricks bubbled with moisture. The place reminded Clara of one of those mausoleums that wealthy families secured for their descendants to lie in perpetuity; except that here the occupants were all too alive, especially the fretful baby and Frau Bessell's five children playing a board game on a table to one side, screaming with alternate jubilation and despair. Though there had been plenty of practices that summer, thus far Berlin had suffered minimal bombing, with the result that many citizens viewed the raids more as an inconvenience than a cause for alarm and most of her neighbours contented themselves with knitting, gossiping and trying to keep their children quiet.

She entered the shelter, noting the stray cat already curled in a corner.

An arch on the far wall led through to a self-contained alcove that was half screened from the main shelter and offered a modicum of privacy. There on a wooden bench Clara's neighbour, Franz Engel, had installed himself. He was reading a novel, but on sighting Clara he put it down and motioned to a space beside him.

'Heard the one about the air-raid shelter?' she said. It had become a habit for them to trade a joke each time they met. *Flüsterwitze,* these jokes were called. Whispered wit. Subversive humour that was not the kind you wanted overheard, but was ideal to allay the boredom of a session entombed underground.

'The man who comes into the shelter and says *Good morning* has already slept. The man who says *Good evening* is yet to sleep. And the man who says *Heil Hitler* is still asleep.'

'That's a new one.' Engel shifted to allow her more space. 'How are you, anyway?'

'Better, thank you. I stayed off the Pervitin, as you warned me. How about you?'

410

A tremor travelled across his features and resolved itself into a bitter smile. In the chalky light of the cellar, he was a waxwork, his complexion blanched with fatigue.

'No one needs help staying awake when we have the services of the Berlin police force.'

'Franz?'

'It was yesterday morning. I was still in bed. I had been to a very enjoyable concert the previous evening and for once I was sound asleep. My two visitors informed me they were under orders to bring Herr Doktor Engel to the station for routine questioning.'

She had not heard a thing. For once her sleep had been deep and dreamless.

'Why?'

'You remember the tests I was carrying out? On the orphans selected for Germanization?'

'Sixty-seven categories.'

'I never failed one. Every child, every category. I passed them all.'

Although there was no chance of being overheard above the shrieks and howls of the children's game, Engel lowered his voice yet further.

'More than that, I falsified the records of my colleagues whenever I could. If I found that a child had been failed, I changed the data. I had access to all the right stationery, the correct forms. I did it late at night at the hospital after everyone else had gone home. I knew sooner or later it would arouse suspicions. Even the limited intelligences of the Lebensborn staff might eventually marvel that such a rich seam of *Volksdeutsche* children had been discovered in the conquered territories.'

'Why did you risk it, Franz?'

'Ah. There's a question.' He removed a handkerchief from his top pocket and devoted himself to the tender cleaning of his spectacles with meticulous care. Then he refolded the handkerchief and only after he had done this and replaced the glasses, said:

'I'm not sure if you know, but our hospital managers recently informed us there is no point caring for the long-term ill. They have put the problem to mathematicians who have concluded that it takes one healthy person to care for three sick people. In the case of sick children, the issue is even more severe. Smaller human beings are more demanding. Their requirements are mathematically incompatible. Unhealthy children sap the energy of nurses who could be usefully employed elsewhere. Seeing as hospital managers lay such great store by logic, my fear was that a logical conclusion of that type might determine the fate of children whose genetic potential is less . . . valuable.'

Clara nodded. A horror was running through her. His meaning was all too clear. She wrenched her mind back to Franz.

'How did they treat you? The police?'

'Adequately.' He offered a tired shrug. 'The information against me seems to have come from one of my colleagues who was recently arrested. He's a courteous chap, and like all doctors he prides himself on professional confidentiality, so I'm sure he wouldn't have parted easily with such a private matter.'

'So what happened?' Clara's fists were bunched on the bench beneath her, her eyes trained on his as if she could barely believe Engel was still right there in front of her.

'Fortunately the police, like us doctors, are great believers in paperwork. Bureaucracy is everything. German doctors have discovered that no condition exists without a paper that is stamped and sealed and signed with the correct signature. In a somewhat ironic turn of events, the documents that would incriminate me beyond doubt have gone missing in the transit to Professor de Crinis' new office.'

'Which meant they had to let you go.'

'When I denied all knowledge they were obliged to release me.'

The screech of a siren cut through the air, signalling that the alert was over. The enemy bombers, if they had even arrived, had now departed the city airspace and moved on to terrify another town or city. There was a mass movement for the door and up the stairs, but after they had climbed the stairwell and emerged into the night, Engel lingered.

'I'm heading back to the hospital to catch up on work.'

'Does that mean what I think it means?'

A flicker of a smile.

'Thank you, by the way, for introducing me to your friend Miss Harker. Mary. She seems a charming woman.'

'She is.'

'If a little immune to the glories of Beethoven, though I'm sure that could be remedied.'

'Perhaps you could help in that direction.'

'Can I trust her?'

'With your life.'

He gave Clara a searching look; a look that seemed to contain within it all the pain and uncertainty and horror that he had seen.

'My life, dear Clara, is not my concern. This is about other lives.'

Then he shrugged himself into his overcoat and disappeared into the night, as though he would far rather disappear altogether.

Chapter Twenty-eight

Until a few years previously, the formidable, eight-storey Bauhaus building towering over Torstrasse and Prenzlauer Allee had been a Jewish-owned department store selling fancy watches, perfumes, clothing and accessories to Berlin's affluent middle classes. Now, however, the building had been stolen, looted and Aryanized and its arching marble chambers were in the process of being transformed into the headquarters of the six-million-strong Hitler Youth. The location was an intensely appealing one for Baldur von Schirach, the plump blond Nazi Youth leader, not only because it was plum in the centre of a solidly Jewish area of town, thus rubbing the swastika banner firmly in the faces of the residents, but also because it overlooked the grave of Horst Wessel, the young activist and thug whose messy death in a brawl had made him the unlikely candidate for first Nazi martyr.

Being a temple to youth, the building was also an inspired venue for Emmy Goering's orphan fundraiser, despite the institutional air and the fact that the Hitler Jugend was generally dedicated to more hearty entertainments such as ten-mile runs and folk singing. Posters of wholesome youthful activities – mountain climbing, rifle shooting and tank driving – were bizarrely interposed on the walls with studio stills of that evening's A-list entertainers, Ludwig Manfred Lommel, Jupp Hussels and Heinz Rühmann.

In many ways a comedy cabaret was a risk. Humour was more dangerous than dynamite now and an explosive joke could land its teller in a camp, yet Emmy Goering's choice of repertoire lay closer to home. While Joseph Goebbels had recently launched a newspaper diatribe about 'tearing out subversive comedy at its roots', Hermann Goering saw jokes as a valuable escape valve – a way for the population to express their daily exasperation about the shortages and petty bureaucracy without ever truly challenging them. So in some ways the evening itself was a big joke at Goebbels' expense, a fact not lost on the Propaganda Minister, judging by his thunderous expression as he hobbled through the crowded foyer.

Unusually for a Nazi entertainment, a very superior white burgundy was circulating, fresh from some Rothschild cellar, as the stars assembled in the lobby, bathed in press flashlights, ready for the next day's papers. While the performers may have been glamorous, most of the VIPs looked as if they had been pulled straight off the suspects' line at a murder trial, as well they might have been. Von Ribbentrop, the Foreign Minister, was sounding off to Robert Ley, head of the German Labour Front, with a wine stain on his white SS summer uniform and a sadistic glitter in his puffy drinker's eyes. Alongside them was the mentally unstable Bernhard Rust, whose rumoured fondness for small boys had, through some bureaucratic mischief, led to him being made Education Minister. Rudolf Hess, who would not understand a joke unless it was summarized, analysed and costed on a ministerial briefing paper, was glaring impatiently across the throng at Heinz Rühmann. Hess had ordered cuts to Rühmann's latest film, *The Gas Man*, because the actor performed a Nazi salute that was unacceptably sloppy, and even though the star had divorced his wife at the regime's request, questions about his allegiance were still circulating.

'Rühmann will be fine,' murmured Irene Schönepauck, coming up to Clara as she skirted the crowd. Irene's Schwarzkopf-blonde hair was styled in a *Dutt*, the braided bun that was every Nazi's favourite hairstyle, though a stripe of brunette at the hairline suggested her own darker roots. Her eye-catching form was encased in a shimmering fuchsia cocktail dress and she smelled of talcum powder and Chanel No. 5.

'Hess might hate Rühmann but he's on the Führer's list.'

The list of approved performers had been compiled after prolonged consultation between Hitler and Goebbels. For comedians a slot on the list meant exemption from military service, but it also meant exemption from most kinds of comedy, as anything remotely political was deemed foreign, Communist or Jewish. Usually all three. In particular, all jokes about the army were off-limits. Any suggestion of undermining the armed forces or questioning the war meant death. Wartime humour – at least the official Party version – was no laughing matter.

'You know who really makes the boss laugh, though?' Irene gave a demure smile in deference to the cameras around them. 'Goering. Hitler can't get enough of Goering jokes. He loves anything about Goering's medals. He had his photographer make up some tinfoil medals and presented them to Goering for him to wear on his pyjamas. Poor Hermann had to laugh along. So humiliating.' She glanced around.

'Watch out. Here comes the Merry Widow.'

Irene skipped smartly away and Clara turned to see a figure in black, evening gown stretched tightly across her pregnant belly and her hair furled savagely from her face, heading towards her. Irene's nickname was cruelly accurate. It was going to take more than a comedy cabaret to cheer the existential misery of the Propaganda Minister's wife.

'Fräulein Vine. What a coincidence. We were talking about you on the way here,' said Magda Goebbels resentfully, as if it were Clara's fault. 'Apparently my husband has plans for you.'

'I'm flattered.' Clara's gayest smile. 'Plans in what way, or shouldn't I ask?'

'Oh, don't worry. It's a perfectly respectable way. Joseph was talking about your role in his new film, *Jud Süss*.'

Magda's voice was thick, clotted with alcohol. She must have been drinking all afternoon. She had one elbow cupped in her hand and was smoking aggressively.

'He never stops talking about it. He thinks it's going to be a historical masterpiece. Right up there with *Battleship*

Potemkin. His own epic contribution to film posterity. At least I think that's what he said. It's probably dreadful. What do you make of it?'

Clara thought of the script in the leather bag. How the dead weight of it had winded the man who accosted her in the darkness.

'The dialogue's a bit leaden.'

'Is it? Perhaps you should decline it then. Joseph did mention that your career is taking you in new directions. Not literally, one assumes. Do tell me you're not leaving us.'

There was an undercurrent of hysteria in Magda's voice. It had been there for years. As if the moorings of her life were shifting, the ground still giving way beneath her as marriage to an overbearing, abusive man took her ever further from the life she once expected. Unimaginably far from her early days as Magda Friedlander, student of Hebrew, engaged to a young Zionist, dwelling in the Jewish quarter of Berlin.

'I don't have any plans.'

'Well, I'm sure that puts all our minds at rest.'

For a second Magda remained silent, a pensive scowl on her face, and Clara wondered what she really believed. Did she see Clara as a convinced Nazi, a loyal follower of the Führer like herself, or did she suspect there were depths that Clara kept well hidden, secrets far below the surface, just as Magda did herself?

True Berliner humour was black as tar and sharp enough to cut yourself on, but that kind of joke was in shorter supply than petrol now and instead the evening was dominated by anodyne jests about Neville Chamberlain 'the umbrella fella', Winston Churchill 'the drunk' and anti-Semitic clichés. The crowd, fuelled by fine wine and coaxed by the presence of celebrity, laughed easily and BDM girls, dressed as usherettes, only with WHW tins instead of cigarettes in the trays round their necks, barred the end of each row until every guest had made their contribution.

As the curtain fell, most of the audience held back to make way for the top brass and senior Nazi officials, who processed like clergy leaving a church before the congregation. Joseph Goebbels left by a side door, followed at a short interval by a brunette with a high flush on her cheeks who had not yet mastered the art of an inconspicuous exit. Eventually, as the vast throng of guests streamed into the damp evening air, Clara spotted the person she had come to see.

Emmy Goering.

The Reich Marshal's wife was, as Clara had expected, only too happy to grant her request.

'Of course I will. After all it was me who gave you the idea in the first place. I'm glad you've come round to my way of thinking. We all have to do what we can. Where have you been, anyway?'

'I was in Lisbon.'

'Another of Goebbels' entertaining missions?'

'Only a short stay. I bumped into some old friends of yours. The Duke and Duchess of Windsor.'

'Did you! What a charming couple they are. How were they?'

'They're off to the Bahamas.'

'Thank God. At least they'll be out of England and well away from the first phase, though, as the dear Duke said, a short burst of heavy bombing will be exactly what England needs to see sense.'

'The Duke said that?"

'His very words. Now if that's all, my husband will be waiting ...'

'Actually, Frau Goering ...' After everything Emmy Goering had done, it seemed almost greedy to ask more, yet in the matter of influence, as well as intelligence, Clara had learned that the more one asked, the more one generally received.

'I hate to mention this, but there is another matter I wanted to raise with you. I have a godson called Erich Schmidt. He's almost seventeen, a very bright boy, an intellectual really, right at the top of his class – and he absolutely worships the Herr Reich Marshal.'

Emmy Goering's face softened in an indulgent smile. There was nothing unusual in that. Such was her own adoration for her husband it was impossible for her to envisage anyone not sharing it.

'Working for the Luftwaffe is Erich's greatest dream. Ernst Udet gave him an autograph once and Erich still has it posted on his wall. But the thing is, Doktor Goebbels has made some remarks about my godson – comments that make me think perhaps he might look ... unfavourably ... on Erich if at any time I didn't please him.'

Emmy Goering's face changed in precisely the way Clara had hoped. Her entire body seemed to shudder at the womanizing tendencies of Joseph Goebbels. Anyone who knew the Propaganda Minister would understand Clara's insinuation: that he was perfectly prepared to use an innocent boy to bend an actress to his will. And every bit of what she had said was true, after all. Yet it helped that the Goerings and the Goebbels were hardened rivals from a private feud that had simmered since the early days of the Reich and any opportunity to thwart the Propaganda Minister would be seized with relish.

'That man! Will nothing stop him! I will see what I can do. If your lad comes under the protection of the Luftwaffe, there's very little Goebbels can do about it. Give me his name and address.'

Clara took out her pen.

'And if he's a bright boy, as you say, we don't want to waste him on the front line. There's a Luftwaffe leadership school right here in Berlin. They take them in the Air Ministry. He'd be round the corner from you. At least to begin with. And then ... Well, who knows what's going to happen in the next few months? Now that's an interesting pen you have. So pretty.'

Ignoring Emmy Goering's outstretched hand, Clara bundled Ian Fleming's fountain pen quickly back into the bottom of her bag.

Mission accomplished, she was almost at the door when Irene caught up with her again.

'What did you think? That was about as funny as a night in the cells, wasn't it? Thank God it's over.'

They clattered down the steps and towards the doors together.

'By the way, did you see Max? Did you get your coffee?'

'Oh, yes. Thank you for fixing it. Melitta coffee on prescription!'

'Max is an amazing doctor. Such a clever man. Though to tell the truth he frightens me rather.'

'Me too.'

'He's so intelligent you feel him working out every thought in your mind, don't you? At least, I do. When I saw him I said, if you're looking for something deep in my soul don't bother, Max. My soul's as deep as a puddle.'

She gave a little, self-deprecating laugh.

'He's Walter's oldest friend, though, so I suppose we'll be seeing more of him. Walter actually lived with his family for a while, and he totally adores him. He even took Max on that operation he did in Venlo last year.'

'Venlo?'

'You must have heard about it. Last November? It was Walter's finest hour. Venlo's a little town on the Dutch border and Walter masterminded an operation there to catch two very important British spies. They were posing as businessmen from The Hague. Captain Sigismund Payne Best and Major Richard Stevens. I only know their names because Walter loves boasting about them. His plan was so ingenious. He led them to believe he was a disaffected officer wanting to plot a coup against the Führer and when they came to the meeting place they were arrested and brought over the border to Germany. It was a triumph.

423

Walter did the interrogations himself and the men confessed everything. They gave away the entire British network in Europe. Every single name. Can you imagine? It's going to be impossible for the enemy to rebuild. The Führer was delighted. That's why he awarded Walter the Iron Cross.'

A peculiar stillness, like the moment before a detonation, overcame Clara.

'Max got one too. He had to go in disguise, of course. He impersonated a military officer. He called himself Colonel Martini, isn't that funny? After the cocktail! Walter thought it would be useful to have a psychiatrist there when they met the enemy spies. You know, so he could tell what they were thinking. And it *was* useful, apparently. Walter thinks the world of Max. When I mentioned I'd suggested you see him, he agreed it was a wonderful idea. It was he who managed to get your appointment brought forward.'

Beneath Clara's rouge, all colour had drained. The old feeling, the sensation that had haunted her through the years, returned with savage intensity. A high, singing note of danger.

What a fool she had been.

It was evident to her now that Schellenberg had been on her trail all the time. Before Paris. Before Lisbon. Right from the time of his career triumph last year when he had captured two British agents and brought them back in glory to the Reich. Clara pictured the men in their prison cell in Prinz-Albrecht-Strasse, tied to their chairs as the beatings rained down. Necks squeezed repeatedly to the point of strangulation. Blindfolded. Fingernails pulled. Muttering names, choking out their contacts, their faces draped in blood.

The honey trap in Paris had not been Goebbels' idea. It had been Schellenberg's all along. The oldest espionage tactic in the book. Set a spy to catch a spy. It was not Reuber's allegiance he suspected – no doubt the Gestapo already had concrete proof of his treachery – it was Clara's. Probably even the watchers Hans Reuber had seen in the streets of Paris had been there for her and not him. For a moment the horror arose that she might have led German agents to the safe house above the café in the Rue Vavin and compromised the brave Frenchmen hiding escapees there. She tried to reassure herself how careful she had been to follow all procedure. How silent and empty the streets had been the morning she met Ned.

Yet all the time Schellenberg had known.

Black with one sugar?

He knew far more than her coffee preferences; he knew everything about her. She thought of his face like a priest's, calm and patient, presiding over more horrors than most people ever had the misfortune to witness. A man who had spent so long peering into the abyss that now it looked back at him.

How idiotic to imagine that she might have outwitted him. How credulous to accept his blandishments; the fanciful idea that he had wanted her to join his intelligence service. That they were going to work together. That he would run her as his agent. He had known her name for eight months. Even before he met her, he had her grilled by his personal psychiatrist. He would always find her. She would always be in his mile-long shadow. How long would it be before he brought her in?

A light rain was falling and there was a scramble for the limited number of taxis available as the guests dispersed into the nocturnal gloom. Declining Irene's offer, Clara decided to walk. Her entire body was racing with adrenalin, and the need to process what she now knew. Her mind dashed through the possibilities, searching for the right course of action like an animal trapped in a maze. There was nowhere to hide or escape. She could do nothing, immediately, but make for home. She pulled her hat down, turned up the collar of her evening coat and hurried west, past the Schloss, the historic residence of Prussian emperors, across the Schlossbrücke and over the Spree with its greasy waters and soot-blackened walls.

The streets were dipped in shadows. Silence slid along the pavement and through the blackout blinds, while inside the apartments all ears were listening for what might lie beyond it: the distant drone of bombers, the thud of the propellers, the drums of metal beating against the sky. Others lay in bed dreading different sounds, of sudden shouts and boots on the stairwell. Yet everything was quiet for now. The only voices on the streets belonged to advertising posters proclaiming *Berlin raucht Juno!* or the slogans of Party propaganda, *Smash the Enemies of Greater Germany! Victory is with our Flags!*

A sharp wind had got up, slamming into the trees on Unter den Linden, sending sheets of rain scurrying across the street. A cat passed, like a shadow. At the top of Wilhelmstrasse Clara turned left, past the British Embassy, now boarded and abandoned, alongside the Reich ministry buildings looming oppressively, their blinded windows sweeping upwards, crowding out the sky.

Past Voss Strasse and the Air Ministry, she miscalculated, deviated right and was aghast to find herself approaching the dingy, five-storey edifice that formerly housed Berlin's School of Arts. The building where Berlin's students had once studied Holbein, Dürer and Caspar David Friedrich was a forbidding, Wilhelmine construction, a warren of corridors with doors leading off and the high vaulted halls of a railway station. Except that this was a place no traveller would voluntarily visit and the destinations of those arriving were generally grim. For in an act of horrifying remodelling, 8, Prinz-Albrecht-Strasse had been transformed into Gestapo HQ and darker arts were now practised within its sombre walls.

The building was blacked out but still alive. It was the one place that never slept, beating on through the night like a malign heart. Even at that hour people were coming and going in the gloom, rifle-bearing sentries standing like statues flanking the doors. It was too late to turn round. As the click of Clara's heels rang unnaturally loud on the paving, she could not help but be conscious of the deep underground beneath her feet, the subterranean network of tunnels like mediaeval catacombs linking Heydrich's headquarters next door with the central office of the Sicherheitsdienst behind. Directly beneath were a series of tiled cells, claustrophobic dungeons where she had herself once been briefly imprisoned. The thought of it quickened her steps, as though the pavement itself might abruptly crater and send her spiralling down into darkness.

She passed the front doors and could not help glancing sideways at one of the guards. The soldier's face was a flat, impassive shield but his Weimaraner dog registered her presence and cocked its ears, nose sniffing the air.

At the end of the street a clanking and hissing sounded in the air, emanating from the network of railway tracks alongside the Anhalter Bahnhof. The rails were singing as a series of covered wagons rattled along the track; a freight train perhaps, bearing weapon parts or troop supplies to the distant outposts of the Greater Reich. Clara heard the groan of metal and the clicking of point switchings. The air was acid with dust.

She felt a throb of danger she could not explain. Diverting into an alley she became aware of something behind her, a scratch on the stone, too slight even to be a tread. A rush of something intangible spiked the air but when she looked round, the street was empty.

Nothing at all.

All the same, she checked and rechecked her surroundings with practised care. What reason was there for anyone to be around here, in the governmental centre, well past midnight? A snap that sounded like the breech of a gun accompanied the rustle of movement and her gaze slipped past the entrance to an apartment block, froze for a second then doubled back. There it was. A shift in the texture of the darkness. A smudge of deeper grey against the gloom.

Fear soaked like grime through the pores of her skin.

How long had this man been there, gliding behind her? Since the moment she left the cabaret? Or since last November, when Schellenberg had first heard her name on the lips of two British agents and set about finding the truth?

Clara quickened her step but another glance behind revealed that the man was keeping pace. His face was not visible but there was something about him, some aspect of his demeanour that clung in her subconscious.

She strained, as though her memory was a muscle, to reach the part of her brain that said where she had seen this figure before. His shape had snagged in her brain, unpinned to any location, date, or name. In her mind she heard Leo Quinn's voice.

'*You should always encode the memory. It's basic training.*'

One of the first things an agent learned was to create context. To make connections in the brain so that a name belonged to a face, and if not to a face then to a location, an object, or anything that meant when they were encountered again they could be categorized. That was how memory worked, after all. Proust needed that madeleine to bring the story of his younger life surging back to him. Songs, names, tastes and smells were all ways into memories that might otherwise be wiped out. But with this person Clara had neglected the basic steps. She had not provided context. She knew she knew the man, but she didn't know why or how.

She tried to reason. This man knew how to remain invisible, which meant that he minded about being seen. That in itself was strange. The Gestapo didn't much care if their surveillance was detected; in fact it was better that way. They liked their prey frightened because frightened people were more likely to make mistakes.

Besides, if Schellenberg wanted to arrest her he had an army of SS men to do it here in Berlin, complete with cars and dogs and the dungeons of Prinz-Albrecht-Strasse in which to inter her. Why put a tail on her?

It was not until she had neared the canal that a gap in the clouds allowed a sliver of moonlight to reach down and pick out a speck of light.

A luminous swastika.

Instantly the shape fitted into the jigsaw in her brain and realization dawned with a fresh horror. That anonymous cast, the lean, pale face. The regular features. Dark hair with a widow's peak. He could have been anyone – a bank clerk, a shop assistant, a low-ranking ministerial official over-burdened with orders for Wehrmacht supplies and making his way home after working late. Yet while he may have appeared unremarkable, in fact he was quite the opposite. He was the man on the train, the one who had accosted her in the street outside her apartment. The S-Bahn man.

He had emerged from the railway sidings by the Anhalter Bahnhof. He had almost certainly been loitering by the train tracks waiting for a woman to pass. It didn't even need to be her. He had seen a lone female and she was his prey.

Incredulity bubbled in her mind. How ironic, that a life

lived in the shadow of a murderous regime might be ended by an act of random violence. That despite the attentions of Germany's head of counter-intelligence, she should become the ultimate quarry of an amateur, dying alone on the street, blood inking the cobbles. That after years of evading imprisonment and pursuit in the Third Reich she might face death by a lone psychopath, rather than at the hands of Nazi thugs.

There was no time to think. Hands shaking, fighting the panic, she ran. The man followed, a hundred yards behind, picking up speed with long, loping strides. He was younger than her, and she was in heels.

Running was hard. The air seemed to have a clogged, distorted texture so that she was moving in slow motion. Sweat was trickling down her back and between her breasts and fear was humming in her blood. Panic dulled her senses.

She reached the Tirpitzufer, where the serried buildings of the Abwehr, the German intelligence service, stretched behind a length of chain-linked wire. A litter of white fragments scattered the street in front of her like torn-up tickets, and she realized they were petals, remnants of the roses that had been thrown at the Führer's car during the recent celebratory parade. The BDM girls had been drilled to cast flowers in a spontaneous act of enthusiasm and tiny children had been permitted to break through the police cordon and approach the Führer's car with posies. Now the flowers were brown at the edges and soaked by the rain into a treacherous mass of decay.

She slipped and fell.

Staggering to her feet she ran across the road, but her slip had allowed the man to gain ground so now he was at most fifty yards behind. Ahead of her lay the greasy waters of the Landwehrkanal, the moon splintered in its oily surface, a flight of steps leading down. The towpath was liquefying in the worsening rain, the mud glittering like pulverized diamonds. Even in normal times there was no lighting along the canal bank, but now the shadow was massed and bulky, the willows above shuddering in the wind.

Blood rushed in her ears and, swifter than any human speed, a succession of images sped through her mind. Herself and the ten-year-old Erich on the roundabout swings at Luna Park, spinning faster and faster, and in the process spinning her own life out of its orbit. How would Erich survive? She hoped Emmy Goering's intervention would spare him from the worst of any action and keep him out of the clutches of Goebbels. From what she knew of her godson he would detest being stuck in an office away from the fighting, but his obedience and sense of duty to the Fatherland was stronger than any other sentiment within him. Stronger, she felt sometimes, than love.

Then came the faces of the people back home. Angela and Kenneth. Her father. The journalist Rupert Allingham, who had first suggested she try her luck in Berlin. Her old acting friend Ida McCloud, who had long since given up the stage for the job of vicar's wife, an occupation that perfectly matched her deportment.

And Ned Russell.

That conversation they had, the morning in Lisbon,

looking out at the harbour and waiting for the Windsors to board their ship. His large hand entirely enclosing her own. His talk about migratory terns, compelled by instinct to cross the globe, from wintering to breeding grounds, ending up at the same place each time. The crystal compass in their beaks guiding them through the invisible magnetic fields, connecting to magnetic north.

You know you have someone to return to.

Ned said he felt serene when he thought he would die, but there was no such serenity for Clara. She picked up her pace, but the path was slippery with darkness and her steps were sludgy, fenced in by railings blooming with rust. The way was narrower now, veering in towards the bank. The canal was clogged with weeds and smelled of rotting wood and dank slime. She was aware of the murk of movement and debris floating past, the surface arrowed with trails from half-submerged planks and other discarded objects. Suicides, perhaps, pecked by fish. This grim spot was a favourite for those Berliners desperate to end their lives. An image of herself flailing, sinking, flashed through her brain and galvanized her.

She was in a horror film, a pathway of jagged shadows and tilted perspectives, the way ahead fraught with uncertainty. Then, suddenly, a crust of mud gave way beneath her and she skidded, costing her precious seconds, and before she knew it the man behind had gained ground and in the next second he was standing over her.

The universe condensed around her so that it was just the two of them. A man and a woman. A scream froze in her throat. She saw nothing but the wild white of his eyes.

She hit him with her fist once, in the windpipe, and he grunted and stepped back, then staggered forward again towards her. Another thrust, straight to his chest, pushed him dangerously close to the slow darkness of the canal, but he sidestepped and recovered himself.

As if from far away she heard the man's voice raised in protest, but she was locked in a cocoon of survival, her mind focused only on self-preservation. As he advanced again, she recalled their last encounter. This time she had no heavy bag to defend herself, but digging in her pocket she found something else. Ian Fleming's pen.

It's useful in emergencies but be careful how you handle it. It emits a large amount of tear gas if you press the clip.

Grappling with it, she reached up and pressed the clip hard, releasing a burst of vapour in the direction of his face. The man reeled and reached out a hand to his eyes, then lurched forward, clamping a hand over her mouth.

'For God's sake, stop! Listen to me! It's not what you think.'

It was an English voice. A voice that carried in its ether a world deeply known to her and, in the subconscious split second that she heard it, a tumult of images attached themselves; of London squares and pubs and parks. Of terraces and teashops and Victorian churches of hearty brick. Of grammar school, and the 5.15 from Waterloo to somewhere in the suburbs. The very sound of it silenced her.

'I didn't mean to scare you, Miss Vine.'

The use of her name shocked her into speech. She sucked in a deep breath.

'I . . . don't . . . believe . . . you.'

Her chest was heaving. She could feel the blood pulse in her throat. The words came out as gasps.

'It's the truth.'

'Who are you?'

'My name is Kolchev. Ljubo Kolchev. I work at the Romanian Embassy.'

The Romanian Embassy? What had Hans Reuber said? *A British agent. He's posing as a press attaché at the Romanian Embassy.*

'Real name Wilson. Roger Wilson.'

'What do you want?'

'I'll tell you. Only please, let's keep walking. It's less conspicuous that way.'

They stumbled on through the rutted mud, then he led the way up from the towpath and she saw no option but to follow. He had dragged a handkerchief from his pocket and was rubbing at his eyes, trying to dissipate the tear gas.

'Bloody hell. Where did you get that stuff? I'm half blind.'

She gave no reply, so he added, 'I mean you no harm. You must trust me.'

'I have no intention of trusting you.'

'For God's sake.'

His face was beaded with sweat, his voice at once urgent and aggrieved.

'How can I convince you?'

'You'd better make it good.'

'I know where you work.'

'Like anyone who visits the cinema.'

'I know your address.'

'So does everyone with a telephone directory.'

'I know your code name.'

That mystified her.

'I don't have a code name.'

'But you do. You must know. It's been in place for years. I heard you mentioned by your code name long before I knew it was you.'

'What is it then?'

'Solitaire.'

Solitaire. In a flash she was back in 1933, and Leo Quinn was preparing to return to his work with the British secret service. Ten minutes earlier she had refused his proposal of marriage in order to stay in Berlin. She heard his protest. *Do you really want to be a solitary? On your own? Because that's what staying in Germany will mean, Clara. You'll be a solitary.* A solitary. What harsh, ungilded truth that name contained. It was the word they used for a lone operative, an isolated agent in the field. For years the word had burned in her as though it was written in fire, but now, hearing it spoken out loud, she wanted to cry because it was the last gift he had given her. *Solitaire.* Leo had made a name for her because she wouldn't take his own.

They were walking northwards up Hermann-Goering-Strasse. To the left lay the crepuscular gloom of the Tiergarten and to the right slumbered the long back gardens of the ministerial palaces. Wilson was still panting from the chase. Ruefully he rubbed the place on his throat where she had hit him.

'Christ. I'd rather go ten rounds with Max Schmeling. You winded me pretty effectively before. I should have remembered what you were like.'

'So it *was* you that night. In the street. I thought you were that man who has been attacking women on the S–Bahn.'

'I suppose your caution does you credit.' There was a resentful note to his voice. 'It's not been easy. I've been frantic at work, so there hasn't been much opportunity to track you down. I've been trying to get in touch for weeks. I found you on the train, but we were interrupted. Then I approached you in the street, but you left me pretty much doubled up in pain. By the time I tried again you'd disappeared to Paris.'

'How did you know I was in Paris?'

He was brushing the mud off his lapels.

'I had a message from Hans Reuber. He was worried. He'd been told to expect you in Paris and assumed you were somebody's spy. I couldn't give anything away. I couldn't tell him your precise status – I wouldn't do that, Miss Vine. But I did my best to allay his fears.'

So that was how Reuber had known that Clara was not working for the Nazis. It was not an unguarded slip on her part. Not carelessness or intuition. He had already been reassured about Clara's allegiances.

'Then before I knew it, you'd vanished.'

Despite everything, she was not prepared to lower her guard. She would not tell him she had been in Lisbon, or what had happened there.

'You'd better tell me what you wanted me for.'

'To warn you, firstly.'

'About the two agents captured at Venlo?'

'So you heard.'

'Are they still alive?'

'I hope so. They're in Sachsenhausen. Schellenberg was responsible for interrogating them. He wanted as many names as possible.'

The leaden confirmation of her fears resounded within her.

'And they gave him mine?"

'We can't be sure.'

'What do you think?'

'We have no proof.' Wilson shook his head. 'What we do know is that the damage inflicted on Britain's espionage network in Europe has been immense. Disastrous. That's why they want to contact you so urgently.'

'Who does?'

'London. They want you over there.'

'What for?'

'They need to reactivate you.'

She was silent a while.

'I don't know. I need time to think about it.'

'Time? There's no time. Besides, you've had all the time you need, surely. You've been shutting yourself up in that apartment for months, going to work every day like a good citizen, keeping your head down. You must have done your thinking by now. You must have worked out what drives you.'

Wilson was right, she could no longer stay still. The

forces that drove her were the same as they had always been; friends murdered, forced into hiding or exile, the comfortable laughter of their persecutors, England, and a father who would rather appease a regime of murderers than stand up to them. Erich in a Luftwaffe uniform. A man who loved Latin and another who told her there was someone to return to.

'Who exactly wants to see me?'

Wilson's voice, already quiet, lowered further.

'Winston Churchill.'

That silenced her. Eyes widened, she turned and stared at him but he carried on walking, a faceless mass with a luminous swastika bobbing in the dark.

'Are you saying the Prime Minister has a message for me?'

'A direct request. He wants to meet you.'

Shock caught the breath in her throat.

'What for?'

'He's establishing a new agency. They're calling it the Special Operations Executive. And they want you to join them.'

'Are you sure?'

'They believe you have exceptional access. They'll never be able to insert another agent with the connections that you have in Berlin. It's not that we won't get people in – there'll be foreign workers sent to Germany for forced labour and we'll be able to place some agents in that way to sabotage railways, power lines, telephone networks. To organize supply lines and link up resistance groups. But those are all low-level. To have a woman like you in the upper echelons, who's been there from the beginning. That's invaluable.'

Clara felt unsteady on her feet, as if the paving stones of Hermann-Goering-Strasse had tipped and tilted beneath her.

'So ... what exactly will they want of me?'

'If, as seems to be the case, the German counter-espionage services are suspicious of you, then you're highly vulnerable, Miss Vine. You may be able to duck and dive for some time, God knows you've managed so far, but it might be that you find yourself in situations that are somewhat more challenging than a ministerial drinks party. So the SIS want you properly trained. They have a place out in Hertfordshire, at Knebworth.'

'What would I learn?'

'How to kill with a single blow. Forge papers, make skeleton keys, pick locks. Morse code. Break into properties. Use a weapon. There are various psychological tests too. They get their people to walk along the tracks of the London Underground in the face of an approaching train.'

'Did you do that yourself, Mr Wilson?'

He shrugged, his face professionally deadened, blank enough to resist a Nazi interrogator, let alone an actress on a Berlin street. Roger Wilson was far too well versed in reserve to give away secrets. She wondered how old he was, and with what psychic blows that composure had been hammered into him.

'The idea is to test your control under stress, but from what I've seen tonight, I think you might be able to handle that.'

'How would you get me out?'

'Not sure yet. I warn you, you may not have much notice. You need to be ready to leave immediately.'

'Not immediately. I still have some matters here to settle.'

'Does that mean you'll come?'

Chapter Twenty-nine

Onkel Toms Hütte was located in Zehlendorf at the end of the U3 line. When it was developed, the area had been envisaged as a revolution in communal living, a Utopian society at one with nature and a way for children to escape the squalid inner-city tenements and thrive in the fresh forest air. The eccentric name was the legacy of a nineteenth-century tavern and the buildings were just as unusual: modernist constructions inspired by Mondrian and Kandinsky, interspersed with paths and parks. Woodpeckers chirped away in the trees, deer skittered in the brushwood and geese flocked to the rush-fringed lakes. On that early August day however, the bucolic tranquillity was rent with the clatter and drill of construction workers. A very different development, commissioned by Heinrich Himmler, was underway on adjacent ground: a precisely symmetrical estate of traditional rustic cottages with neat wooden shutters and gabled windows, perfect for SS families. Utopia was no longer to be the preserve of the poor, with their wretched pallor and sun-starved faces. From now on the air and beauty of the area would be devoted to the cream of Nazi children. Already a competition had been held in Berlin's schools to select suitable names for the streets and so far the winning entries included Führerstrasse, Victory Street and Duty Way. Originality was not an option.

Not far away, Clara and Katerina sat at a café beside Krumme Lanke under a candy-striped awning. Katerina was taking small sips from a bottle of Coca-Cola with a straw, rationing herself strictly to make the unexpected luxury last. Close by a heron, like an untidy grey umbrella, unfolded its limbs and lifted off from the crystal lake, transforming the drops into glittering prisms.

Only two hours earlier Clara had entered the NSV home in Lichterfelde for an interview with the most senior of the Brown Sisters. After listening to Clara's speech in silence, Frau Schneider had delivered her verdict with a deference that only thinly veneered her disdain.

'Normally, Fräulein Vine, the adoption of children would be unacceptable unless by families, and preferably those of the SS. In addition, there is something I must in all conscience tell you. I wouldn't be doing my duty if I failed to alert you and besides, it's on her files. The girl you have selected suffers from a congenital impairment. A leg problem.'

'I didn't notice.'

'I thought I should point it out. In fact, she is what we call a category four child. Technically she is not eligible for adoption. It is most irregular. But in this case, we are prepared to make an exception, especially,' she stopped and scrutinized again the paper in front of her with a mixture of bewilderment and annoyance, 'for someone recommended by Frau Reich Marshal Goering herself.'

'I hoped that would help. My position on the NSV orphan committee encouraged me to think about taking in a child myself.'

'Of course. But it is important that you know the implications of the disability. As it happens, arrangements were in place for her to be transferred to a special hospital. The paperwork is all complete . . .'

'That won't be necessary. I'd like the adoption to take place immediately, Frau Schneider. I have filming commitments, you understand, and I would love to spend some time with Katerina before that happens.'

Within half an hour she had completed the formalities while Katerina's small case was packed and then the iron gates clanged shut behind them. With almost indecent haste Clara hurried them onto the U–Bahn, as though the supervisor might have second thoughts and reel them back in, and rode as far as possible, right to the outskirts of the city, so that Katerina would feel safe.

It was a perfect afternoon. High clouds floated like dandelion clocks and linden blossom spiralled in the scintillating air. On a weekend the lakeside would have been packed with Berliners fleeing the city to sunbathe in the sandy reaches at the water's edge, picnicking and playing cards and relaxing from the stress of city life, but that day they were the only customers at the café.

Katerina sat with her peculiar stillness, watching a flock

of black geese lift off the blank dazzle of the lake like letters unsticking from a page.

'You don't have any children yourself, do you?'

'I have a godson. Erich. Perhaps you can meet him.'

That morning Clara had received a call from Erich. His voice had that high pitch of excitement that told her in a second that her wish had been granted.

'Clara! You'll never guess what. I've been conscripted. To the Luftwaffe! I'm to report to the Air Ministry next week. I don't even have to complete my school year. I was marked out, they said.'

'Erich, that's wonderful! Will you be flying planes?'

'Not at first. There's a lot of learning to do, technical stuff.'

He skated over the detail, anxious to play down the disappointment of being office-bound.

'But Clara,' a note of sweetness entered his voice, the sweetness that had been there from the very first time she met him, an awkward ten-year-old, brimming with affection, 'it's near your apartment so I'll still be able to see you.'

Katerina knitted her brows and a slight breeze plucked at the snow-blonde hair.

'Does Erich live with you?'

'No. But I don't expect you'll be living with me for long either.'

'Oh.' The girl's eyes dipped again.

'Don't look like that. I wanted to wait until we were here before I told you.'

'Am I to be sent somewhere else?'

The way she said it, she might have been a parcel to be

packaged, posted and dispatched to the distant reaches of the Reich. A piece of luggage to be delivered into the hands of people who would not care for her.

'Your sister's coming back.'

'Sonja!'

'She'll be home very soon.'

The child turned towards her rapt, her face splintered by sun and shadow. Her look was everything Clara might have imagined and more. She thought of all the tendernesses she had seen, of Wallis Simpson and her exiled king, stroking his cheek in Estoril. The radiance of Hans Reuber when he talked of his wife, Cici. Of Erich, remembering his mother and how he had knocked a boy out for her. Of Ned, his quiet intensity, his hand feeling for hers, their bodies moving together in a dance they had yet to learn. And she held that tenderness close and cherished it, as though it might protect her from everything time and future had to bring.

Author's Note

Operation Willi, the attempted kidnap of the Duke and Duchess of Windsor in July 1940, had the valuable effect of delaying Hitler's planned invasion of the UK, giving Britain longer to prepare for the Battle of Britain air campaign, which eventually began in August. The Duke and Duchess of Windsor saw out the war in the Bahamas, and returned to live in France. It was the German Ambassador to Portugal, Oswald, Baron von Hoyningen-Huene, who recorded the Duke's conviction that 'had he remained on the throne, war could have been avoided'. In a memo to Berlin, von Hoyningen-Huene wrote that the ex-King 'describes himself as a firm supporter of a compromise peace with Germany. The Duke believes with certainty that continued heavy bombing will make England ready for peace.'

After Ian Fleming had assisted the evacuation of King Zog from Bordeaux in June 1940, he visited Lisbon, but his activities there are not recorded. He returned to Lisbon in 1941 as an intelligence officer in the Royal Navy to devise

Operation Goldeneye, the Allied plan to monitor Spain and defend Gibraltar.

The Venlo Incident, a plot to capture two British SIS officers, Captain Sigismund Payne Best and Major Richard Stevens, at the Dutch border town of Venlo in November 1939, was a coup for Walter Schellenberg. The two British agents were sent to concentration camps and although they survived the war, the information revealed by one of them under interrogation severely compromised European SIS networks. This led Winston Churchill to initiate plans for a new network in Europe, the Special Operations Executive or SOE.

The SS *Eindeutschung* programme was a plan formulated by Heinrich Himmler in 1940 to kidnap thousands of 'racially valuable' children from conquered territory to make up for the loss of German lives. They were declared *Volksdeutsche*, ethnically Aryan children of the German diaspora, and were subjected to Germanization, which involved a period of re-education at Lebensborn centres, where they were forcibly encouraged to reject and forget their birth parents. They were then fostered out to German families. The programme was covert, partly because it was believed that German parents would not want a Polish or other race child in their family. Of the estimated two hundred thousand Polish children deported for Germanization purposes only fifteen to twenty per cent were recovered at war's end. Those who did not pass the initial racial screening mostly perished in concentration camps.

Professor Max de Crinis took over as Director of Psychiatry at Berlin's Charité hospital from Karl Bonhoeffer, the father of

Dietrich Bonhoeffer. De Crinis was a medical expert for the secret Action T4 experiment, named after its headquarters at 4, Tiergartenstrasse, and established in spring 1940. Initially planned for the euthanasia of mentally ill adults, the scheme was widened to encompass children with mental and physical deformities, and claimed seventy thousand victims. De Crinis' curious involvement in the Venlo operation came about because of his close friendship with Walter Schellenberg, who wrote that he regarded him as a father. De Crinis died on May 1st, 1945, after poisoning his family then himself with potassium cyanide.

Between 1940 and 1941 Berliners were gripped by the case of the man dubbed the S-Bahn murderer, a serial killer who stalked women on or near railways in the city. He proved highly elusive and exploited the blackout to his advantage. Male police officers in drag were placed on trains as bait. Confounding expectations that the murderer would be a Jew or a foreigner, it was twenty-nine-year-old assistant signalman Paul Ogorzow, a Nazi Party and SA member, who eventually confessed to eight murders, six attempted murders and thirty-one cases of sexual assault.

Acknowledgements

Many thanks to my publishers, Simon & Schuster, and in particular to Suzanne Baboneau and Clare Hey. Also to my agent, Caradoc King, for his generous support and incisive suggestions. In the course of writing and talking about the Clara Vine series I have encountered and befriended many wonderful people and amongst them I'm especially endebted to Jim Mitchell, whose enthusiasm and steady supply of research material has been gratefully received. Lastly, thanks go, as ever, to my children, William, Charlie and Naomi, for enhancing the solitary writing process with YouTube videos, cups of tea and endless teenage banter.

Faith and Beauty

Jane Thynne

Berlin, on the eve of war ...

As soldiers muster on the streets, spies circle in the
shadows and Lotti Franke, a young woman from the
Faith and Beauty Society – the elite finishing school
for Nazi girls – is found in a shallow grave.

Clara Vine, Anglo-German actress and spy, has been
offered the most ambitious part she has ever played. And
in her more secret life, British Intelligence has recalled
her to London to probe reports that the Nazis and the
Soviet Union are planning to make a pact.

Then Clara hears of Lotti's death, and is determined to
discover what happened to her. But what she uncovers is
something of infinite value to the Nazi regime –
the object that led to Lotti's murder – and
now she herself is in danger.

'An irresistible page-turner packed with historical detail
and told from a most unusual perspective'
Kirkus Reviews

PAPERBACK ISBN 978-1-4711-3194-3
EBOOK ISBN 978-1-4711-3195-0

A War of Flowers

Jane Thynne

August, 1938. Paris is a city living on its nerves as the threat of war hangs heavy . . .

British actress, Clara Vine, is in Paris to film her latest movie, having left Berlin under a cloud. Joseph Goebbels has become increasingly suspicious that Clara has been mingling in Berlin society and passing snippets of information to her contacts in the British Embassy. It would have been absurd, if it hadn't also been true . . .

With war becoming increasingly likely, Clara is approached by an undercover British operative, Guy Hamilton, who asks her to perform a task for her country: to befriend Eva Braun, Hitler's girlfriend, and to pass on any information she can gather.

Clara knows that to undertake this task is to put herself back in danger. But she also knows that soon she may have to do everything in her power to protect her country . . .

'Thynne's grasp of the period is first-class, and she has woven in a tender wartime love story' *Mail on Sunday*

PAPERBACK ISBN 978-1-4711-3190-5
EBOOK ISBN 978-1-4711-3191-2

The Winter Garden

Jane Thynne

**Berlin, 1937. The city radiates glamour and ambition.
But danger lurks in every shadow ...**

Clara Vine is an actress at the famous Ufa studios by day
and an undercover British Intelligence agent by night.
When a young girl is found brutally murdered in the
gardens of Berlin's notorious bride school, where young
women are schooled on the art of being an SS officer's
wife, Clara soon discovers that the murder is linked
to a far more ominous secret.

With the newly abdicated Edward VIII and his wife
Wallis set to arrive in Berlin, and the Mitford sisters
dazzling on the social scene, Clara must work in the
darkness to find the truth and send it back to London. It
is a dangerous path she treads, and it will take everything
she has to survive ...

'A thoroughly enjoyable read: fast-paced, atmospheric
and genuinely suspenseful'
Mail on Sunday

PAPERBACK ISBN 978-1-84983-989-1
EBOOK ISBN 978-1-84983-990-7

Black Roses

Jane Thynne

1933 and warning bells ring across Europe as Hitler comes to power ...

Clara Vine, a young, talented British actress, finds herself in Berlin and, unwittingly, in the midst of an uneasy circle of Nazi wives, among them Magda Goebbels.

There she meets Leo Quinn, an undercover British intelligence agent, and is soon recruited to spy on her new acquaintances.

But when Magda Goebbels reveals to Clara a dramatic secret and entrusts her with an extraordinary mission, Clara feels threatened, compromised and desperately caught between duty and love.

'Superbly atmospheric'
Kate Saunders

PAPERBACK ISBN 978-1-84983-985-3
EBOOK ISBN 978-1-84983-986-0